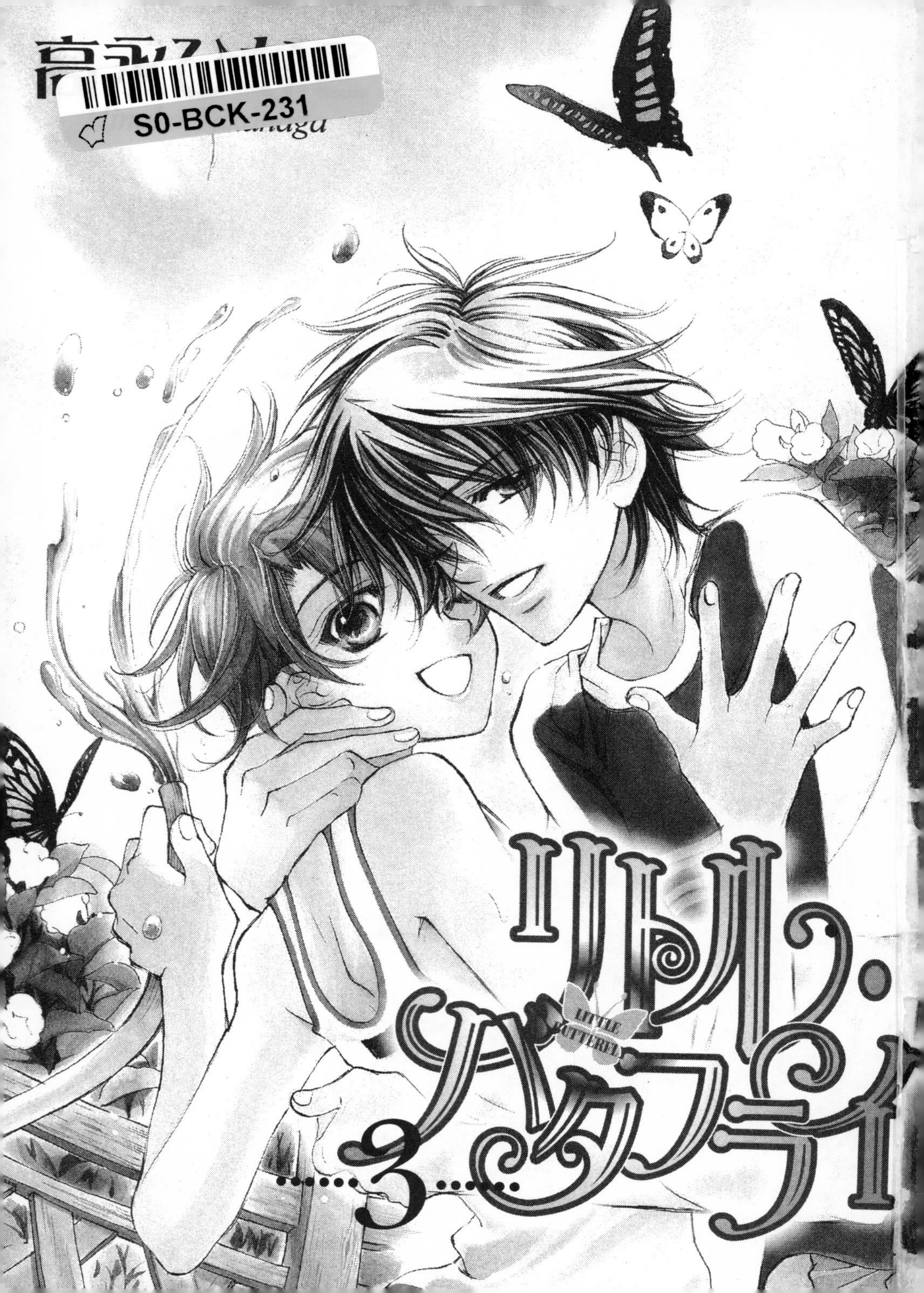
リトル・バタフライ
LITTLE BUTTERFLY
3

Little Butterfly 3

Translation	Sachiko Sato
Editing	Stephanie Donnelly
Lettering	Melanie Lewis
Graphic Design	Wendy Lee
Print Production	Fred Lui
Publisher	Hikaru Sasahara

English Edition Published by
DIGITAL MANGA PUBLISHING
A division of DIGITAL MANGA, Inc.
1487 W 178th Street, Suite 300
Gardena, CA 90248

www.dmpbooks.com

First Edition: November 2006
ISBN: 1-56970-905-X

1 3 5 7 9 10 8 6 4 2

Printed in China

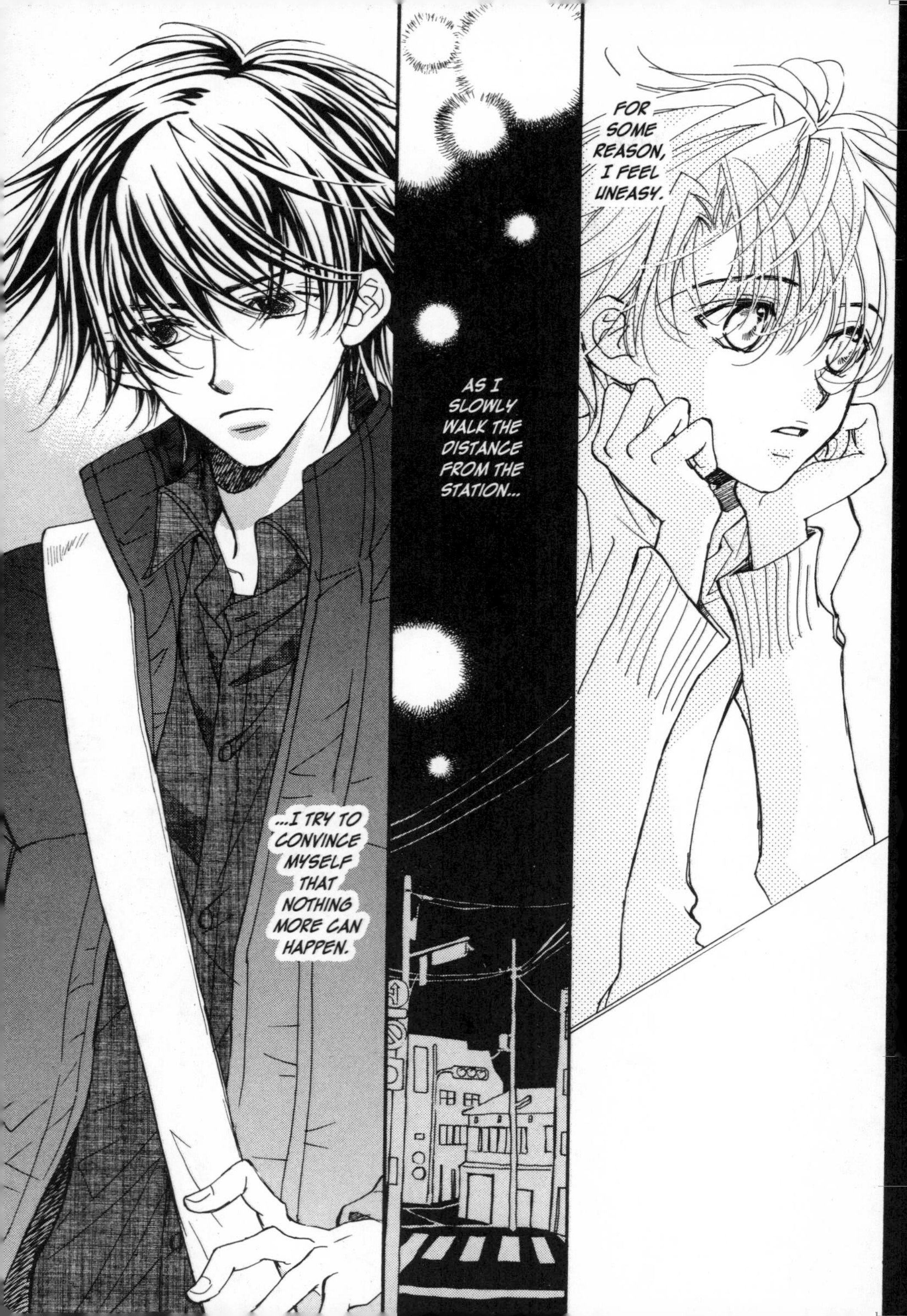
FOR SOME REASON, I FEEL UNEASY.
AS I SLOWLY WALK THE DISTANCE FROM THE STATION...
...I TRY TO CONVINCE MYSELF THAT NOTHING MORE CAN HAPPEN.

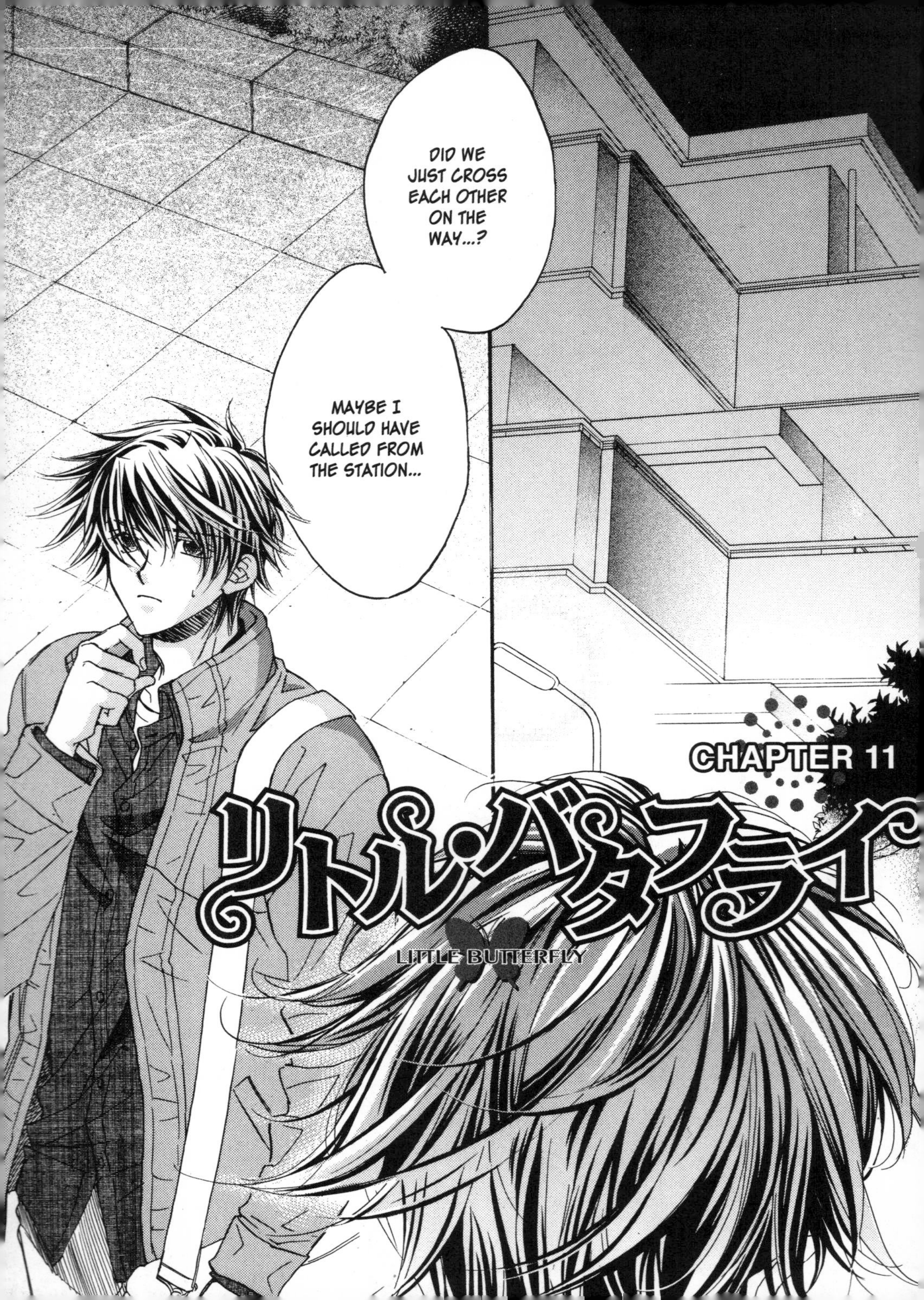
DID WE JUST CROSS EACH OTHER ON THE WAY...?
MAYBE I SHOULD HAVE CALLED FROM THE STATION...
CHAPTER 11
リトル・バタフライ
LITTLE BUTTERFLY

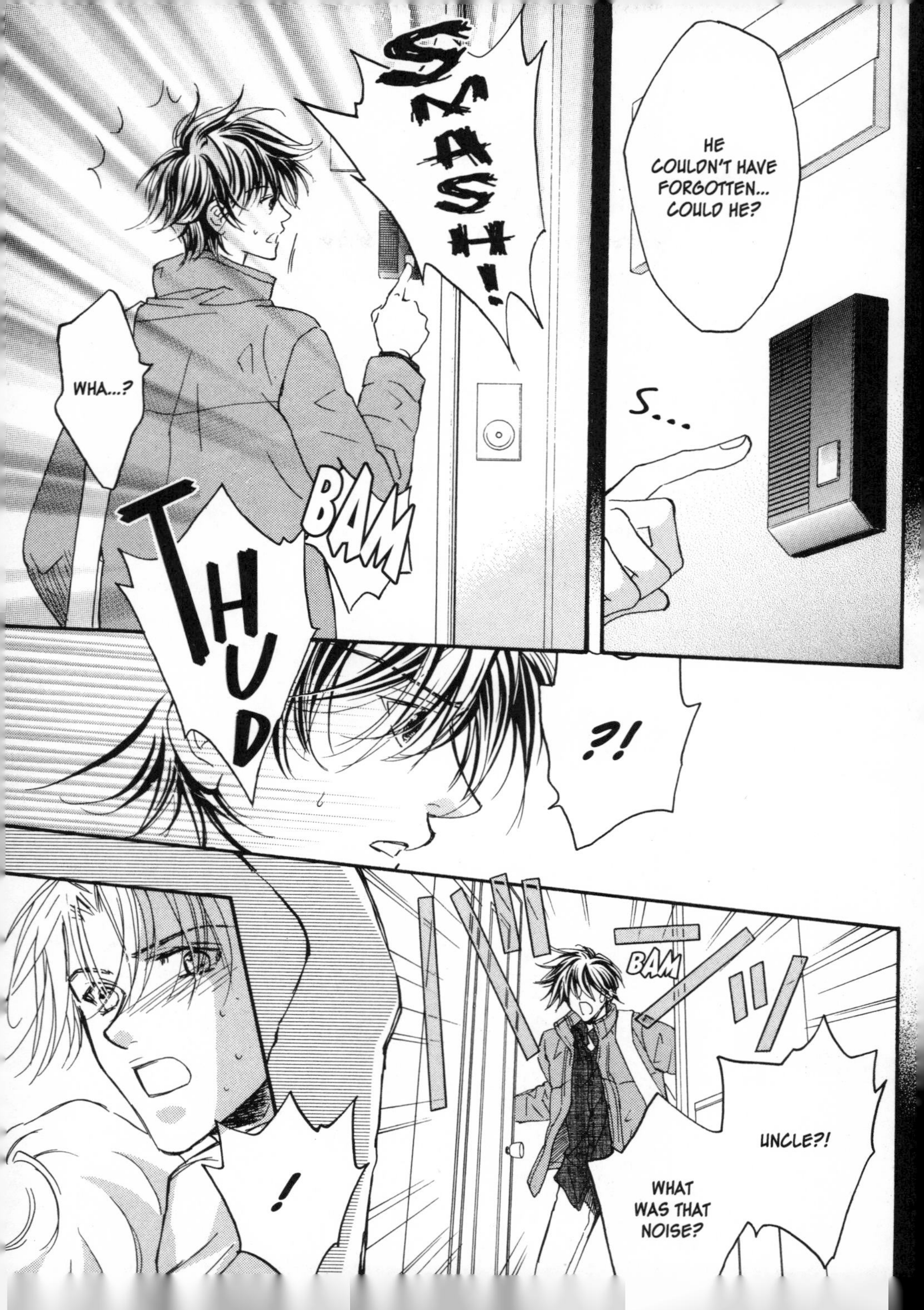
HE COULDN'T HAVE FORGOTTEN... COULD HE?
S...
SMASH!
WHA...?
BAM
THUD
?!
UNCLE?!
WHAT WAS THAT NOISE?
BAM
!

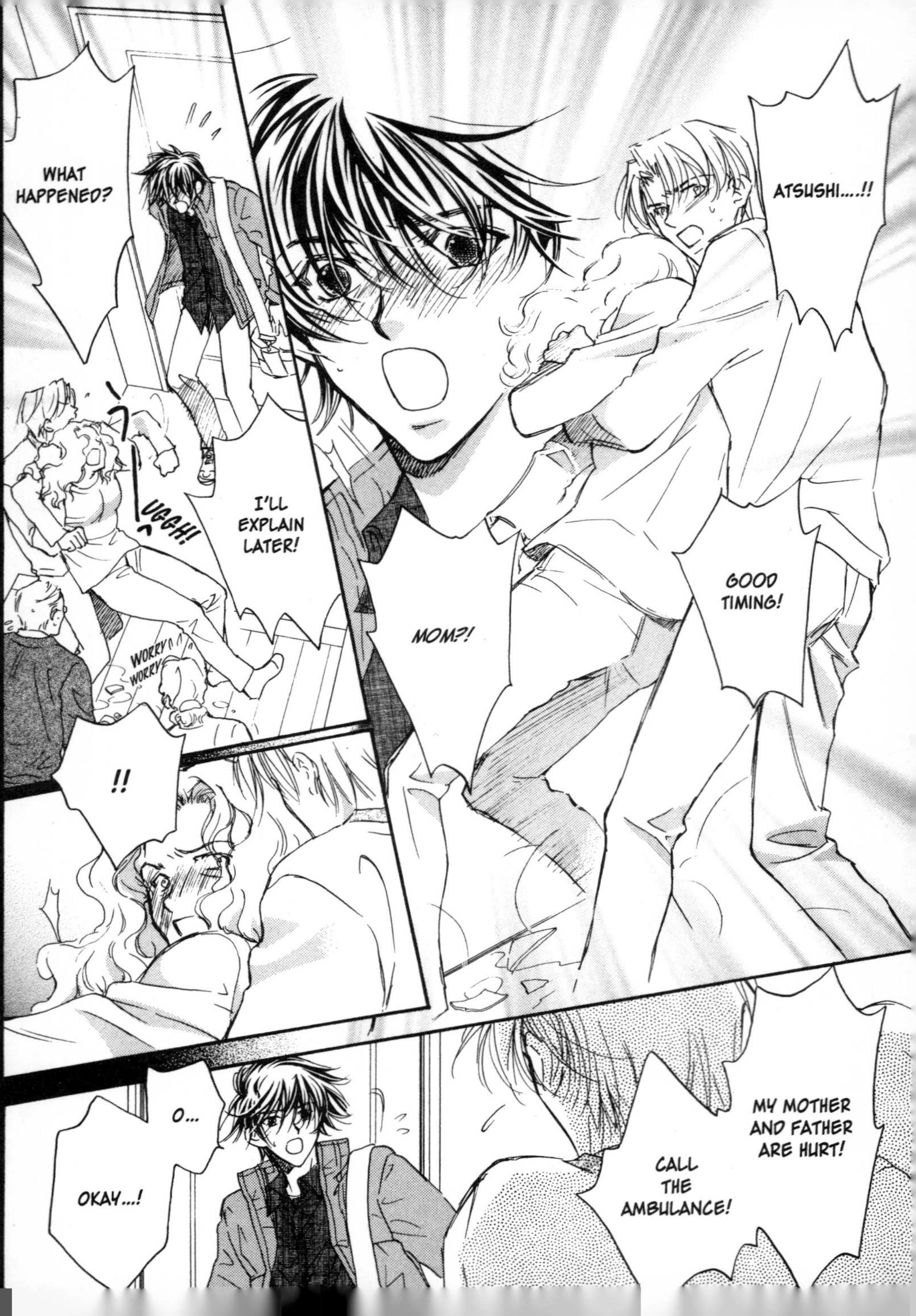
ATSUSHI....!!
GOOD TIMING!
MOM?!
WHAT HAPPENED?
I'LL EXPLAIN LATER!
UGGH!
WORRY WORRY
!!
MY MOTHER AND FATHER ARE HURT!
CALL THE AMBULANCE!
O...
OKAY...!

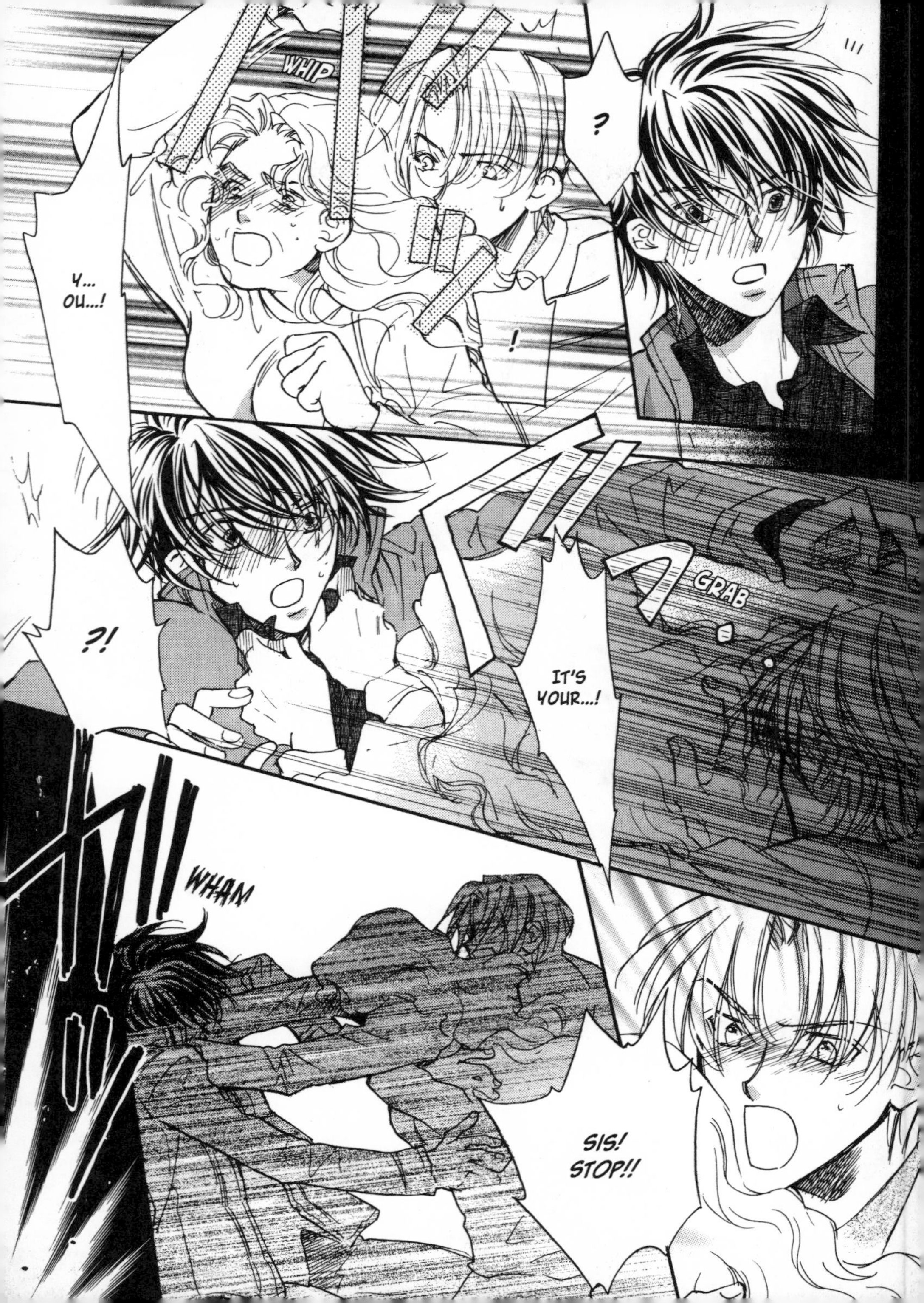
?
WHIP
Y...
OU...!
!
GRAB
IT'S
YOUR...!
?!
SIS!
STOP!!
WHAM

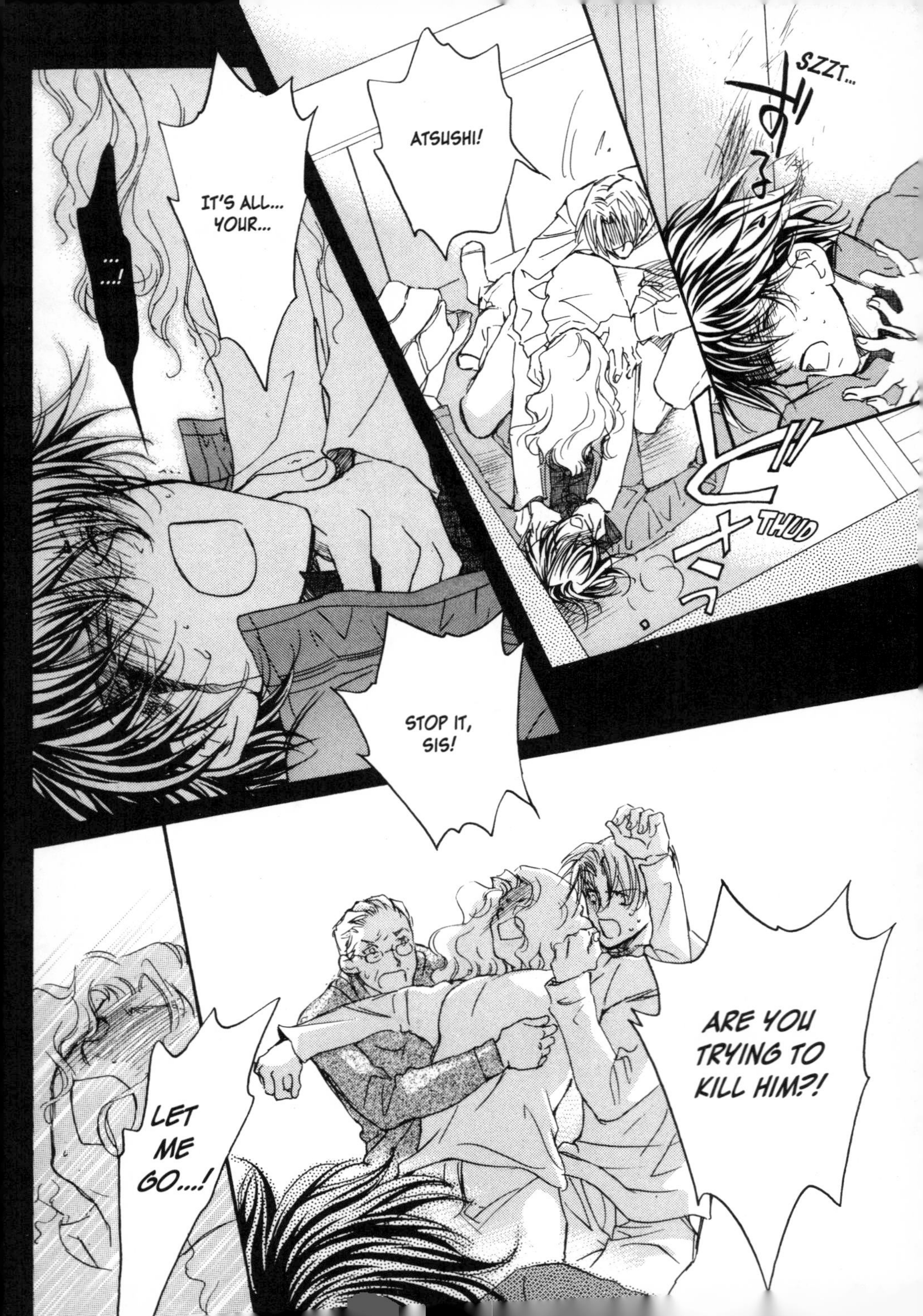
SZZT...
THUD
ATSUSHI!
IT'S ALL... YOUR...
......!
STOP IT, SIS!
ARE YOU TRYING TO KILL HIM?!
LET ME GO...!

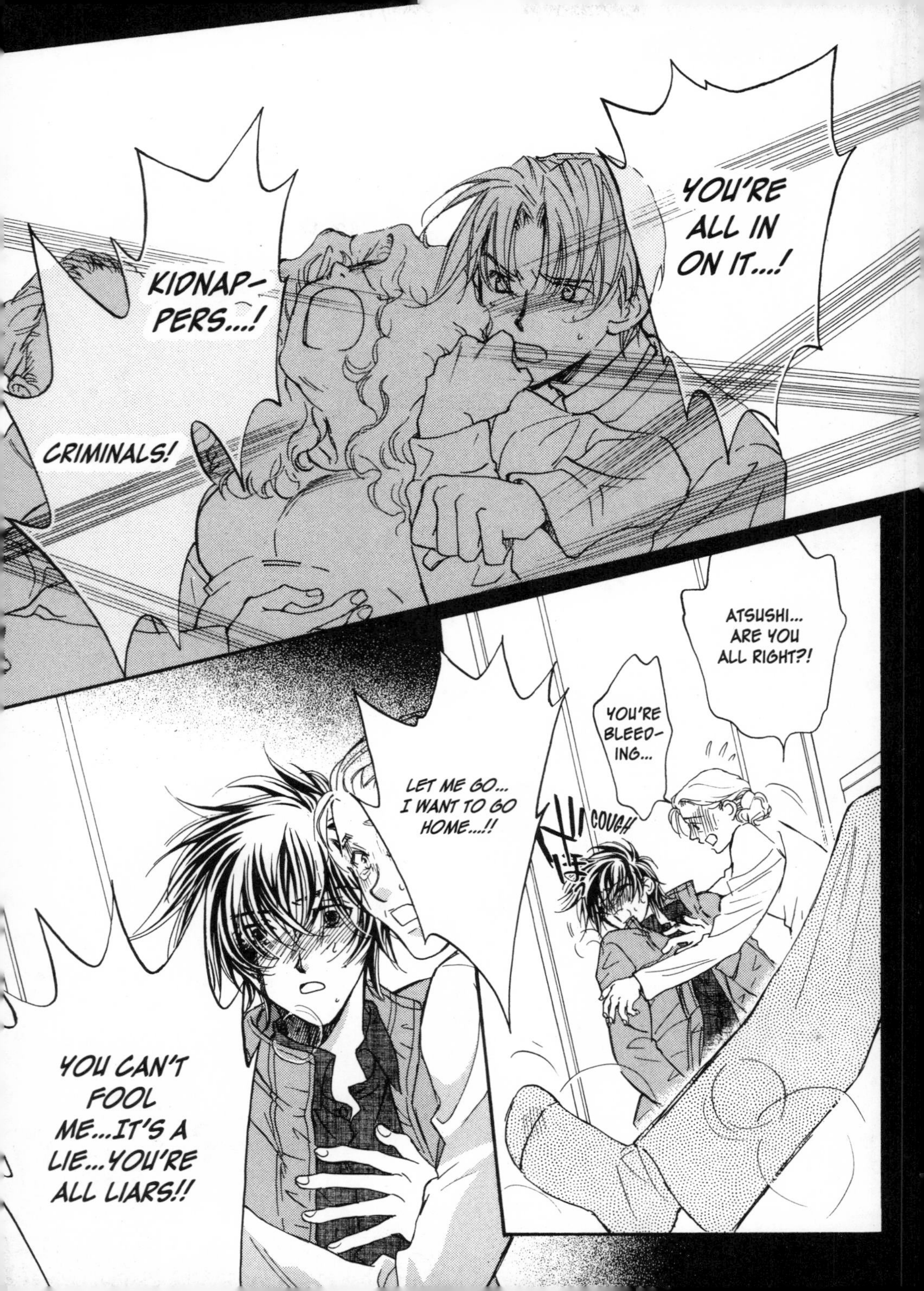
YOU'RE ALL IN ON IT...!
KIDNAP-PERS...!
CRIMINALS!
ATSUSHI... ARE YOU ALL RIGHT?!
YOU'RE BLEED-ING...
COUGH
LET ME GO... I WANT TO GO HOME...!!
YOU CAN'T FOOL ME...IT'S A LIE...YOU'RE ALL LIARS!!

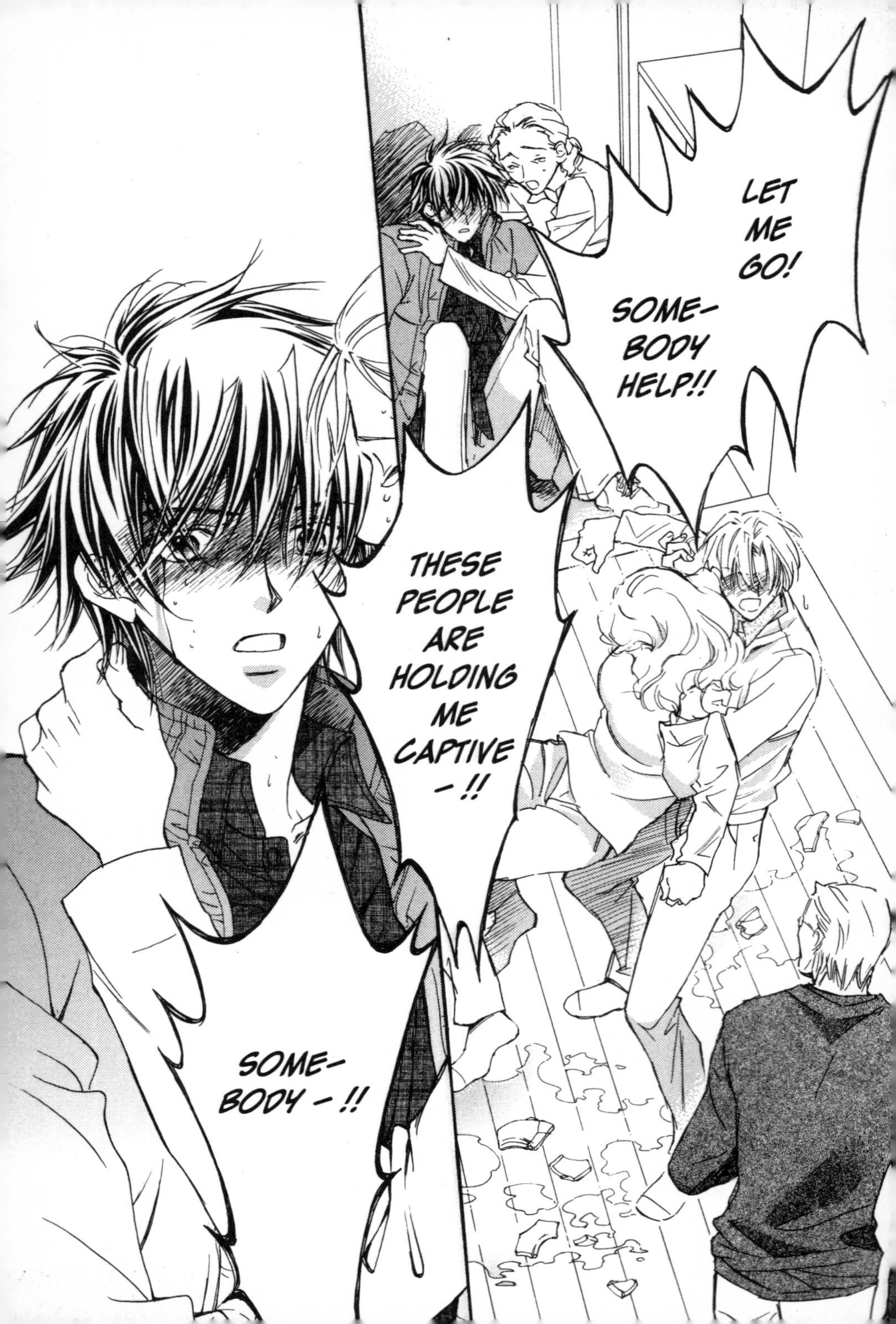
LET ME GO!
SOME-BODY HELP!!
THESE PEOPLE ARE HOLDING ME CAPTIVE -!!
SOME-BODY -!!

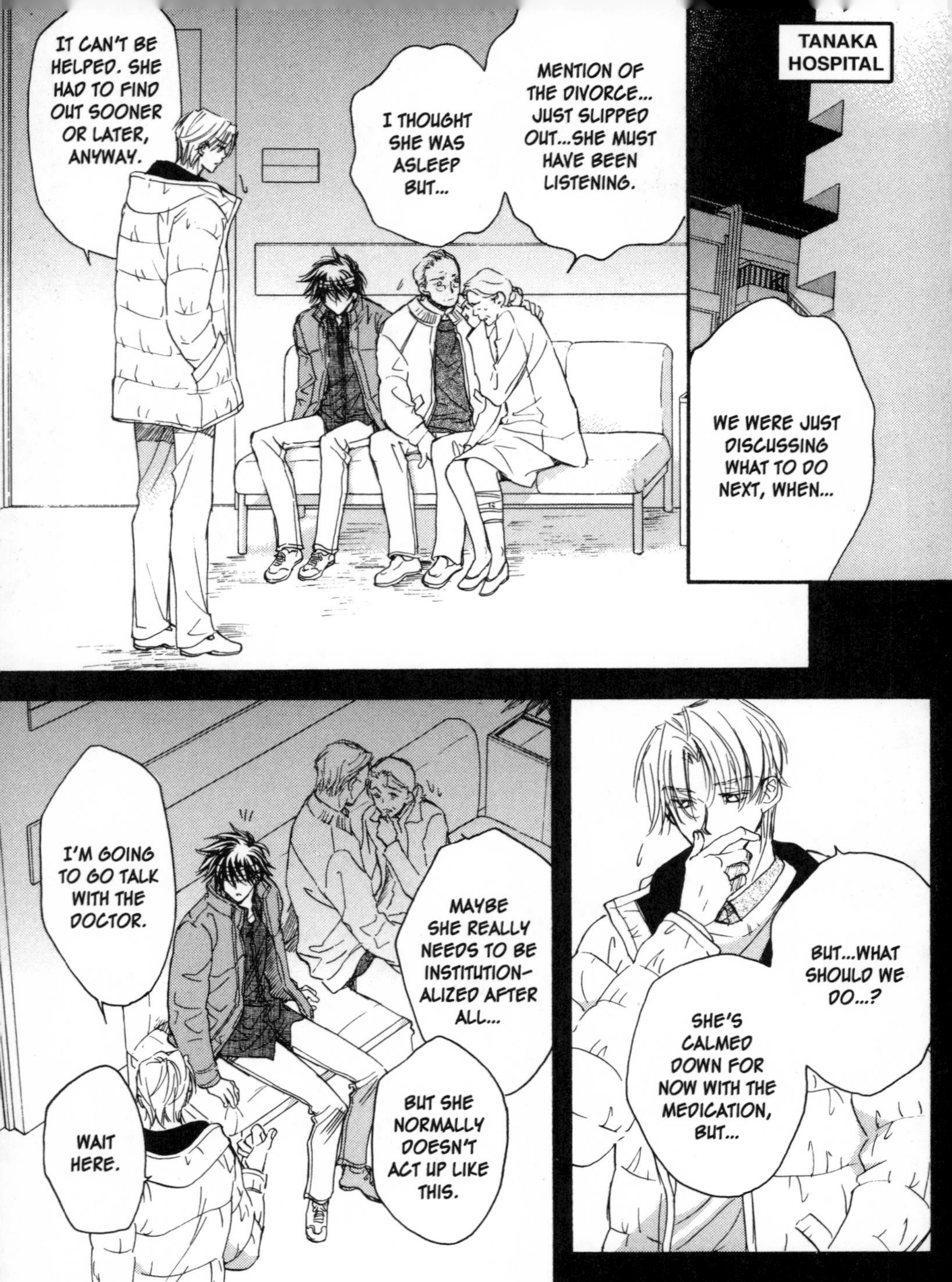
TANAKA HOSPITAL
WE WERE JUST DISCUSSING WHAT TO DO NEXT, WHEN...
MENTION OF THE DIVORCE... JUST SLIPPED OUT...SHE MUST HAVE BEEN LISTENING.
I THOUGHT SHE WAS ASLEEP BUT...
IT CAN'T BE HELPED. SHE HAD TO FIND OUT SOONER OR LATER, ANYWAY.
BUT...WHAT SHOULD WE DO...?
SHE'S CALMED DOWN FOR NOW WITH THE MEDICATION, BUT...
MAYBE SHE REALLY NEEDS TO BE INSTITUTION-ALIZED AFTER ALL...
BUT SHE NORMALLY DOESN'T ACT UP LIKE THIS.
I'M GOING TO GO TALK WITH THE DOCTOR.
WAIT HERE.

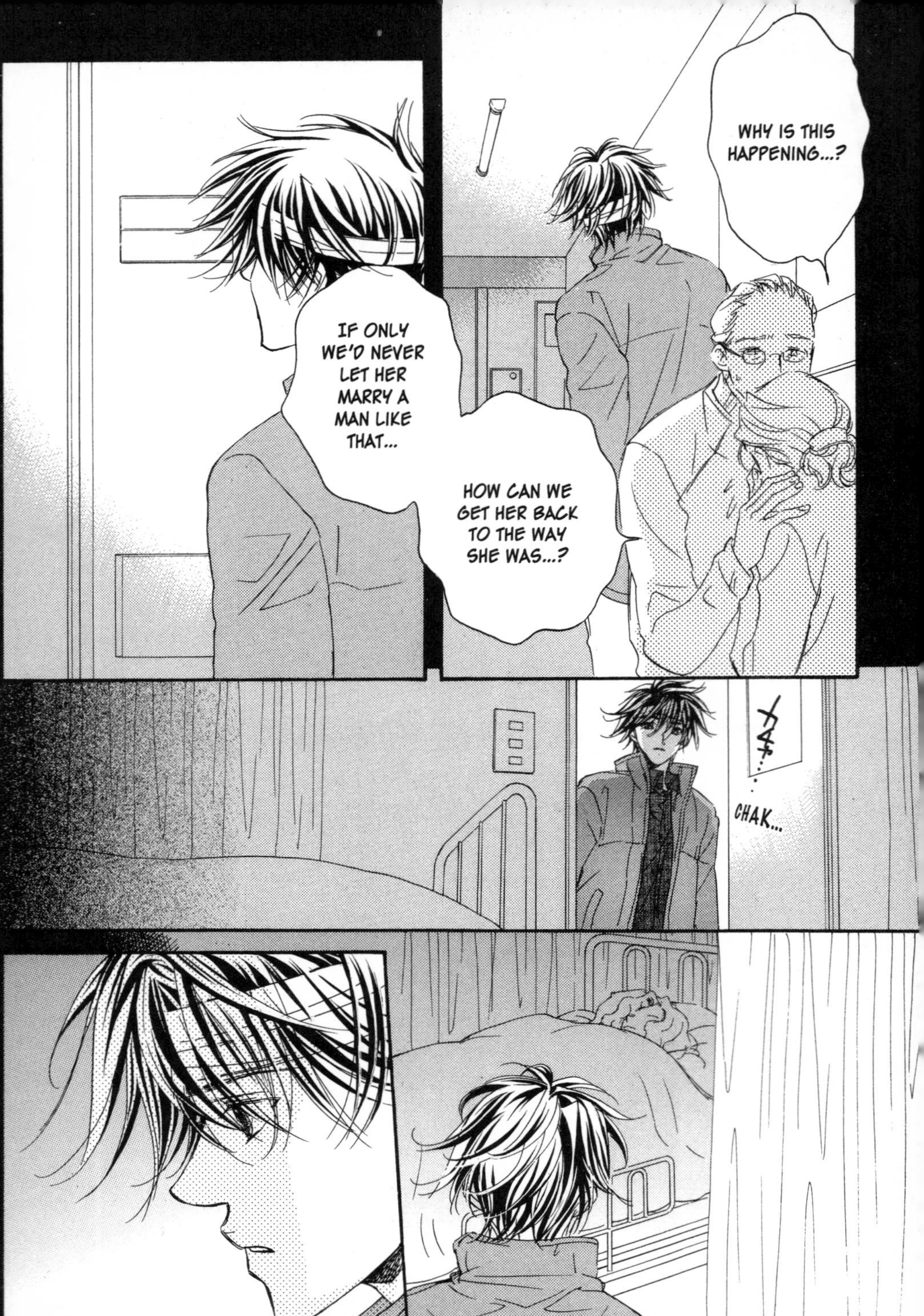
WHY IS THIS HAPPENING...?
IF ONLY WE'D NEVER LET HER MARRY A MAN LIKE THAT...
HOW CAN WE GET HER BACK TO THE WAY SHE WAS...?
CHAK...

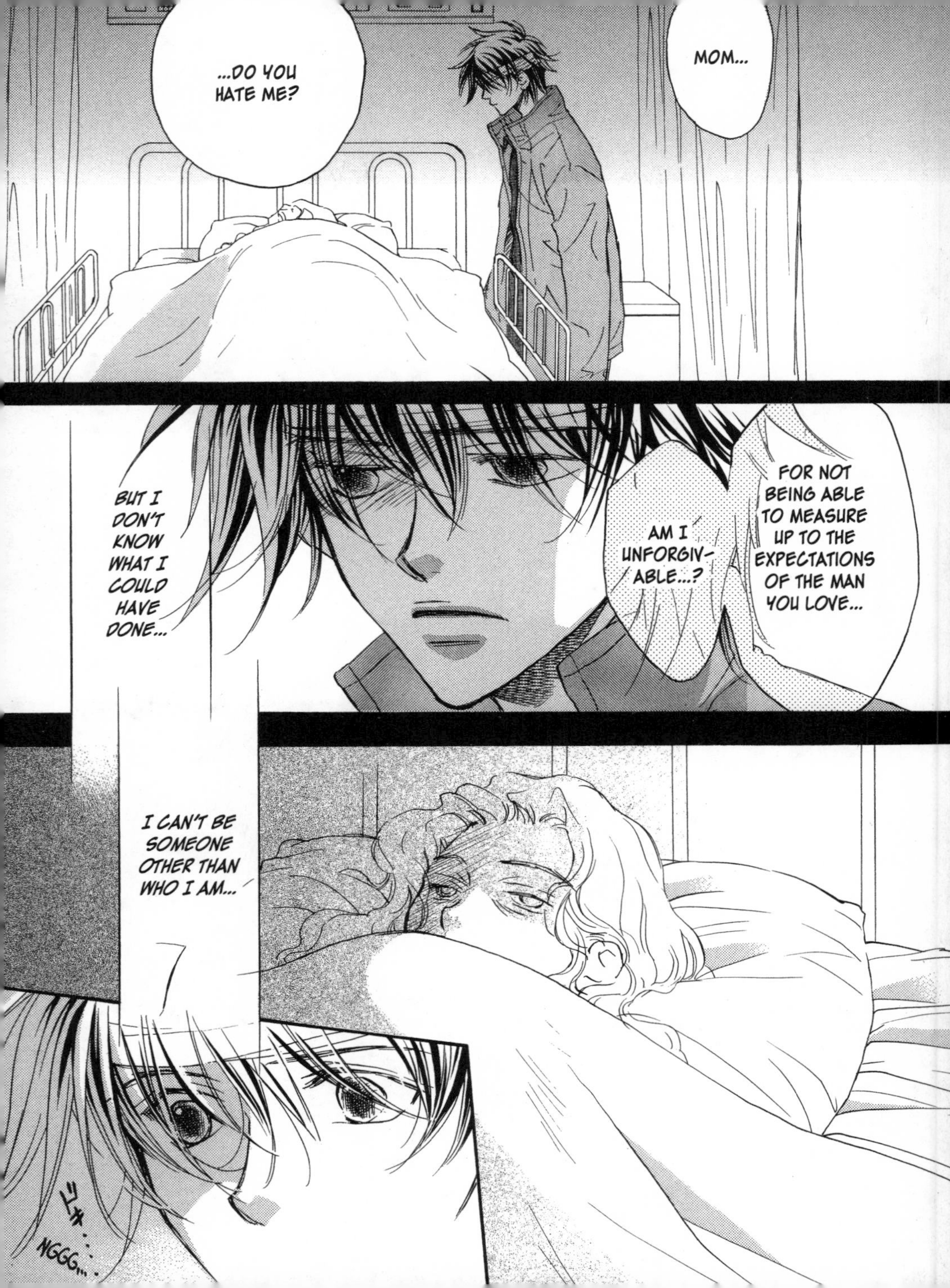
MOM...
...DO YOU HATE ME?
FOR NOT BEING ABLE TO MEASURE UP TO THE EXPECTATIONS OF THE MAN YOU LOVE...
AM I UNFORGIV-ABLE...?
BUT I DON'T KNOW WHAT I COULD HAVE DONE...
I CAN'T BE SOMEONE OTHER THAN WHO I AM...
NGGG...

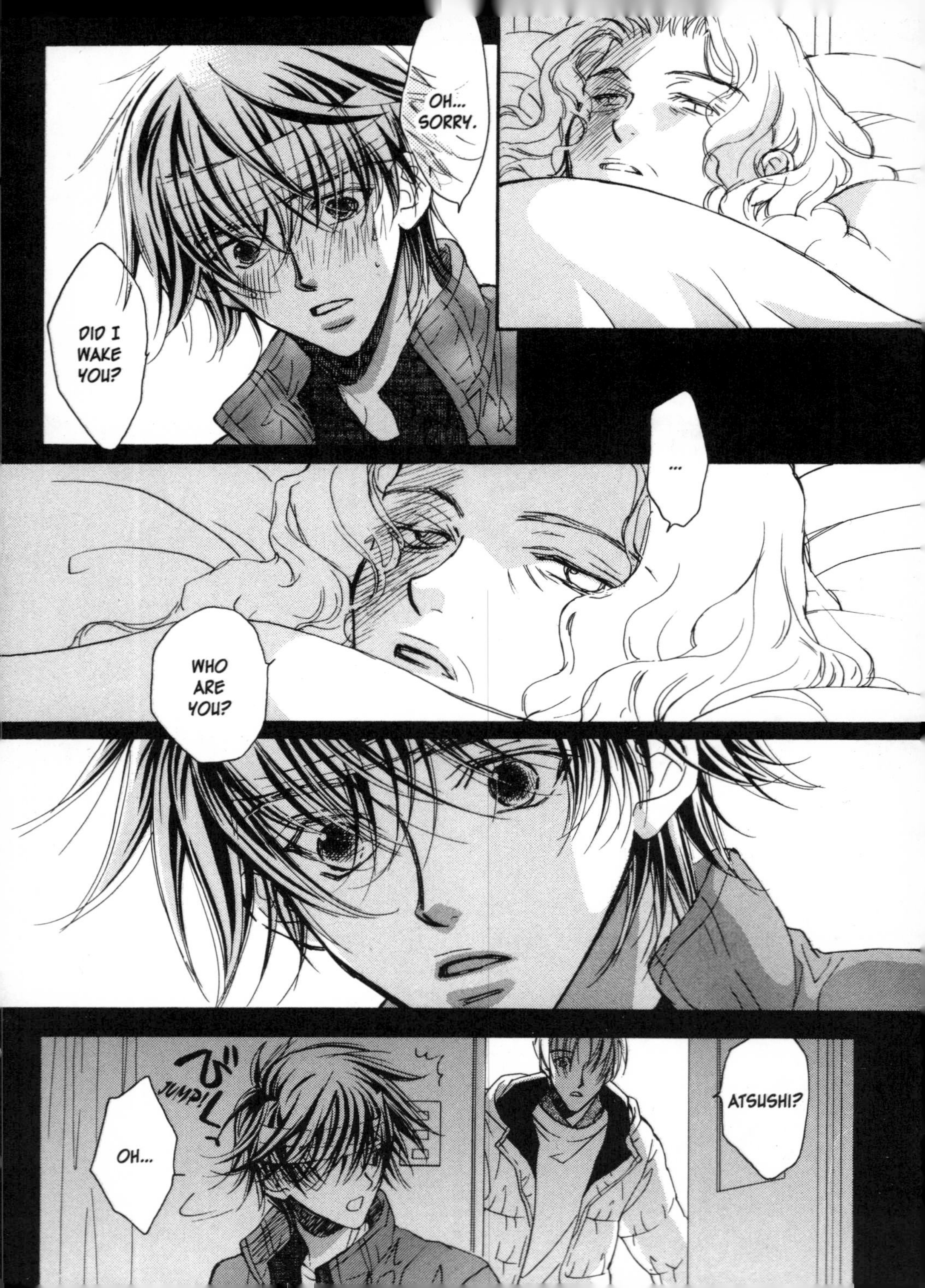
OH... SORRY.
DID I WAKE YOU?
...
WHO ARE YOU?
ATSUSHI?
JUMP!
OH...

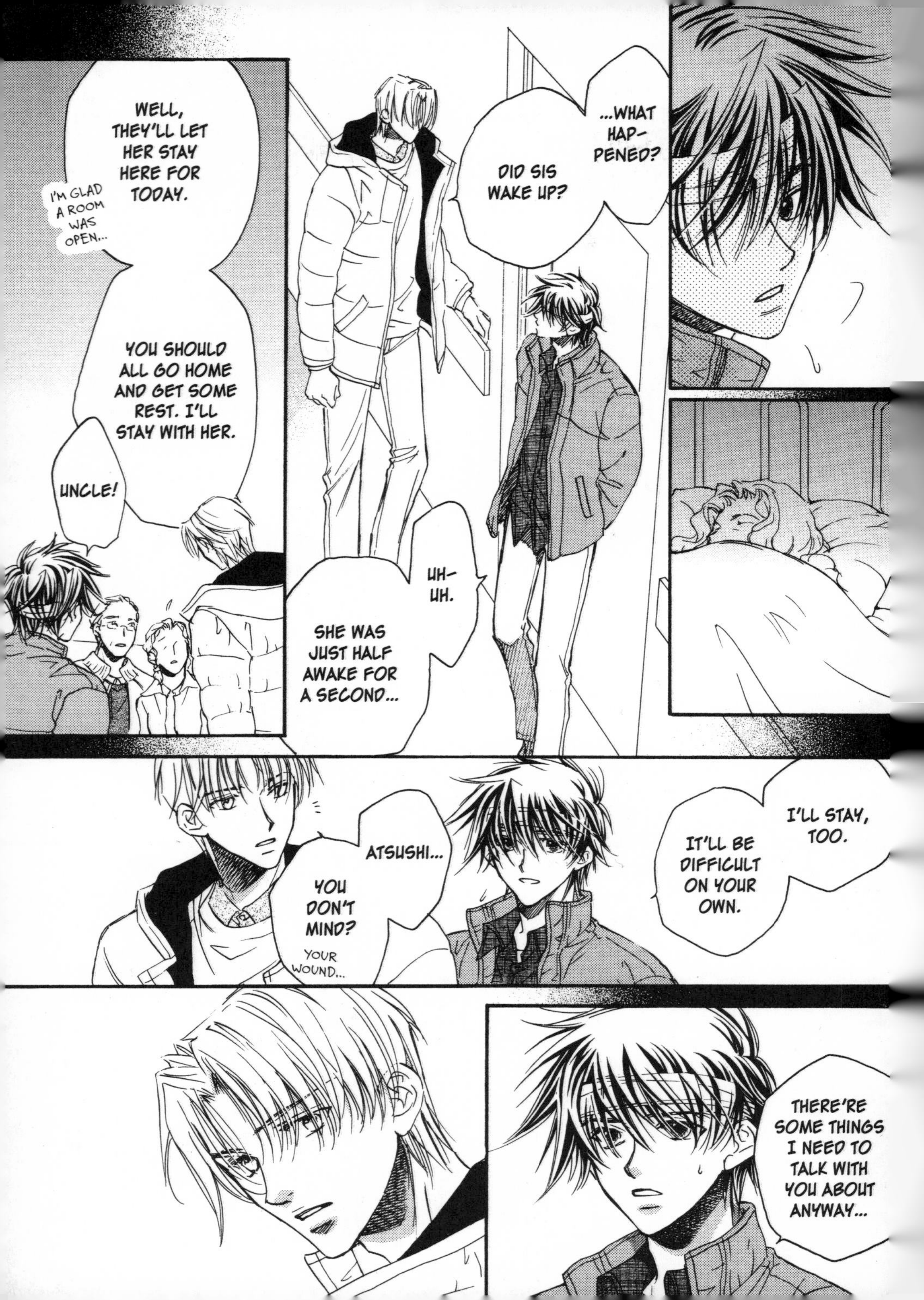
...WHAT HAPPENED?
DID SIS WAKE UP?
UH-UH.
SHE WAS JUST HALF AWAKE FOR A SECOND...
WELL, THEY'LL LET HER STAY HERE FOR TODAY.
I'M GLAD A ROOM WAS OPEN...
YOU SHOULD ALL GO HOME AND GET SOME REST. I'LL STAY WITH HER.
UNCLE!
I'LL STAY, TOO.
IT'LL BE DIFFICULT ON YOUR OWN.
ATSUSHI...
YOU DON'T MIND?
YOUR WOUND...
THERE'RE SOME THINGS I NEED TO TALK WITH YOU ABOUT ANYWAY...

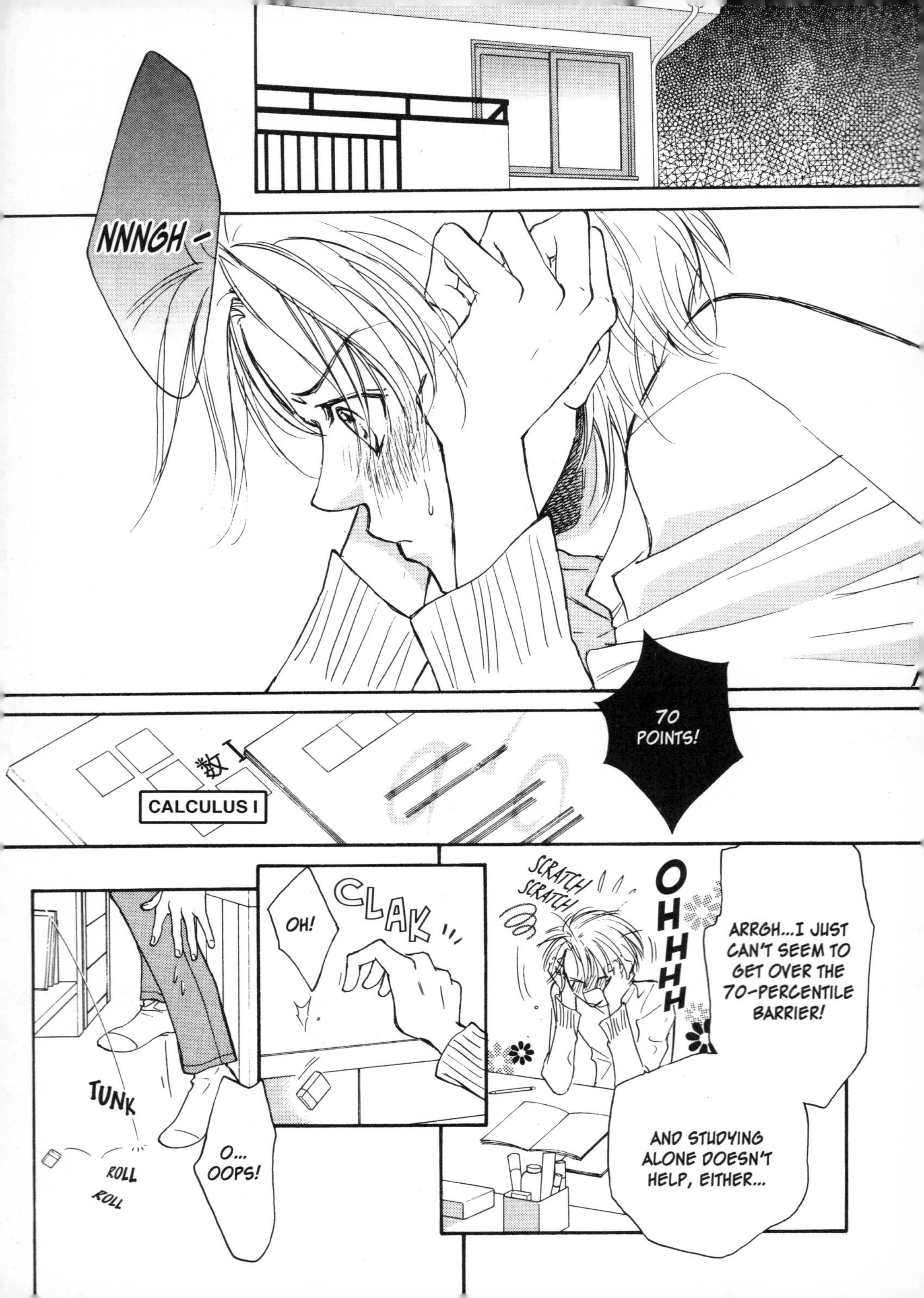

NNNGH –
70 POINTS!
数I
CALCULUS I
ARRGH...I JUST CAN'T SEEM TO GET OVER THE 70-PERCENTILE BARRIER!
OHHHH
SCRATCH SCRATCH
AND STUDYING ALONE DOESN'T HELP, EITHER...
CLAK
OH!
TUNK
ROLL ROLL
O... OOPS!

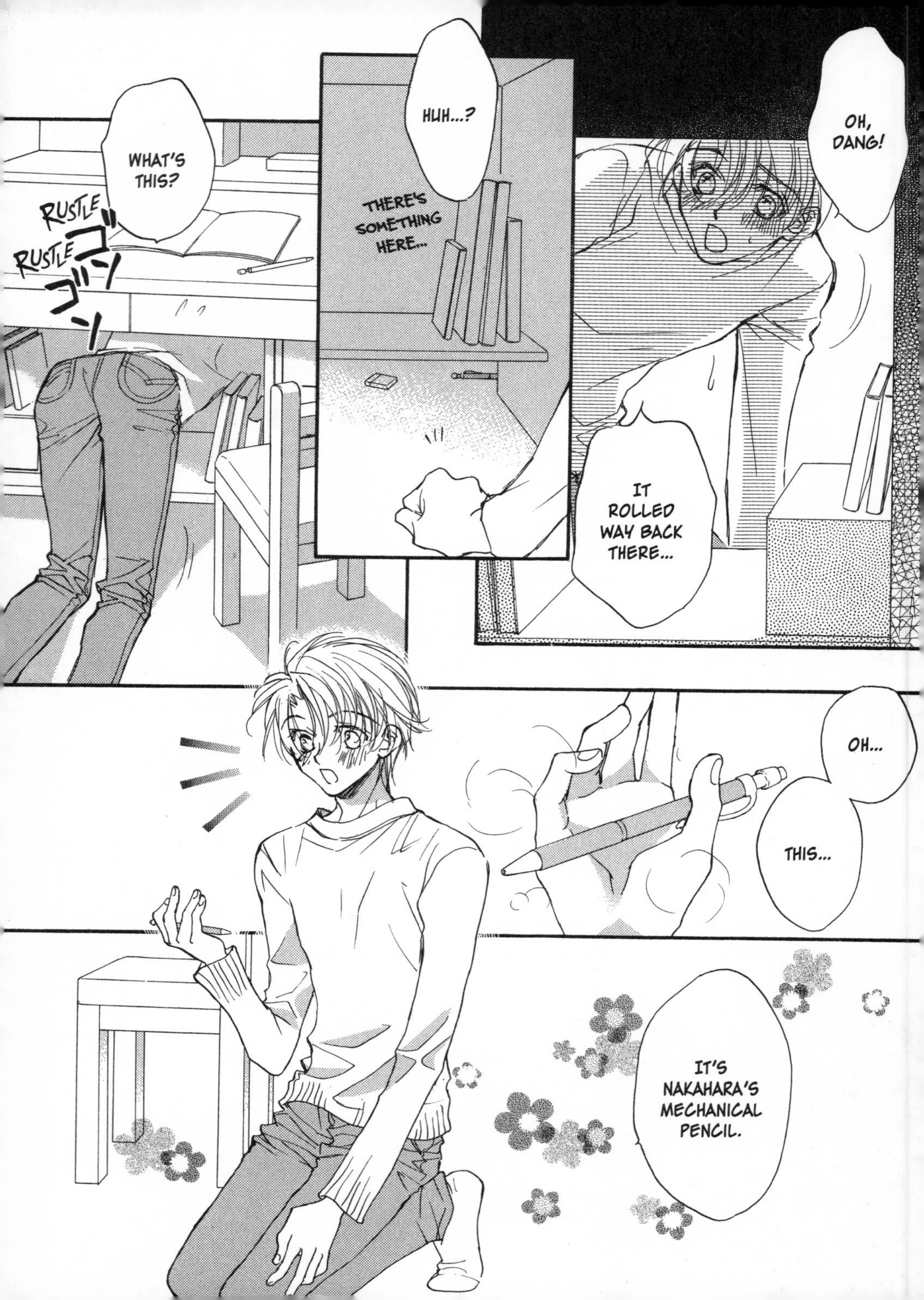

OH, DANG!
IT ROLLED WAY BACK THERE...
HUH...?
THERE'S SOMETHING HERE...
WHAT'S THIS?
RUSTLE RUSTLE
ゴソゴソ
OH...
THIS...
IT'S NAKAHARA'S MECHANICAL PENCIL.

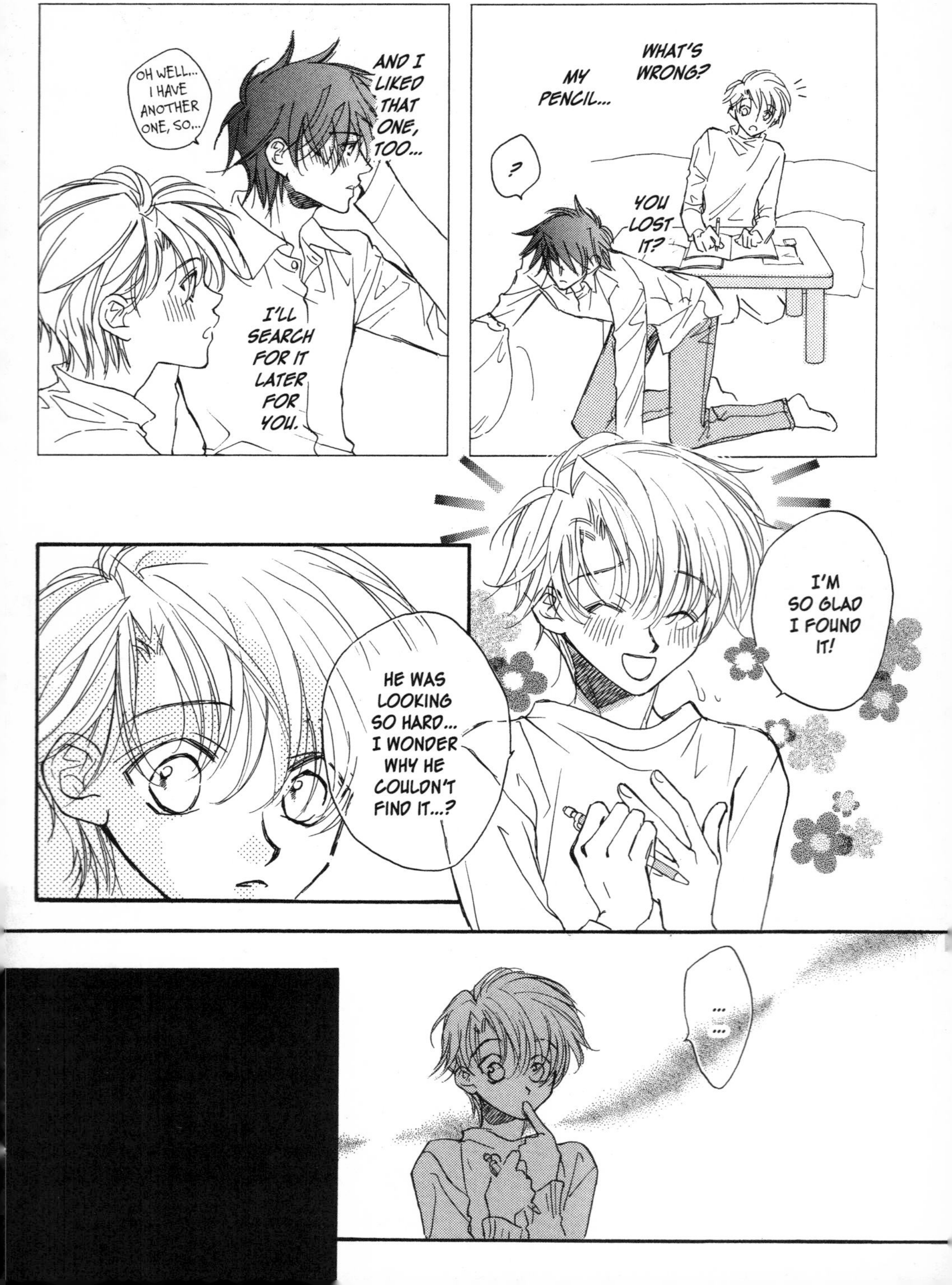
WHAT'S WRONG?
MY PENCIL...
?
YOU LOST IT?
AND I LIKED THAT ONE, TOO...
OH WELL... I HAVE ANOTHER ONE, SO...
I'LL SEARCH FOR IT LATER FOR YOU.
I'M SO GLAD I FOUND IT!
HE WAS LOOKING SO HARD... I WONDER WHY HE COULDN'T FIND IT...?
... ...

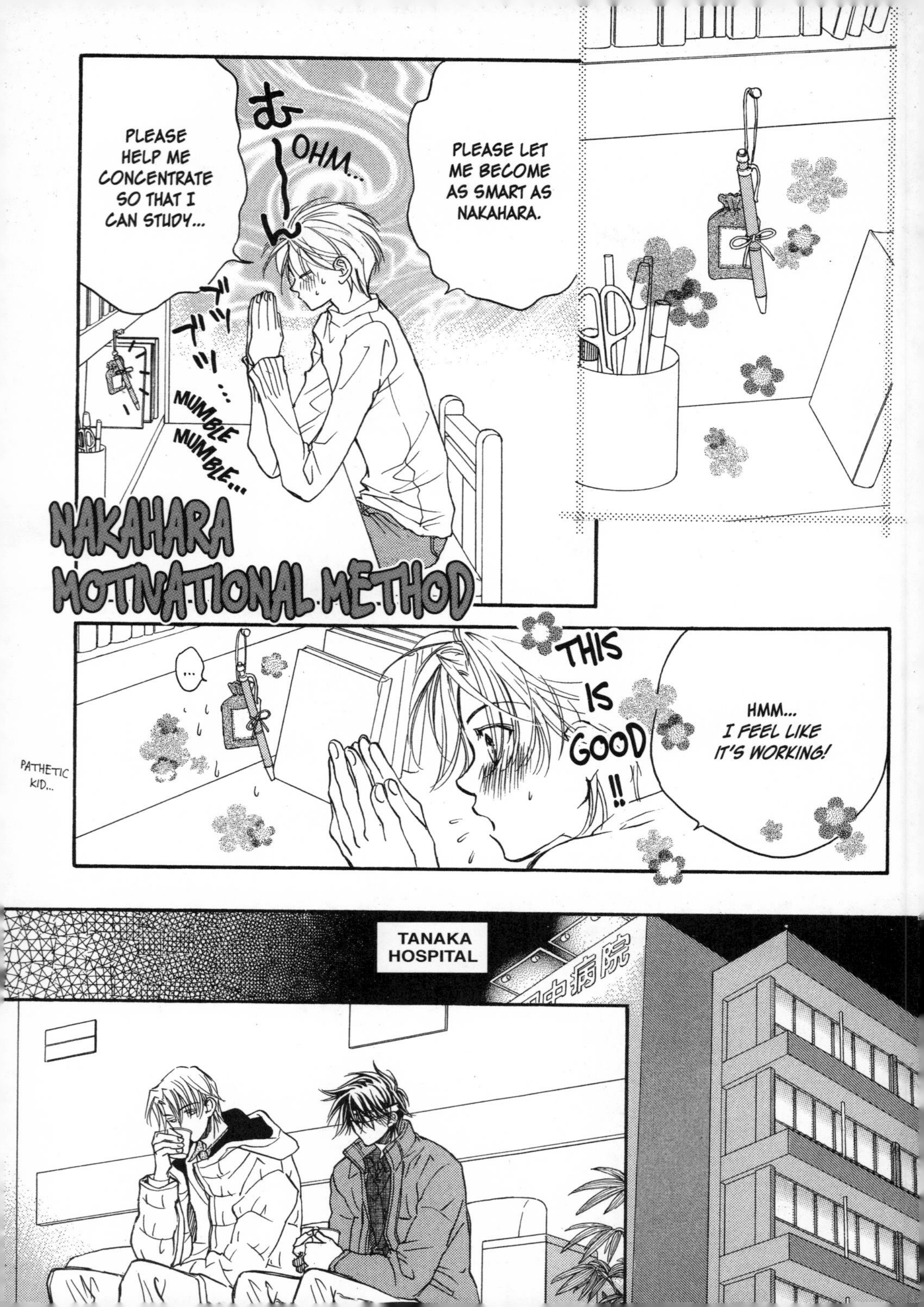
PLEASE LET ME BECOME AS SMART AS NAKAHARA.
むーん
OHM...
PLEASE HELP ME CONCENTRATE SO THAT I CAN STUDY...
ブツブツ...
MUMBLE MUMBLE...
NAKAHARA MOTIVATIONAL METHOD
HMM... I FEEL LIKE IT'S WORKING!
THIS IS GOOD!!
...
PATHETIC KID...
TANAKA HOSPITAL
中病院

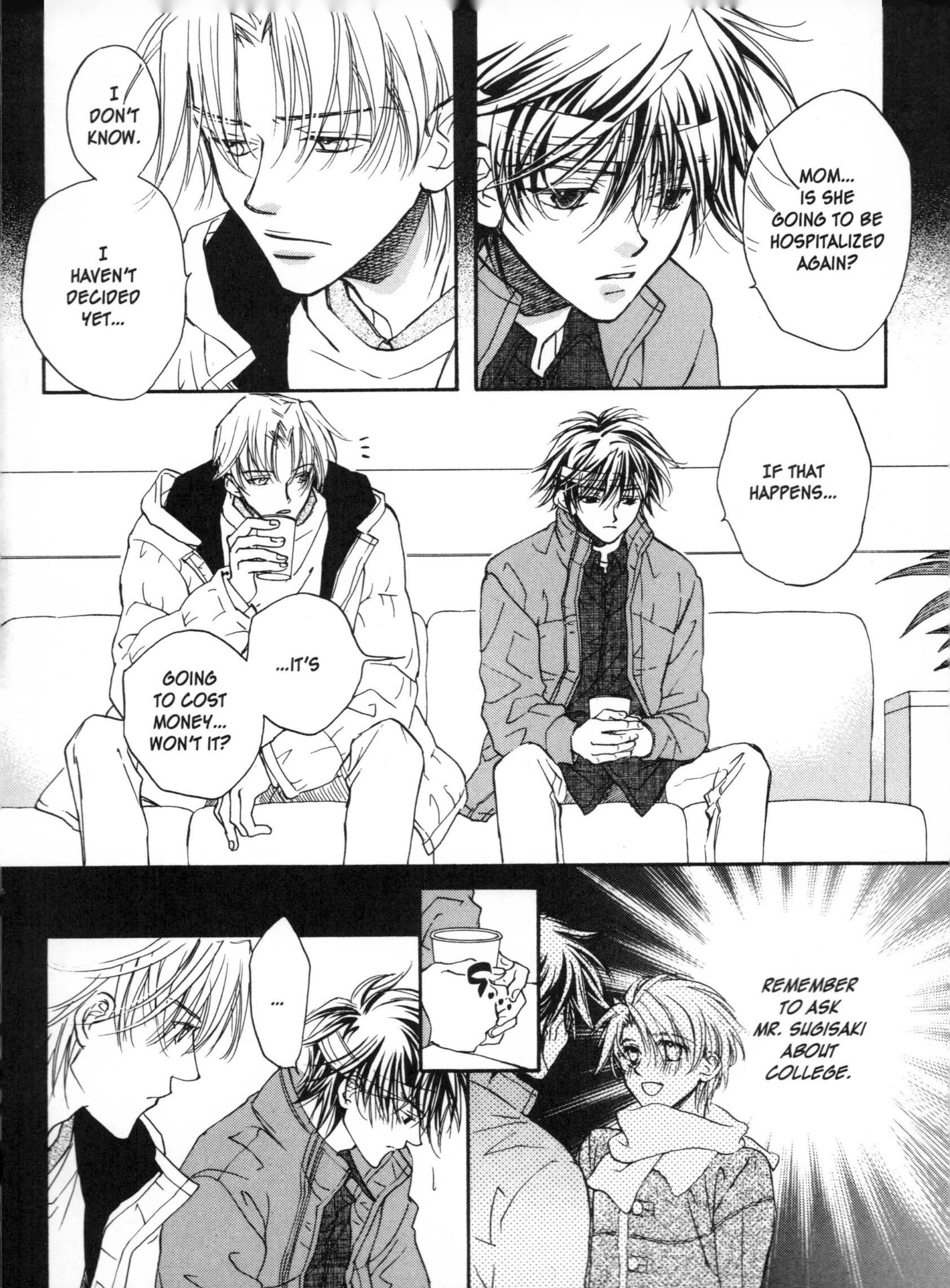
MOM... IS SHE GOING TO BE HOSPITALIZED AGAIN?
I DON'T KNOW.
I HAVEN'T DECIDED YET...
IF THAT HAPPENS...
...IT'S
GOING TO COST MONEY... WON'T IT?
REMEMBER TO ASK MR. SUGISAKI ABOUT COLLEGE.
...

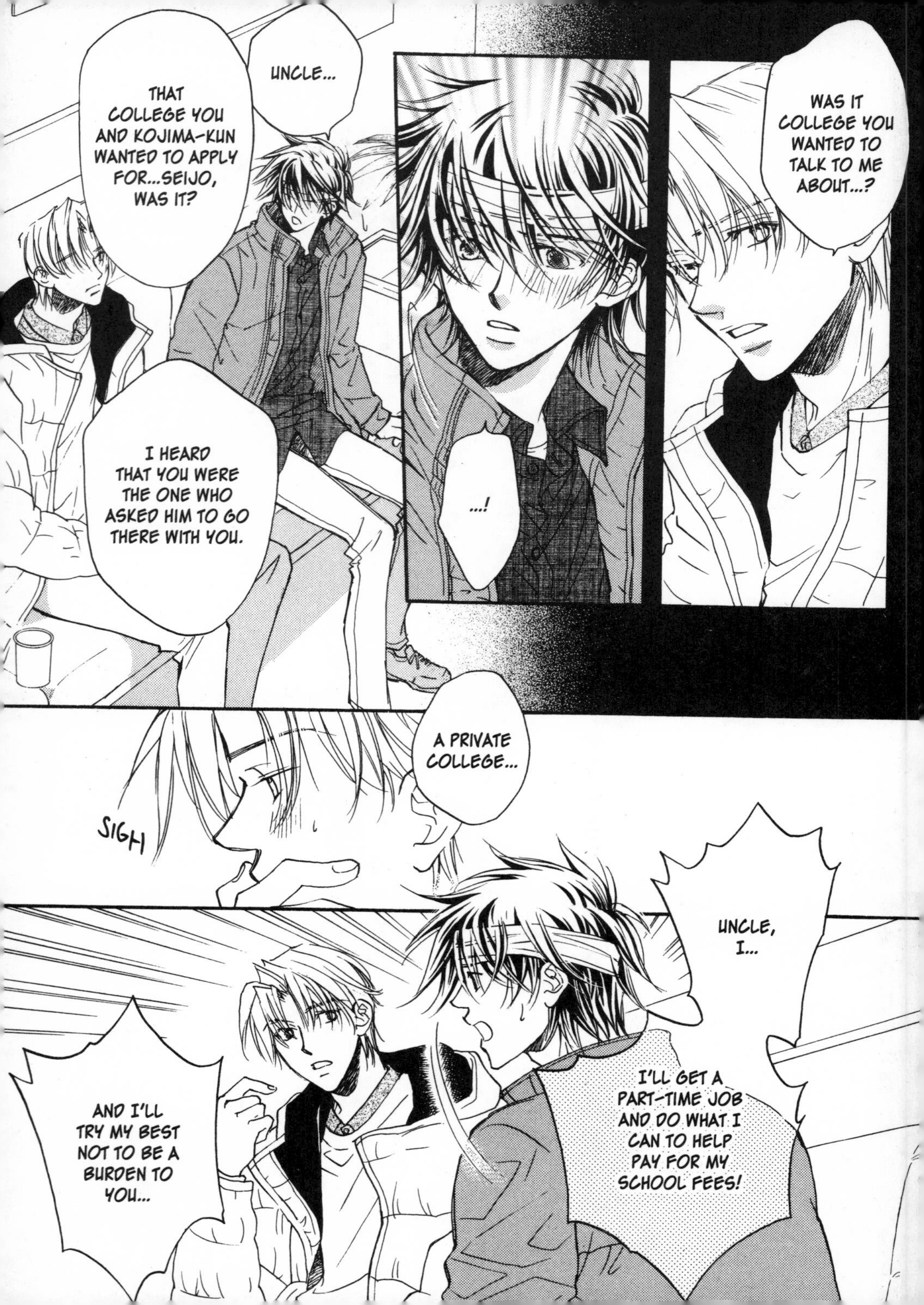
WAS IT COLLEGE YOU WANTED TO TALK TO ME ABOUT...?
...!
UNCLE...
THAT COLLEGE YOU AND KOJIMA-KUN WANTED TO APPLY FOR...SEIJO, WAS IT?
I HEARD THAT YOU WERE THE ONE WHO ASKED HIM TO GO THERE WITH YOU.
A PRIVATE COLLEGE...
SIGH
UNCLE, I...
I'LL GET A PART-TIME JOB AND DO WHAT I CAN TO HELP PAY FOR MY SCHOOL FEES!
AND I'LL TRY MY BEST NOT TO BE A BURDEN TO YOU...

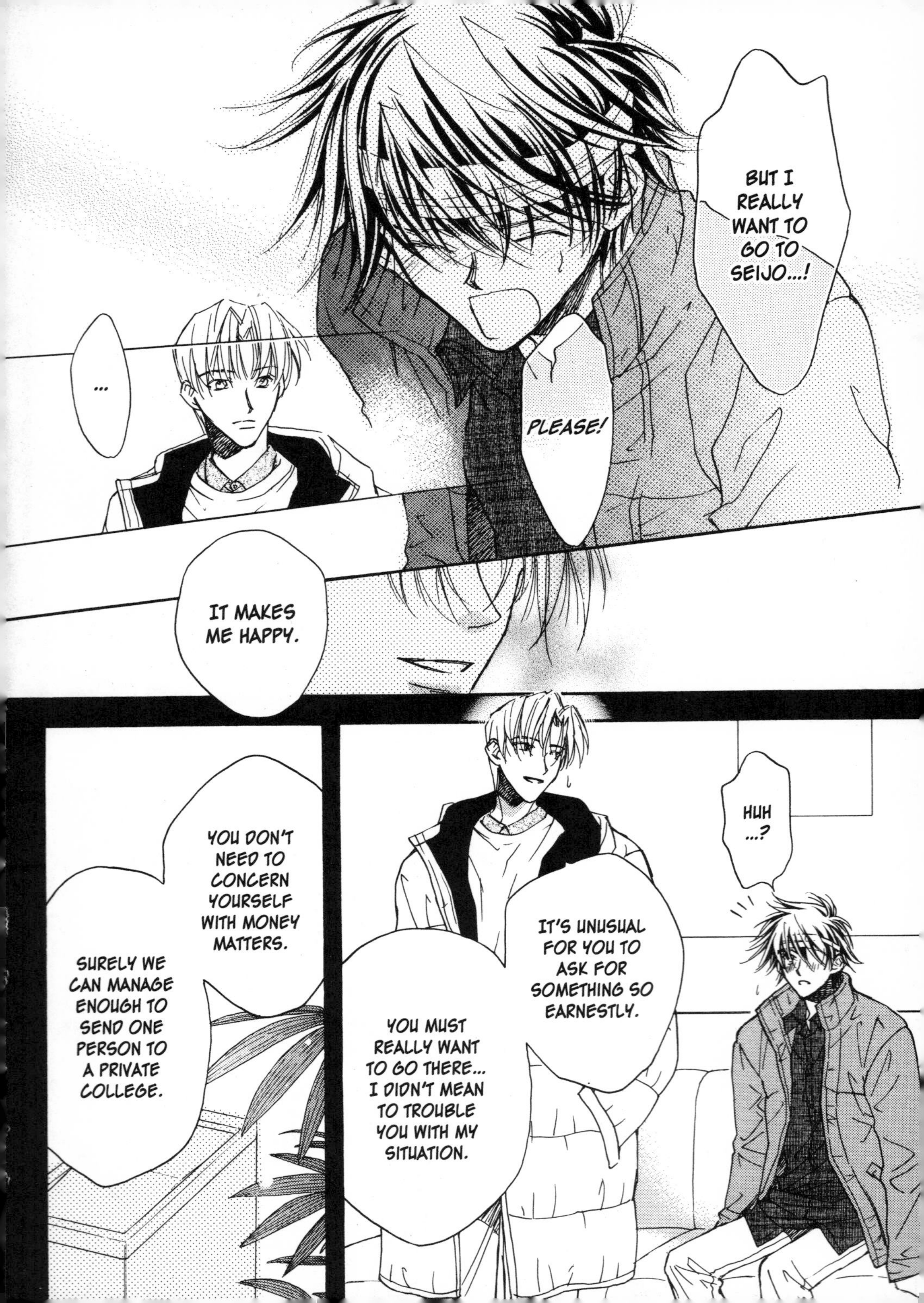
BUT I REALLY WANT TO GO TO SEIJO...!
PLEASE!
...
IT MAKES ME HAPPY.
HUH ...?
IT'S UNUSUAL FOR YOU TO ASK FOR SOMETHING SO EARNESTLY.
YOU MUST REALLY WANT TO GO THERE... I DIDN'T MEAN TO TROUBLE YOU WITH MY SITUATION.
YOU DON'T NEED TO CONCERN YOURSELF WITH MONEY MATTERS.
SURELY WE CAN MANAGE ENOUGH TO SEND ONE PERSON TO A PRIVATE COLLEGE.

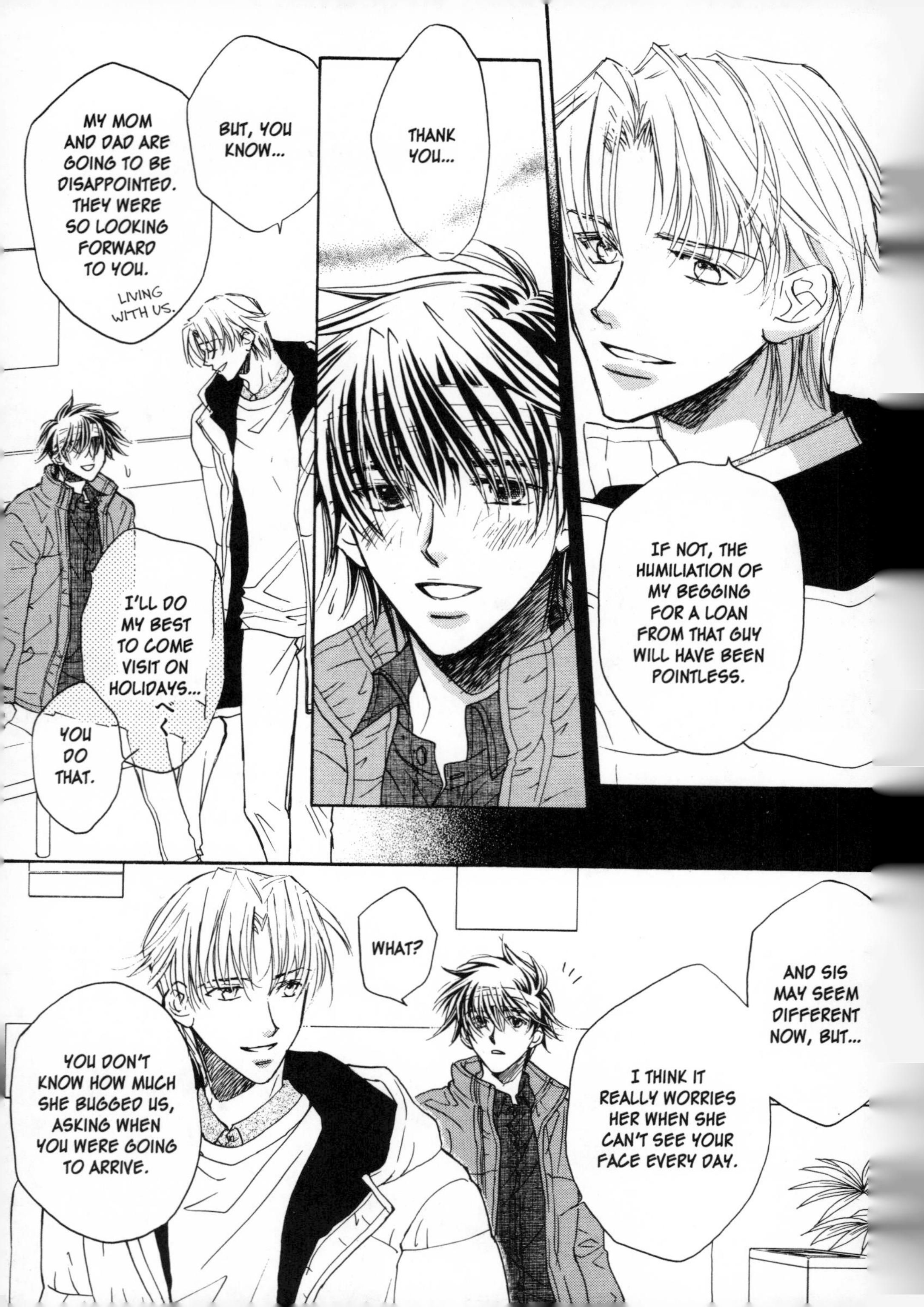
IF NOT, THE HUMILIATION OF MY BEGGING FOR A LOAN FROM THAT GUY WILL HAVE BEEN POINTLESS.
THANK YOU...
BUT, YOU KNOW...
MY MOM AND DAD ARE GOING TO BE DISAPPOINTED. THEY WERE SO LOOKING FORWARD TO YOU.
LIVING WITH US.
I'LL DO MY BEST TO COME VISIT ON HOLIDAYS...
べく
YOU DO THAT.
AND SIS MAY SEEM DIFFERENT NOW, BUT...
I THINK IT REALLY WORRIES HER WHEN SHE CAN'T SEE YOUR FACE EVERY DAY.
WHAT?
YOU DON'T KNOW HOW MUCH SHE BUGGED US, ASKING WHEN YOU WERE GOING TO ARRIVE.

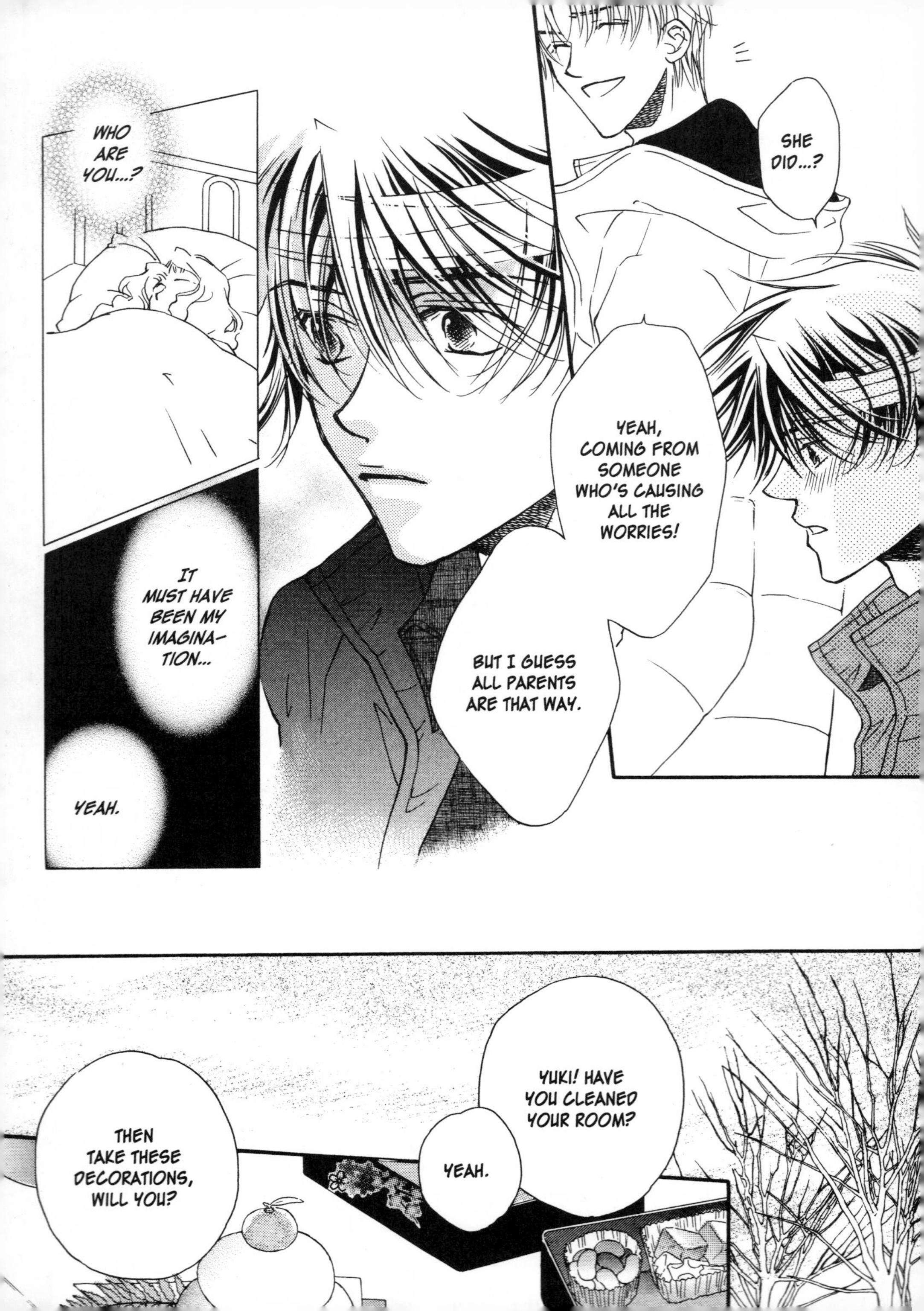
SHE DID...?
YEAH, COMING FROM SOMEONE WHO'S CAUSING ALL THE WORRIES!
BUT I GUESS ALL PARENTS ARE THAT WAY.
WHO ARE YOU...?
IT MUST HAVE BEEN MY IMAGINATION...
YEAH.
YUKI! HAVE YOU CLEANED YOUR ROOM?
YEAH.
THEN TAKE THESE DECORATIONS, WILL YOU?

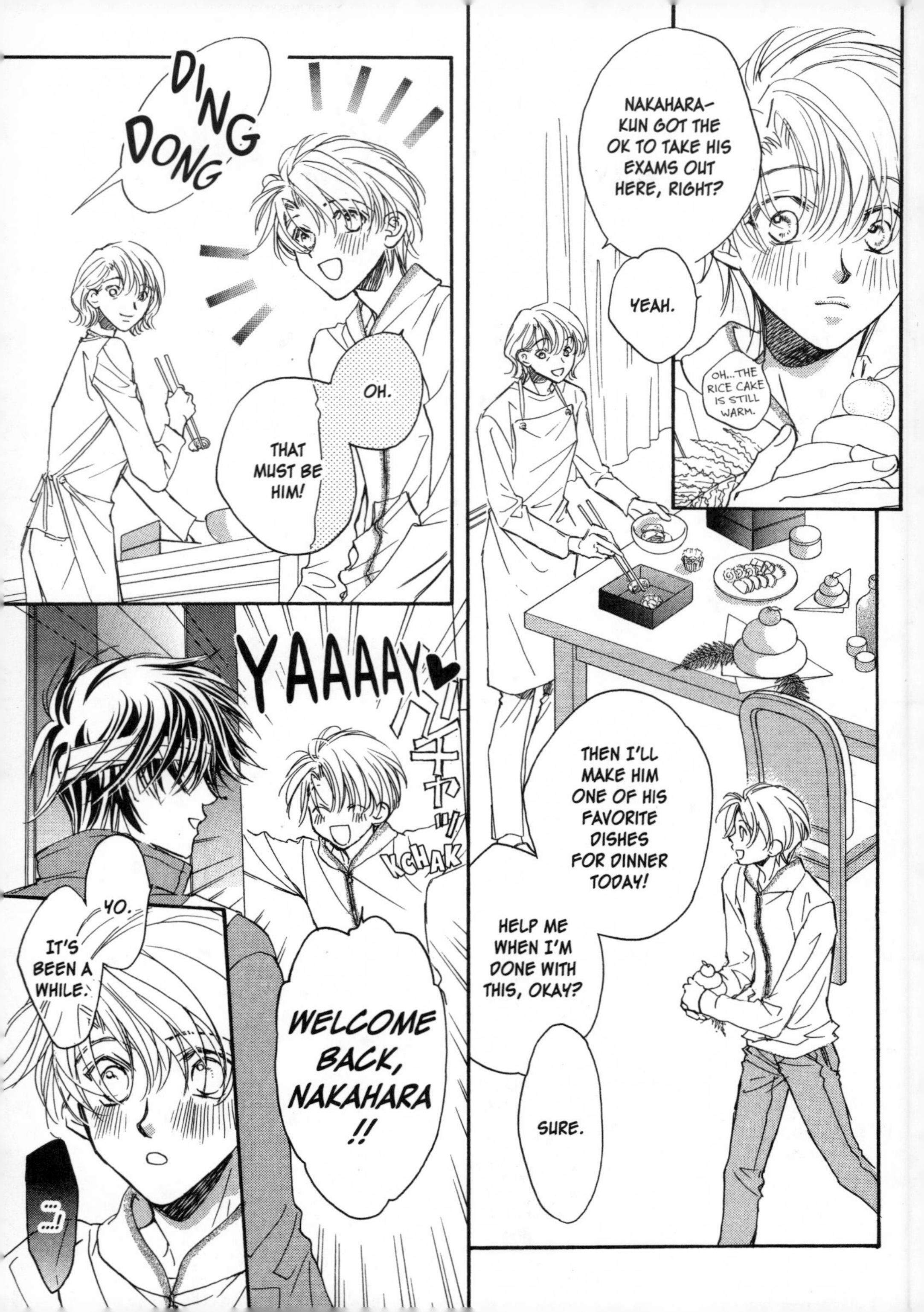
NAKAHARA-KUN GOT THE OK TO TAKE HIS EXAMS OUT HERE, RIGHT?
YEAH.
OH...THE RICE CAKE IS STILL WARM.
THEN I'LL MAKE HIM ONE OF HIS FAVORITE DISHES FOR DINNER TODAY!
HELP ME WHEN I'M DONE WITH THIS, OKAY?
SURE.
DING DONG
OH.
THAT MUST BE HIM!
YAAAAY♥
KCHAK
WELCOME BACK, NAKAHARA !!
YO.
IT'S BEEN A WHILE.

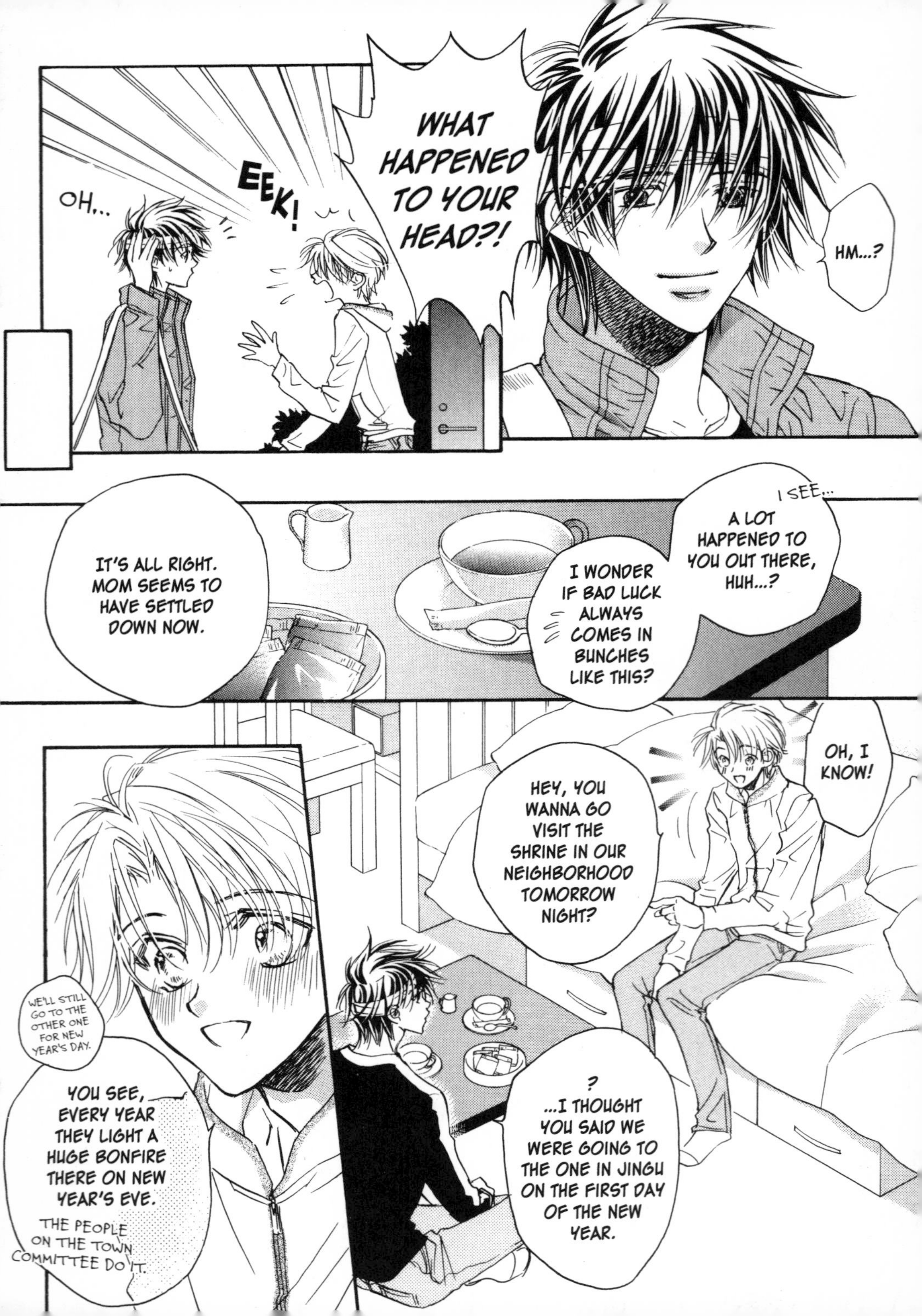
HM...?
WHAT HAPPENED TO YOUR HEAD?!
EEK!
OH...
I SEE...
A LOT HAPPENED TO YOU OUT THERE, HUH...?
I WONDER IF BAD LUCK ALWAYS COMES IN BUNCHES LIKE THIS?
IT'S ALL RIGHT. MOM SEEMS TO HAVE SETTLED DOWN NOW.
OH, I KNOW!
HEY, YOU WANNA GO VISIT THE SHRINE IN OUR NEIGHBORHOOD TOMORROW NIGHT?
? ...I THOUGHT YOU SAID WE WERE GOING TO THE ONE IN JINGU ON THE FIRST DAY OF THE NEW YEAR.
YOU SEE, EVERY YEAR THEY LIGHT A HUGE BONFIRE THERE ON NEW YEAR'S EVE.
THE PEOPLE ON THE TOWN COMMITTEE DO IT.
WE'LL STILL GO TO THE OTHER ONE FOR NEW YEAR'S DAY.

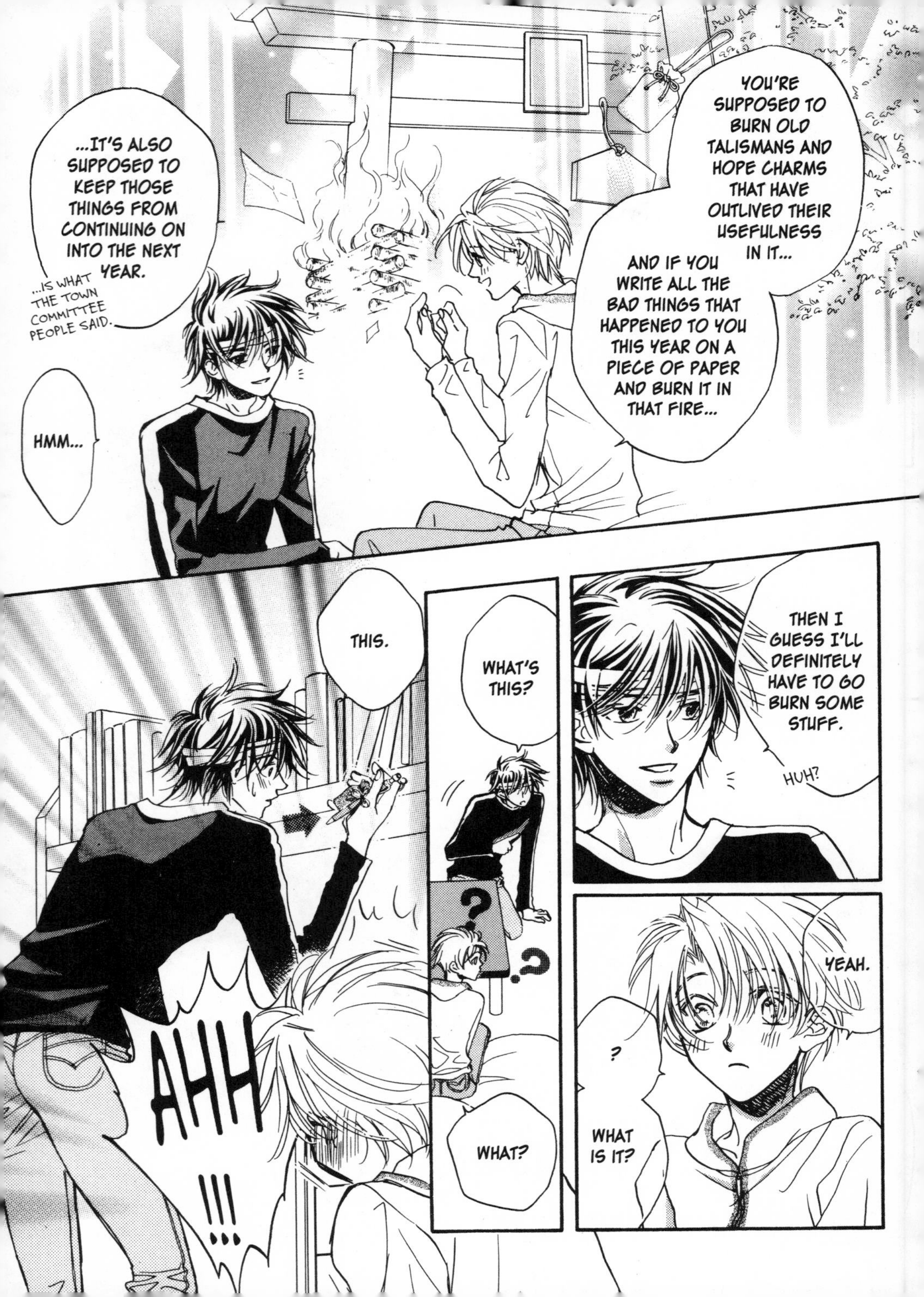
YOU'RE SUPPOSED TO BURN OLD TALISMANS AND HOPE CHARMS THAT HAVE OUTLIVED THEIR USEFULNESS IN IT...
AND IF YOU WRITE ALL THE BAD THINGS THAT HAPPENED TO YOU THIS YEAR ON A PIECE OF PAPER AND BURN IT IN THAT FIRE...
...IT'S ALSO SUPPOSED TO KEEP THOSE THINGS FROM CONTINUING ON INTO THE NEXT YEAR.
...IS WHAT THE TOWN COMMITTEE PEOPLE SAID.
HMM...
THEN I GUESS I'LL DEFINITELY HAVE TO GO BURN SOME STUFF.
HUH?
YEAH.
?
WHAT IS IT?
WHAT'S THIS?
WHAT?
THIS.
AHH
!!!...

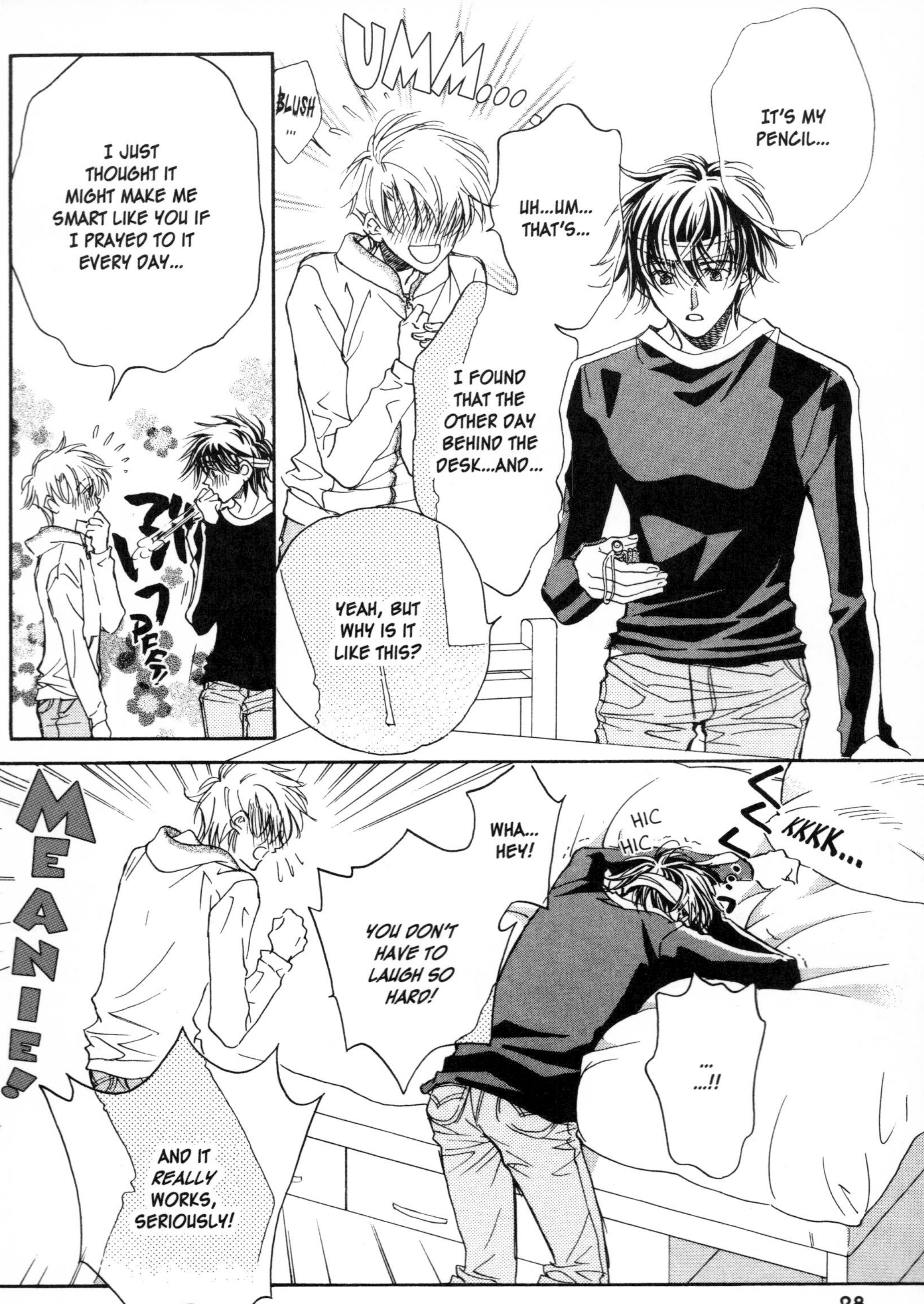
IT'S MY PENCIL...
UH...UM... THAT'S...
UMMOOO
BLUSH ...
I FOUND THAT THE OTHER DAY BEHIND THE DESK...AND...
YEAH, BUT WHY IS IT LIKE THIS?
I JUST THOUGHT IT MIGHT MAKE ME SMART LIKE YOU IF I PRAYED TO IT EVERY DAY...
PFFT!
KKKK...
HIC HIC
WHA... HEY!
... ...!!
YOU DON'T HAVE TO LAUGH SO HARD!
MEANIE!
AND IT REALLY WORKS, SERIOUSLY!

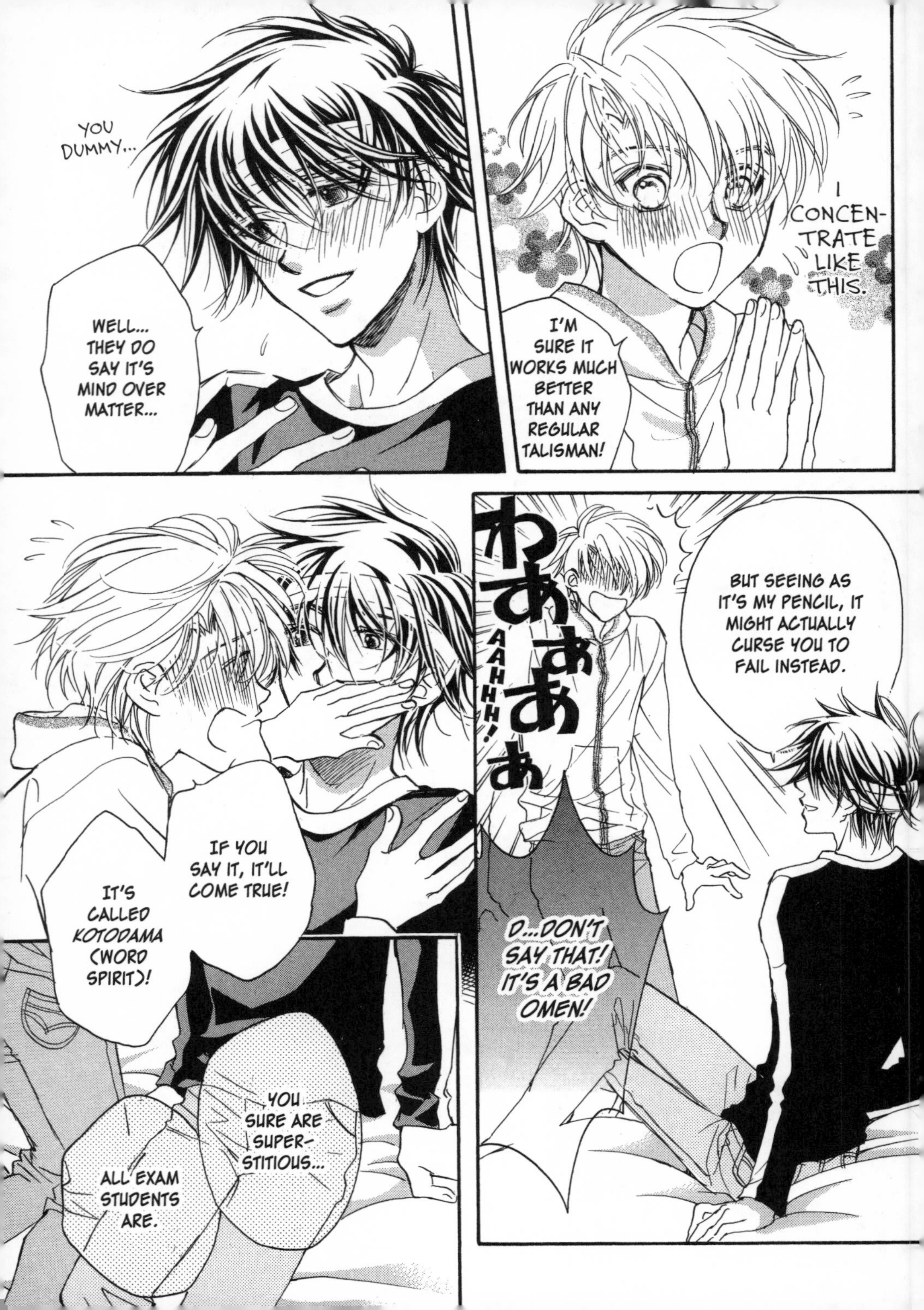
I CONCENTRATE LIKE THIS.
I'M SURE IT WORKS MUCH BETTER THAN ANY REGULAR TALISMAN!
YOU DUMMY...
WELL... THEY DO SAY IT'S MIND OVER MATTER...
BUT SEEING AS IT'S MY PENCIL, IT MIGHT ACTUALLY CURSE YOU TO FAIL INSTEAD.
わぁぁぁぁ
AAHHH!
D...DON'T SAY THAT! IT'S A BAD OMEN!
IF YOU SAY IT, IT'LL COME TRUE!
IT'S CALLED KOTODAMA (WORD SPIRIT)!
YOU SURE ARE SUPER-STITIOUS...
ALL EXAM STUDENTS ARE.

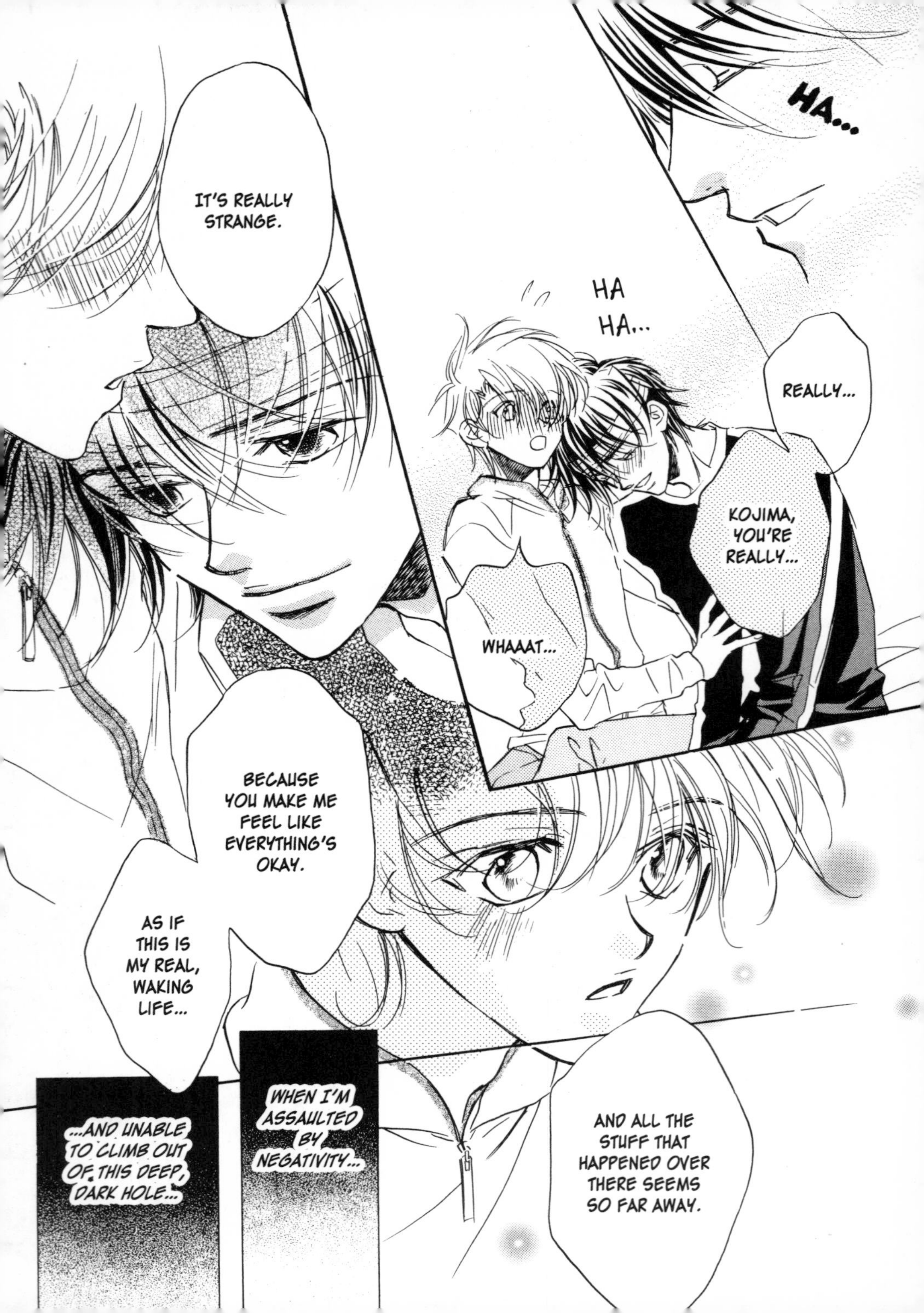
HA...
HA HA...
REALLY...
KOJIMA, YOU'RE REALLY...
WHAAAT...
IT'S REALLY STRANGE.
BECAUSE YOU MAKE ME FEEL LIKE EVERYTHING'S OKAY.
AS IF THIS IS MY REAL, WAKING LIFE...
AND ALL THE STUFF THAT HAPPENED OVER THERE SEEMS SO FAR AWAY.
WHEN I'M ASSAULTED BY NEGATIVITY...
...AND UNABLE TO CLIMB OUT OF THIS DEEP, DARK HOLE...

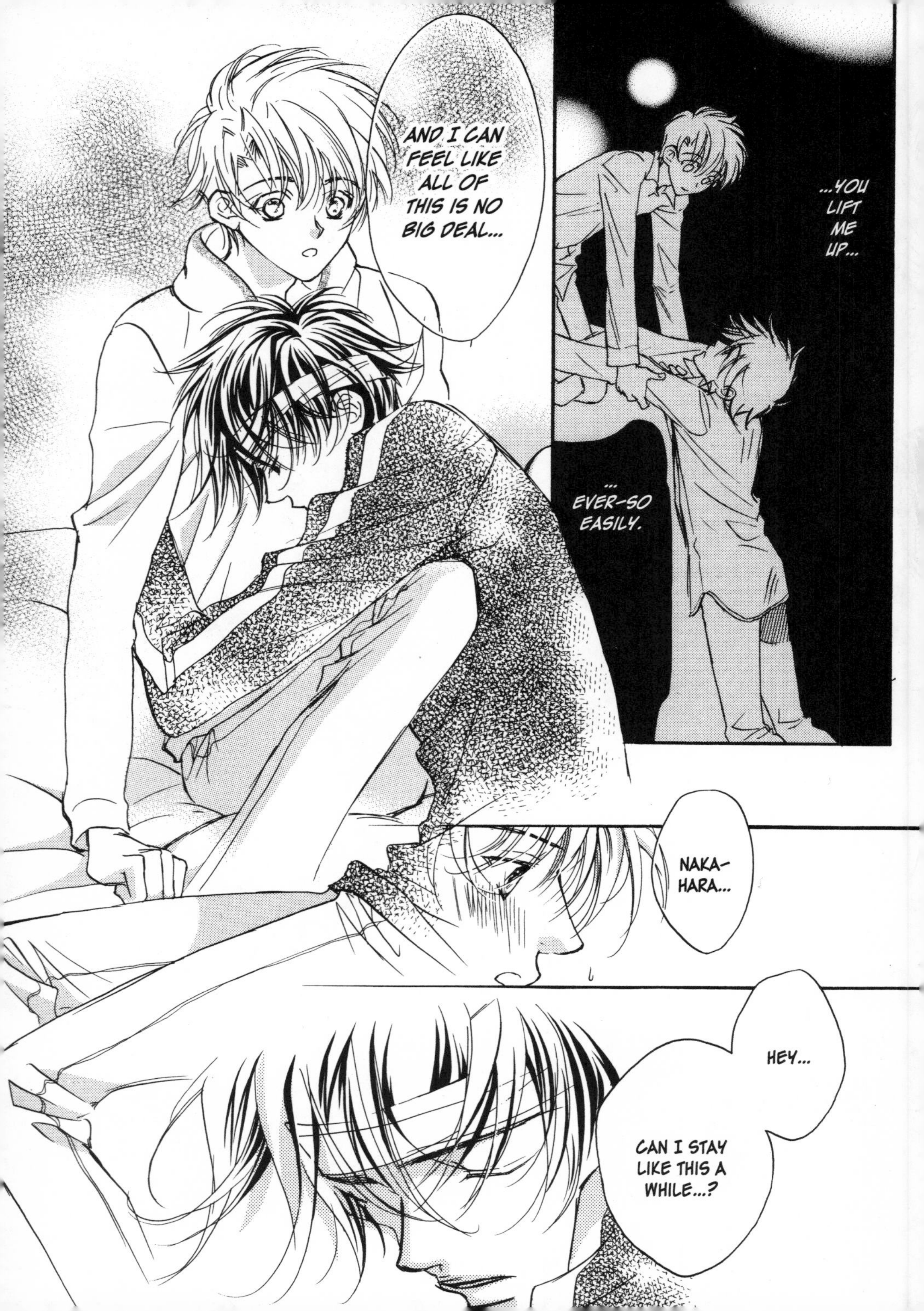
...YOU LIFT ME UP...
... EVER-SO EASILY.
AND I CAN FEEL LIKE ALL OF THIS IS NO BIG DEAL...
NAKA-HARA...
HEY...
CAN I STAY LIKE THIS A WHILE...?

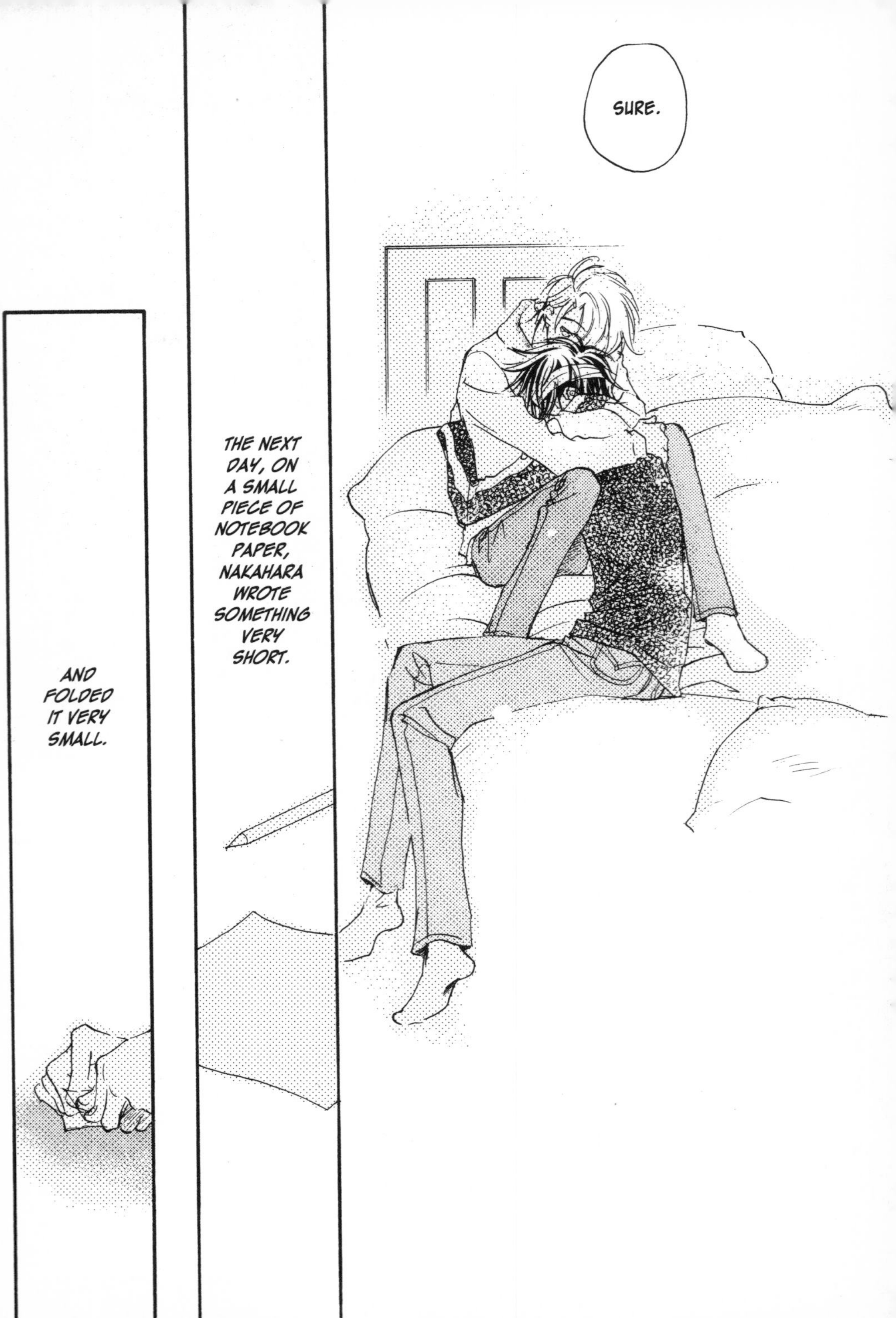
SURE.
THE NEXT DAY, ON A SMALL PIECE OF NOTEBOOK PAPER, NAKAHARA WROTE SOMETHING VERY SHORT.
AND FOLDED IT VERY SMALL.

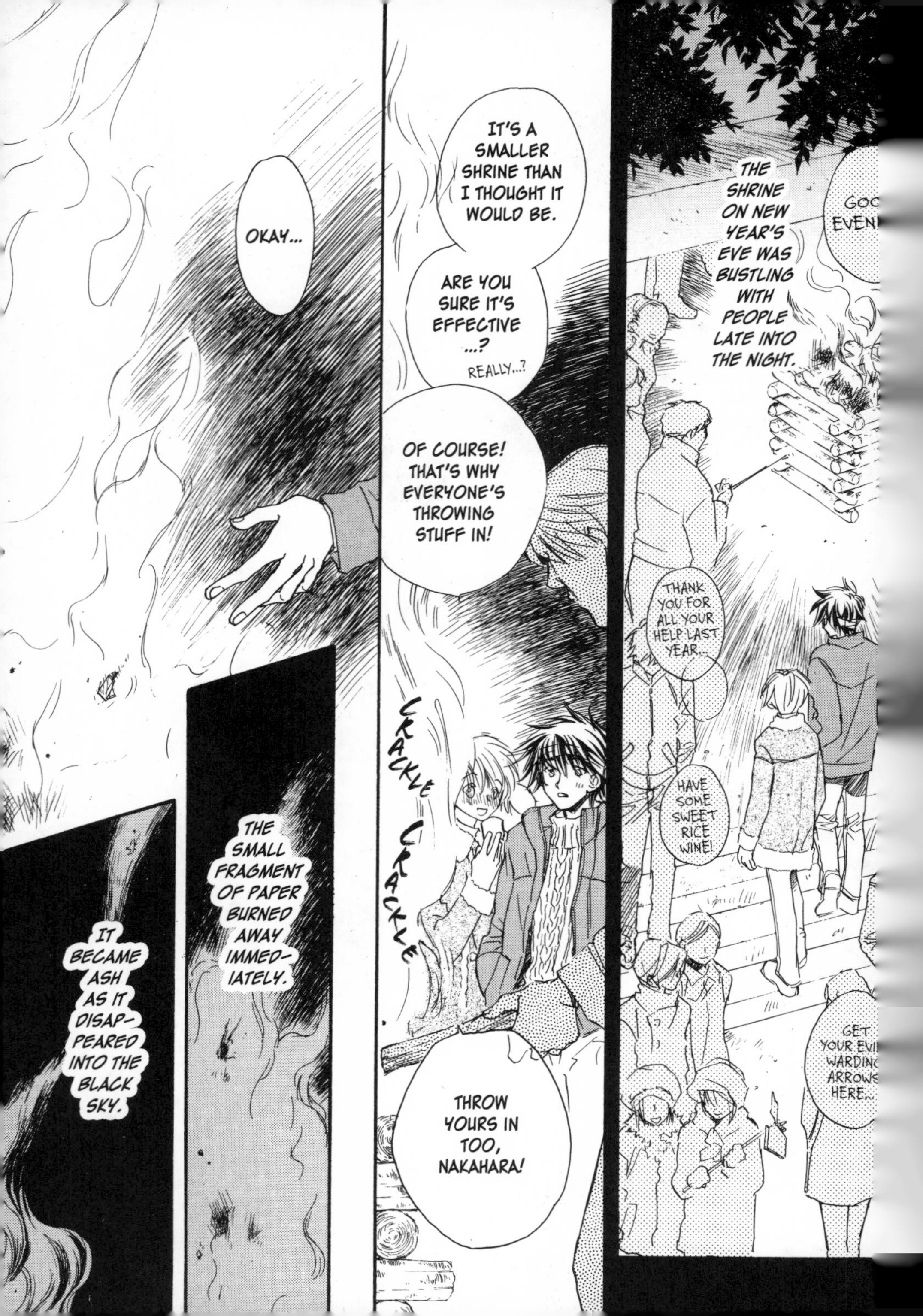
THE SHRINE ON NEW YEAR'S EVE WAS BUSTLING WITH PEOPLE LATE INTO THE NIGHT.
THANK YOU FOR ALL YOUR HELP LAST YEAR...
HAVE SOME SWEET RICE WINE!
GET YOUR EVI WARDING ARROWS HERE...
IT'S A SMALLER SHRINE THAN I THOUGHT IT WOULD BE.
ARE YOU SURE IT'S EFFECTIVE ...?
REALLY...?
OF COURSE! THAT'S WHY EVERYONE'S THROWING STUFF IN!
CRACKLE CRACKLE
THROW YOURS IN TOO, NAKAHARA!
OKAY...
THE SMALL FRAGMENT OF PAPER BURNED AWAY IMMEDIATELY.
IT BECAME ASH AS IT DISAPPEARED INTO THE BLACK SKY.

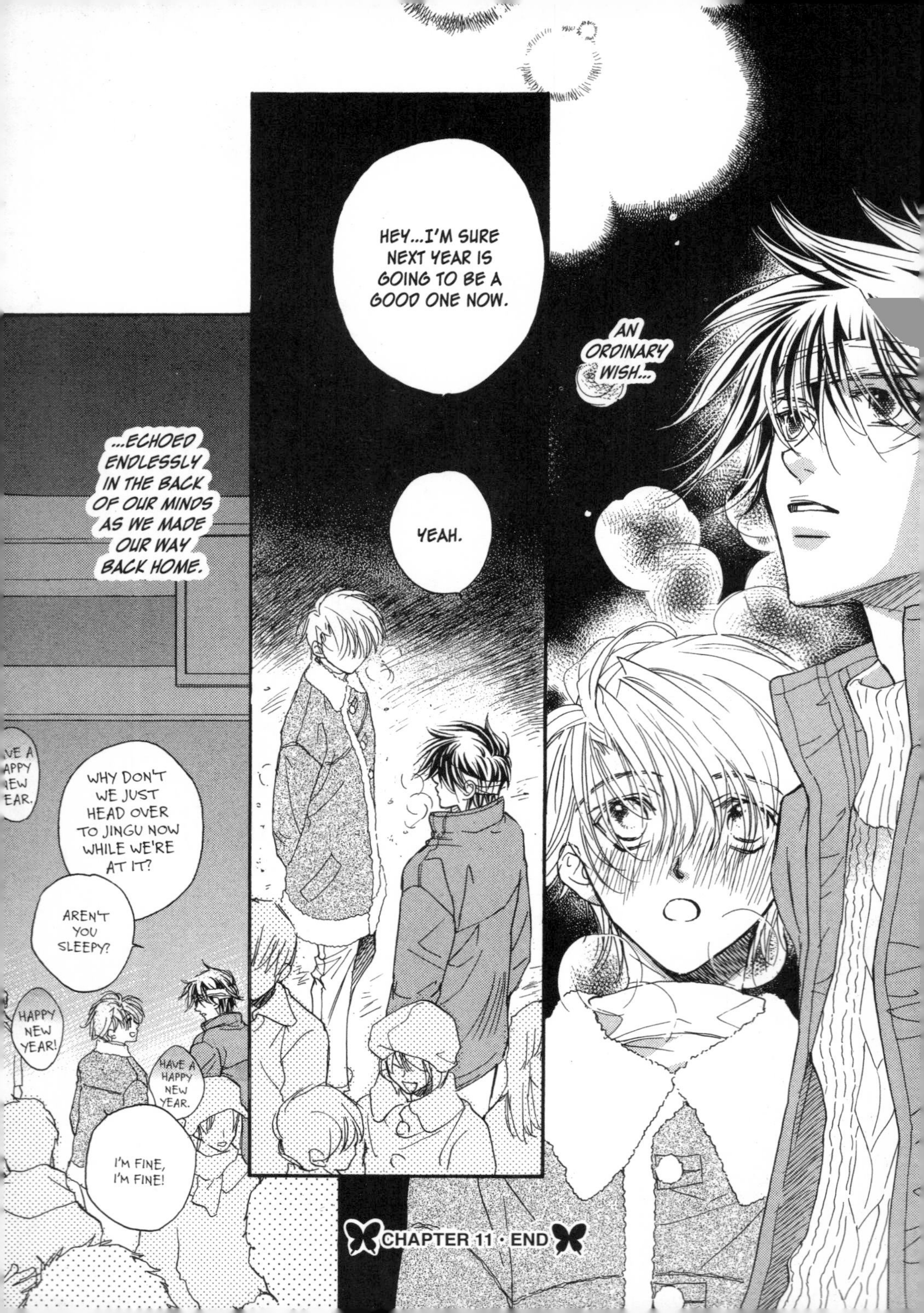
AN ORDINARY WISH...
HEY...I'M SURE NEXT YEAR IS GOING TO BE A GOOD ONE NOW.
YEAH.
...ECHOED ENDLESSLY IN THE BACK OF OUR MINDS AS WE MADE OUR WAY BACK HOME.
WHY DON'T WE JUST HEAD OVER TO JINGU NOW WHILE WE'RE AT IT?
AREN'T YOU SLEEPY?
HAVE A HAPPY NEW YEAR.
HAPPY NEW YEAR!
I'M FINE, I'M FINE!
CHAPTER 11 · END

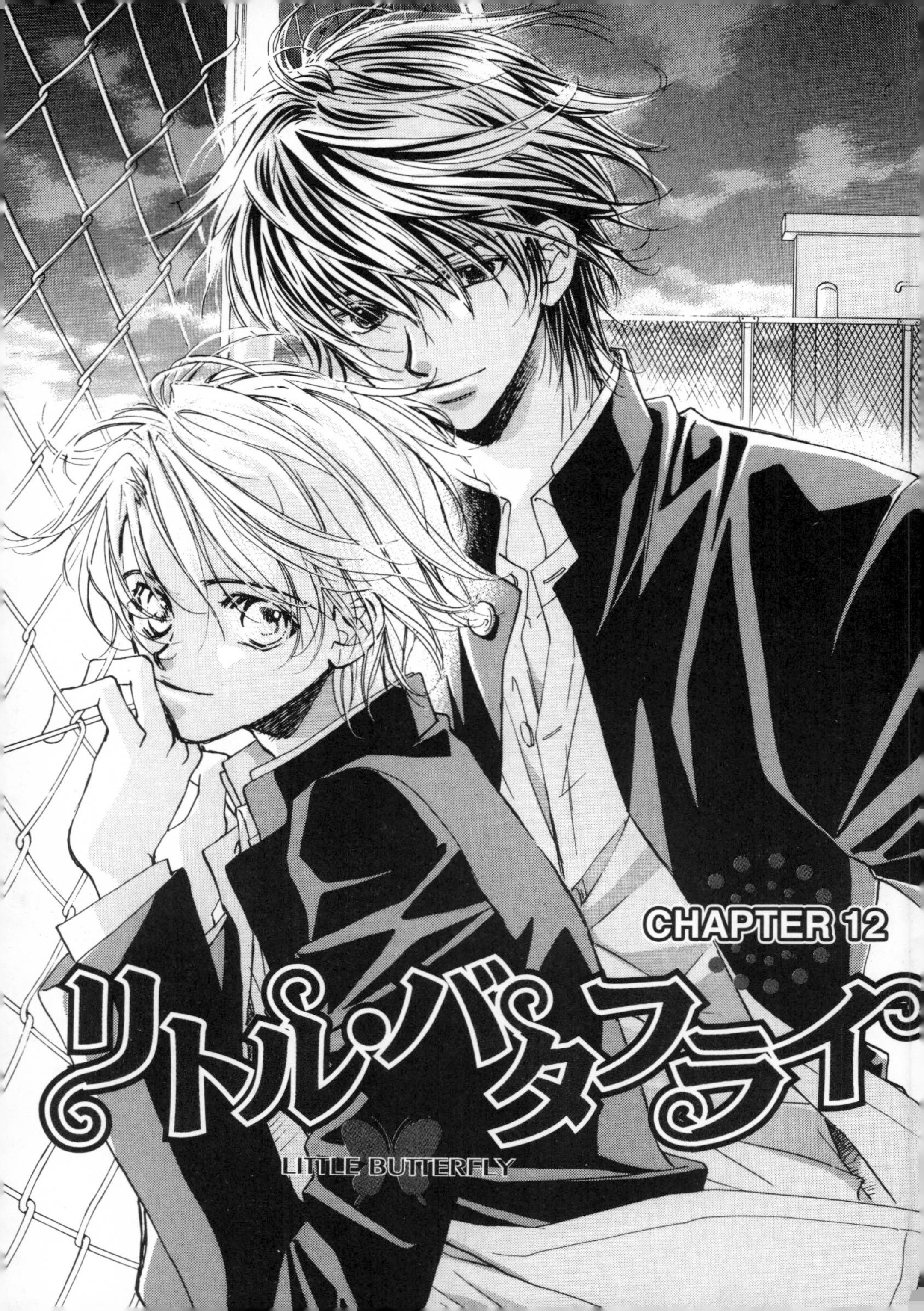
CHAPTER 12
リトル・バタフライ
LITTLE BUTTERFLY

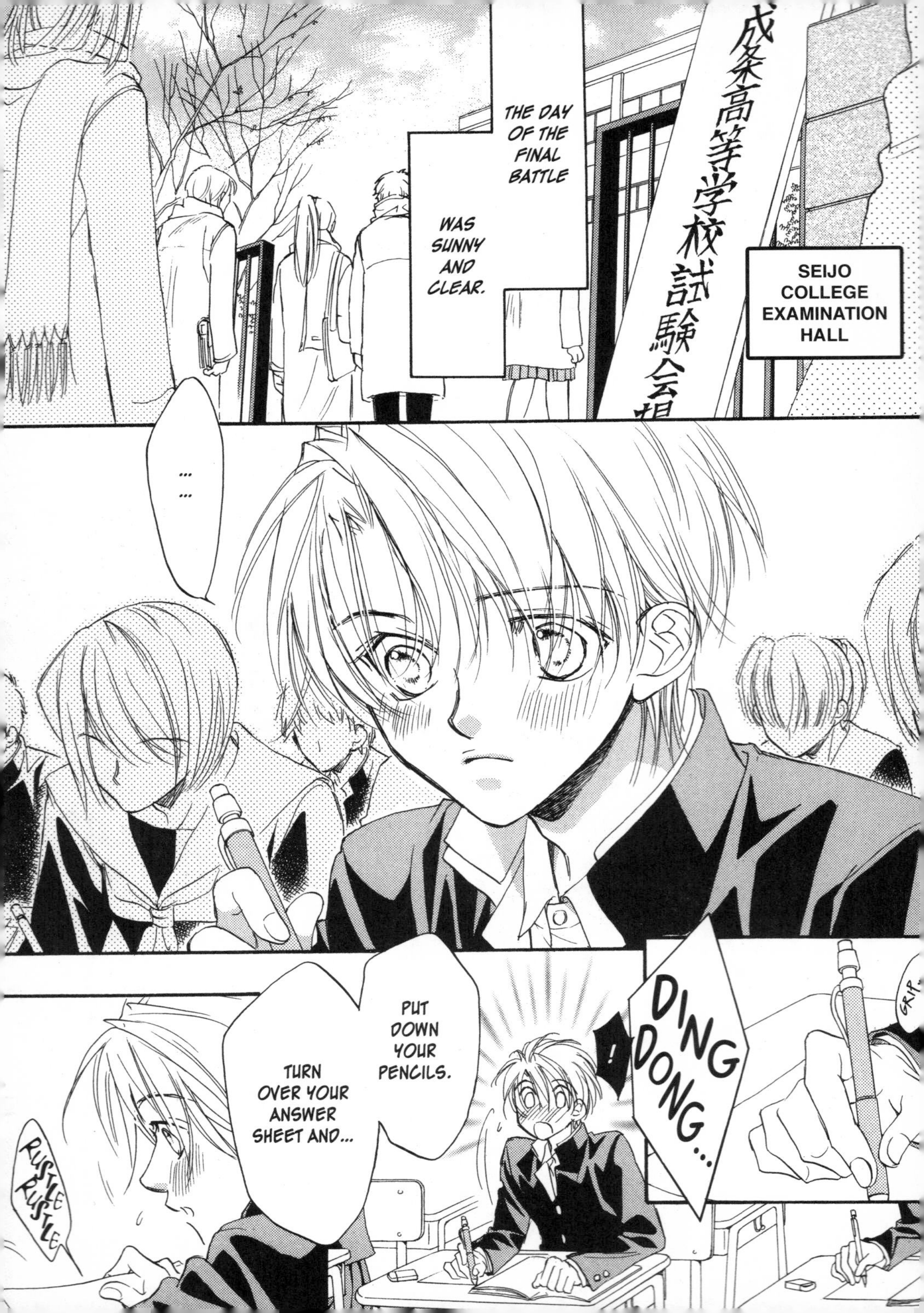
成条高等学校試験会
SEIJO COLLEGE EXAMINATION HALL
THE DAY OF THE FINAL BATTLE
WAS SUNNY AND CLEAR.
... ...
GRIP...
DING DONG...
!
PUT DOWN YOUR PENCILS.
TURN OVER YOUR ANSWER SHEET AND...
RUSTLE RUSTLE

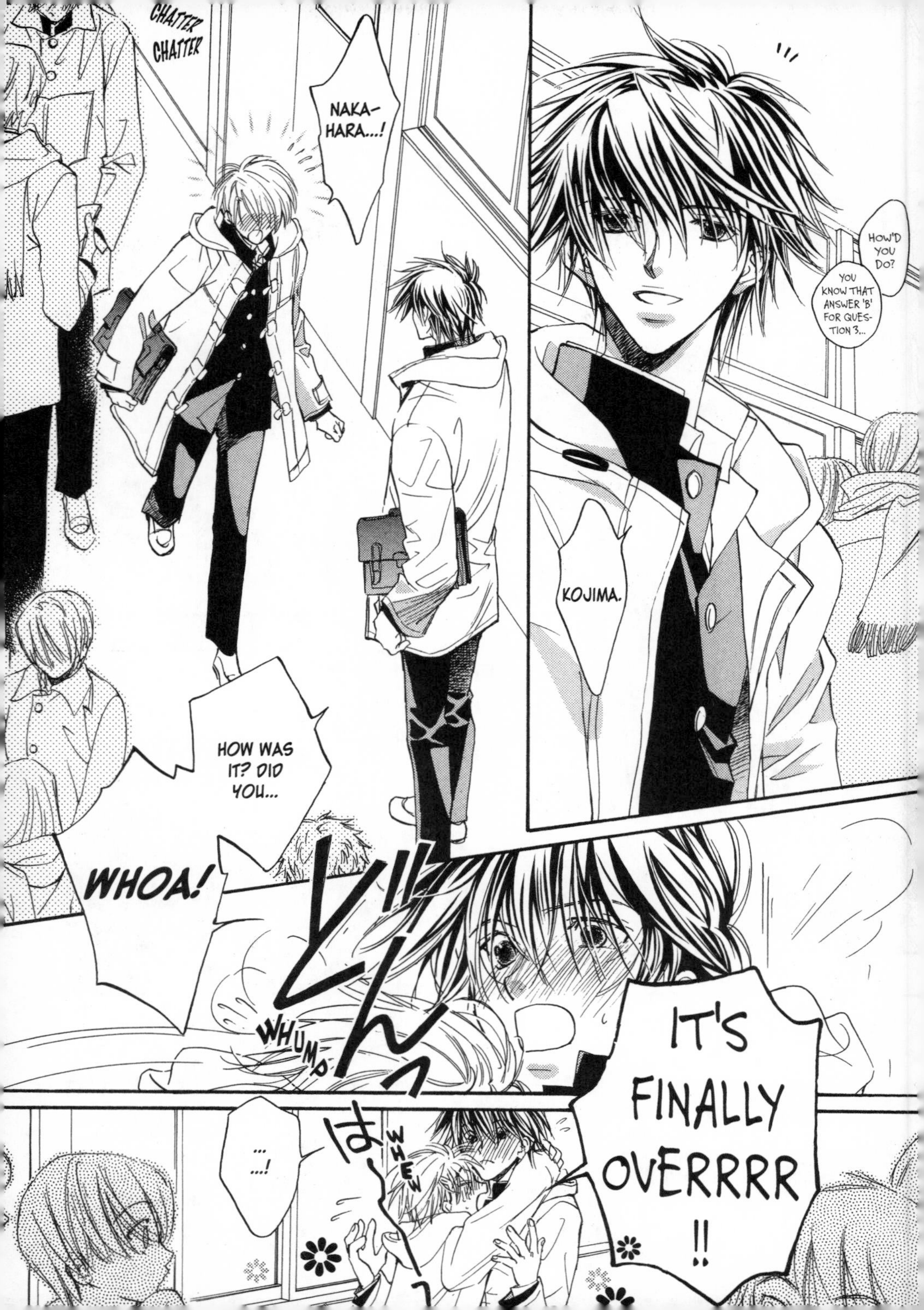
HOW'D YOU DO?
YOU KNOW THAT ANSWER 'B' FOR QUES-TION 3...
KOJIMA.
NAKA-HARA...!
CHATTER CHATTER
HOW WAS IT? DID YOU...
WHOA!
IT'S FINALLY OVERRRR!!
WHUMP
WHEW
...
...!

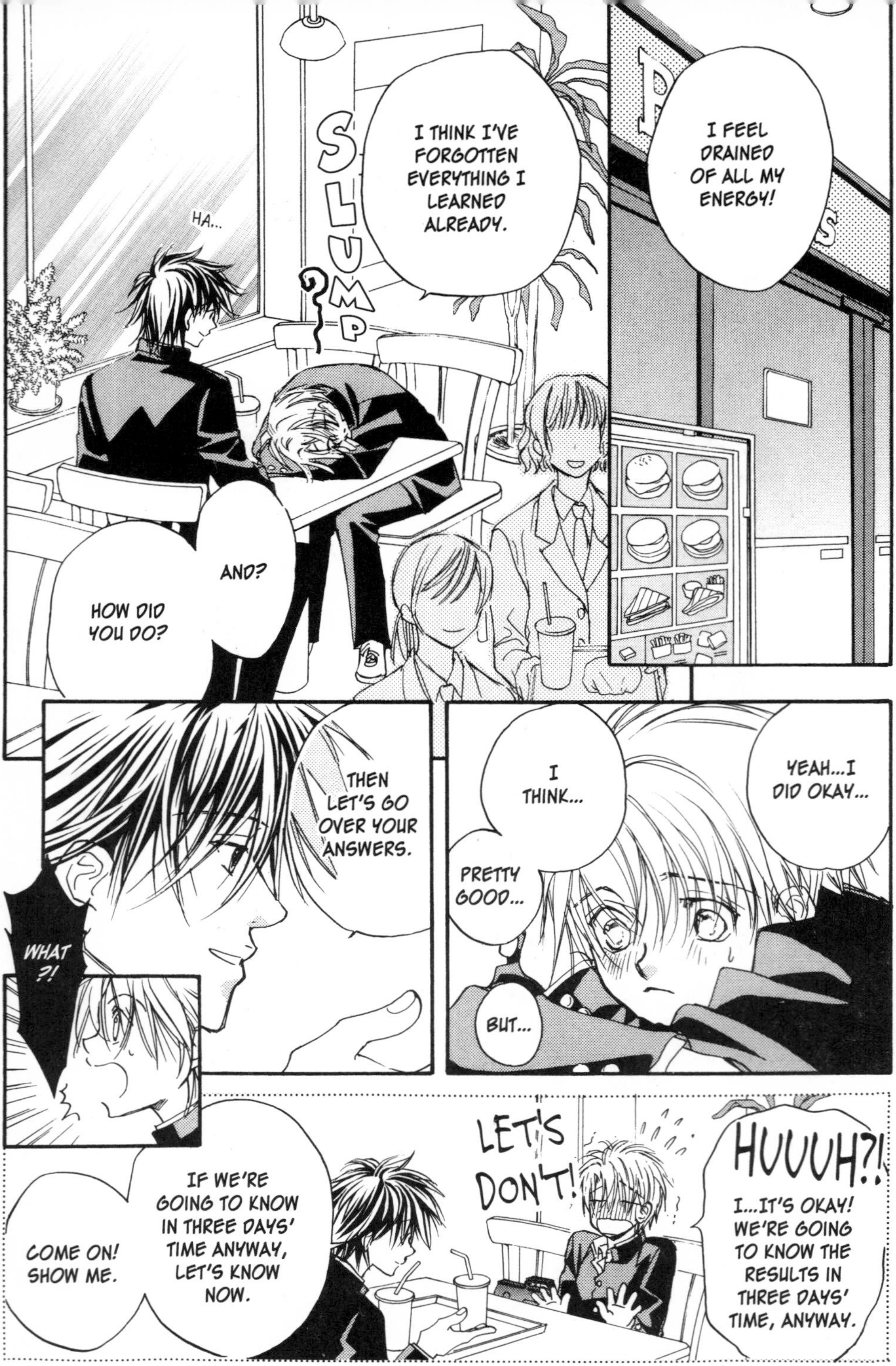
I FEEL DRAINED OF ALL MY ENERGY!
I THINK I'VE FORGOTTEN EVERYTHING I LEARNED ALREADY.
SLUMP
HA...
AND? HOW DID YOU DO?
YEAH...I DID OKAY...
I THINK... PRETTY GOOD...
BUT...
THEN LET'S GO OVER YOUR ANSWERS.
WHAT?!
HUUUH?!
I...IT'S OKAY! WE'RE GOING TO KNOW THE RESULTS IN THREE DAYS' TIME, ANYWAY.
LET'S DON'T!
IF WE'RE GOING TO KNOW IN THREE DAYS' TIME ANYWAY, LET'S KNOW NOW.
COME ON! SHOW ME.

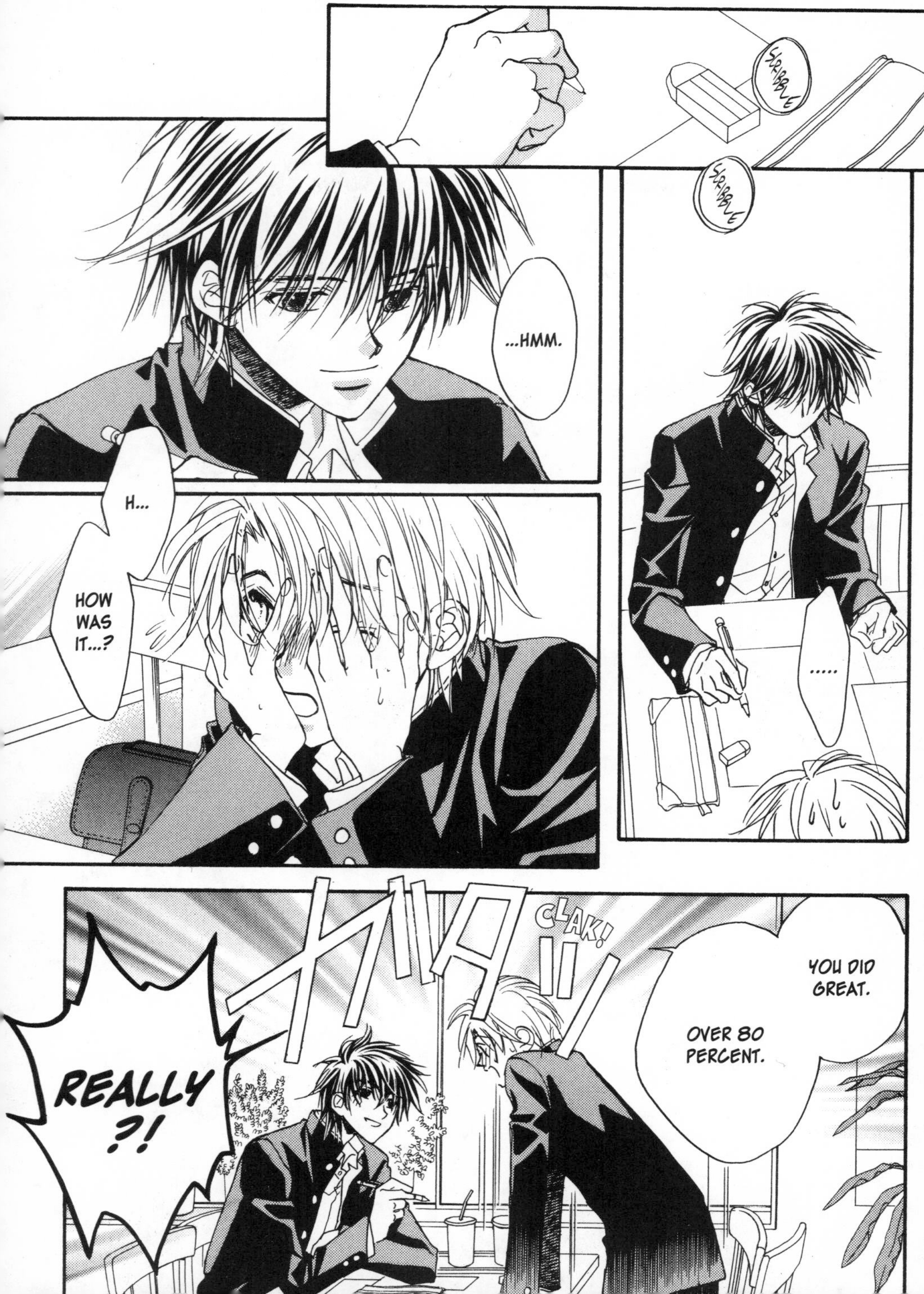
SCRIBBLE
SCRIBBLE
.....
...HMM.
H...
HOW WAS IT...?
YOU DID GREAT.
OVER 80 PERCENT.
CLAK!
REALLY ?!

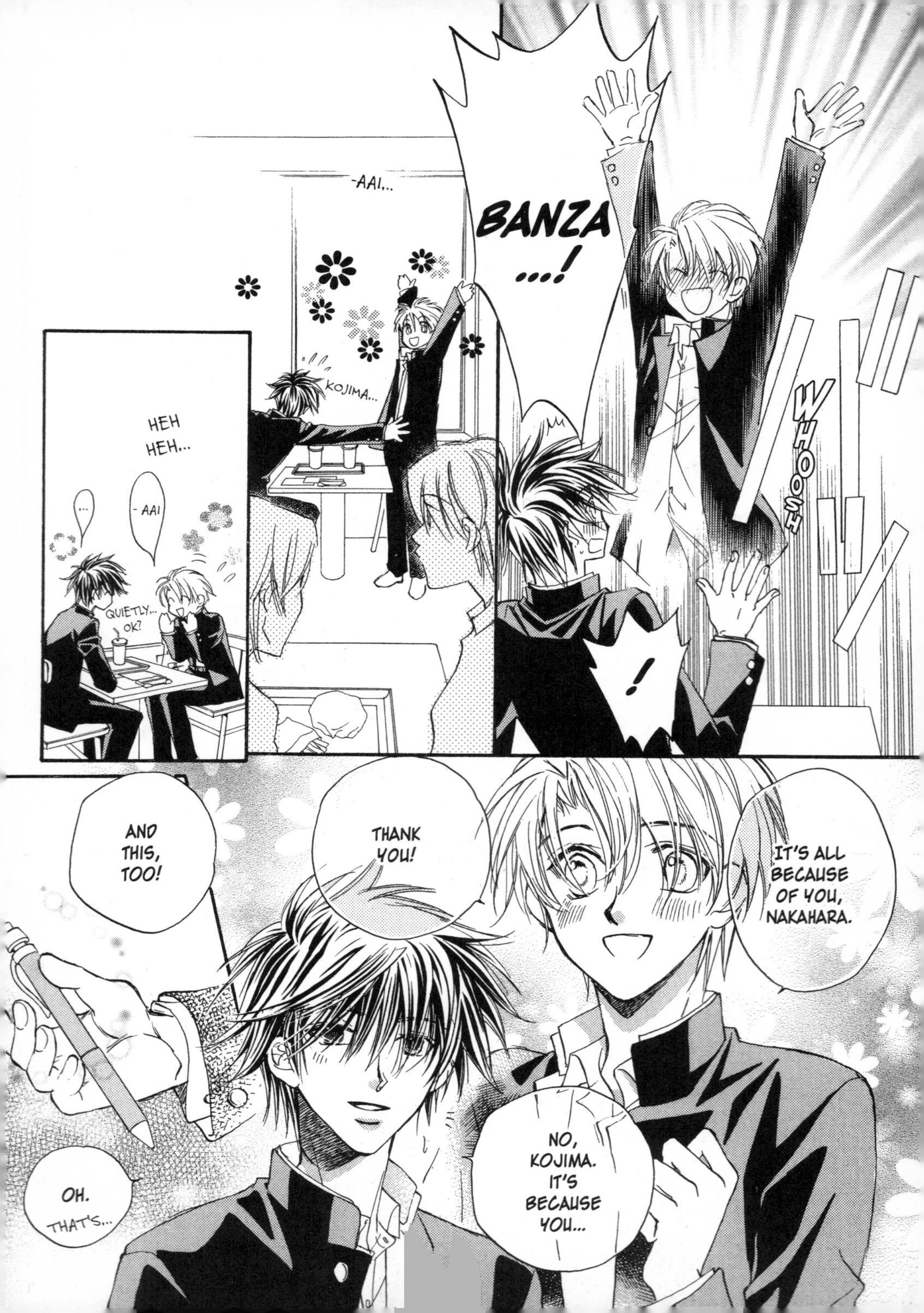
BANZA ...!
WHOOSH
!
-AAI...
KOJIMA...
HEH HEH...
- AAI
...
QUIETLY... OK?
IT'S ALL BECAUSE OF YOU, NAKAHARA.
THANK YOU!
AND THIS, TOO!
NO, KOJIMA. IT'S BECAUSE YOU...
OH. THAT'S...

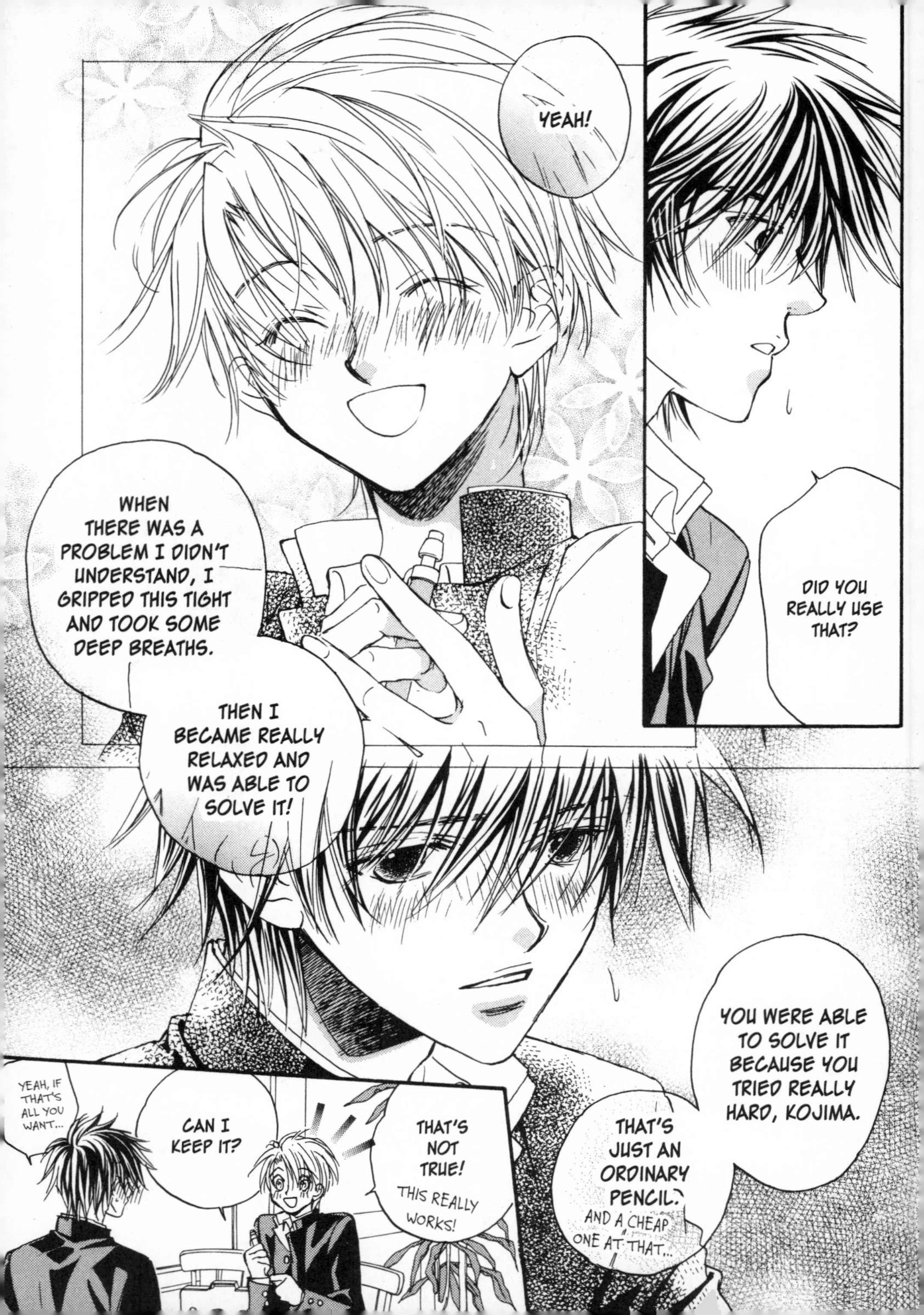
DID YOU REALLY USE THAT?
YEAH!
WHEN THERE WAS A PROBLEM I DIDN'T UNDERSTAND, I GRIPPED THIS TIGHT AND TOOK SOME DEEP BREATHS.
THEN I BECAME REALLY RELAXED AND WAS ABLE TO SOLVE IT!
YOU WERE ABLE TO SOLVE IT BECAUSE YOU TRIED REALLY HARD, KOJIMA.
THAT'S JUST AN ORDINARY PENCIL.
AND A CHEAP ONE AT THAT...
THAT'S NOT TRUE!
THIS REALLY WORKS!
CAN I KEEP IT?
YEAH, IF THAT'S ALL YOU WANT...

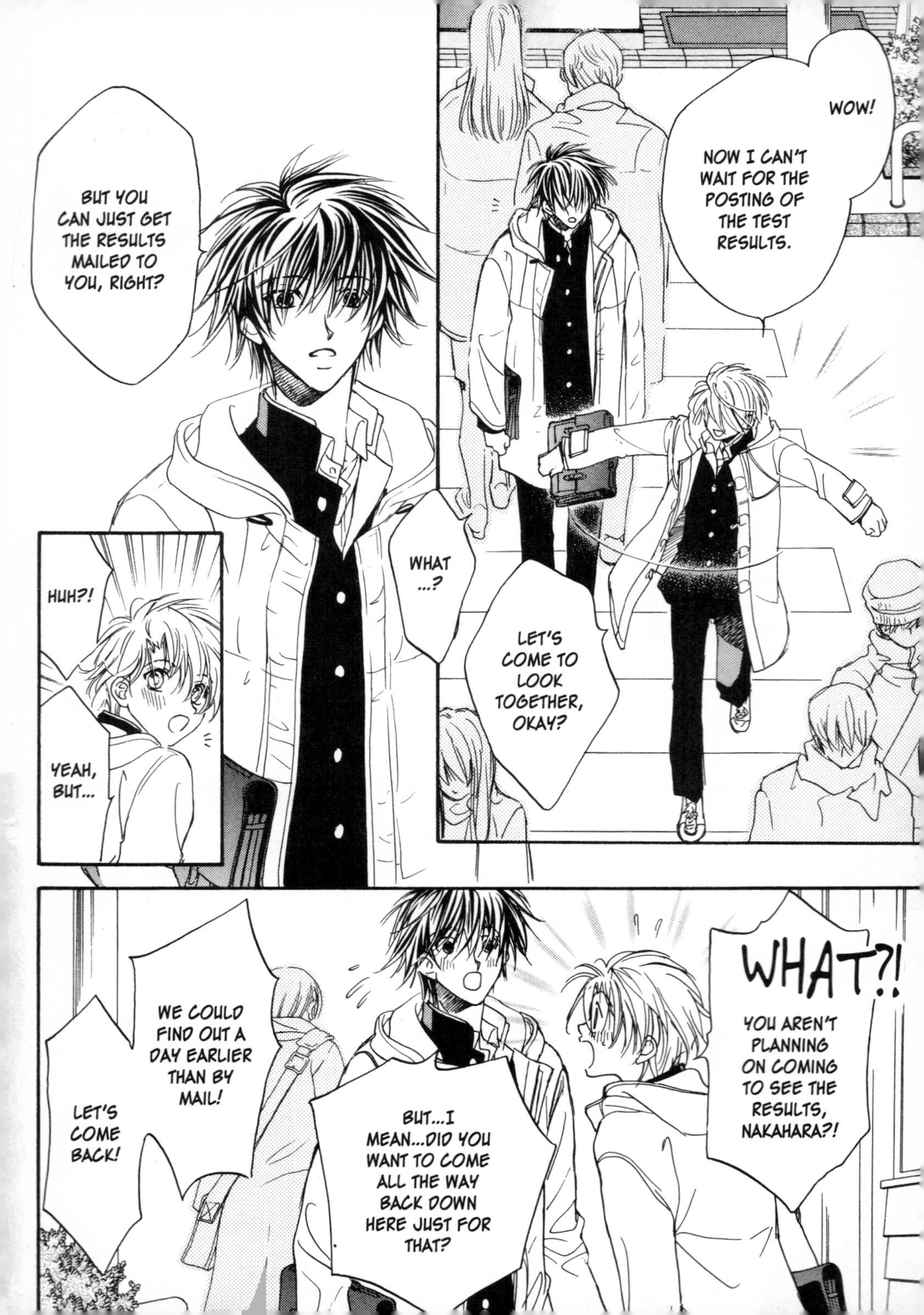
WOW!
NOW I CAN'T WAIT FOR THE POSTING OF THE TEST RESULTS.
WHAT ...?
LET'S COME TO LOOK TOGETHER, OKAY?
BUT YOU CAN JUST GET THE RESULTS MAILED TO YOU, RIGHT?
HUH?!
YEAH, BUT...
WHAT?!
YOU AREN'T PLANNING ON COMING TO SEE THE RESULTS, NAKAHARA?!
BUT...I MEAN...DID YOU WANT TO COME ALL THE WAY BACK DOWN HERE JUST FOR THAT?
WE COULD FIND OUT A DAY EARLIER THAN BY MAIL!
LET'S COME BACK!

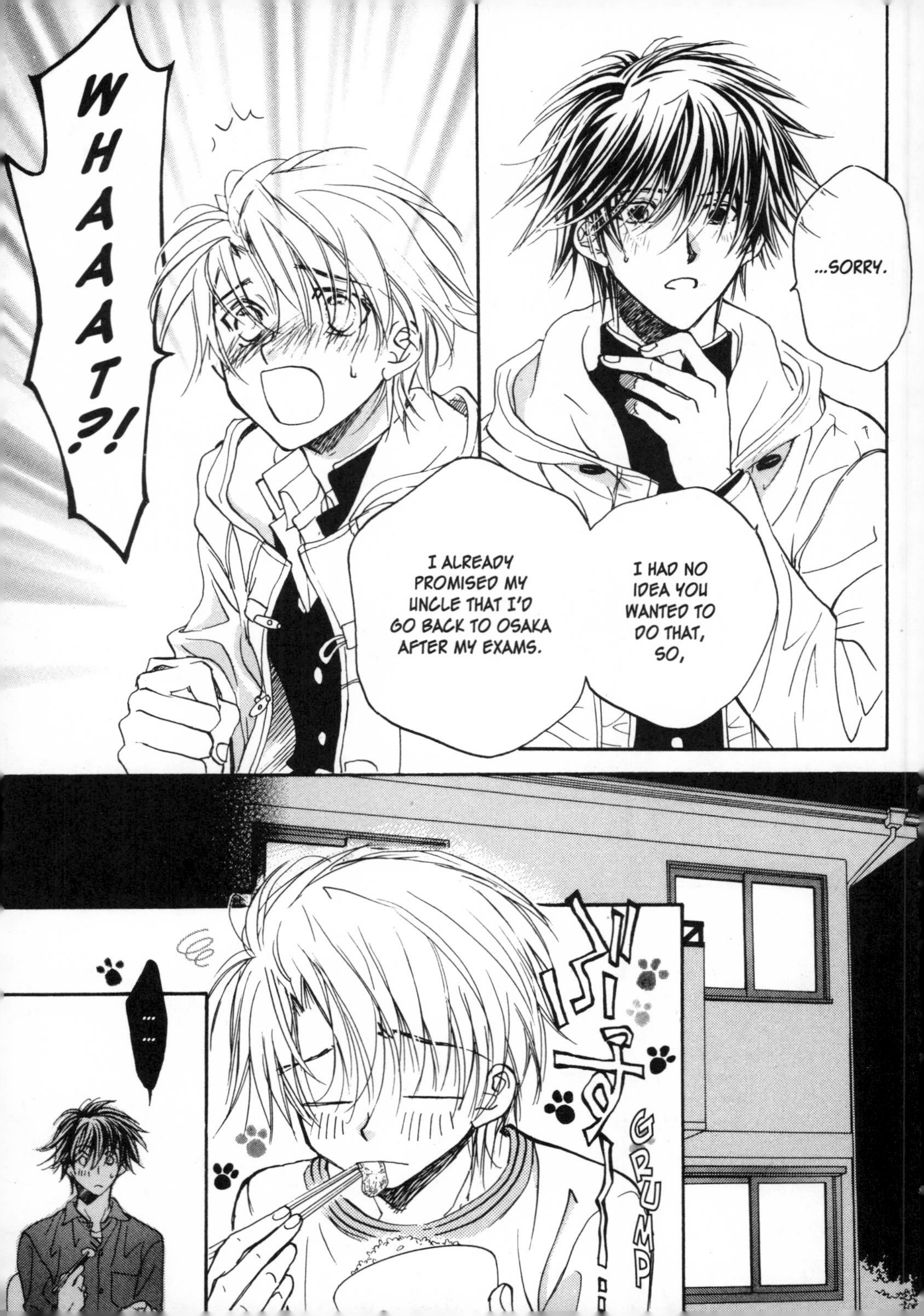
...SORRY.
I HAD NO IDEA YOU WANTED TO DO THAT, SO,
I ALREADY PROMISED MY UNCLE THAT I'D GO BACK TO OSAKA AFTER MY EXAMS.
WHAAAAT?!
GRUMP
......

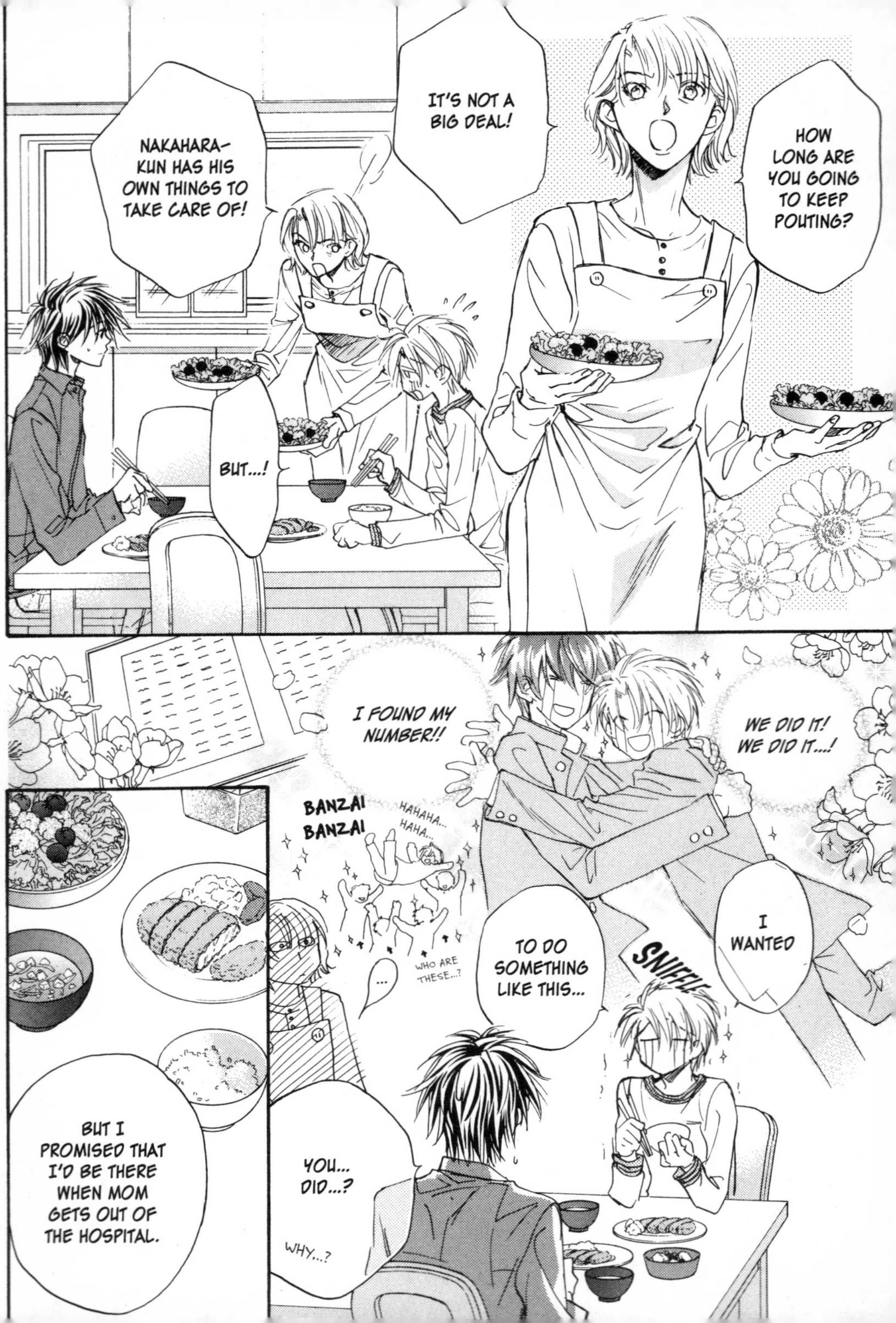
HOW LONG ARE YOU GOING TO KEEP POUTING?
IT'S NOT A BIG DEAL!
NAKAHARA-KUN HAS HIS OWN THINGS TO TAKE CARE OF!
BUT...!
WE DID IT! WE DID IT...!
I FOUND MY NUMBER!!
BANZAI BANZAI
HAHAHA... HAHA...
I WANTED
TO DO SOMETHING LIKE THIS...
SNIFFLE
...
WHO ARE THESE...?
YOU... DID...?
WHY...?
BUT I PROMISED THAT I'D BE THERE WHEN MOM GETS OUT OF THE HOSPITAL.

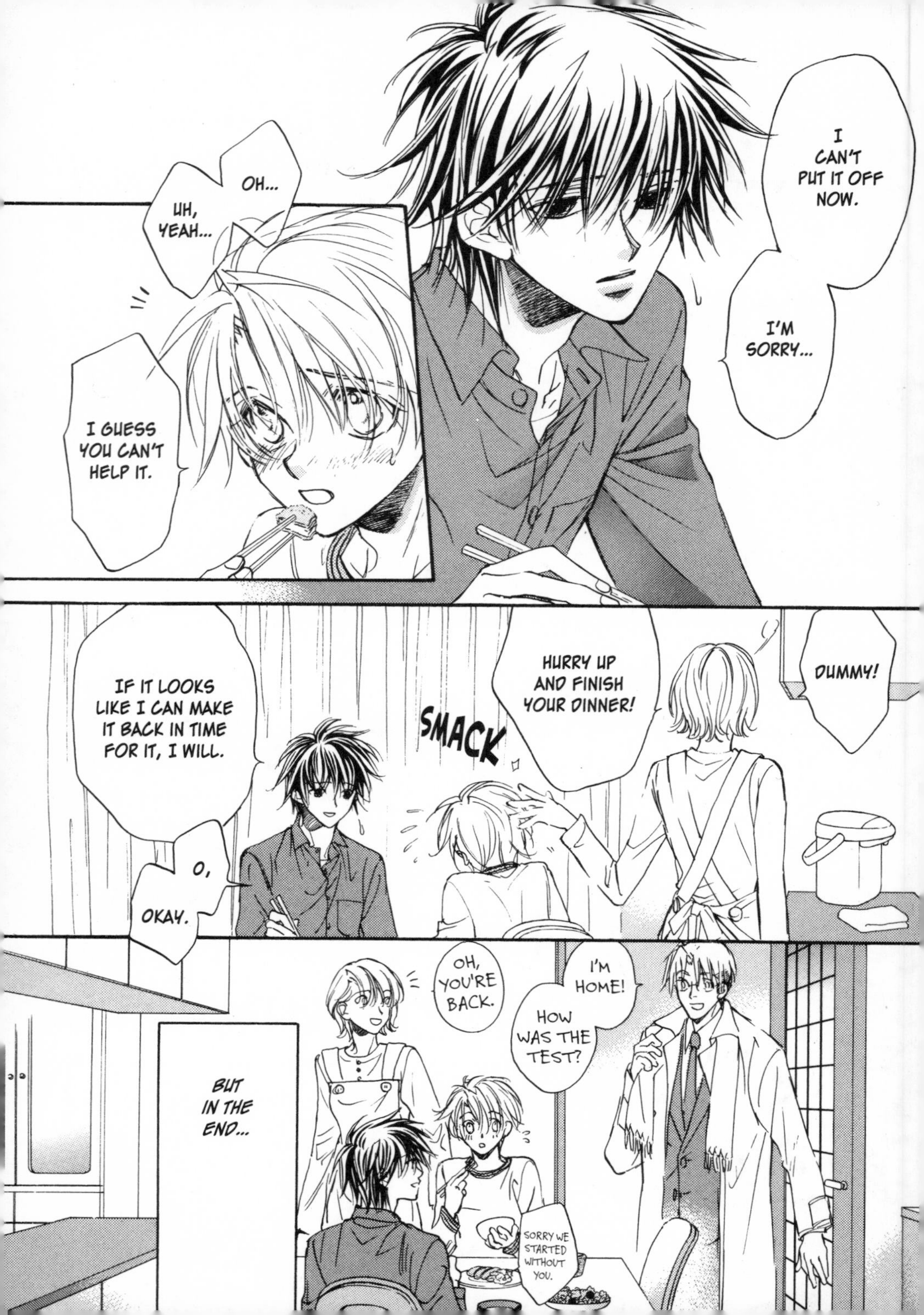
I CAN'T PUT IT OFF NOW.
I'M SORRY...
OH...
UH, YEAH...
I GUESS YOU CAN'T HELP IT.
DUMMY!
HURRY UP AND FINISH YOUR DINNER!
SMACK
IF IT LOOKS LIKE I CAN MAKE IT BACK IN TIME FOR IT, I WILL.
O,
OKAY.
I'M HOME!
HOW WAS THE TEST?
OH, YOU'RE BACK.
SORRY WE STARTED WITHOUT YOU.
BUT IN THE END...

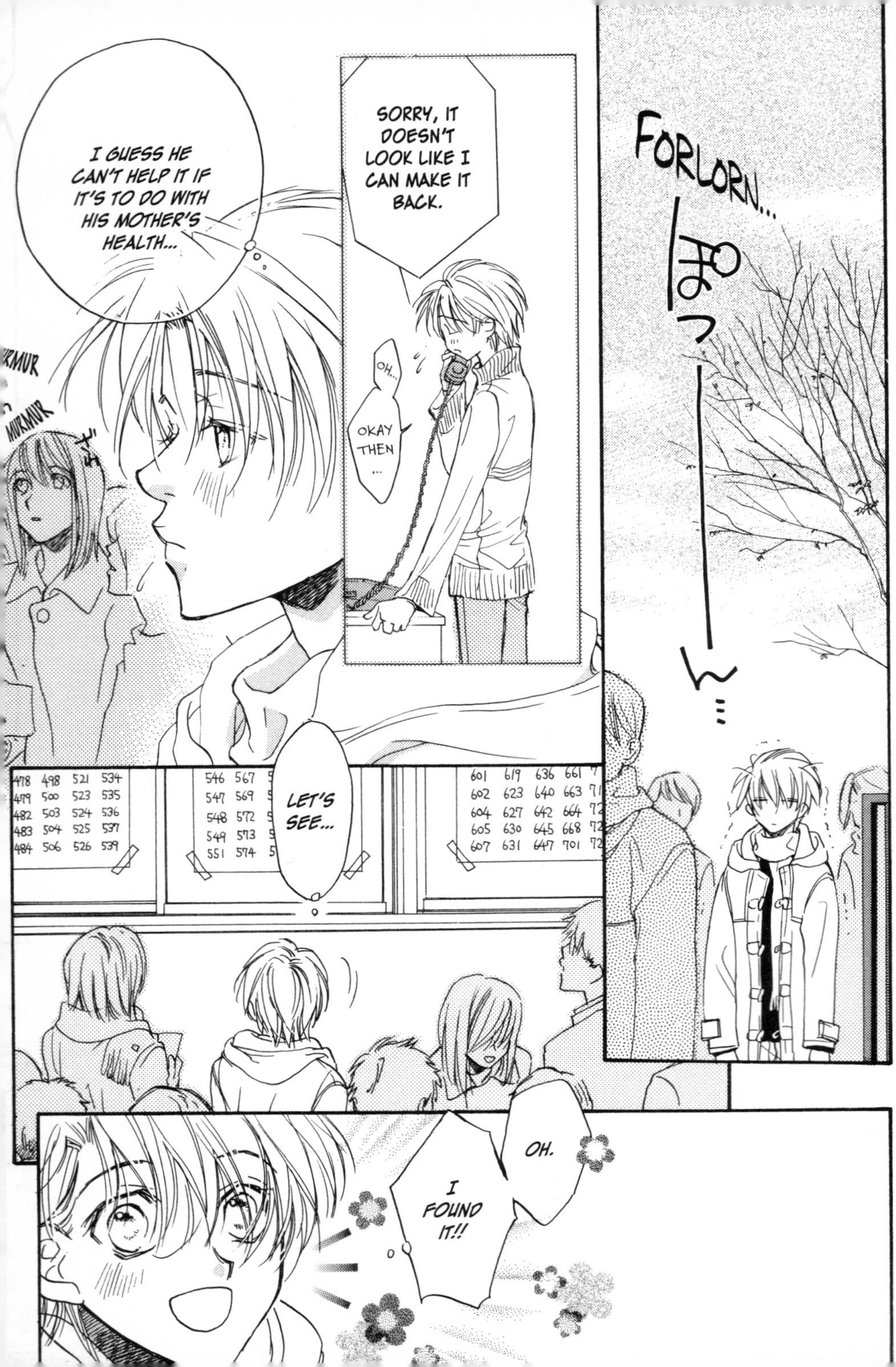
FORLORN...
ぽつーーん
SORRY, IT DOESN'T LOOK LIKE I CAN MAKE IT BACK.
OH...
OKAY THEN ...
I GUESS HE CAN'T HELP IT IF IT'S TO DO WITH HIS MOTHER'S HEALTH...
MURMUR
MURMUR
LET'S SEE...
OH.
I FOUND IT!!

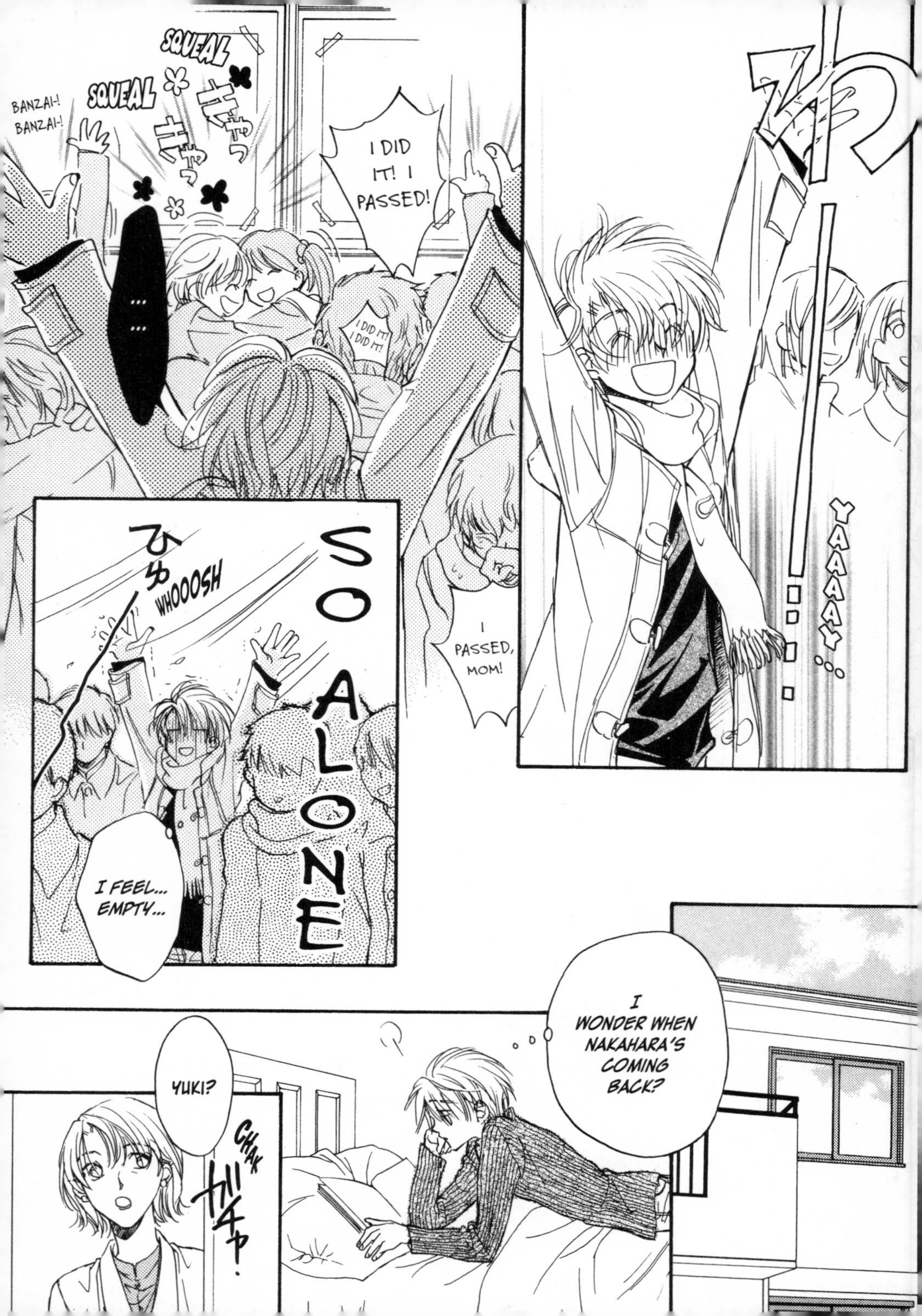
ワッ
YAAAAAY...
SQUEAL
SQUEAL
きゃっ きゃっ
BANZAI-! BANZAI-!
I DID IT! I PASSED!
...
...
I DID IT! I DID IT!
I PASSED, MOM!
SO ALONE
ひゅ
WHOOOSH
I FEEL... EMPTY...
I WONDER WHEN NAKAHARA'S COMING BACK?
YUKI?
CHAK
ガチャ

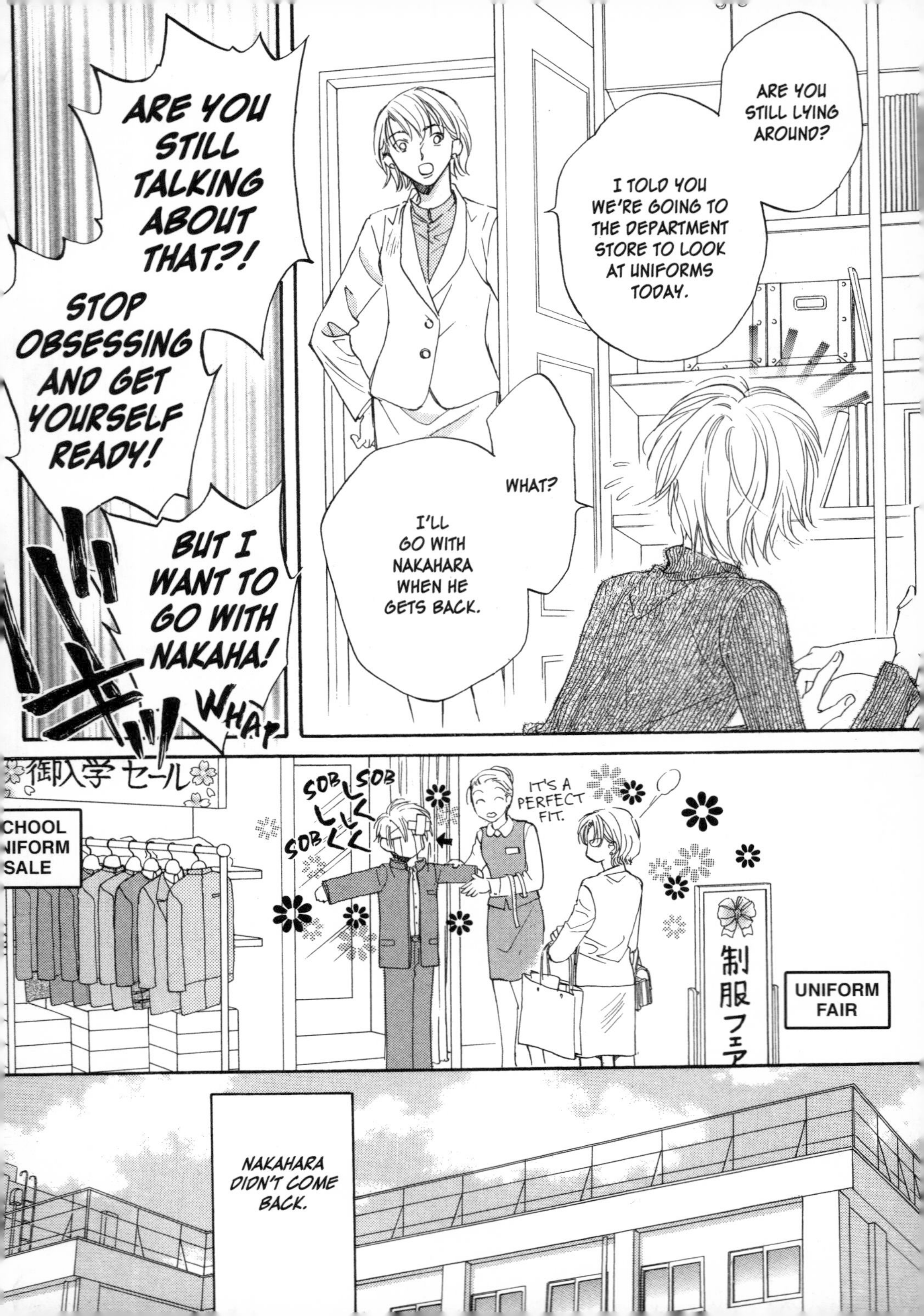
ARE YOU STILL LYING AROUND?
I TOLD YOU WE'RE GOING TO THE DEPARTMENT STORE TO LOOK AT UNIFORMS TODAY.
WHAT?
I'LL GO WITH NAKAHARA WHEN HE GETS BACK.
ARE YOU STILL TALKING ABOUT THAT?!
STOP OBSESSING AND GET YOURSELF READY!
BUT I WANT TO GO WITH NAKAHA!
WHAT
御入学セール
CHOOL NIFORM SALE
SOB SOB SOB
しくしくしく
IT'S A PERFECT FIT.
制服フェア
UNIFORM FAIR
NAKAHARA DIDN'T COME BACK.

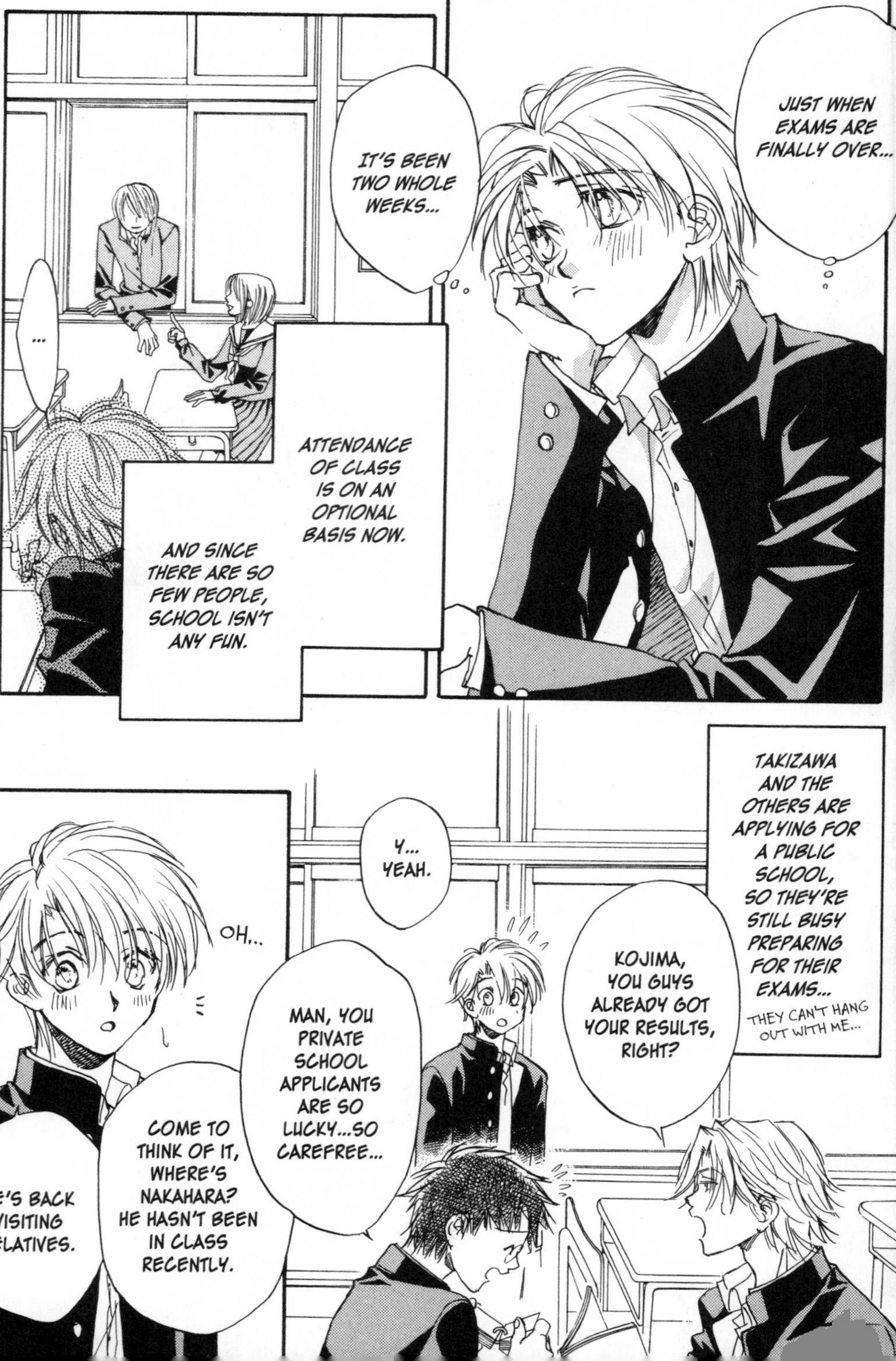
JUST WHEN EXAMS ARE FINALLY OVER...
IT'S BEEN TWO WHOLE WEEKS...
ATTENDANCE OF CLASS IS ON AN OPTIONAL BASIS NOW.
AND SINCE THERE ARE SO FEW PEOPLE, SCHOOL ISN'T ANY FUN.
...
TAKIZAWA AND THE OTHERS ARE APPLYING FOR A PUBLIC SCHOOL, SO THEY'RE STILL BUSY PREPARING FOR THEIR EXAMS...
THEY CAN'T HANG OUT WITH ME...
KOJIMA, YOU GUYS ALREADY GOT YOUR RESULTS, RIGHT?
Y... YEAH.
MAN, YOU PRIVATE SCHOOL APPLICANTS ARE SO LUCKY...SO CAREFREE...
OH...
COME TO THINK OF IT, WHERE'S NAKAHARA? HE HASN'T BEEN IN CLASS RECENTLY.
HE'S BACK VISITING RELATIVES.

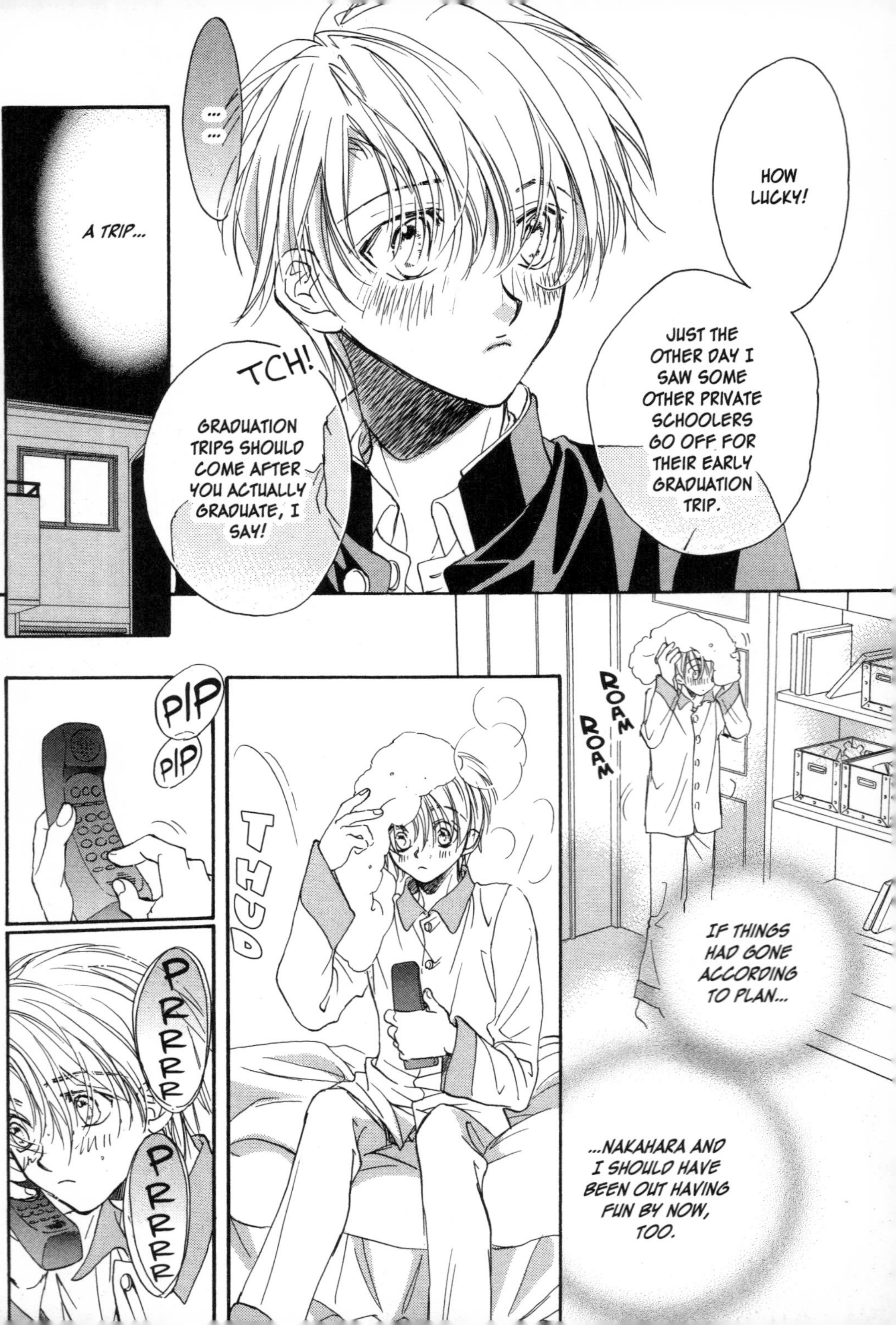
HOW LUCKY!
JUST THE OTHER DAY I SAW SOME OTHER PRIVATE SCHOOLERS GO OFF FOR THEIR EARLY GRADUATION TRIP.
TCH!
GRADUATION TRIPS SHOULD COME AFTER YOU ACTUALLY GRADUATE, I SAY!
...
...
A TRIP...
ROAM ROAM
IF THINGS HAD GONE ACCORDING TO PLAN...
...NAKAHARA AND I SHOULD HAVE BEEN OUT HAVING FUN BY NOW, TOO.
THUD
PIP
PIP
PRRRR
PRRRR

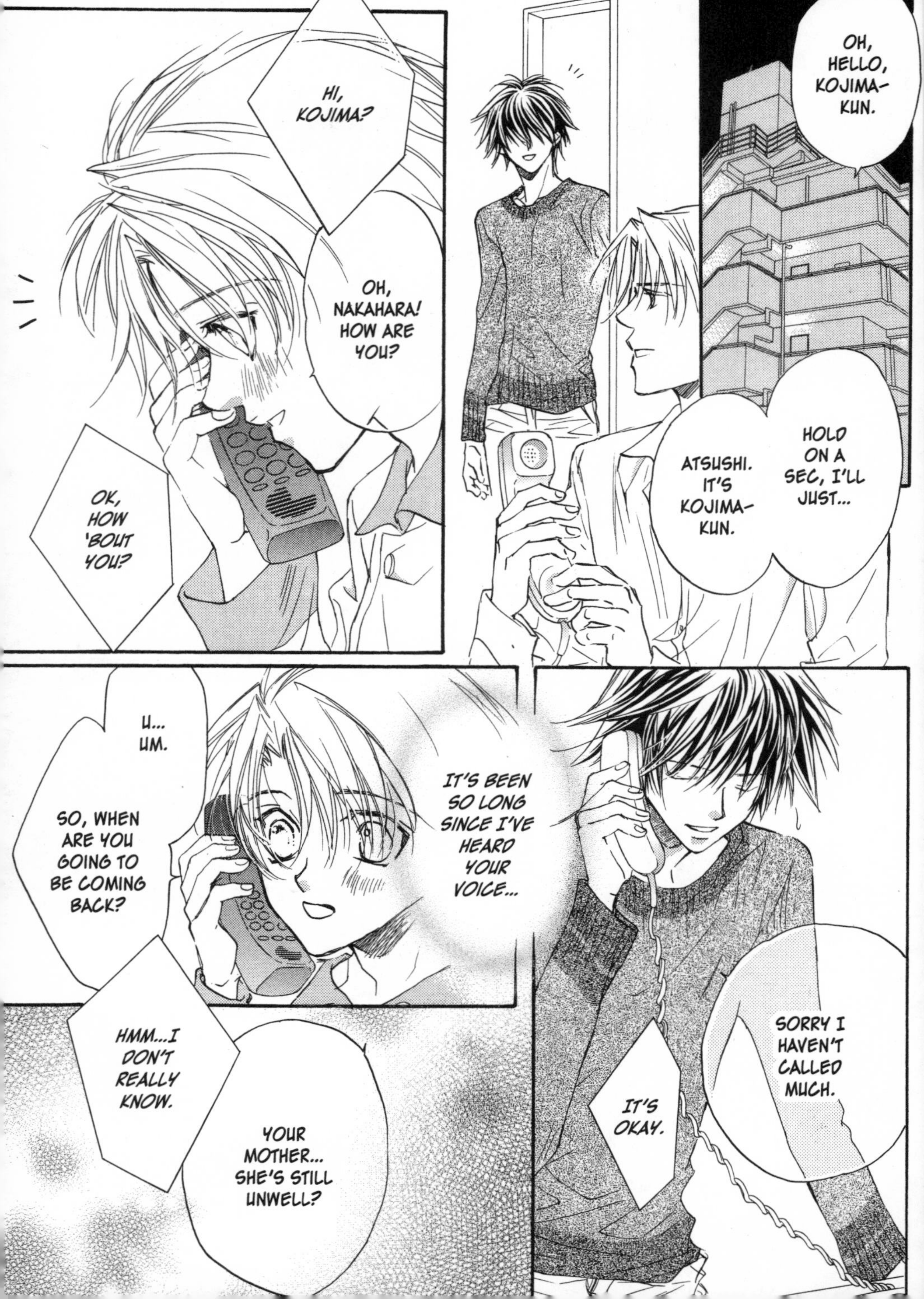
OH, HELLO, KOJIMA-KUN.
HOLD ON A SEC, I'LL JUST...
ATSUSHI. IT'S KOJIMA-KUN.
HI, KOJIMA?
OH, NAKAHARA! HOW ARE YOU?
OK, HOW 'BOUT YOU?
IT'S BEEN SO LONG SINCE I'VE HEARD YOUR VOICE...
SORRY I HAVEN'T CALLED MUCH.
IT'S OKAY.
U... UM.
SO, WHEN ARE YOU GOING TO BE COMING BACK?
HMM...I DON'T REALLY KNOW.
YOUR MOTHER... SHE'S STILL UNWELL?

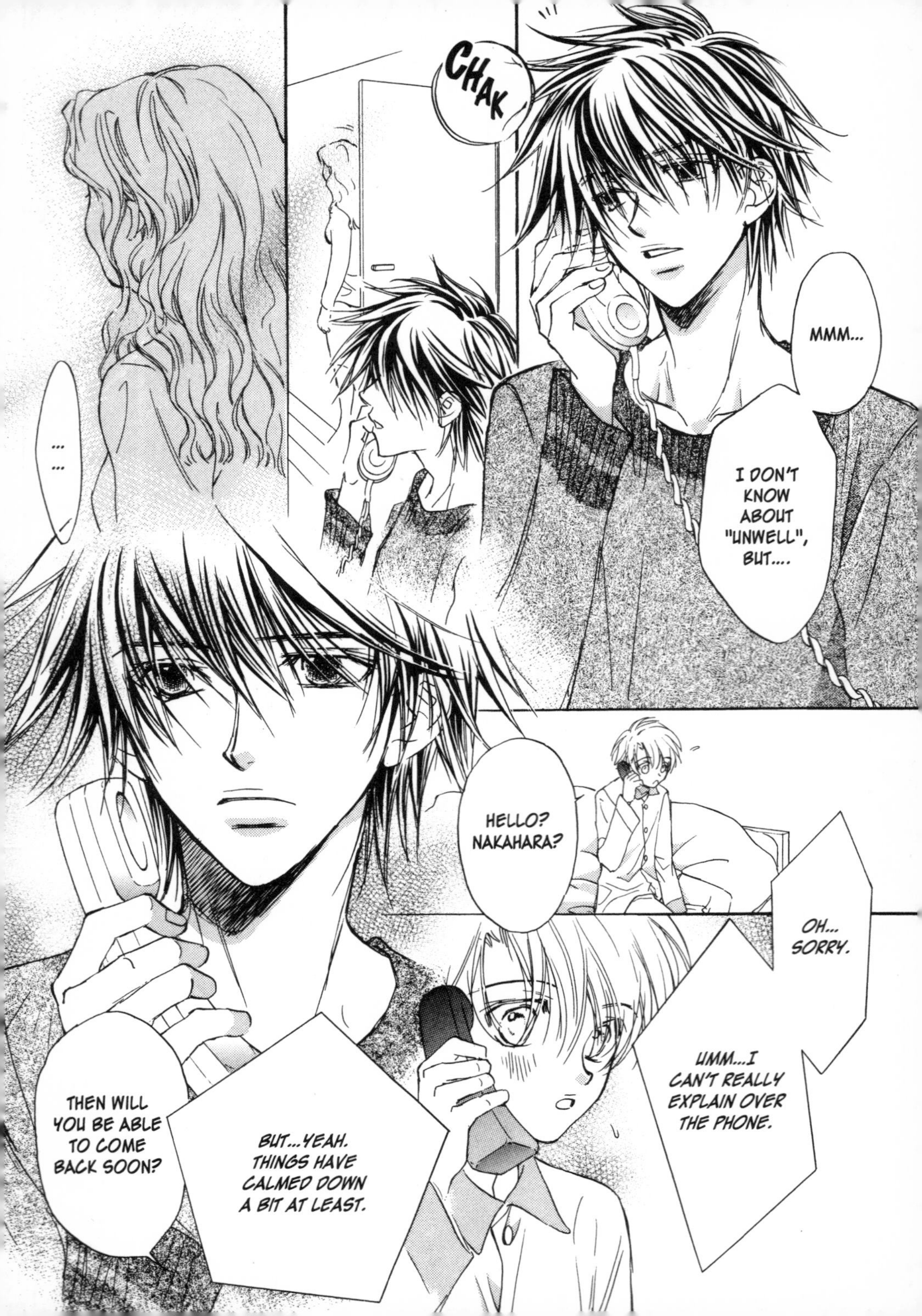
CHAK
MMM...
I DON'T KNOW ABOUT "UNWELL", BUT....
... ...
HELLO? NAKAHARA?
OH... SORRY.
UMM...I CAN'T REALLY EXPLAIN OVER THE PHONE.
THEN WILL YOU BE ABLE TO COME BACK SOON?
BUT...YEAH. THINGS HAVE CALMED DOWN A BIT AT LEAST.

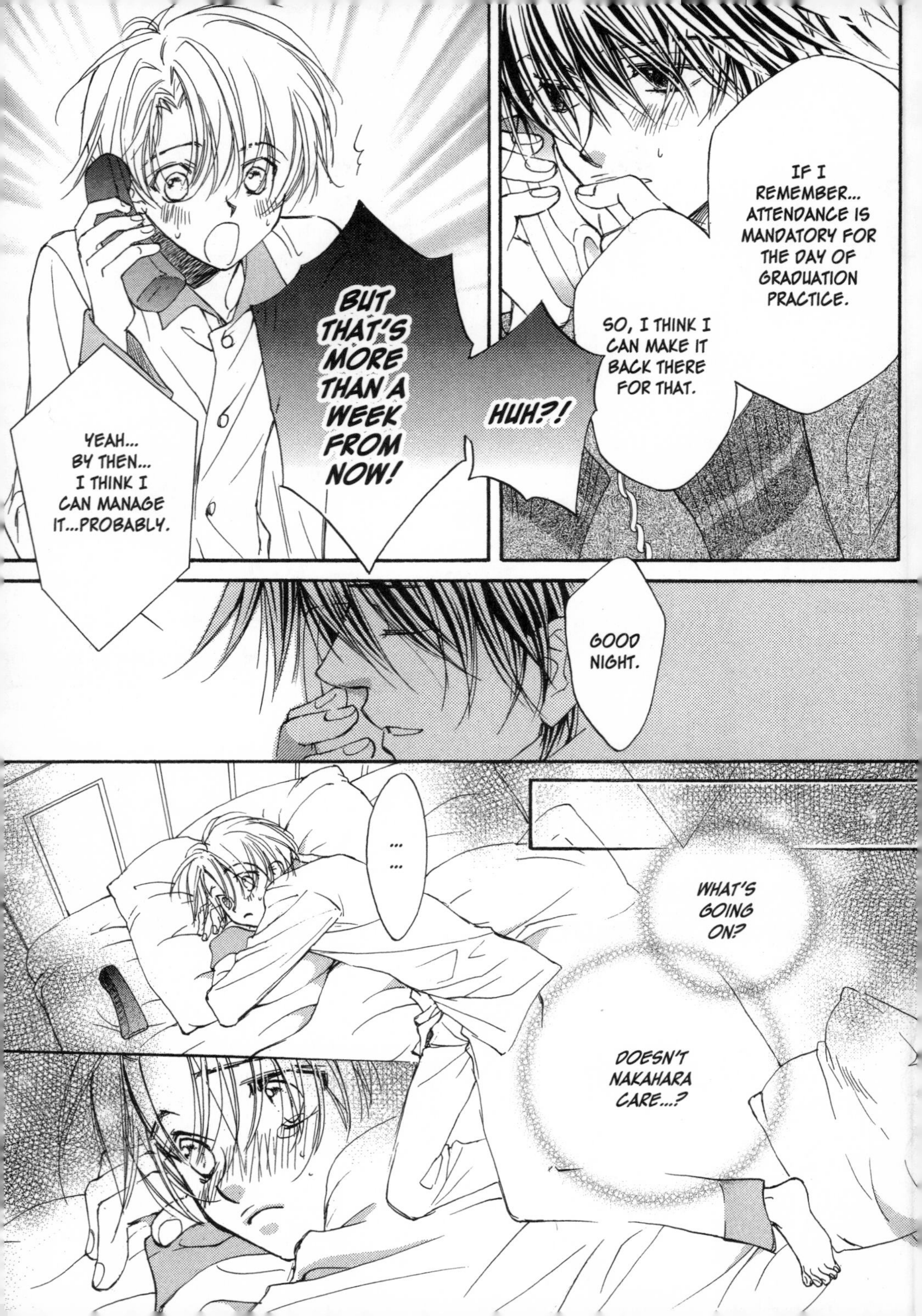
IF I REMEMBER... ATTENDANCE IS MANDATORY FOR THE DAY OF GRADUATION PRACTICE.
SO, I THINK I CAN MAKE IT BACK THERE FOR THAT.
HUH?!
BUT THAT'S MORE THAN A WEEK FROM NOW!
YEAH... BY THEN... I THINK I CAN MANAGE IT...PROBABLY.
GOOD NIGHT.
... ...
WHAT'S GOING ON?
DOESN'T NAKAHARA CARE...?

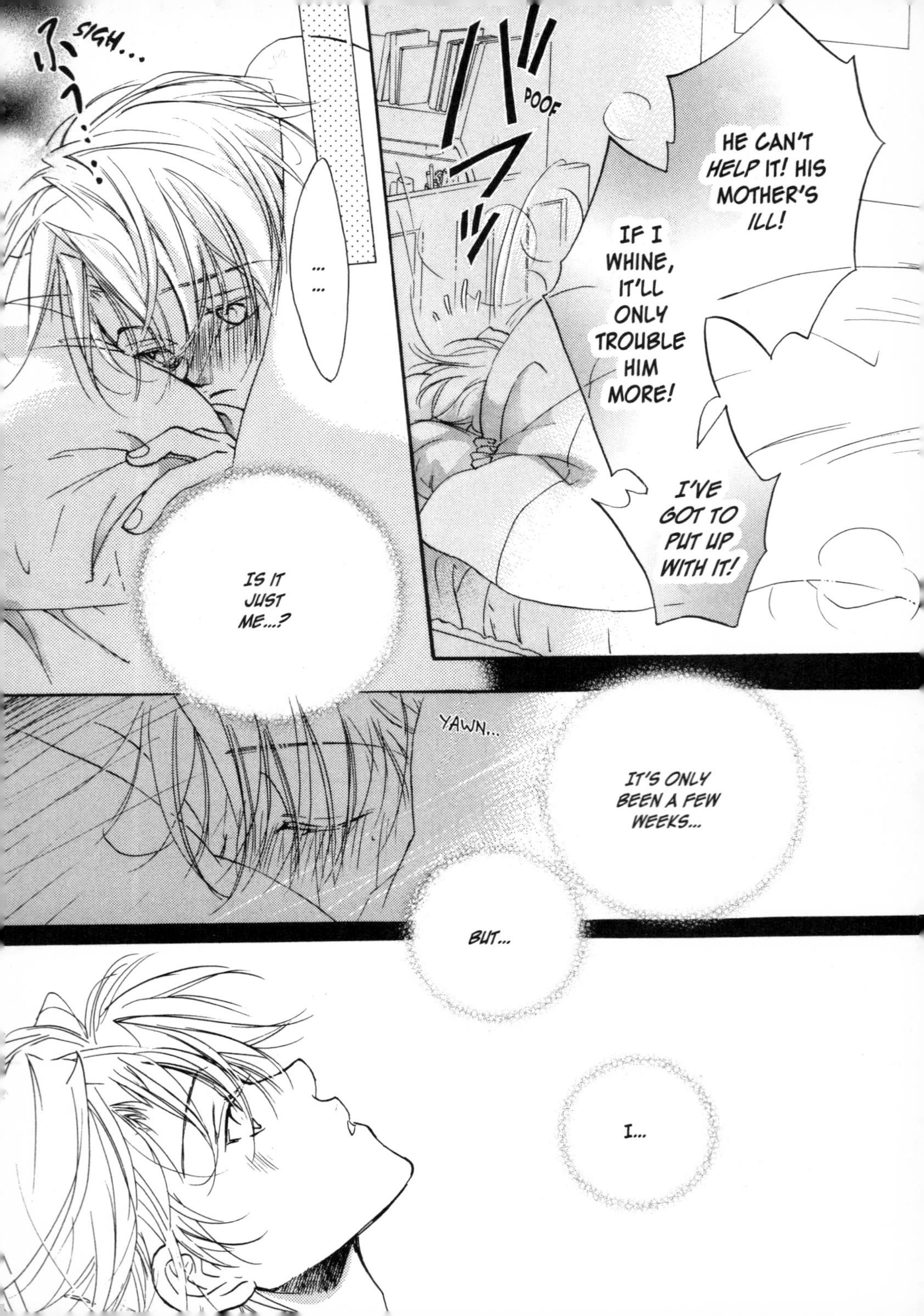
POOF
HE CAN'T HELP IT! HIS MOTHER'S ILL!
IF I WHINE, IT'LL ONLY TROUBLE HIM MORE!
I'VE GOT TO PUT UP WITH IT!
SIGH...
... ...
IS IT JUST ME...?
YAWN...
IT'S ONLY BEEN A FEW WEEKS...
BUT...
I...

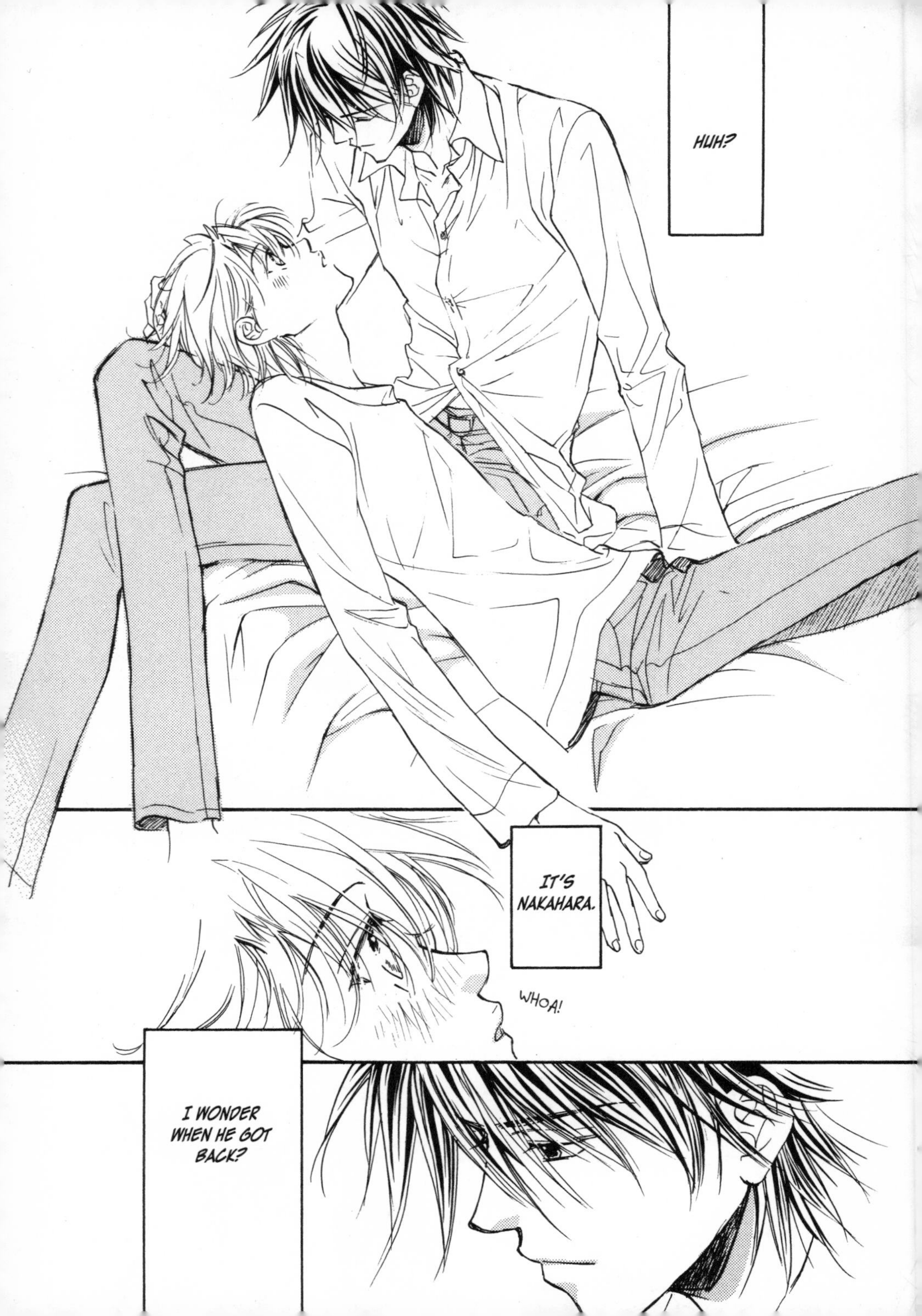
HUH?
IT'S NAKAHARA.
WHOA!
I WONDER WHEN HE GOT BACK?

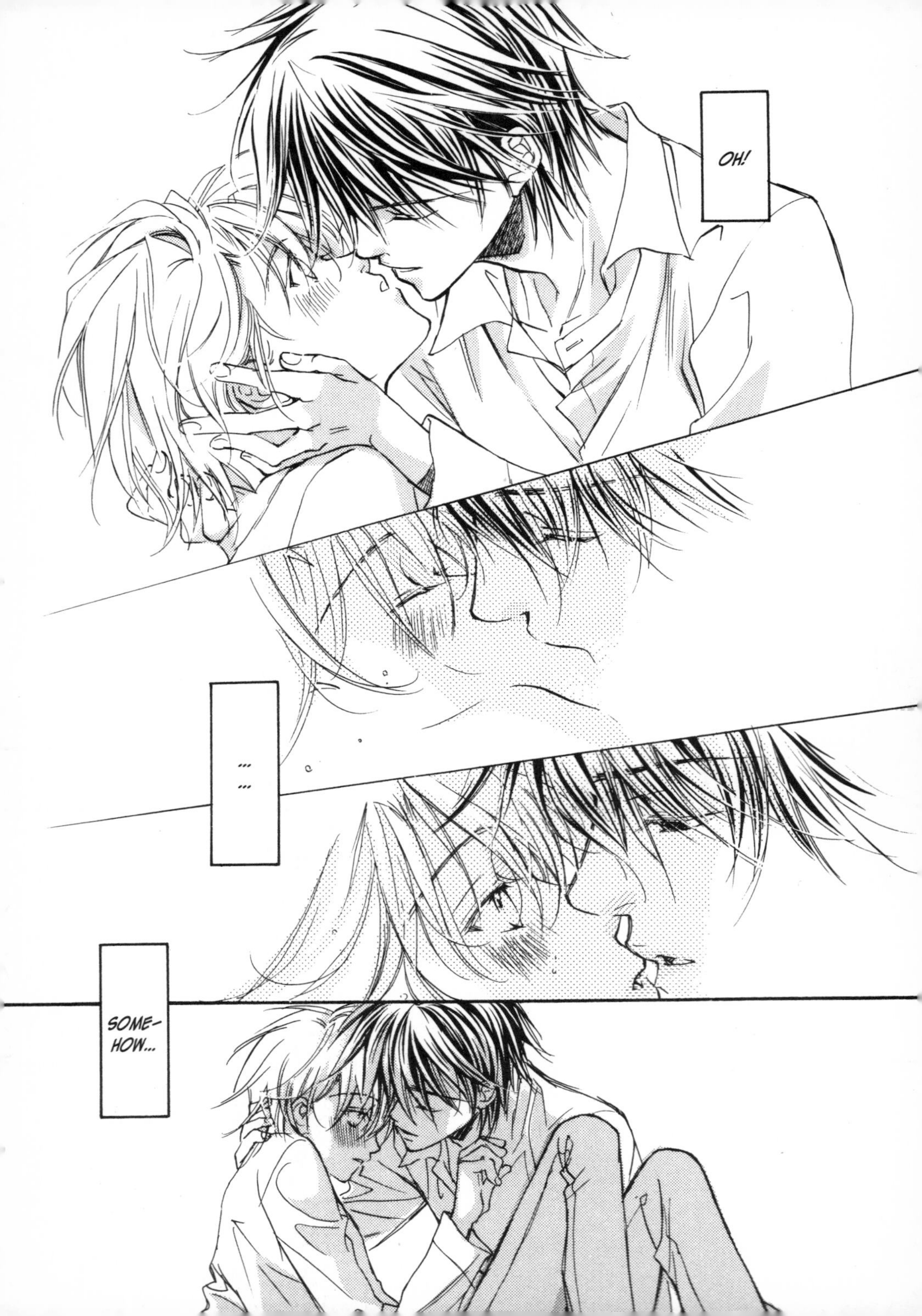
OH!
...
...
SOME-HOW...

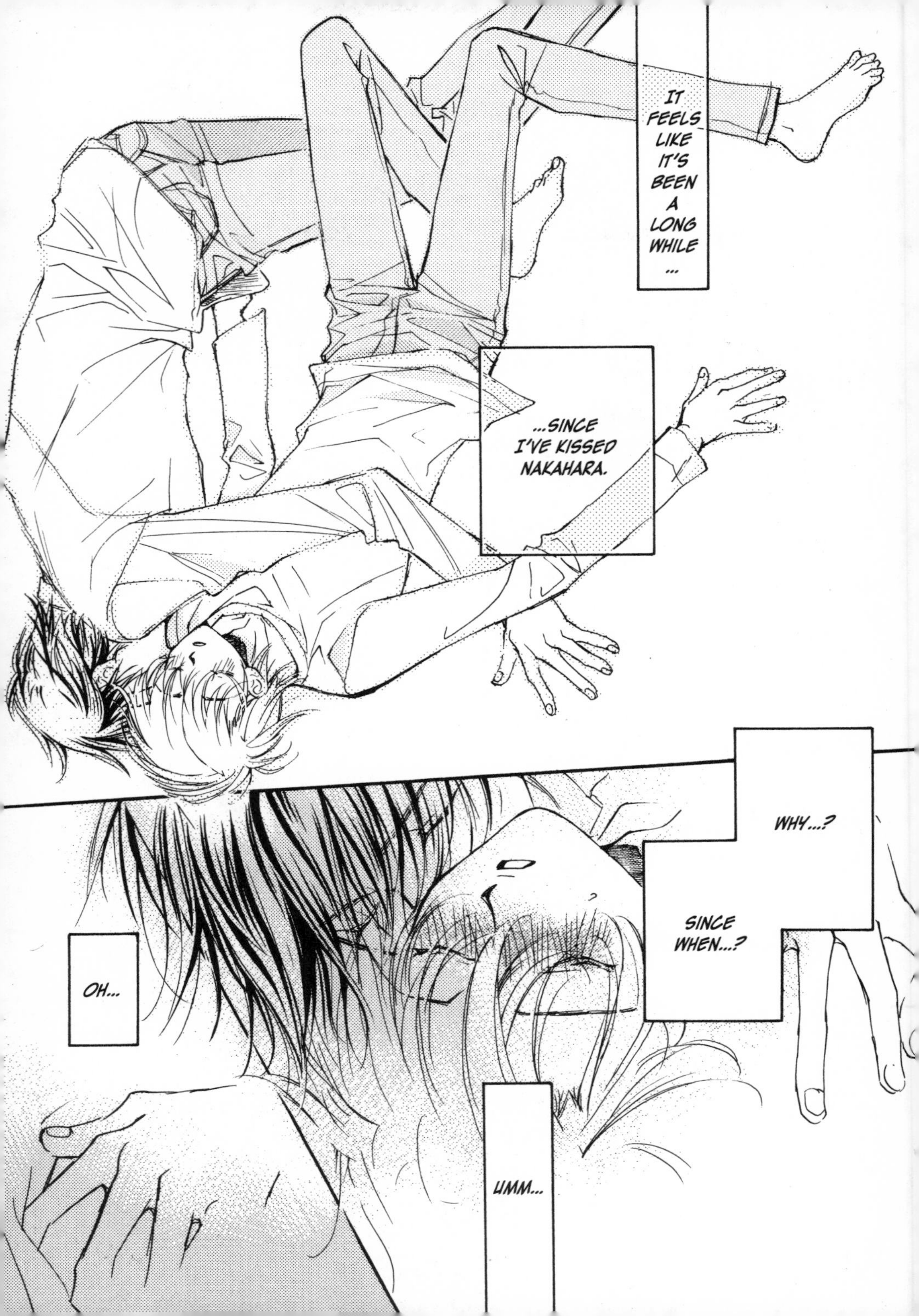
IT FEELS LIKE IT'S BEEN A LONG WHILE ...
...SINCE I'VE KISSED NAKAHARA.
WHY...?
SINCE WHEN...?
UMM...
OH...

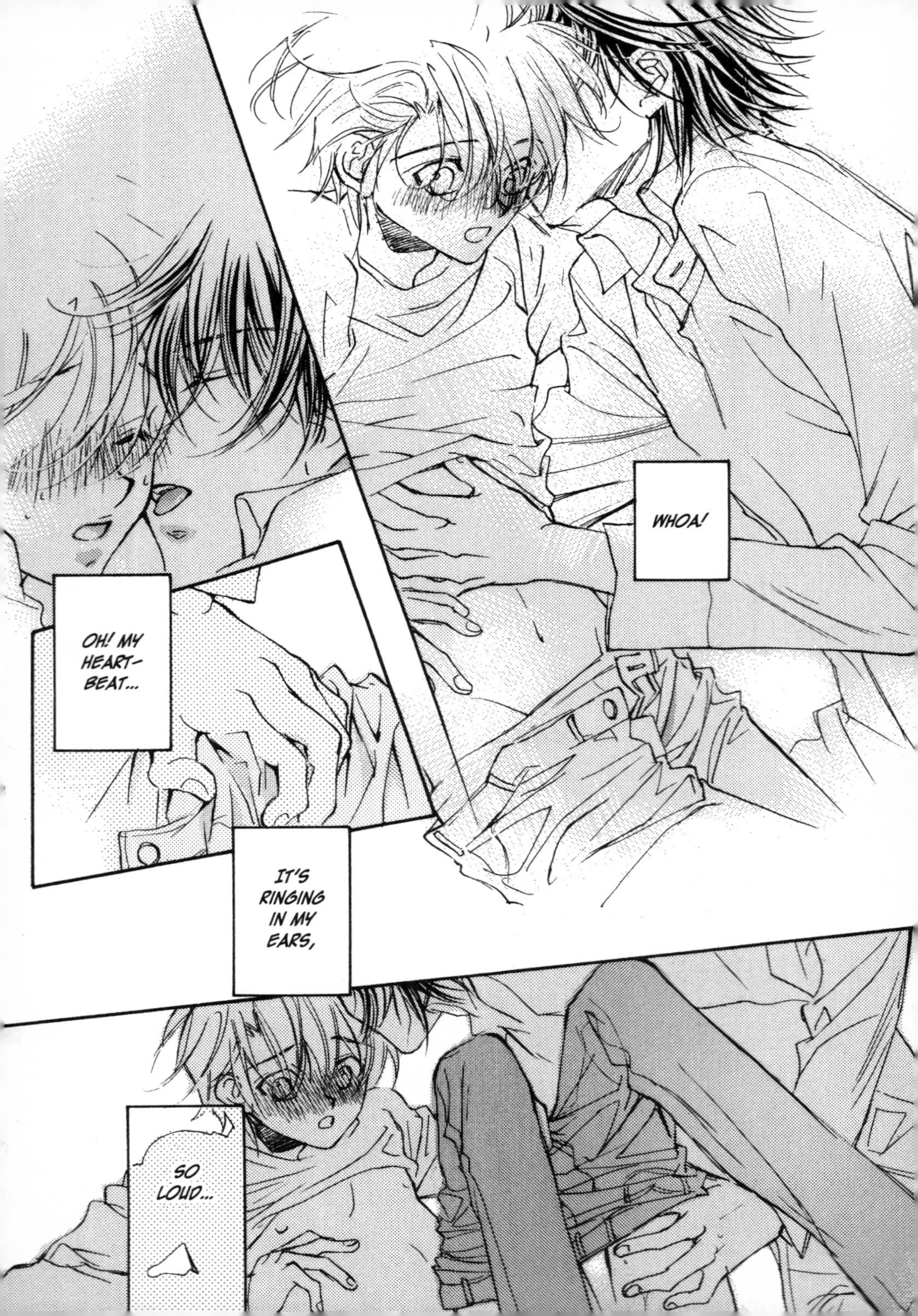
WHOA!
OH! MY HEART-BEAT...
IT'S RINGING IN MY EARS,
SO LOUD...

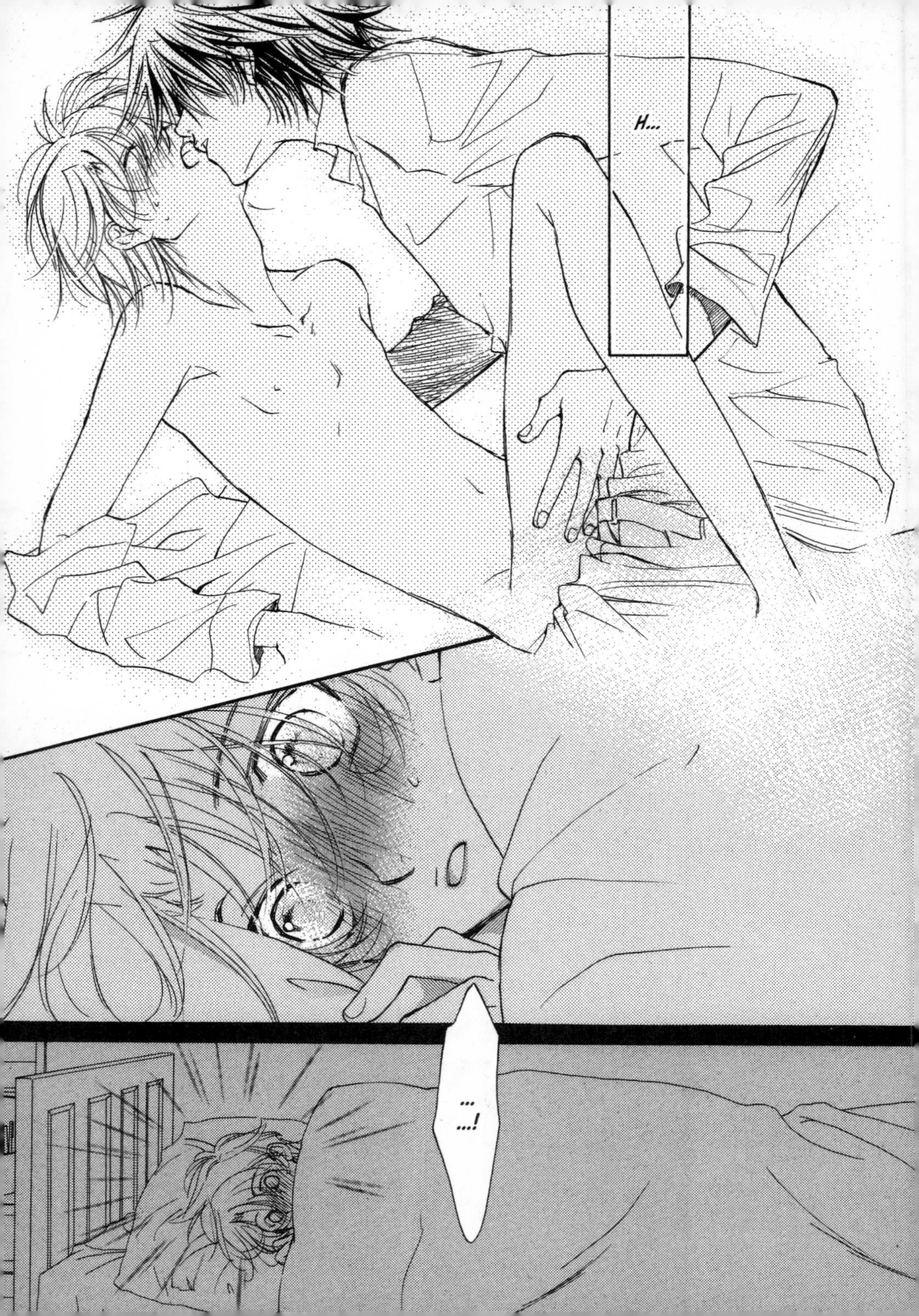
H...
...
...!

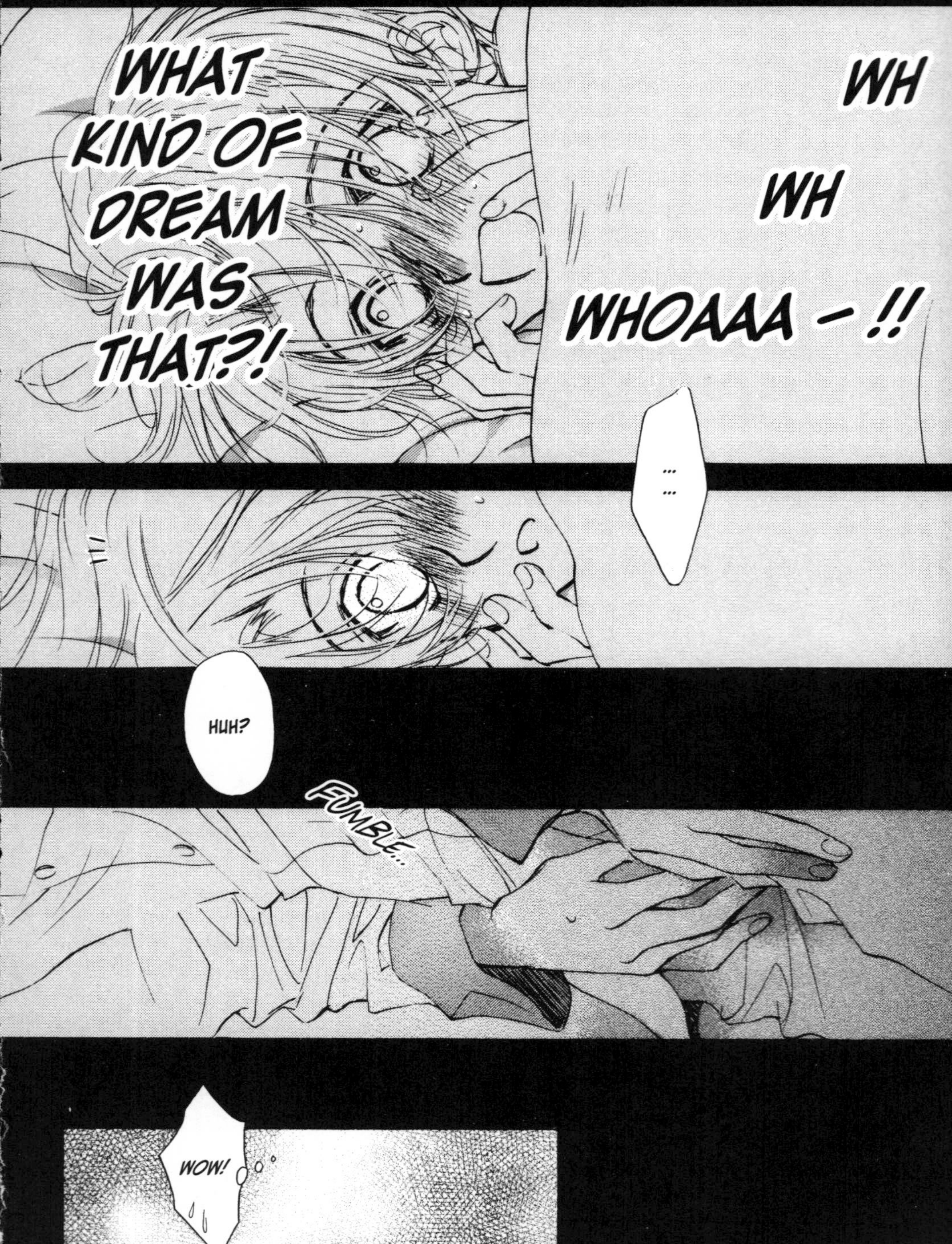
WH WH WHOAAA –!!
WHAT KIND OF DREAM WAS THAT?!
......
HUH?
FUMBLE...
WOW!

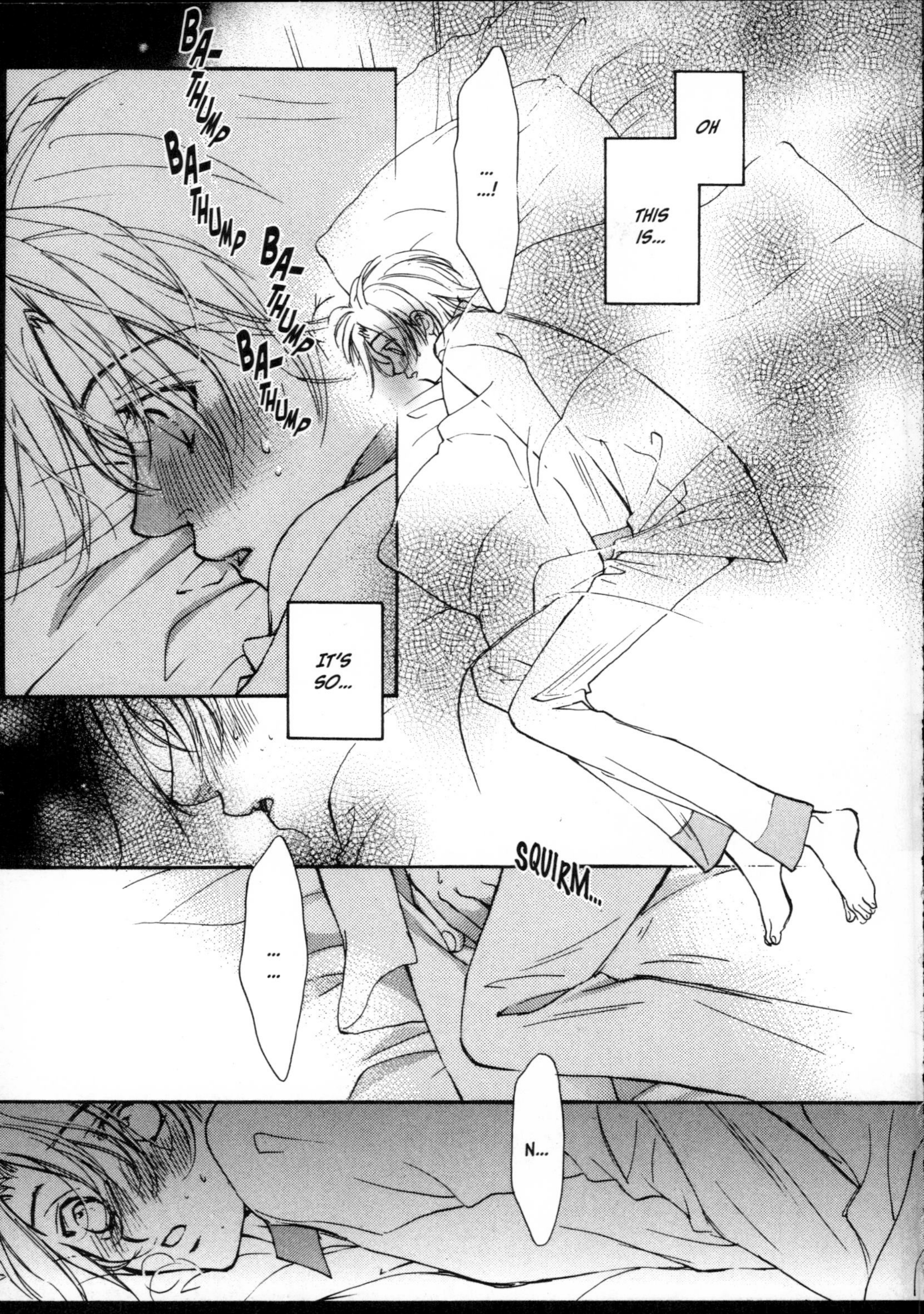
OH
THIS IS...
... ...!
BA-THUMP BA-THUMP
BA-THUMP BA-THUMP
IT'S SO...
SQUIRM...
... ...
N...

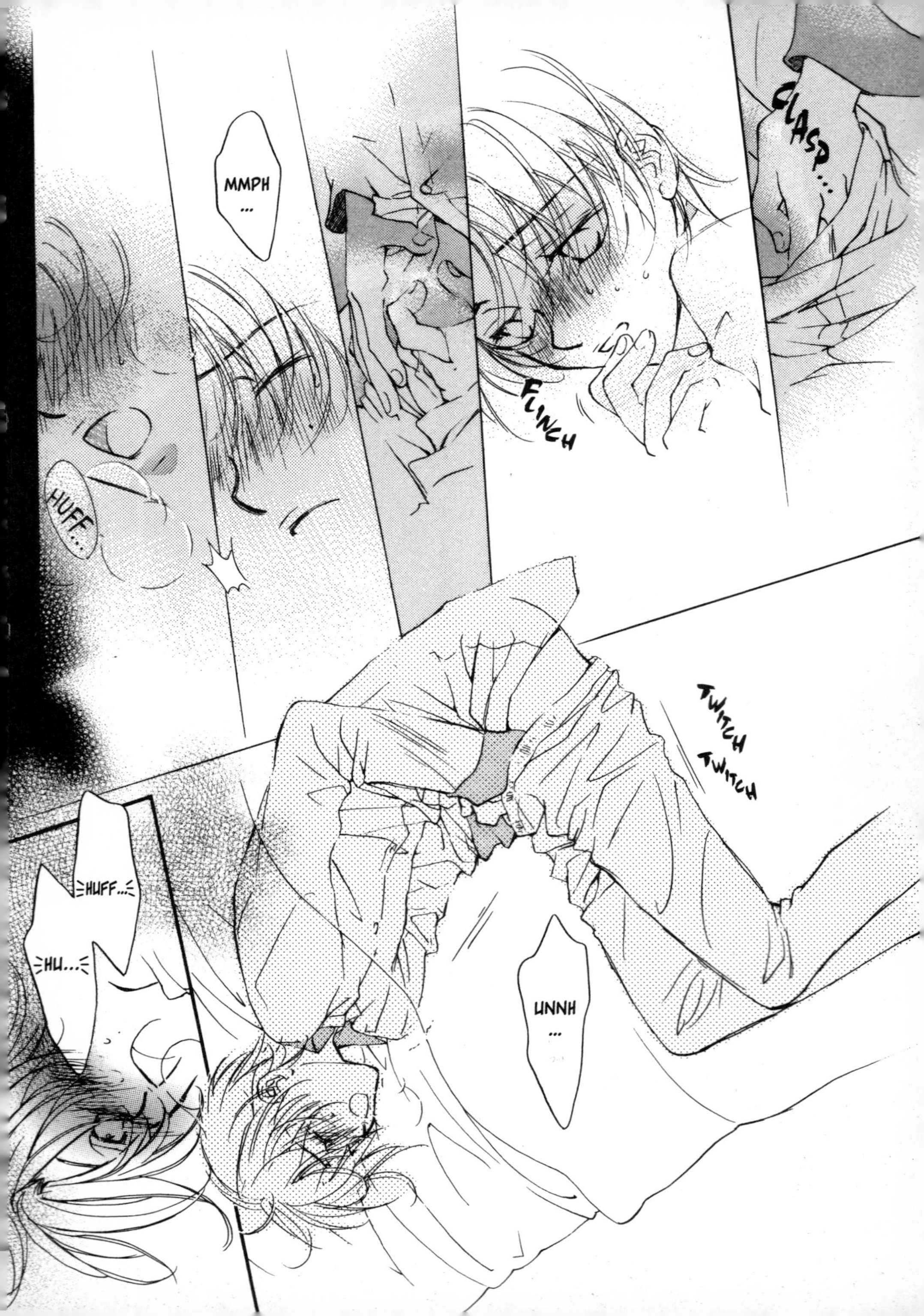
CLASP...
FLINCH
MMPH...
HUFF...
TWITCH TWITCH
UNNH...
HUFF...
HU...

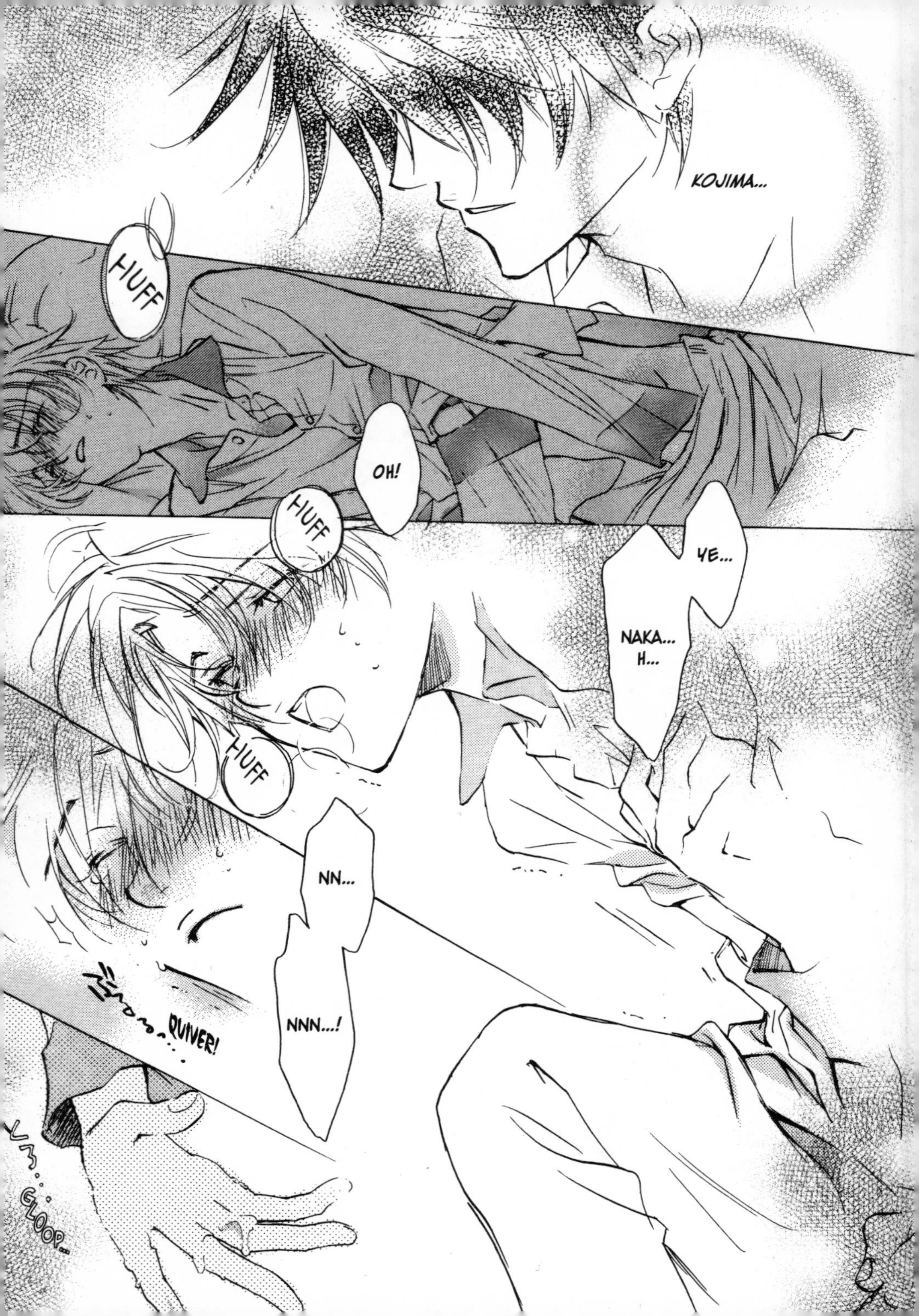
KOJIMA...
OH!
HUFF
HUFF
YE...
NAKA...
H...
HUFF
NN...
NNN...!
QUIVER!
GLOOP...

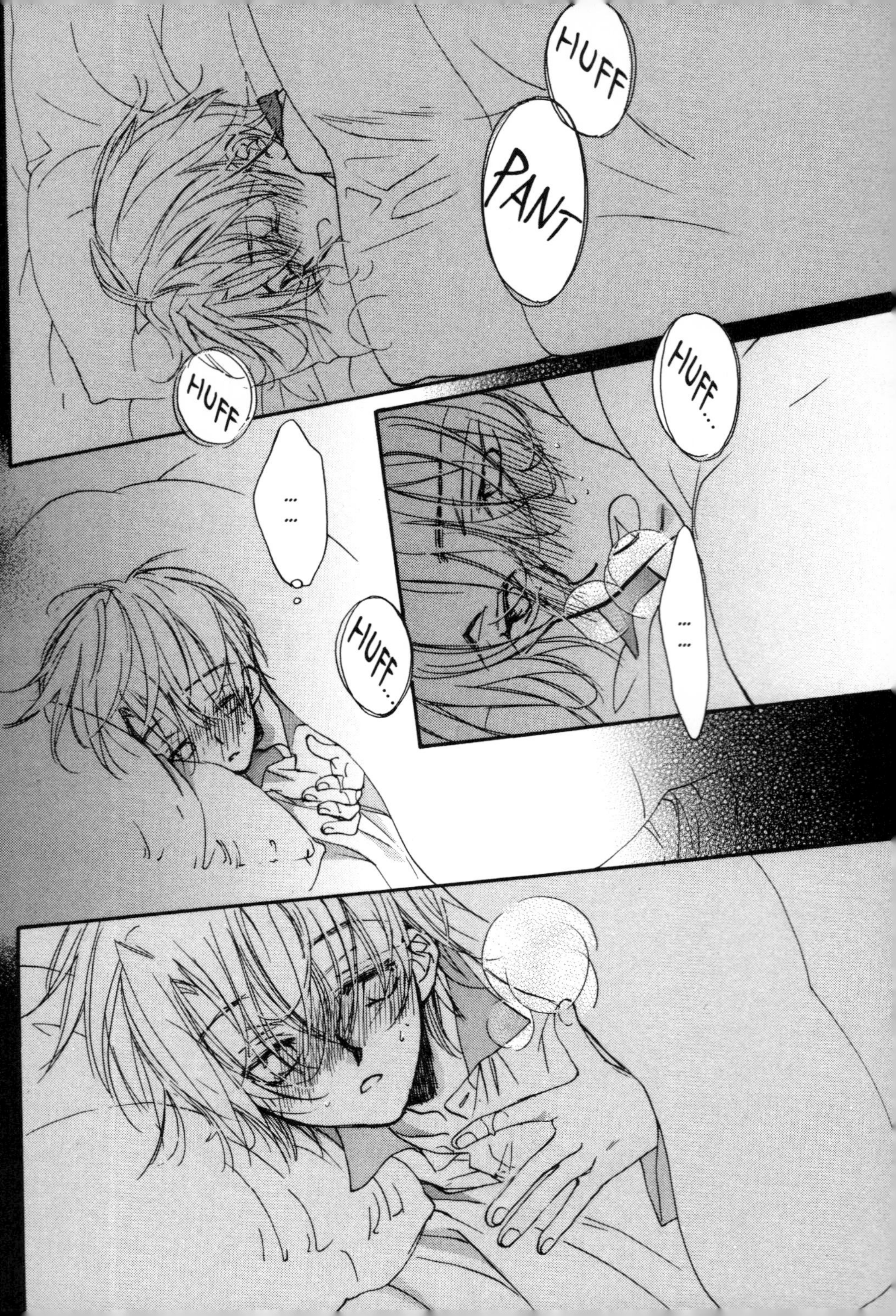
HUFF
PANT
HUFF
HUFF...
......
......
HUFF...

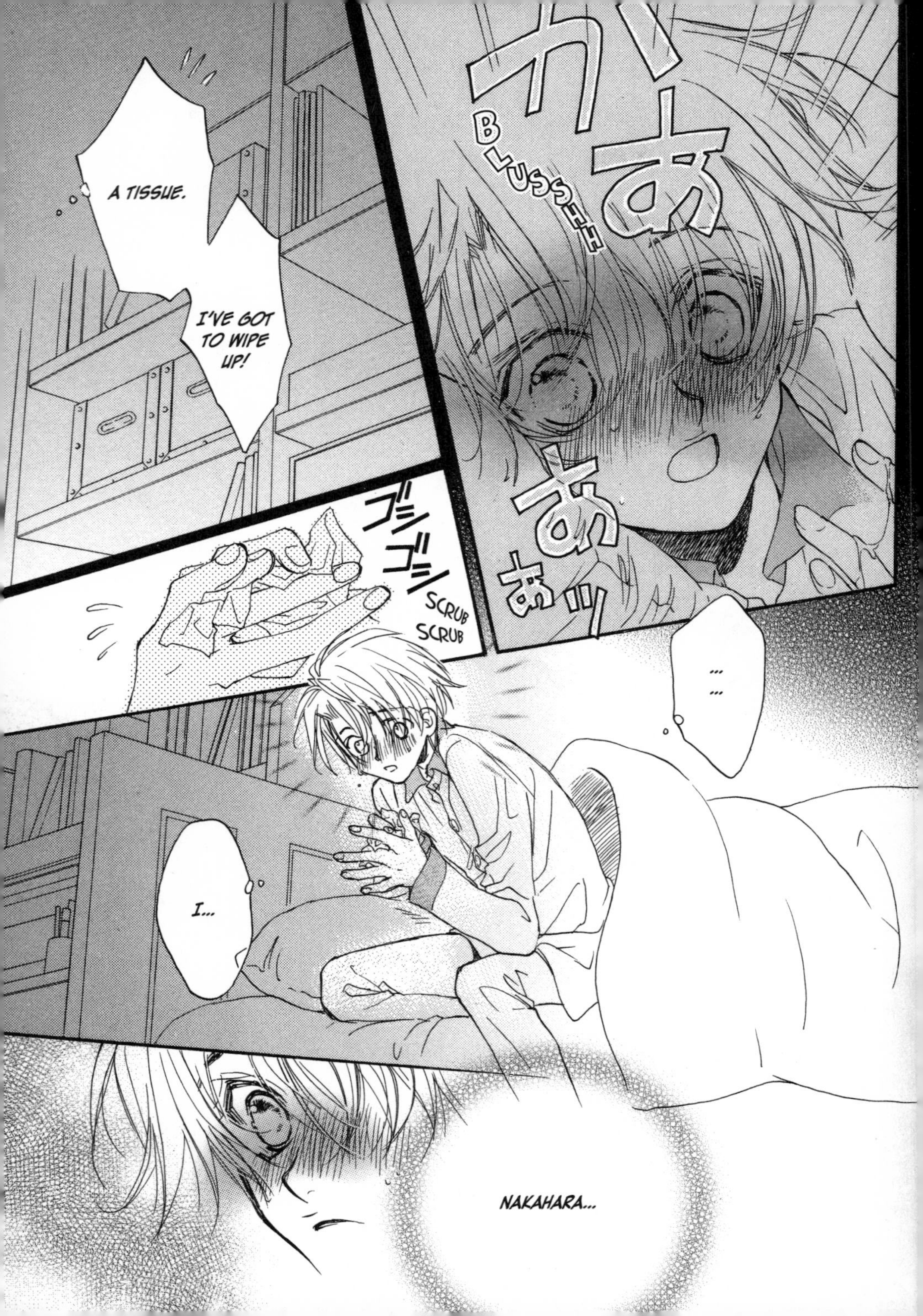
BLUSSHHH
A TISSUE.
I'VE GOT TO WIPE UP!
ゴシゴシ
SCRUB SCRUB
……
I…
NAKAHARA…

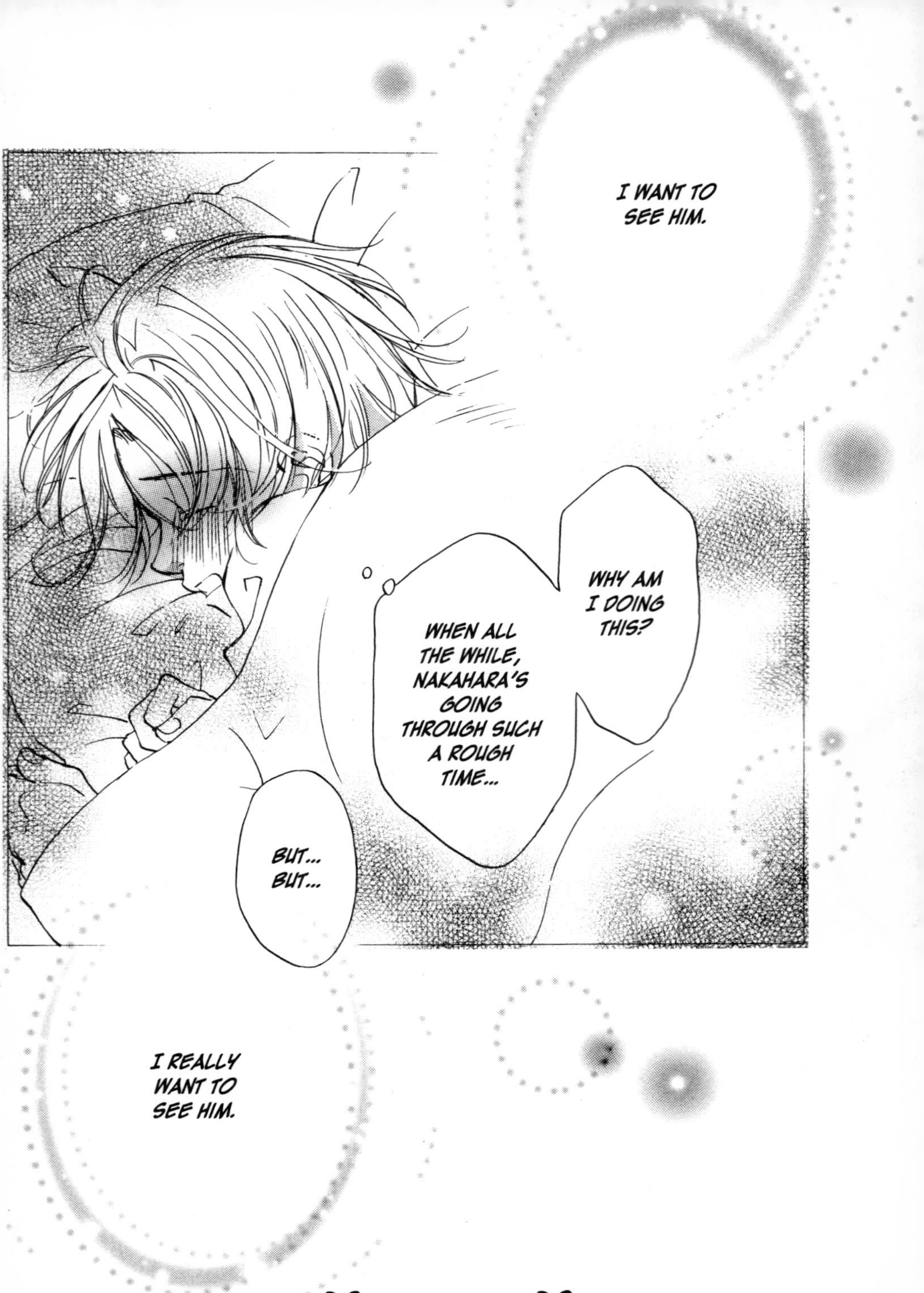
I WANT TO SEE HIM.
WHY AM I DOING THIS?
WHEN ALL THE WHILE, NAKAHARA'S GOING THROUGH SUCH A ROUGH TIME...
BUT... BUT...
I REALLY WANT TO SEE HIM.

CHAPTER 12 · END

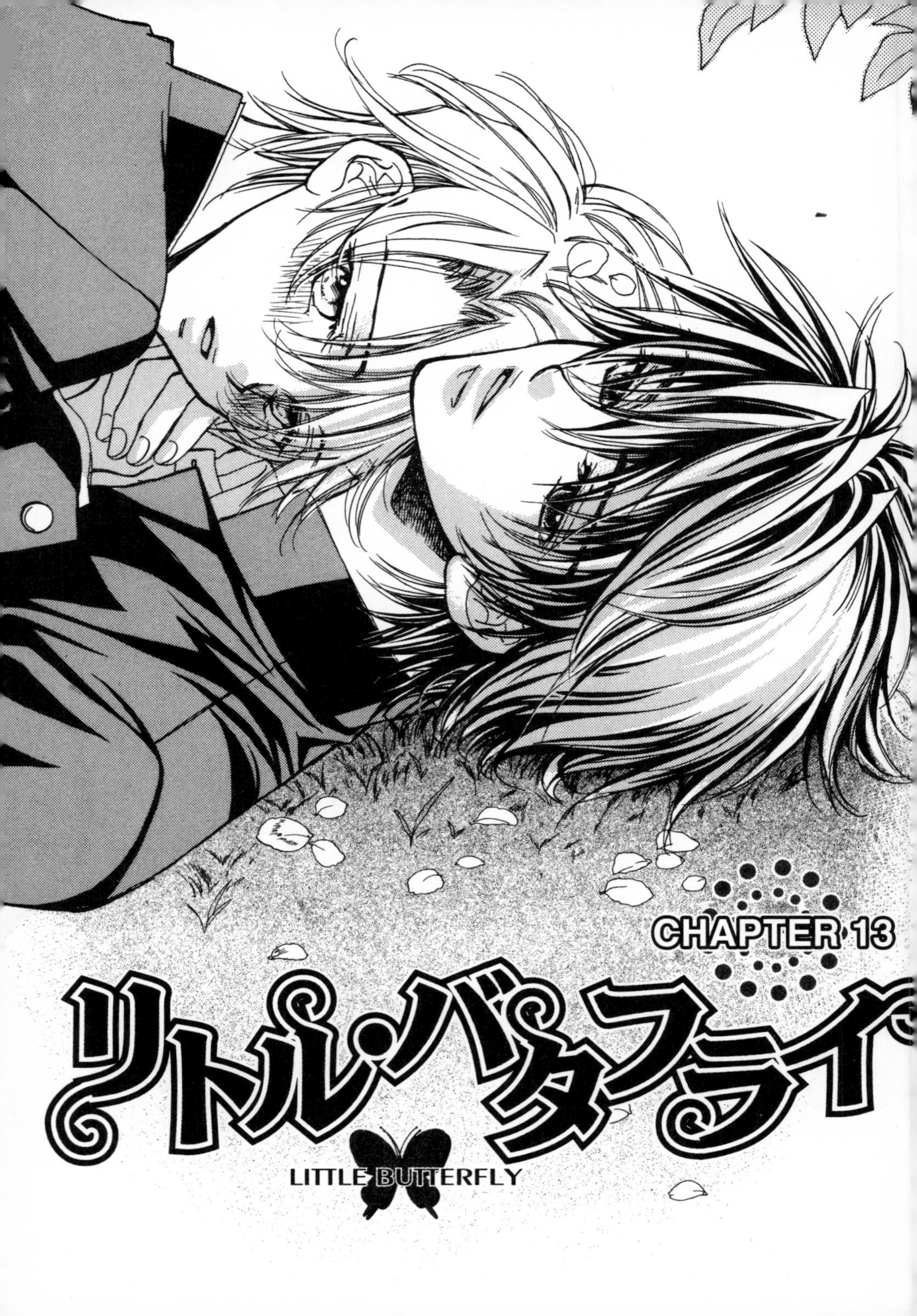

CHAPTER 13
リトル・バタフライ
LITTLE BUTTERFLY

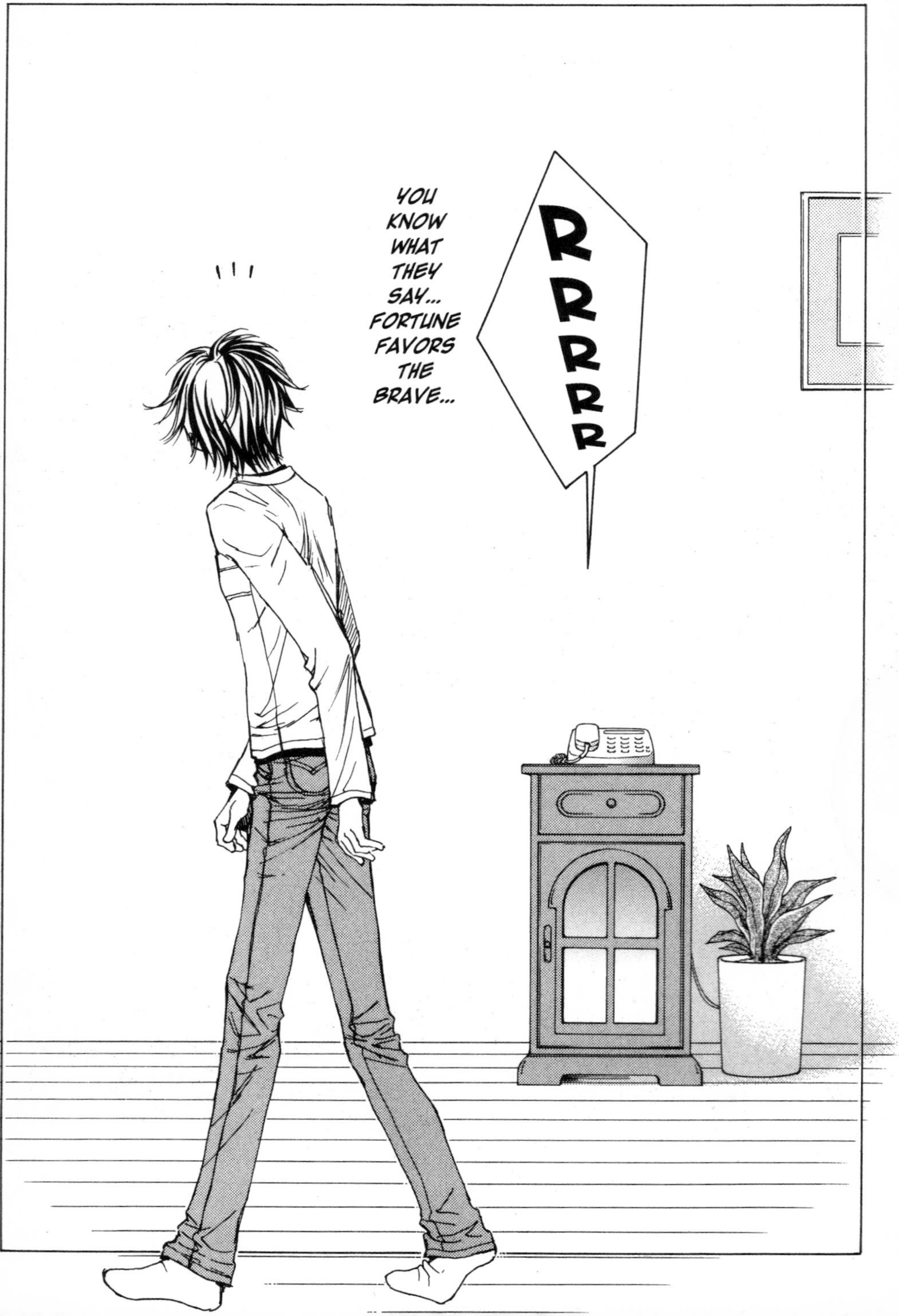
RRRRR
YOU KNOW WHAT THEY SAY... FORTUNE FAVORS THE BRAVE...

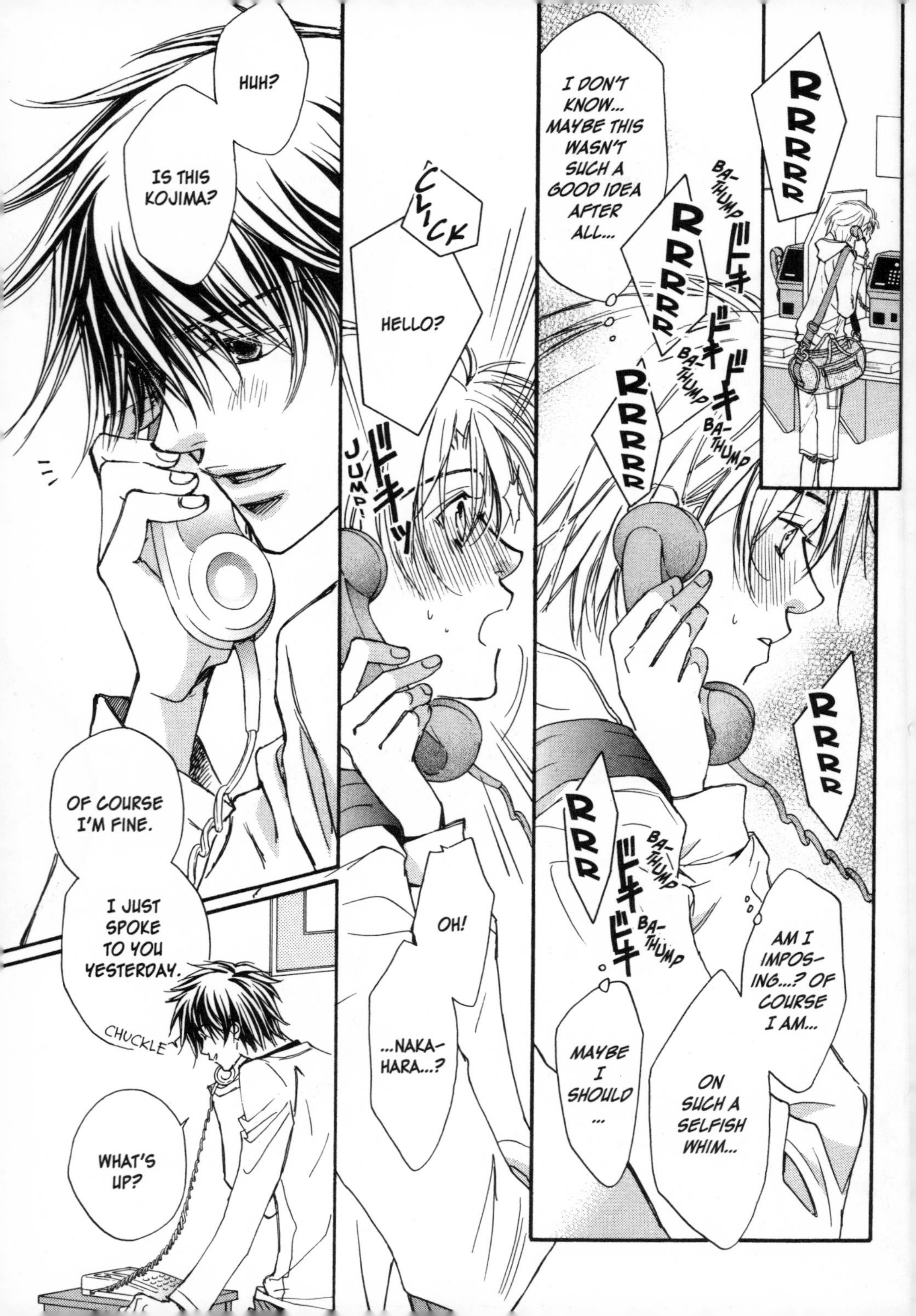
RRRRR
I DON'T KNOW... MAYBE THIS WASN'T SUCH A GOOD IDEA AFTER ALL...
BA-THUMP
RRRRRR
BA-THUMP
BA-THUMP
RRRRR
RRRR
RRR
BA-THUMP
BA-THUMP
AM I IMPOS-ING...? OF COURSE I AM...
ON SUCH A SELFISH WHIM...
MAYBE I SHOULD ...
CLICK
HELLO?
JUMP!
OH!
...NAKA-HARA...?
HUH?
IS THIS KOJIMA?
OF COURSE I'M FINE.
I JUST SPOKE TO YOU YESTERDAY.
CHUCKLE
WHAT'S UP?

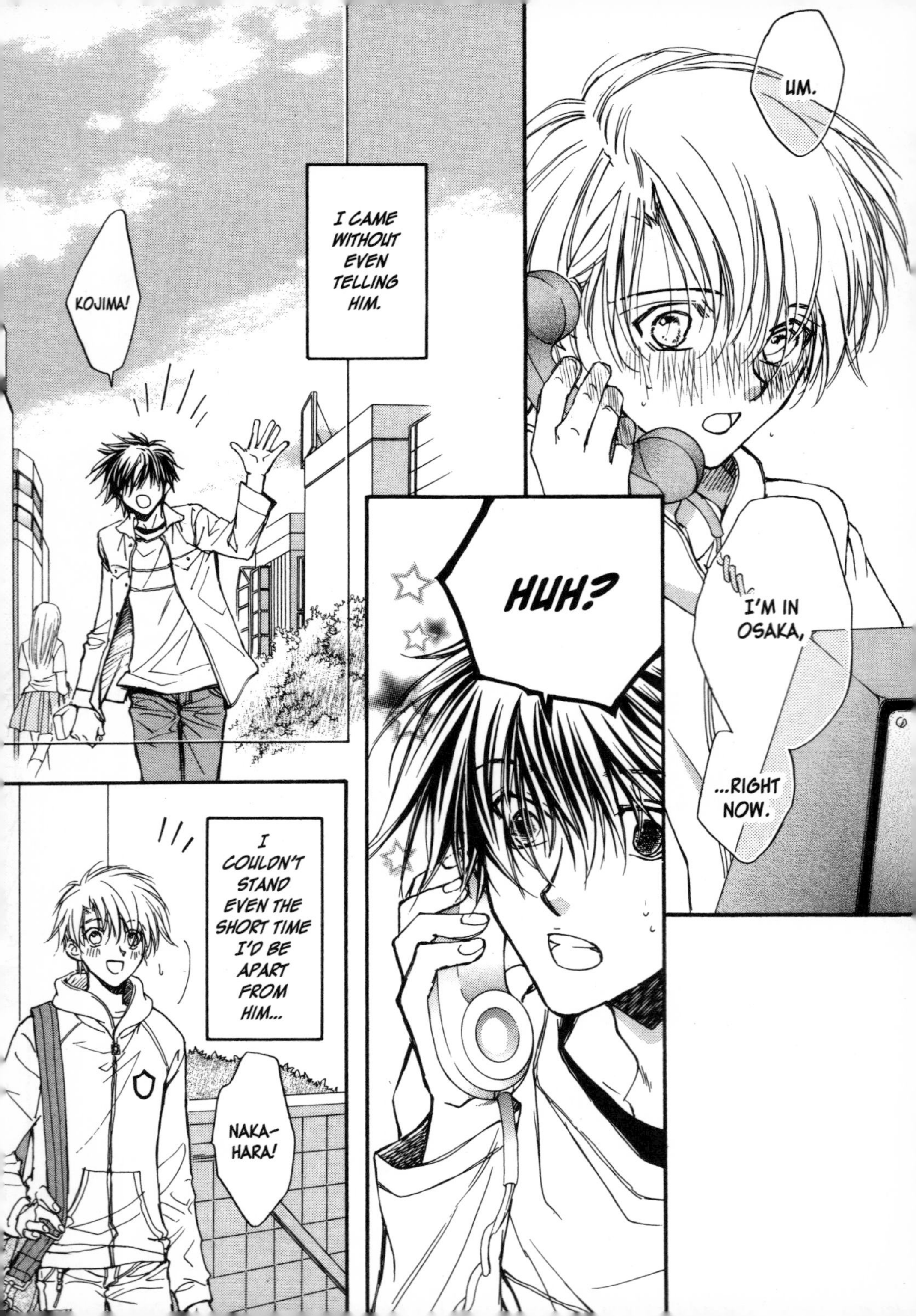
UM.
I'M IN OSAKA,
...RIGHT NOW.
HUH?
I CAME WITHOUT EVEN TELLING HIM.
KOJIMA!
I COULDN'T STAND EVEN THE SHORT TIME I'D BE APART FROM HIM...
NAKA-HARA!

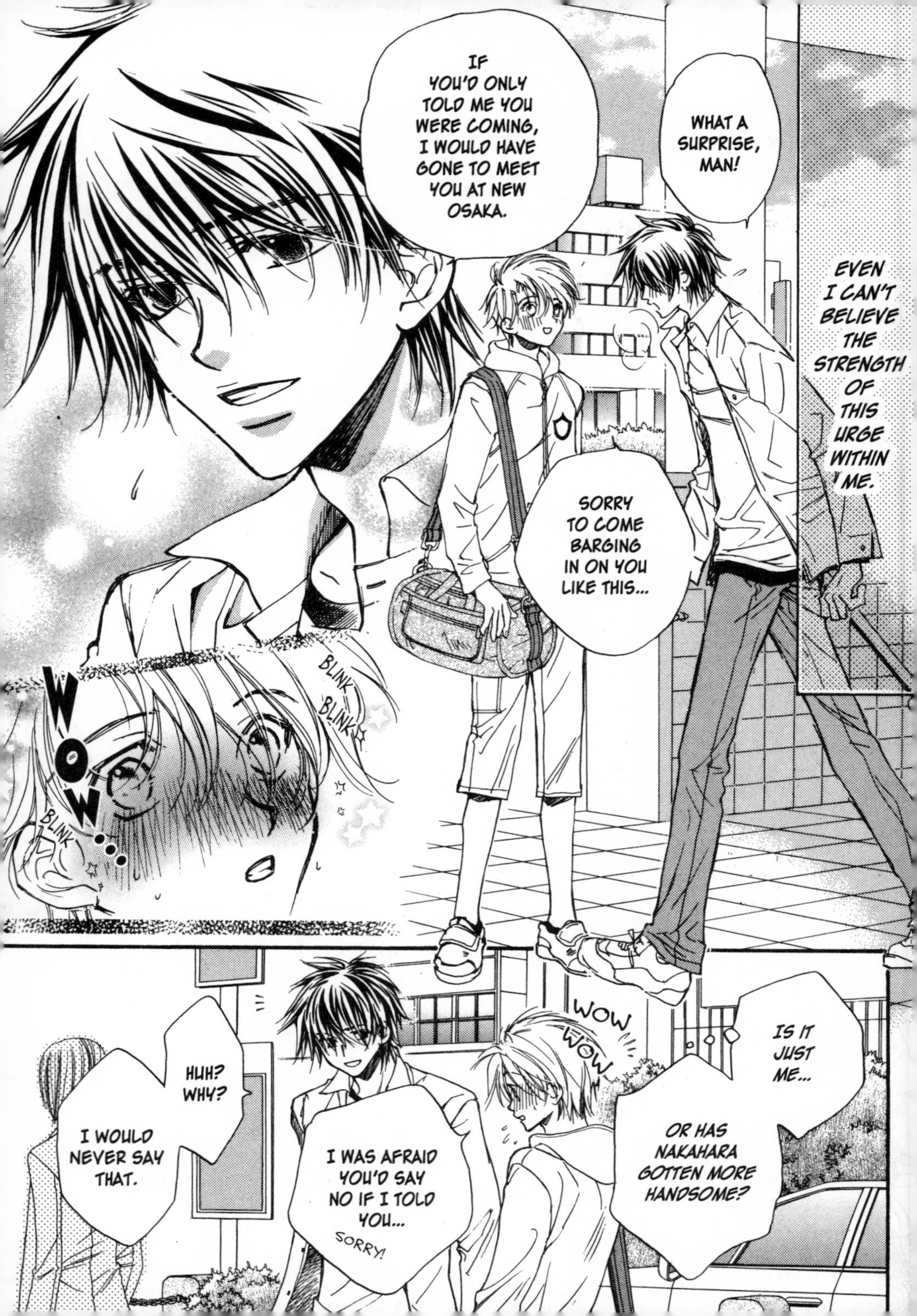
WHAT A SURPRISE, MAN!
EVEN I CAN'T BELIEVE THE STRENGTH OF THIS URGE WITHIN ME.
IF YOU'D ONLY TOLD ME YOU WERE COMING, I WOULD HAVE GONE TO MEET YOU AT NEW OSAKA.
SORRY TO COME BARGING IN ON YOU LIKE THIS...
BLINK BLINK
WOW
BLINK
IS IT JUST ME...
OR HAS NAKAHARA GOTTEN MORE HANDSOME?
WOW WOW
I WAS AFRAID YOU'D SAY NO IF I TOLD YOU...
SORRY!
HUH? WHY?
I WOULD NEVER SAY THAT.

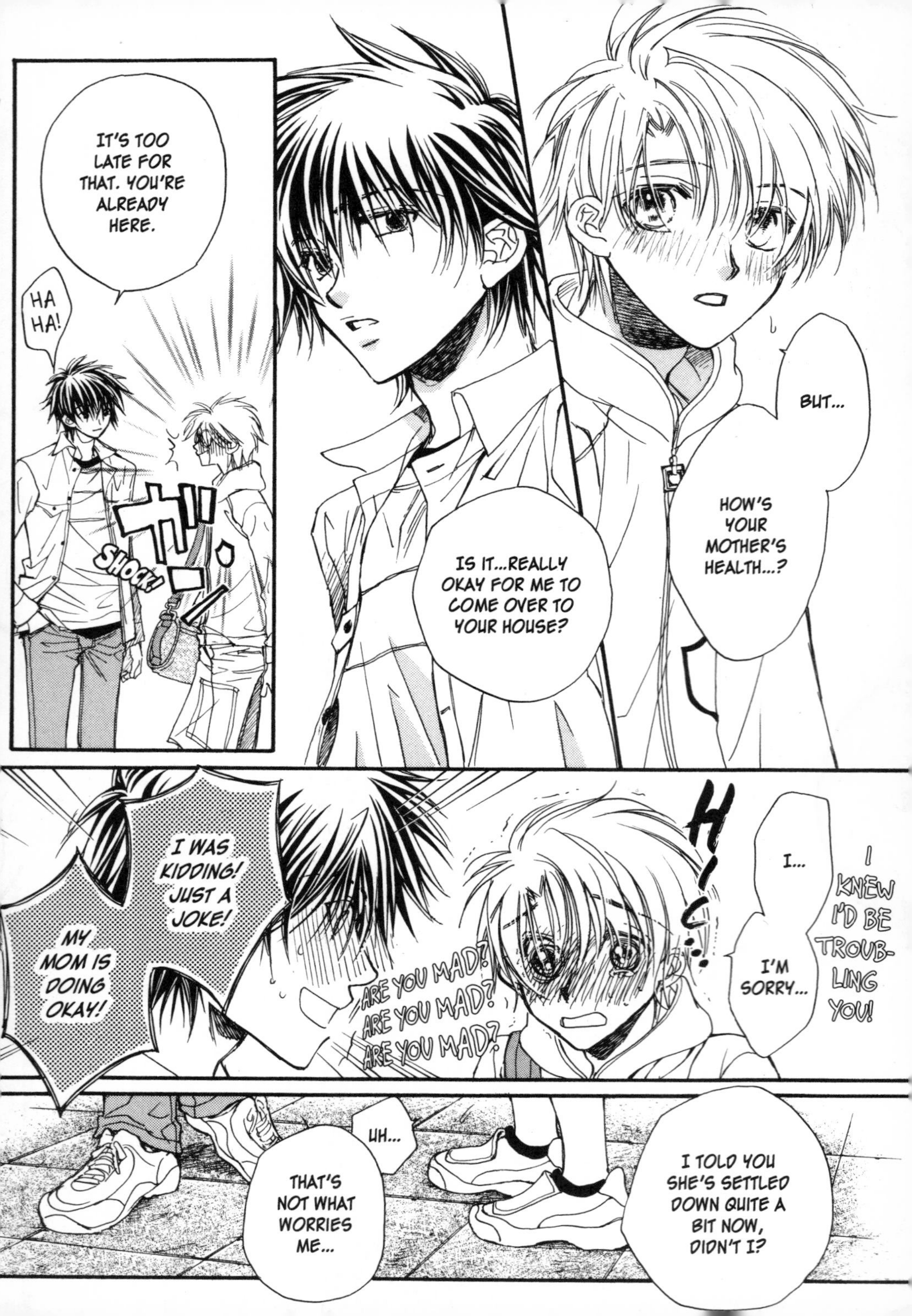

BUT...
HOW'S YOUR MOTHER'S HEALTH...?
IS IT...REALLY OKAY FOR ME TO COME OVER TO YOUR HOUSE?
IT'S TOO LATE FOR THAT. YOU'RE ALREADY HERE.
HA HA!
SHOCK!
I KNEW I'D BE TROUBLING YOU!
I...
I'M SORRY...
HIC...
ARE YOU MAD? ARE YOU MAD? ARE YOU MAD?
I WAS KIDDING! JUST A JOKE!
MY MOM IS DOING OKAY!
I TOLD YOU SHE'S SETTLED DOWN QUITE A BIT NOW, DIDN'T I?
UH...
THAT'S NOT WHAT WORRIES ME...

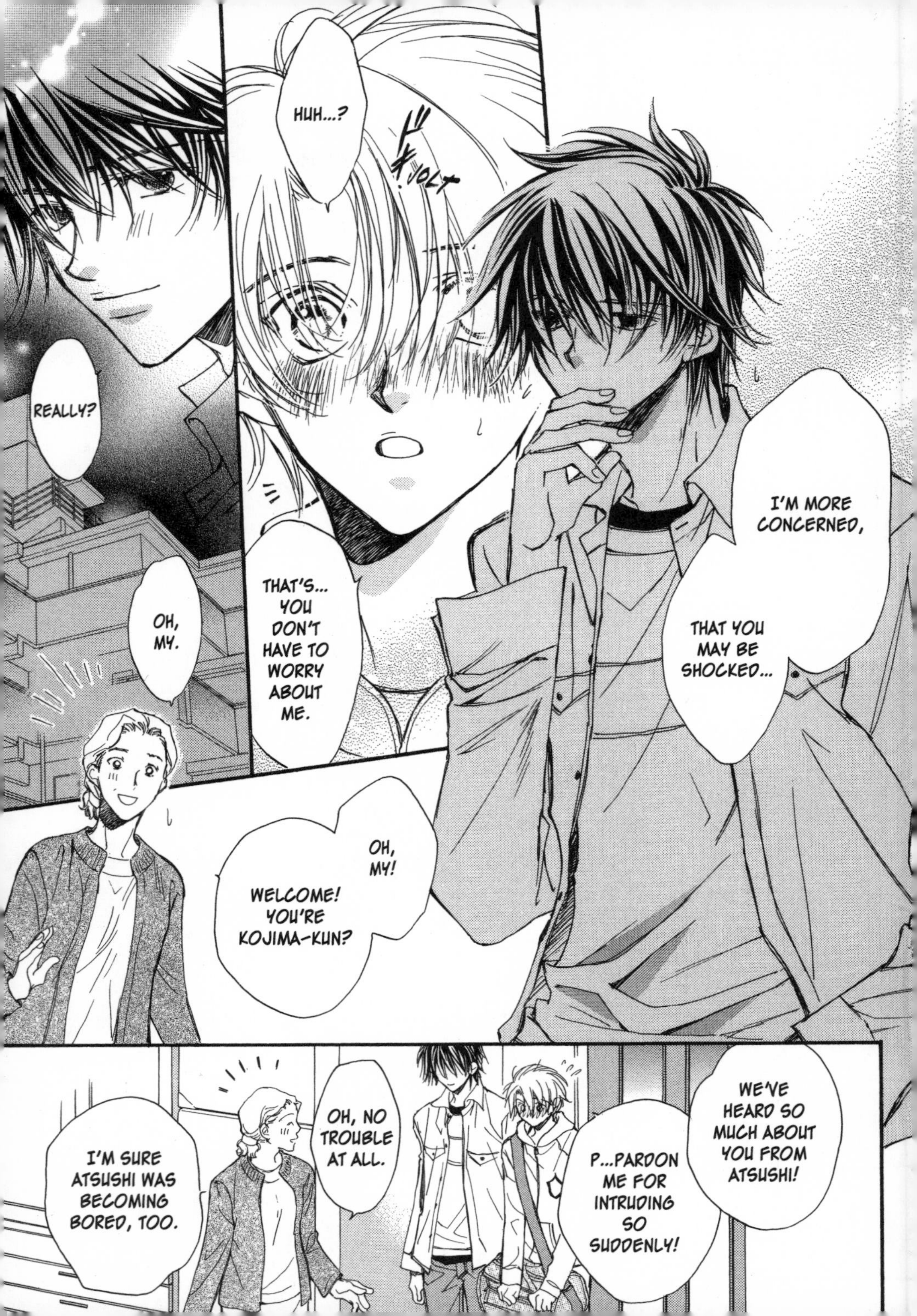
I'M MORE CONCERNED,
THAT YOU MAY BE SHOCKED...
HUH...?
JOLT
THAT'S... YOU DON'T HAVE TO WORRY ABOUT ME.
REALLY?
OH, MY.
OH, MY!
WELCOME! YOU'RE KOJIMA-KUN?
WE'VE HEARD SO MUCH ABOUT YOU FROM ATSUSHI!
P...PARDON ME FOR INTRUDING SO SUDDENLY!
OH, NO TROUBLE AT ALL.
I'M SURE ATSUSHI WAS BECOMING BORED, TOO.

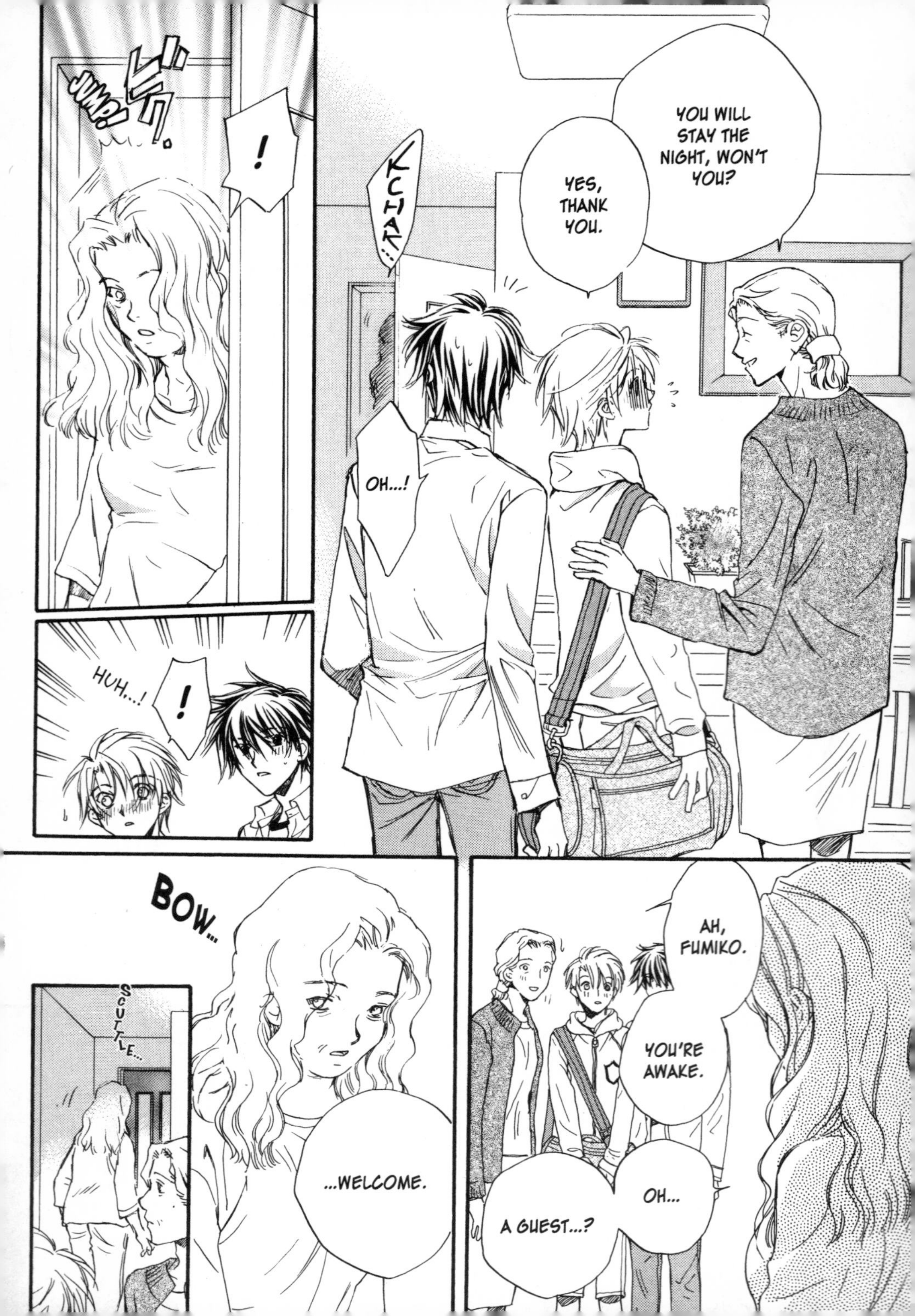

YOU WILL STAY THE NIGHT, WON'T YOU?
YES, THANK YOU.
KCHAK...
OH...!
JUMP!
!
HUH...!
!
AH, FUMIKO.
YOU'RE AWAKE.
OH...
A GUEST...?
BOW...
...WELCOME.
SCUTTLE...

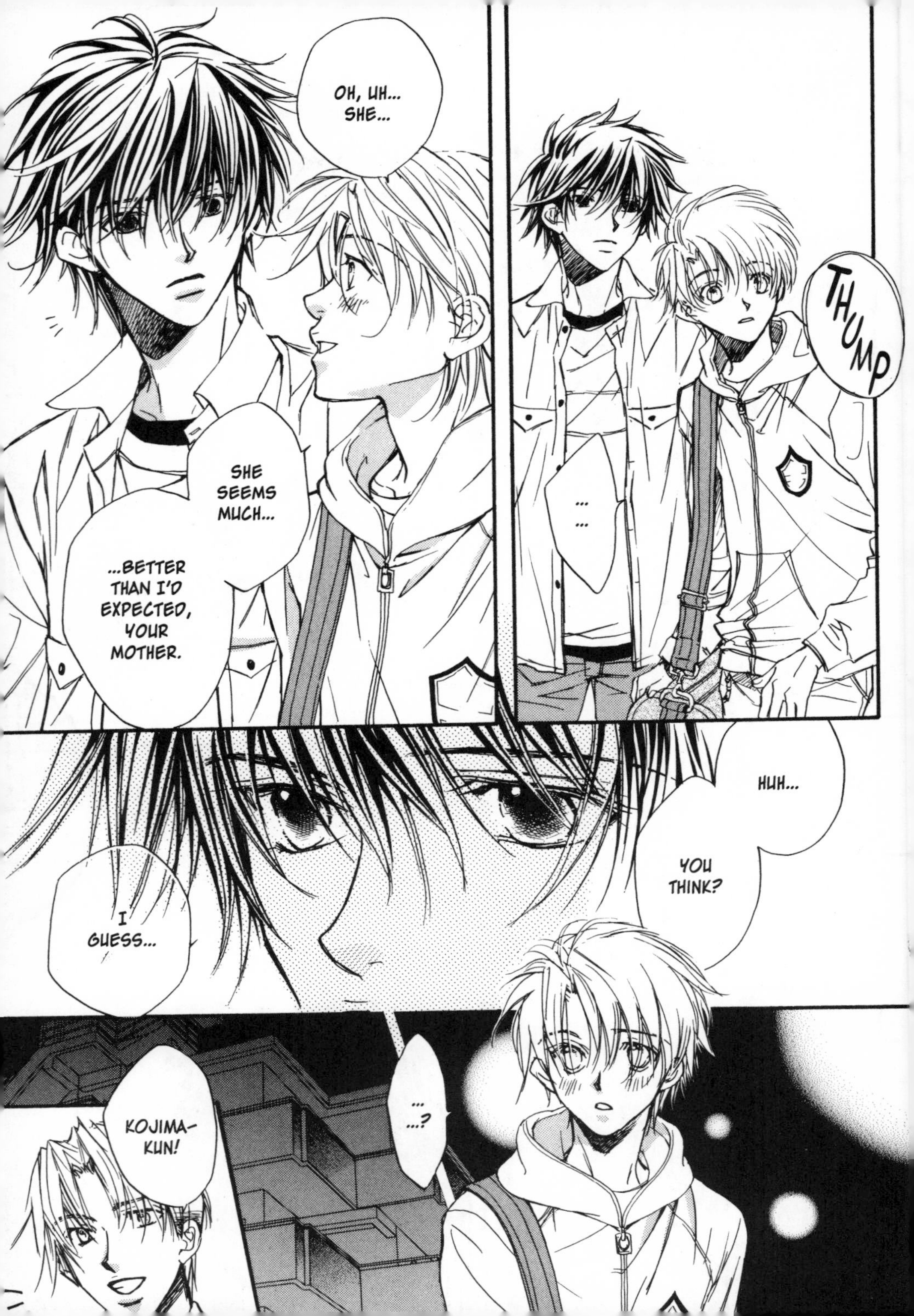
THUMP
...
...
OH, UH... SHE...
SHE SEEMS MUCH...
...BETTER THAN I'D EXPECTED, YOUR MOTHER.
HUH...
YOU THINK?
I GUESS...
...
...?
KOJIMA-KUN!

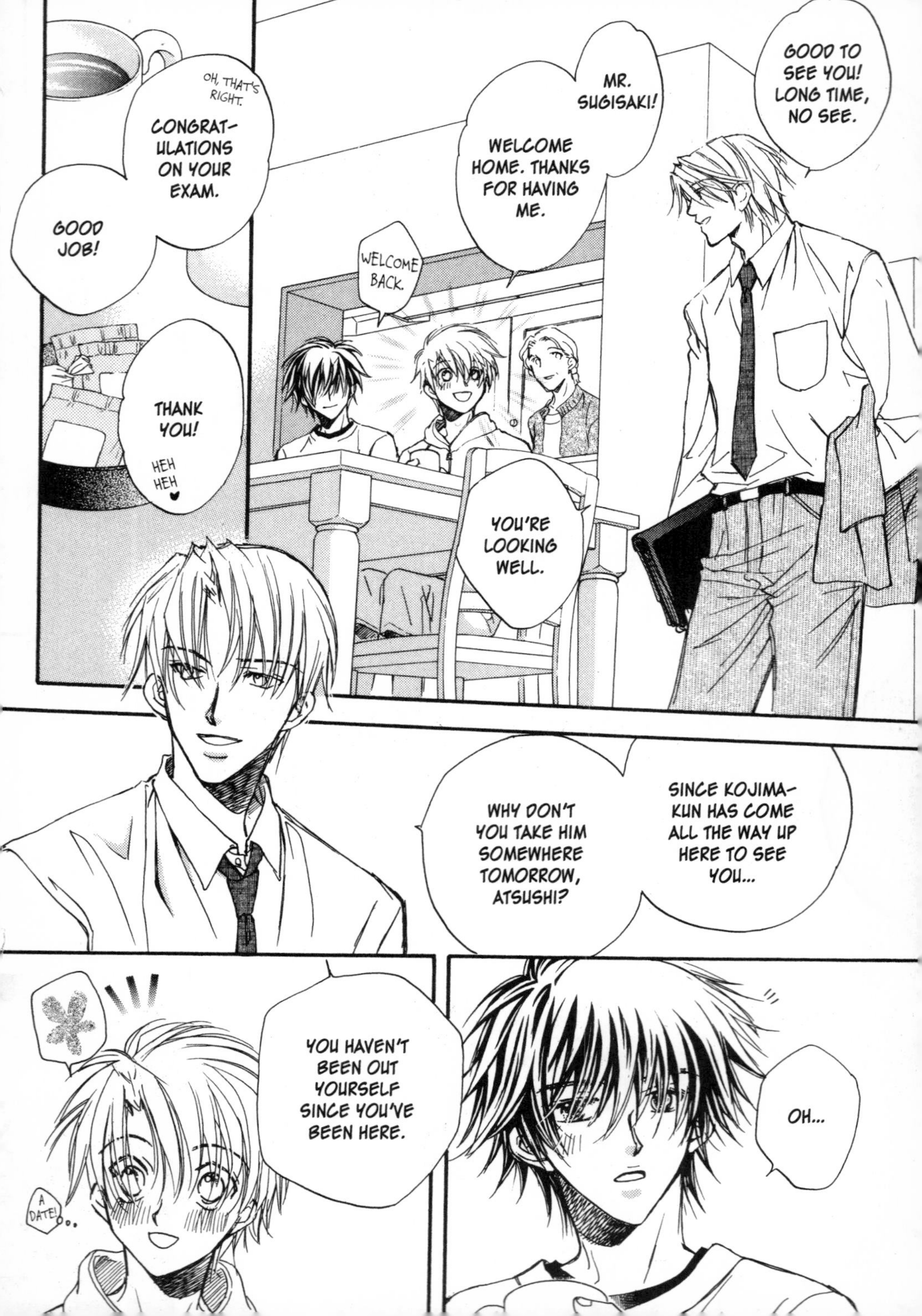
GOOD TO SEE YOU! LONG TIME, NO SEE.
MR. SUGISAKI!
WELCOME HOME. THANKS FOR HAVING ME.
WELCOME BACK.
OH, THAT'S RIGHT.
CONGRAT-ULATIONS ON YOUR EXAM.
GOOD JOB!
YOU'RE LOOKING WELL.
THANK YOU!
HEH HEH ♥
SINCE KOJIMA-KUN HAS COME ALL THE WAY UP HERE TO SEE YOU...
WHY DON'T YOU TAKE HIM SOMEWHERE TOMORROW, ATSUSHI?
OH...
YOU HAVEN'T BEEN OUT YOURSELF SINCE YOU'VE BEEN HERE.
A DATE!

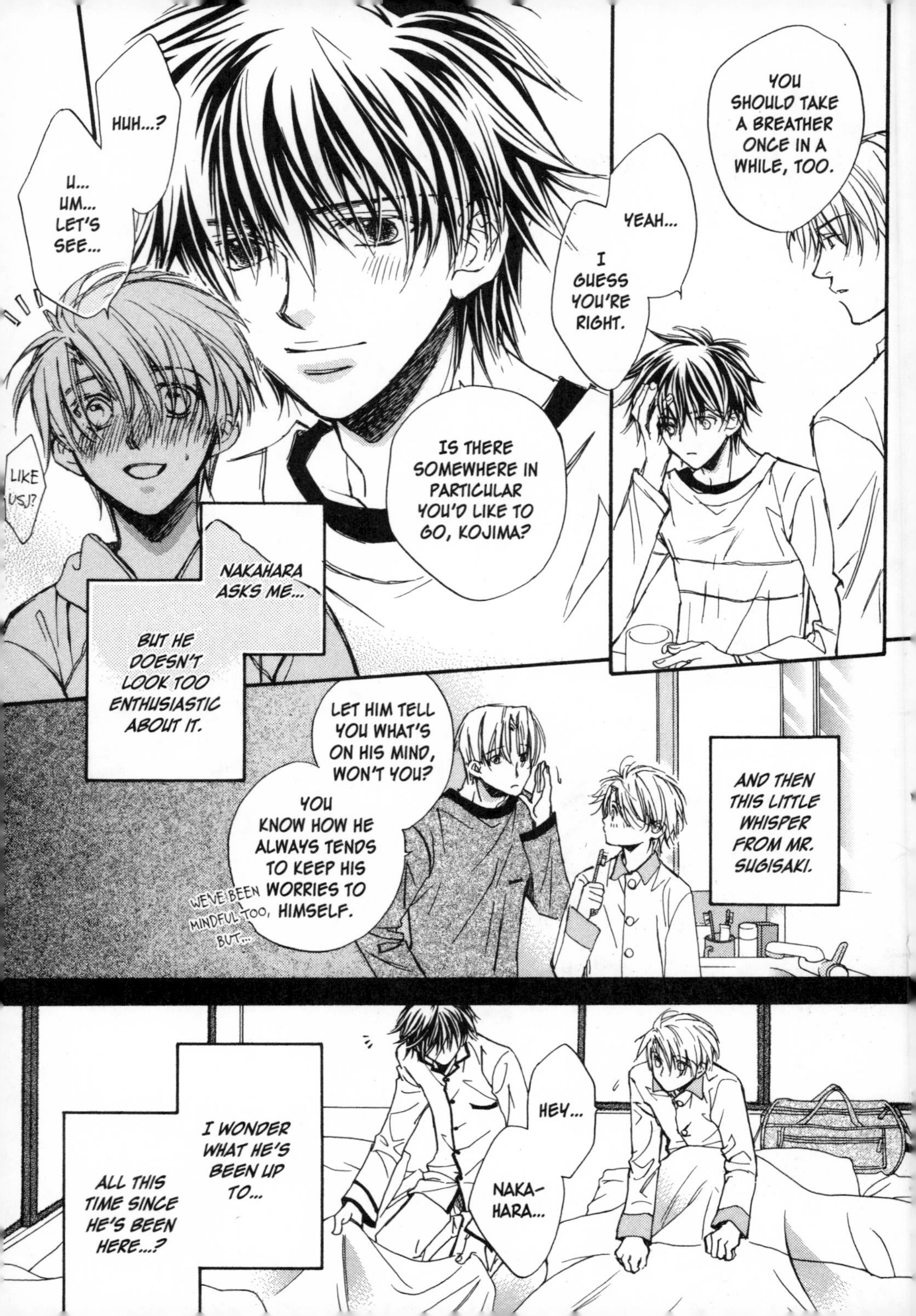
YOU SHOULD TAKE A BREATHER ONCE IN A WHILE, TOO.
YEAH...
I GUESS YOU'RE RIGHT.
IS THERE SOMEWHERE IN PARTICULAR YOU'D LIKE TO GO, KOJIMA?
HUH...?
U... UM... LET'S SEE...
LIKE USJ?
NAKAHARA ASKS ME...
BUT HE DOESN'T LOOK TOO ENTHUSIASTIC ABOUT IT.
AND THEN THIS LITTLE WHISPER FROM MR. SUGISAKI.
LET HIM TELL YOU WHAT'S ON HIS MIND, WON'T YOU?
YOU KNOW HOW HE ALWAYS TENDS TO KEEP HIS WORRIES TO HIMSELF.
WE'VE BEEN MINDFUL TOO, BUT...
HEY...
NAKA-HARA...
I WONDER WHAT HE'S BEEN UP TO...
ALL THIS TIME SINCE HE'S BEEN HERE...?

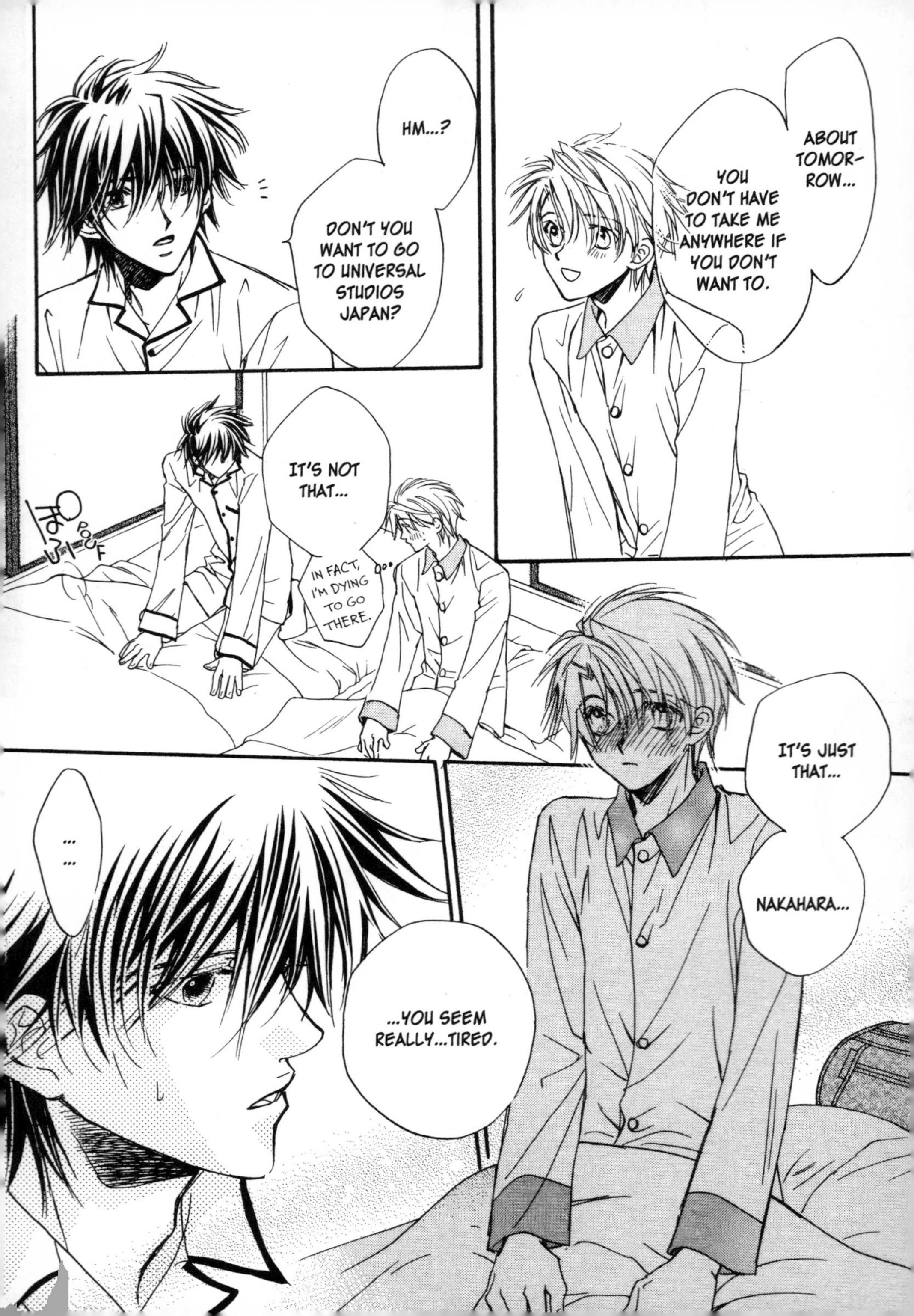
ABOUT TOMORROW...
YOU DON'T HAVE TO TAKE ME ANYWHERE IF YOU DON'T WANT TO.
HM...?
DON'T YOU WANT TO GO TO UNIVERSAL STUDIOS JAPAN?
IT'S NOT THAT...
IN FACT, I'M DYING TO GO THERE.
POUF
IT'S JUST THAT...
NAKAHARA...
...YOU SEEM REALLY...TIRED.
... ...

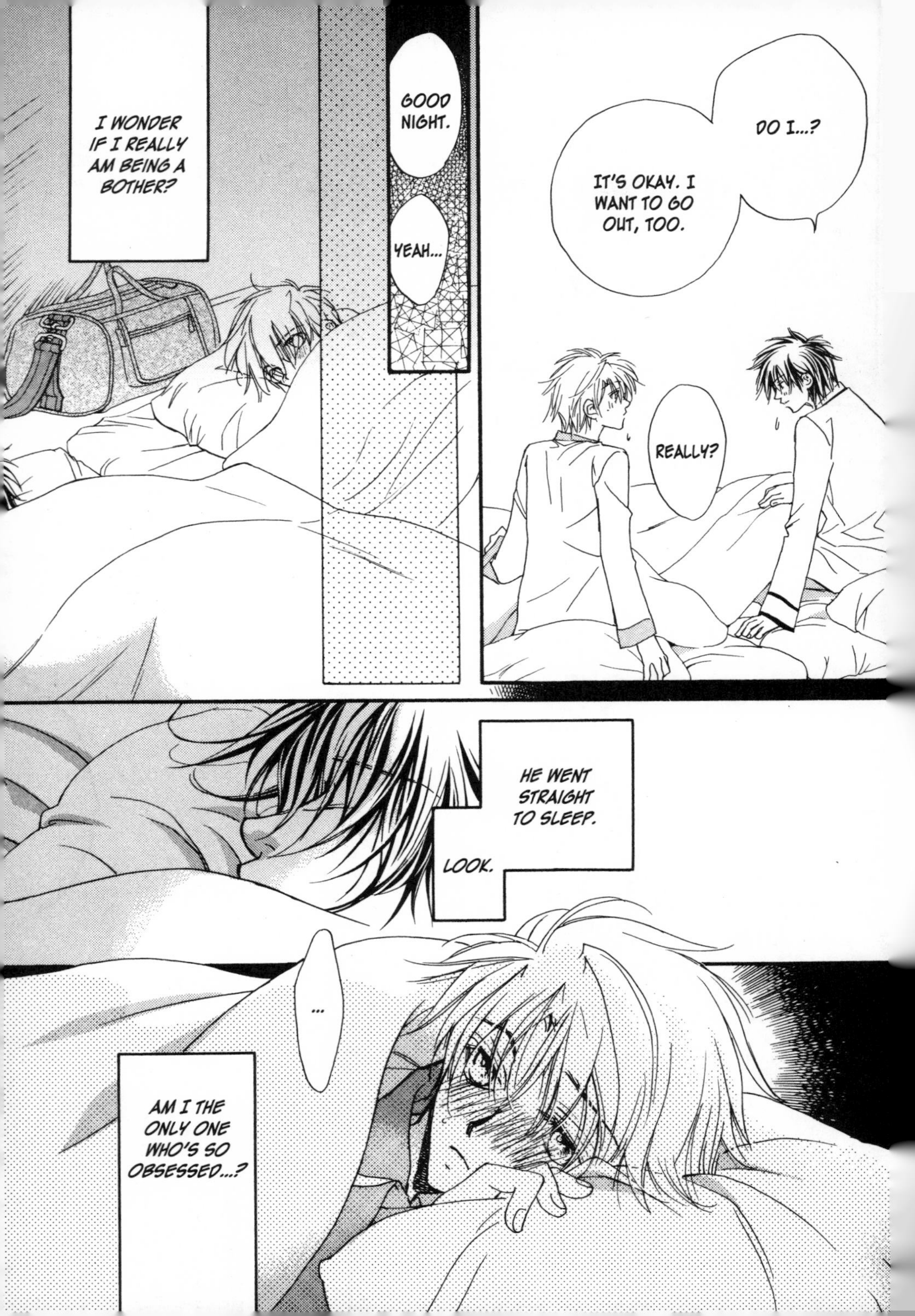
DO I...?
IT'S OKAY. I WANT TO GO OUT, TOO.
REALLY?
GOOD NIGHT.
YEAH...
I WONDER IF I REALLY AM BEING A BOTHER?
HE WENT STRAIGHT TO SLEEP.
LOOK.
...
AM I THE ONLY ONE WHO'S SO OBSESSED...?

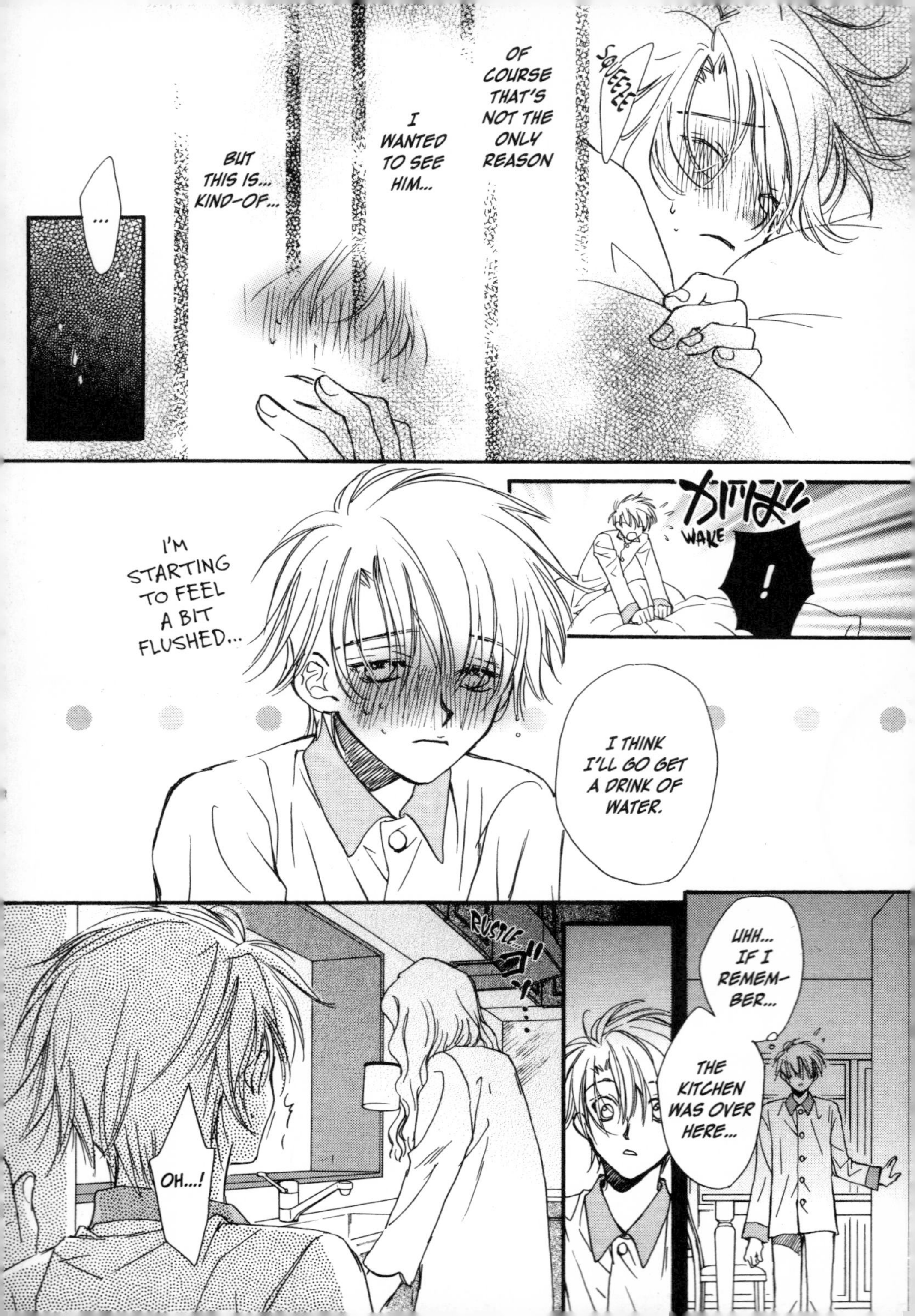
SQUEEZE
OF COURSE THAT'S NOT THE ONLY REASON
I WANTED TO SEE HIM...
BUT THIS IS... KIND-OF...
...
WAKE
!
I'M STARTING TO FEEL A BIT FLUSHED...
I THINK I'LL GO GET A DRINK OF WATER.
UHH... IF I REMEMBER...
THE KITCHEN WAS OVER HERE...
RUSTLE...
...
OH...!

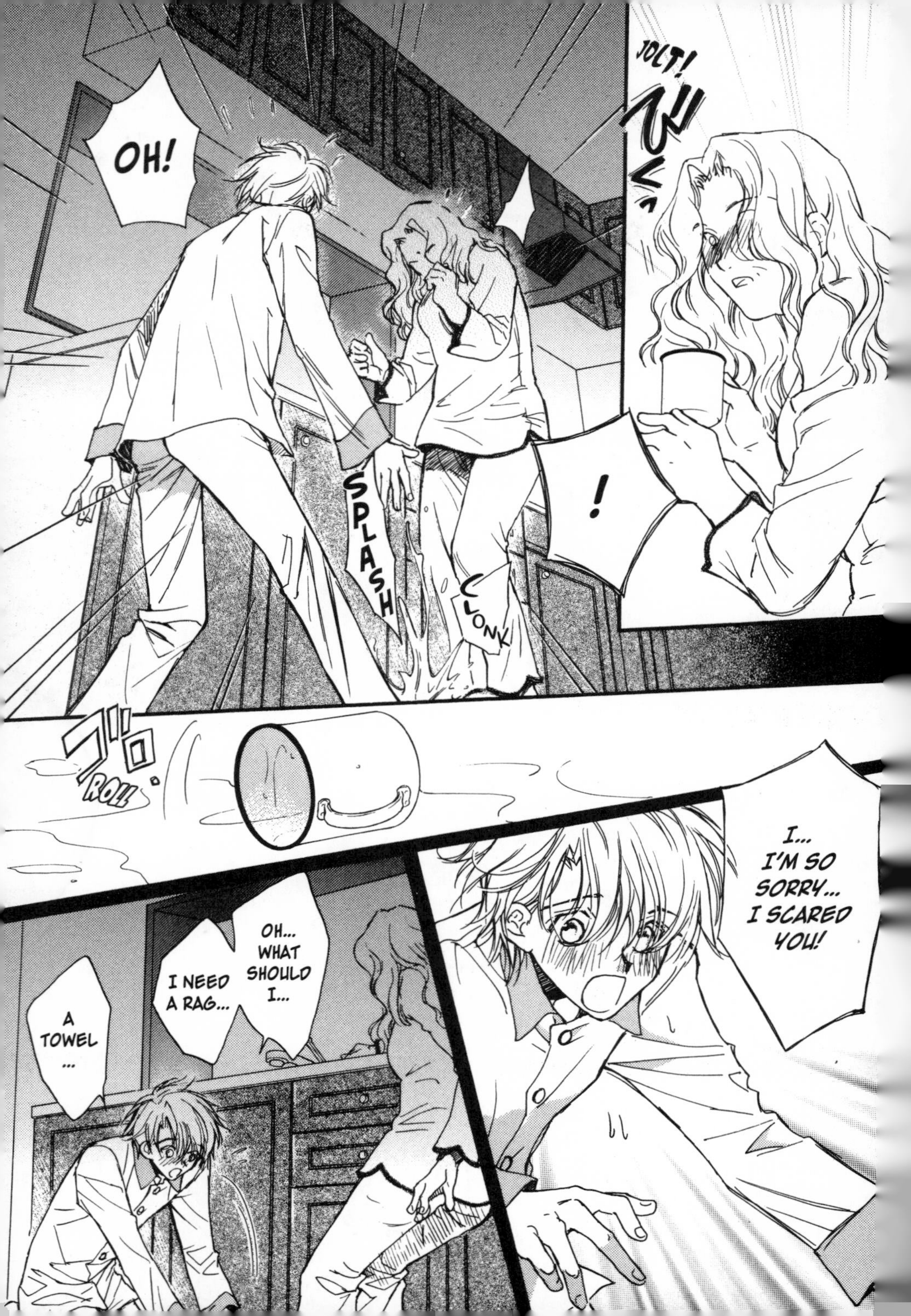

JOLT!
!
OH!
SPLASH
CLONK
ROLL
I... I'M SO SORRY... I SCARED YOU!
OH... WHAT SHOULD I...
I NEED A RAG...
A TOWEL ...

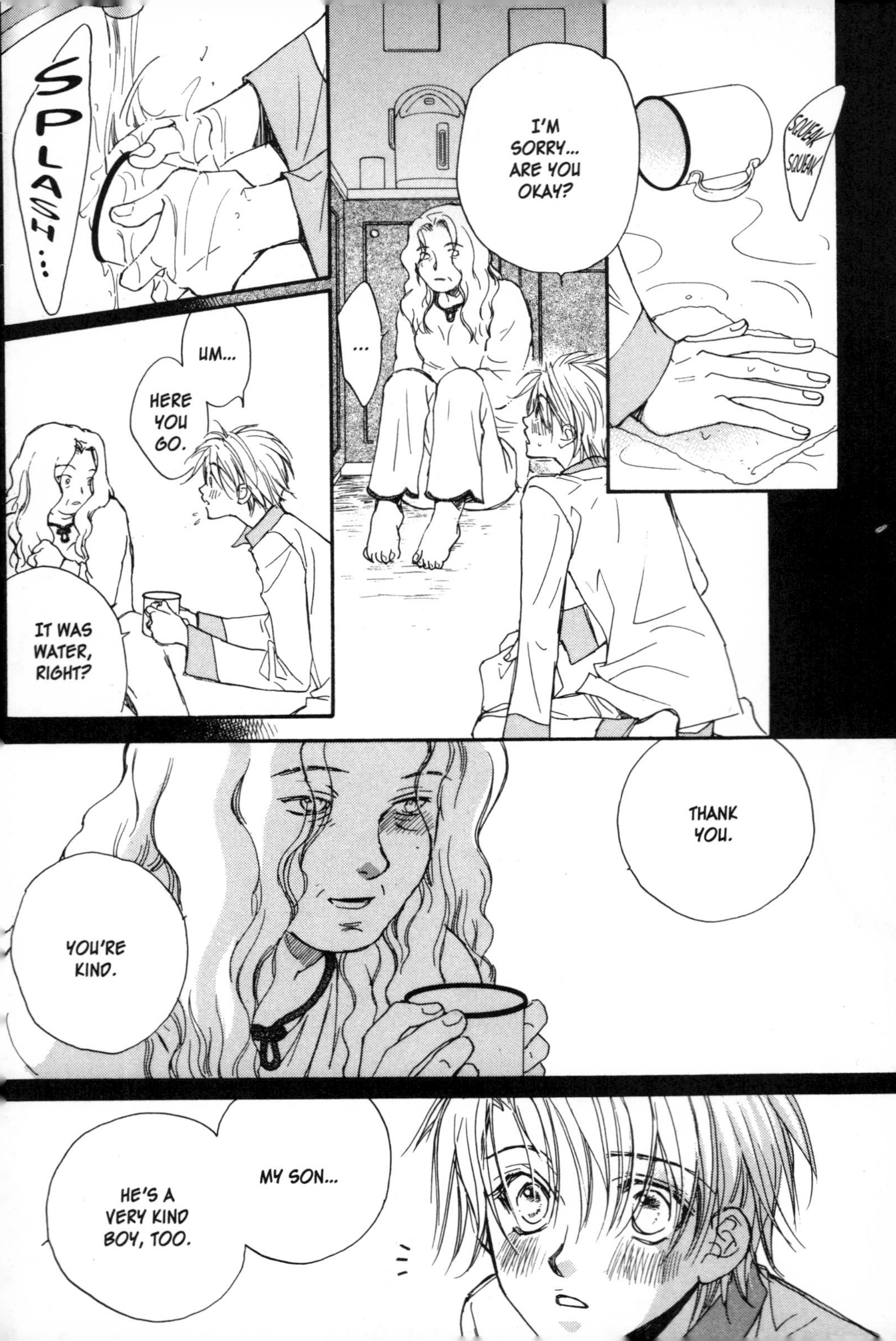
SQUEAK SQUEAK
I'M SORRY... ARE YOU OKAY?
...
SPLASH...
UM...
HERE YOU GO.
IT WAS WATER, RIGHT?
THANK YOU.
YOU'RE KIND.
MY SON...
HE'S A VERY KIND BOY, TOO.

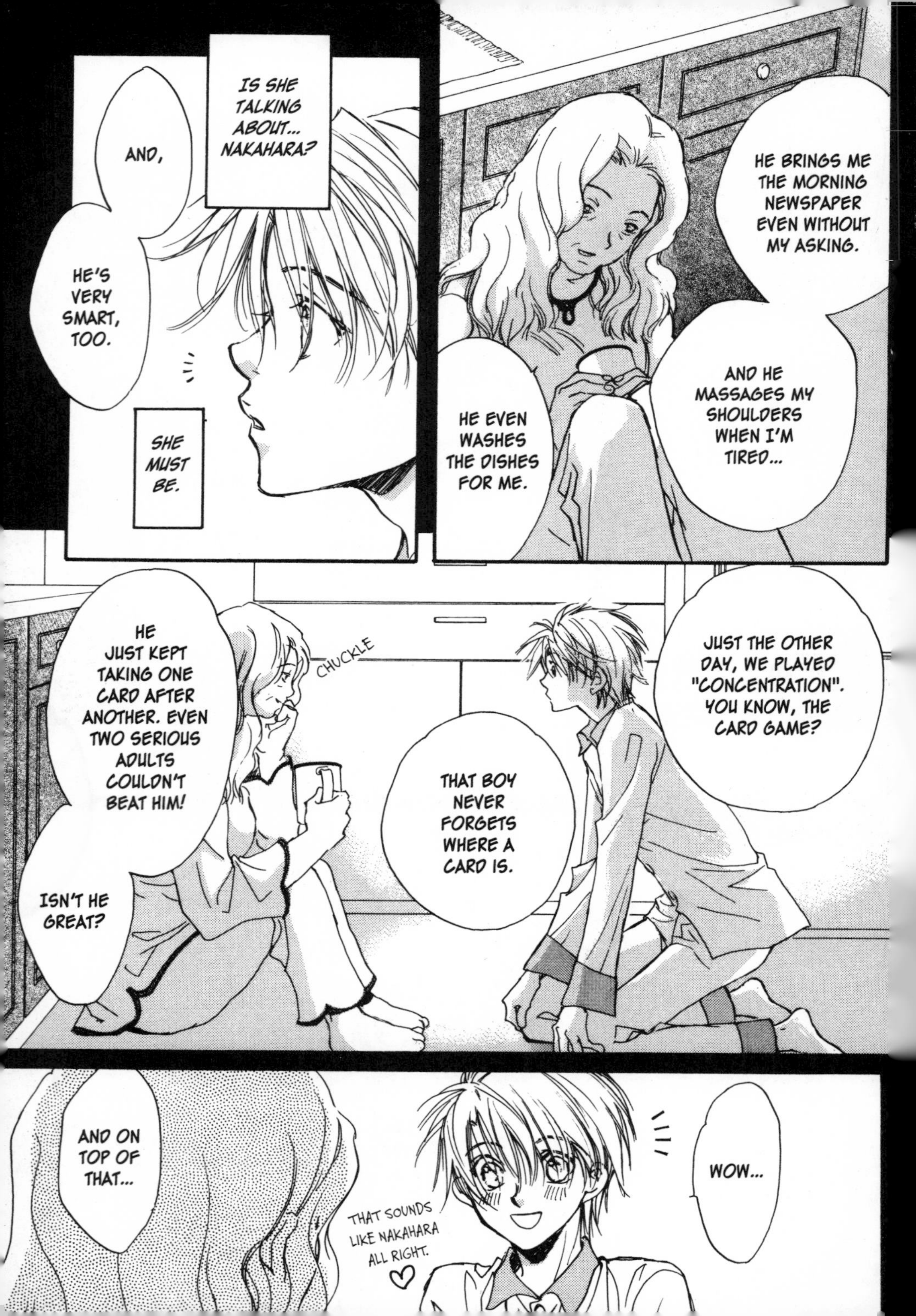
HE BRINGS ME THE MORNING NEWSPAPER EVEN WITHOUT MY ASKING.
AND HE MASSAGES MY SHOULDERS WHEN I'M TIRED...
HE EVEN WASHES THE DISHES FOR ME.
IS SHE TALKING ABOUT... NAKAHARA?
AND,
HE'S VERY SMART, TOO.
SHE MUST BE.
JUST THE OTHER DAY, WE PLAYED "CONCENTRATION". YOU KNOW, THE CARD GAME?
THAT BOY NEVER FORGETS WHERE A CARD IS.
CHUCKLE
HE JUST KEPT TAKING ONE CARD AFTER ANOTHER. EVEN TWO SERIOUS ADULTS COULDN'T BEAT HIM!
ISN'T HE GREAT?
WOW...
THAT SOUNDS LIKE NAKAHARA ALL RIGHT.
AND ON TOP OF THAT...

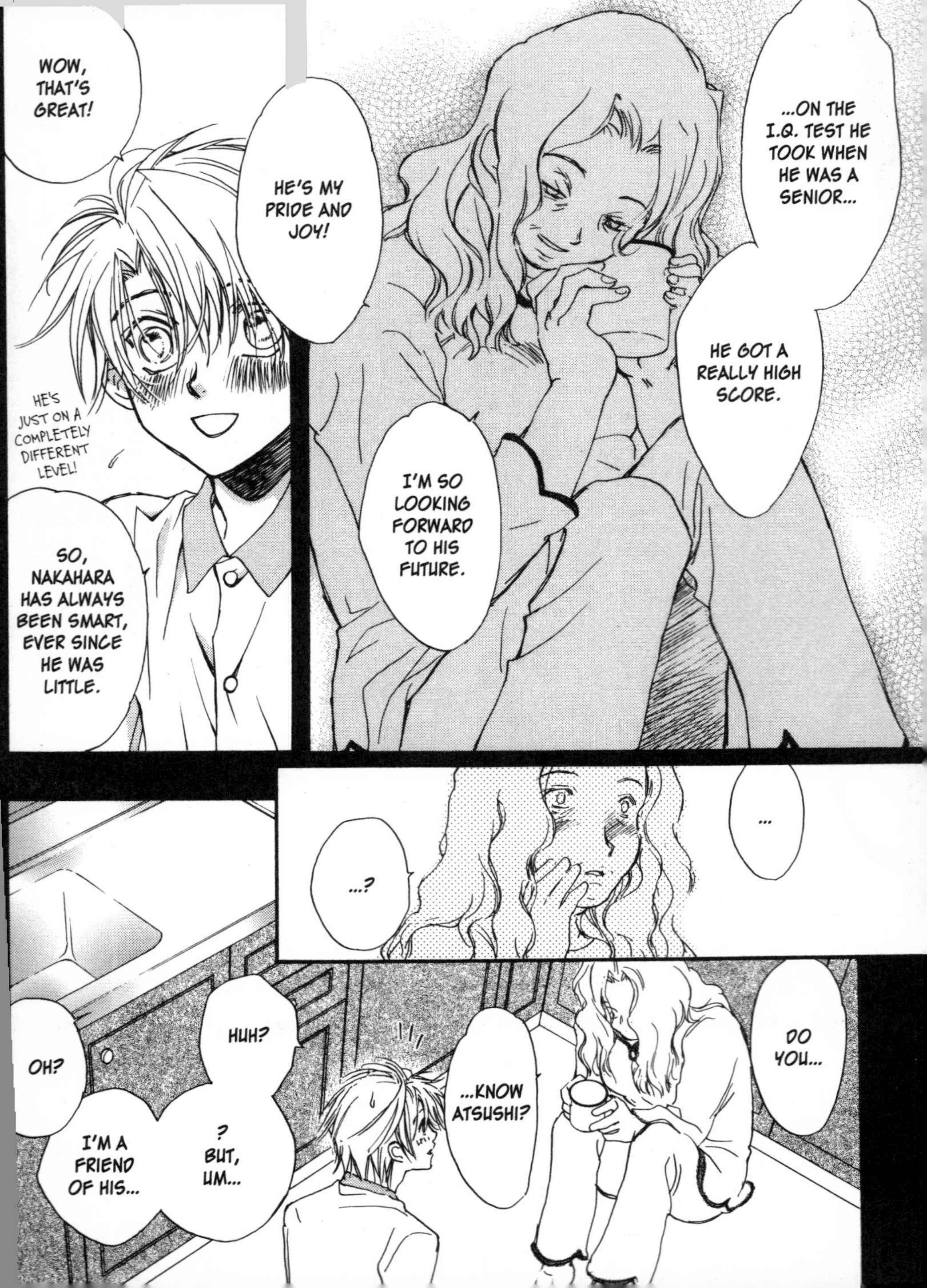
...ON THE I.Q. TEST HE TOOK WHEN HE WAS A SENIOR...
HE GOT A REALLY HIGH SCORE.
HE'S MY PRIDE AND JOY!
I'M SO LOOKING FORWARD TO HIS FUTURE.
WOW, THAT'S GREAT!
HE'S JUST ON A COMPLETELY DIFFERENT LEVEL!
SO, NAKAHARA HAS ALWAYS BEEN SMART, EVER SINCE HE WAS LITTLE.
...
...?
DO YOU...
...KNOW ATSUSHI?
HUH?
? BUT, UM...
OH?
I'M A FRIEND OF HIS...

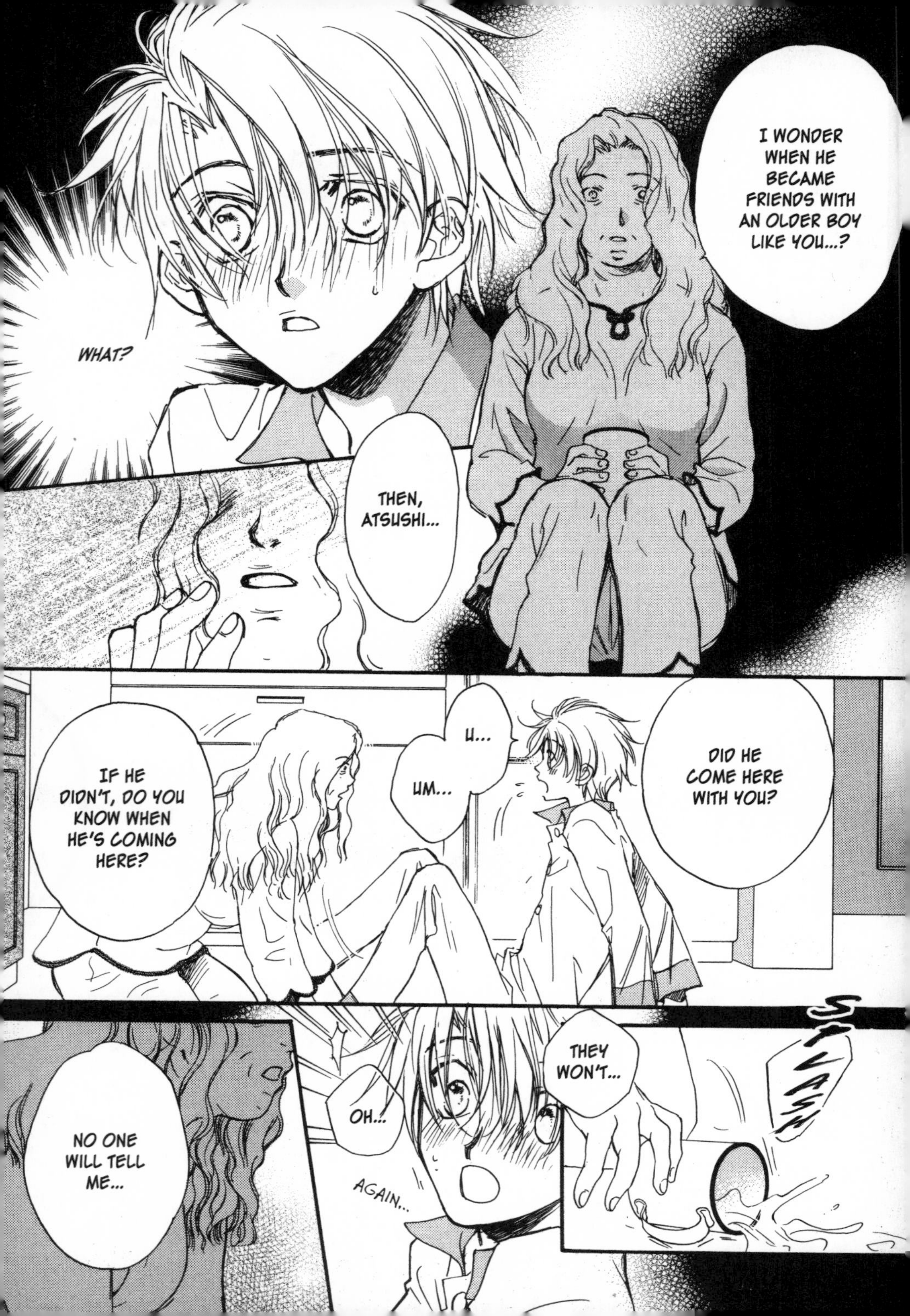
I WONDER WHEN HE BECAME FRIENDS WITH AN OLDER BOY LIKE YOU...?
WHAT?
THEN, ATSUSHI...
DID HE COME HERE WITH YOU?
U...
UM...
IF HE DIDN'T, DO YOU KNOW WHEN HE'S COMING HERE?
SPLASH
THEY WON'T...
OH...
AGAIN...
NO ONE WILL TELL ME...

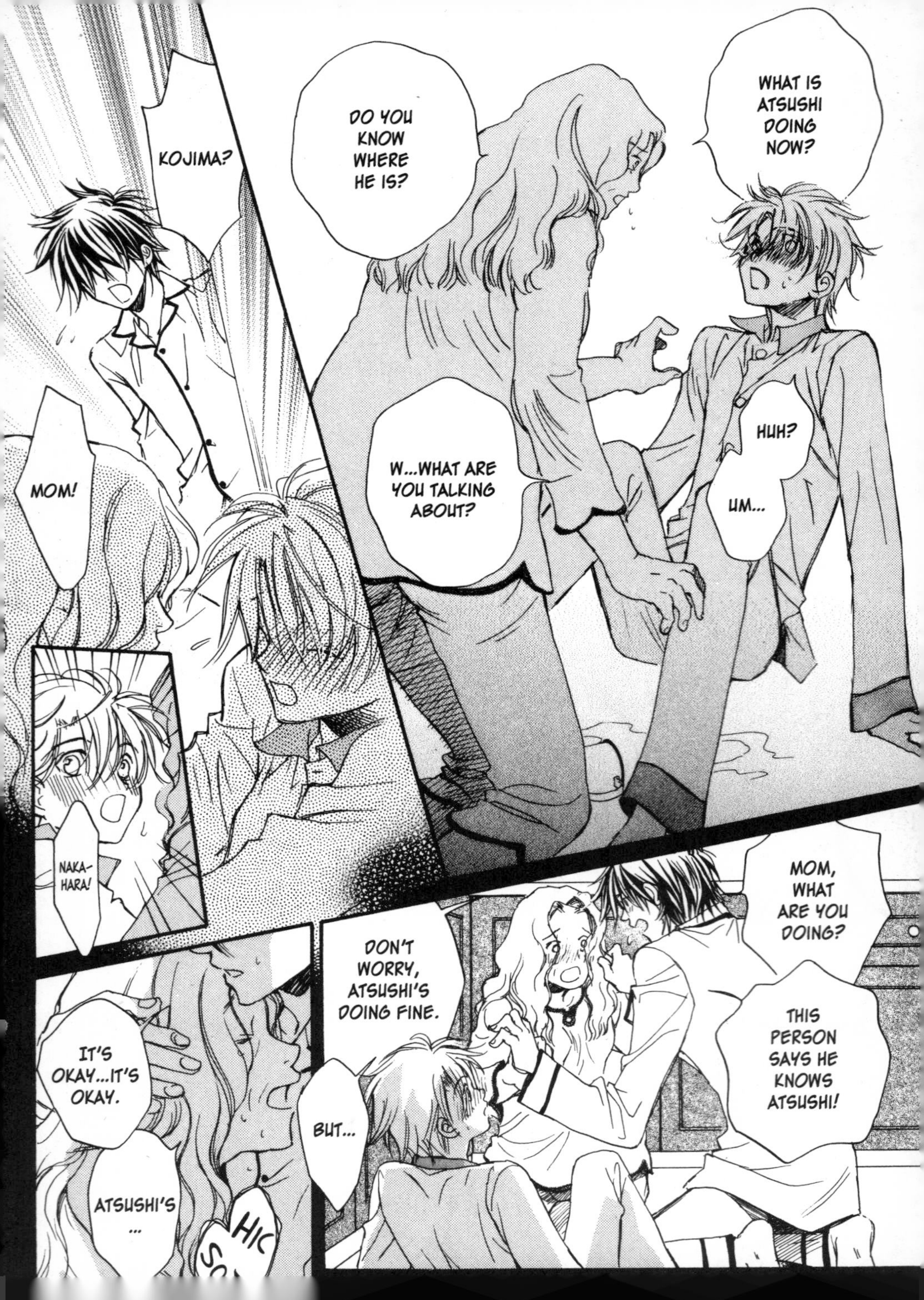

WHAT IS ATSUSHI DOING NOW?
DO YOU KNOW WHERE HE IS?
HUH?
UM...
W...WHAT ARE YOU TALKING ABOUT?
KOJIMA?
MOM!
NAKA-HARA!
MOM, WHAT ARE YOU DOING?
THIS PERSON SAYS HE KNOWS ATSUSHI!
DON'T WORRY, ATSUSHI'S DOING FINE.
BUT...
IT'S OKAY...IT'S OKAY.
ATSUSHI'S ...
HIC

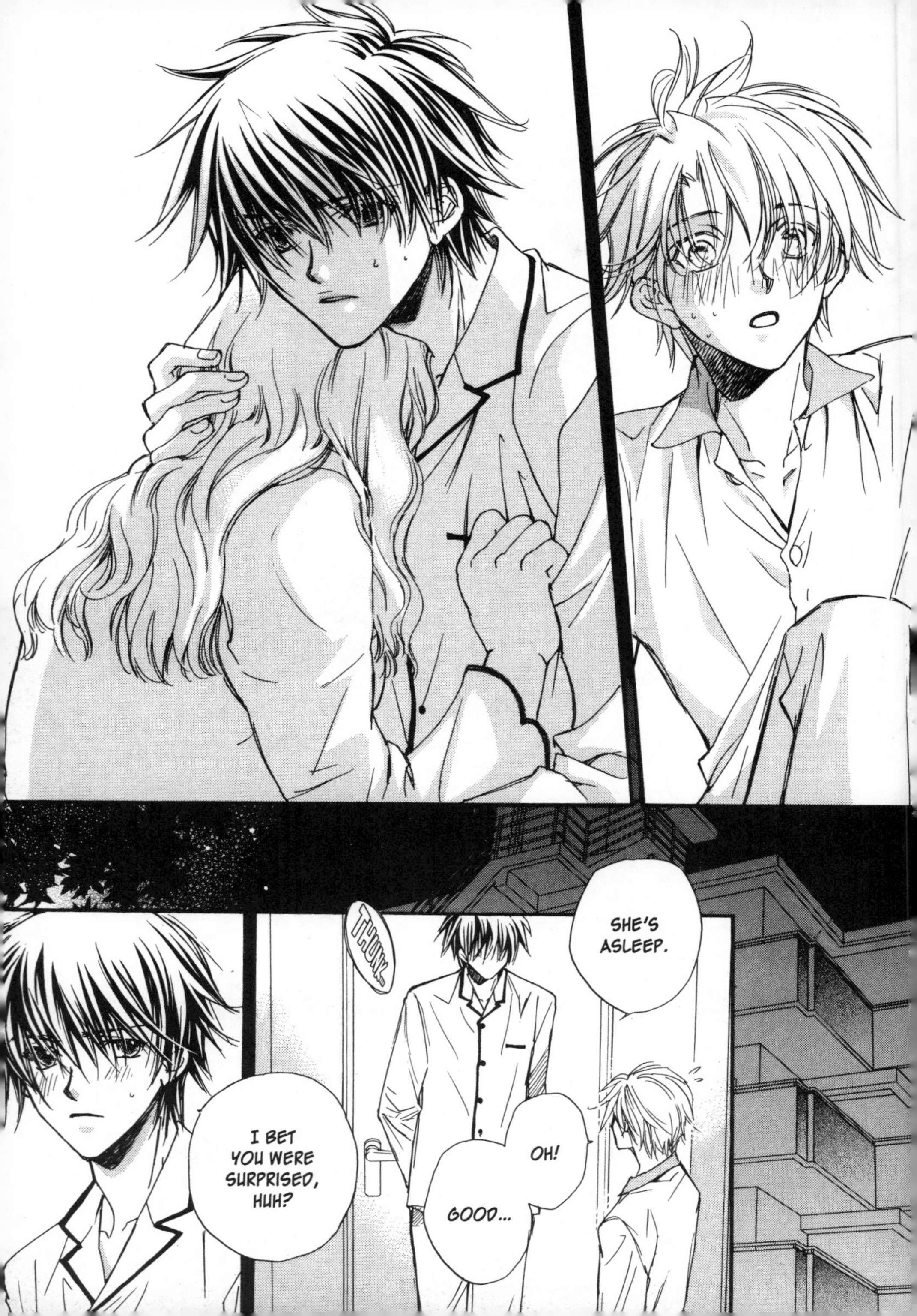
SHE'S ASLEEP.
THUNK...
OH!
GOOD...
I BET YOU WERE SURPRISED, HUH?

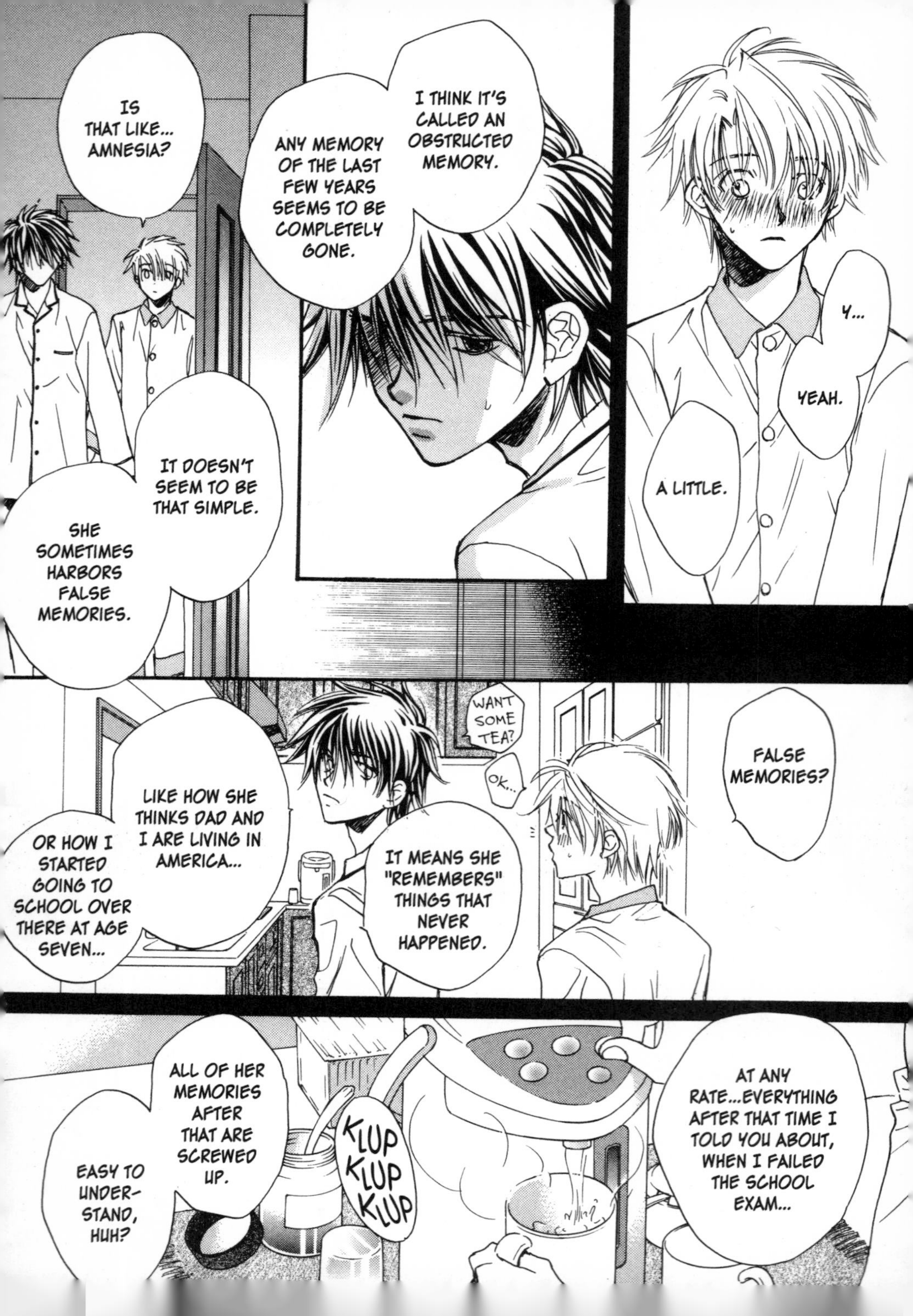
Y...
YEAH.
A LITTLE.
I THINK IT'S CALLED AN OBSTRUCTED MEMORY.
ANY MEMORY OF THE LAST FEW YEARS SEEMS TO BE COMPLETELY GONE.
IS THAT LIKE... AMNESIA?
IT DOESN'T SEEM TO BE THAT SIMPLE.
SHE SOMETIMES HARBORS FALSE MEMORIES.
FALSE MEMORIES?
WANT SOME TEA?
OK...
IT MEANS SHE "REMEMBERS" THINGS THAT NEVER HAPPENED.
LIKE HOW SHE THINKS DAD AND I ARE LIVING IN AMERICA...
OR HOW I STARTED GOING TO SCHOOL OVER THERE AT AGE SEVEN...
AT ANY RATE...EVERYTHING AFTER THAT TIME I TOLD YOU ABOUT, WHEN I FAILED THE SCHOOL EXAM...
ALL OF HER MEMORIES AFTER THAT ARE SCREWED UP.
KLUP KLUP KLUP
EASY TO UNDER-STAND, HUH?

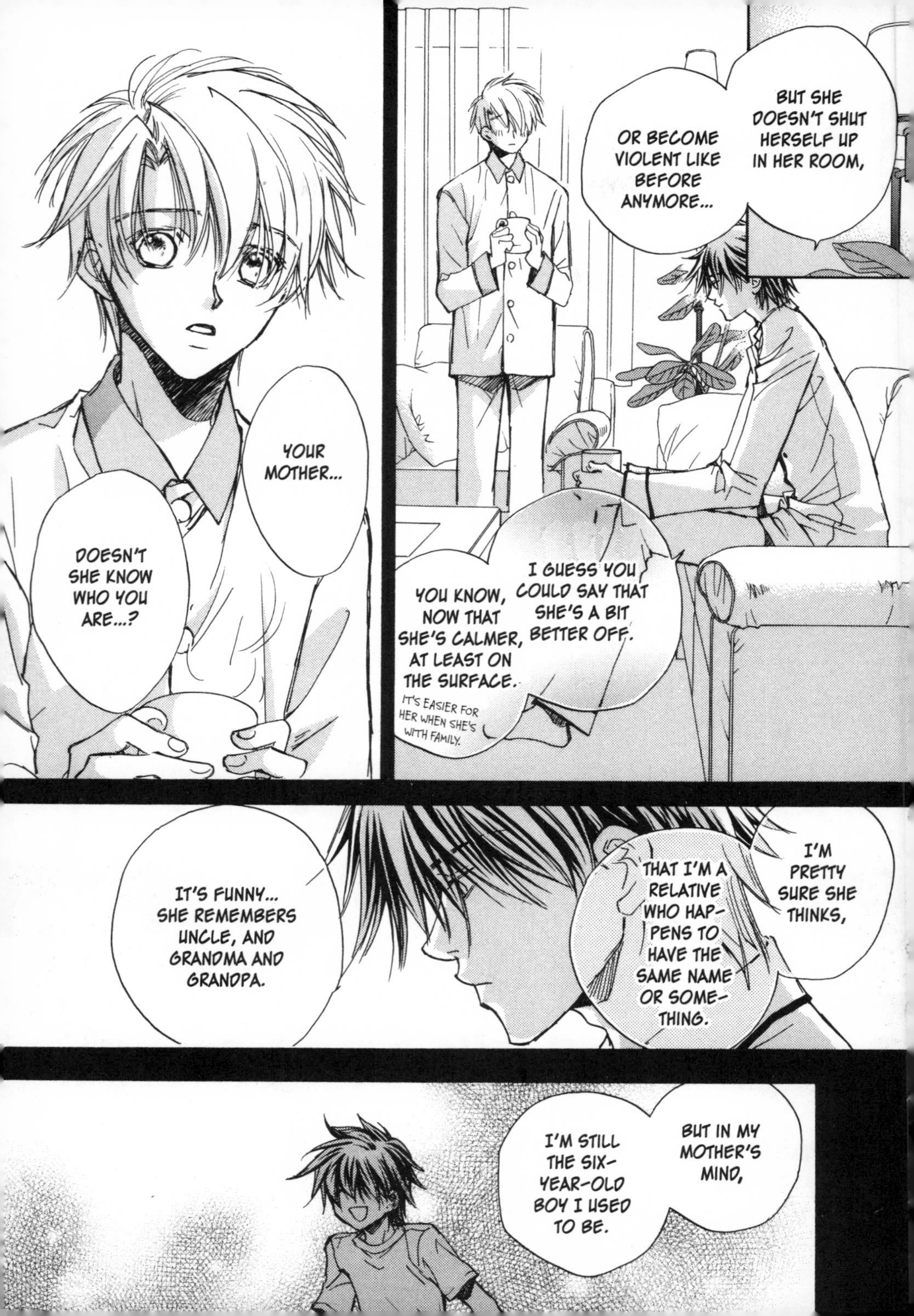
BUT SHE DOESN'T SHUT HERSELF UP IN HER ROOM,
OR BECOME VIOLENT LIKE BEFORE ANYMORE...
I GUESS YOU COULD SAY THAT SHE'S A BIT BETTER OFF.
YOU KNOW, NOW THAT SHE'S CALMER, AT LEAST ON THE SURFACE.
IT'S EASIER FOR HER WHEN SHE'S WITH FAMILY.
YOUR MOTHER...
DOESN'T SHE KNOW WHO YOU ARE...?
I'M PRETTY SURE SHE THINKS,
THAT I'M A RELATIVE WHO HAPPENS TO HAVE THE SAME NAME OR SOMETHING.
IT'S FUNNY... SHE REMEMBERS UNCLE, AND GRANDMA AND GRANDPA.
BUT IN MY MOTHER'S MIND,
I'M STILL THE SIX-YEAR-OLD BOY I USED TO BE.

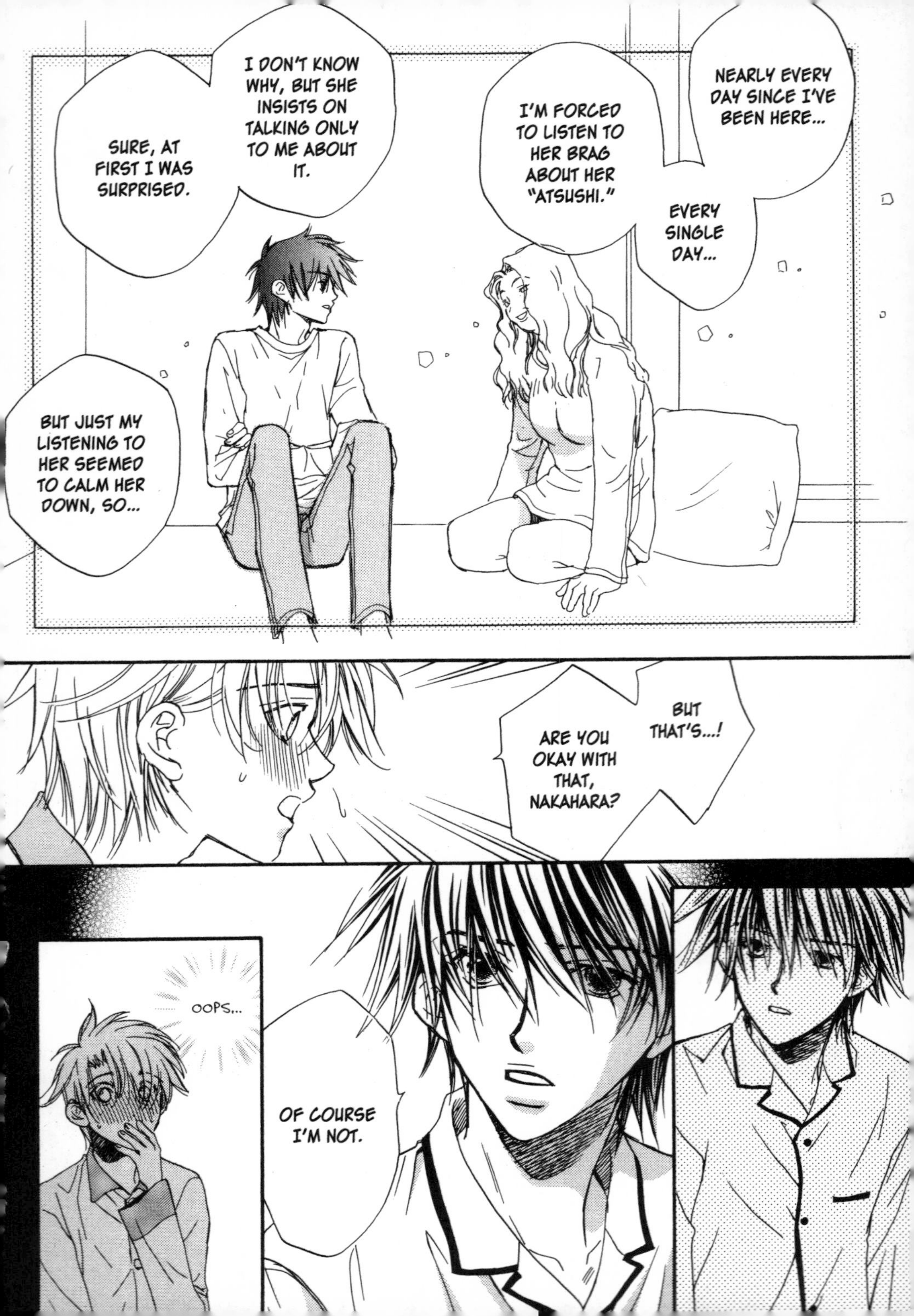
NEARLY EVERY DAY SINCE I'VE BEEN HERE...
EVERY SINGLE DAY...
I'M FORCED TO LISTEN TO HER BRAG ABOUT HER "ATSUSHI."
I DON'T KNOW WHY, BUT SHE INSISTS ON TALKING ONLY TO ME ABOUT IT.
SURE, AT FIRST I WAS SURPRISED.
BUT JUST MY LISTENING TO HER SEEMED TO CALM HER DOWN, SO...
BUT THAT'S...!
ARE YOU OKAY WITH THAT, NAKAHARA?
OF COURSE I'M NOT.
OOPS...

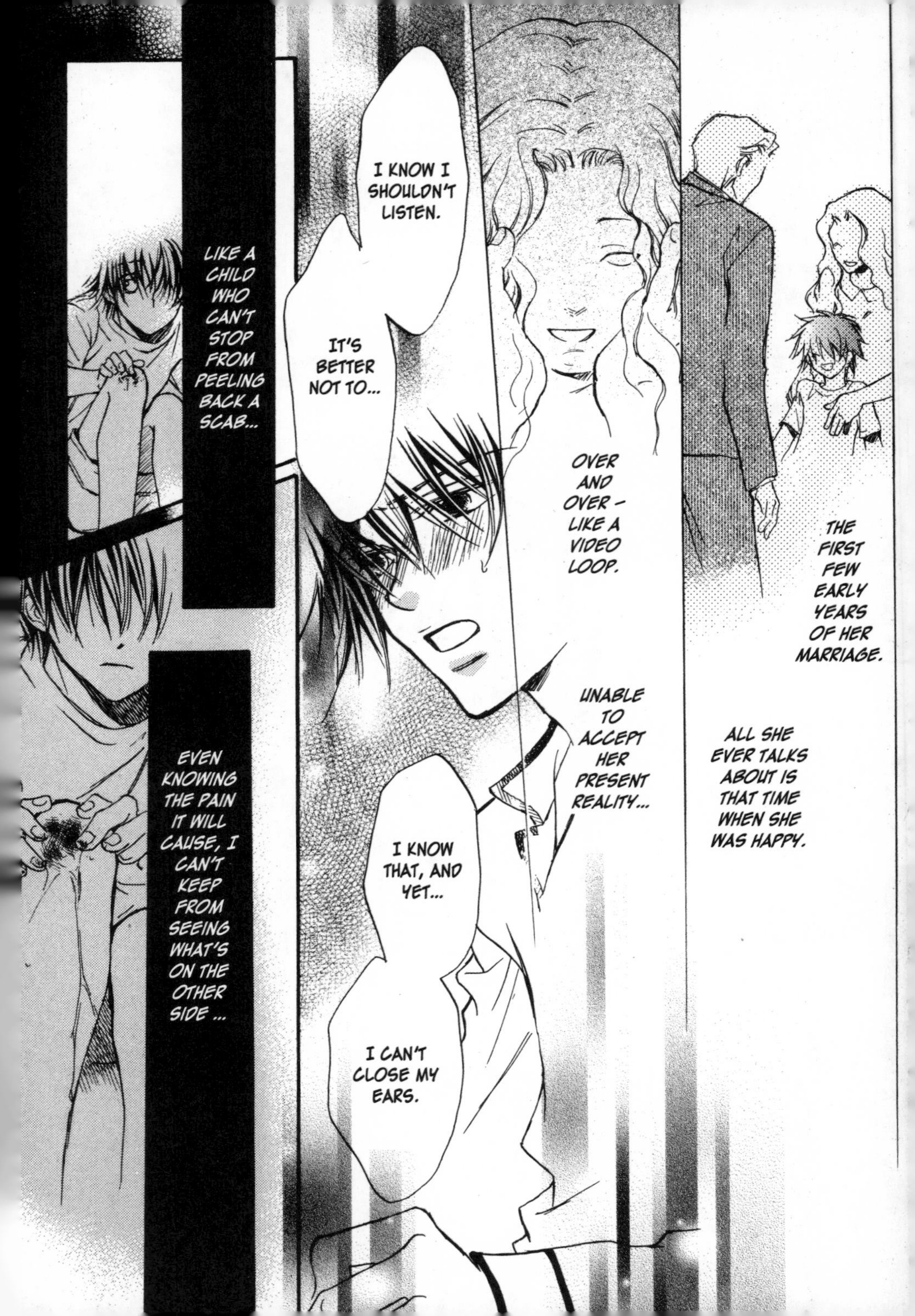
THE FIRST FEW EARLY YEARS OF HER MARRIAGE.
ALL SHE EVER TALKS ABOUT IS THAT TIME WHEN SHE WAS HAPPY.
OVER AND OVER - LIKE A VIDEO LOOP.
UNABLE TO ACCEPT HER PRESENT REALITY...
I KNOW I SHOULDN'T LISTEN.
IT'S BETTER NOT TO...
I KNOW THAT, AND YET...
I CAN'T CLOSE MY EARS.
LIKE A CHILD WHO CAN'T STOP FROM PEELING BACK A SCAB...
EVEN KNOWING THE PAIN IT WILL CAUSE, I CAN'T KEEP FROM SEEING WHAT'S ON THE OTHER SIDE ...

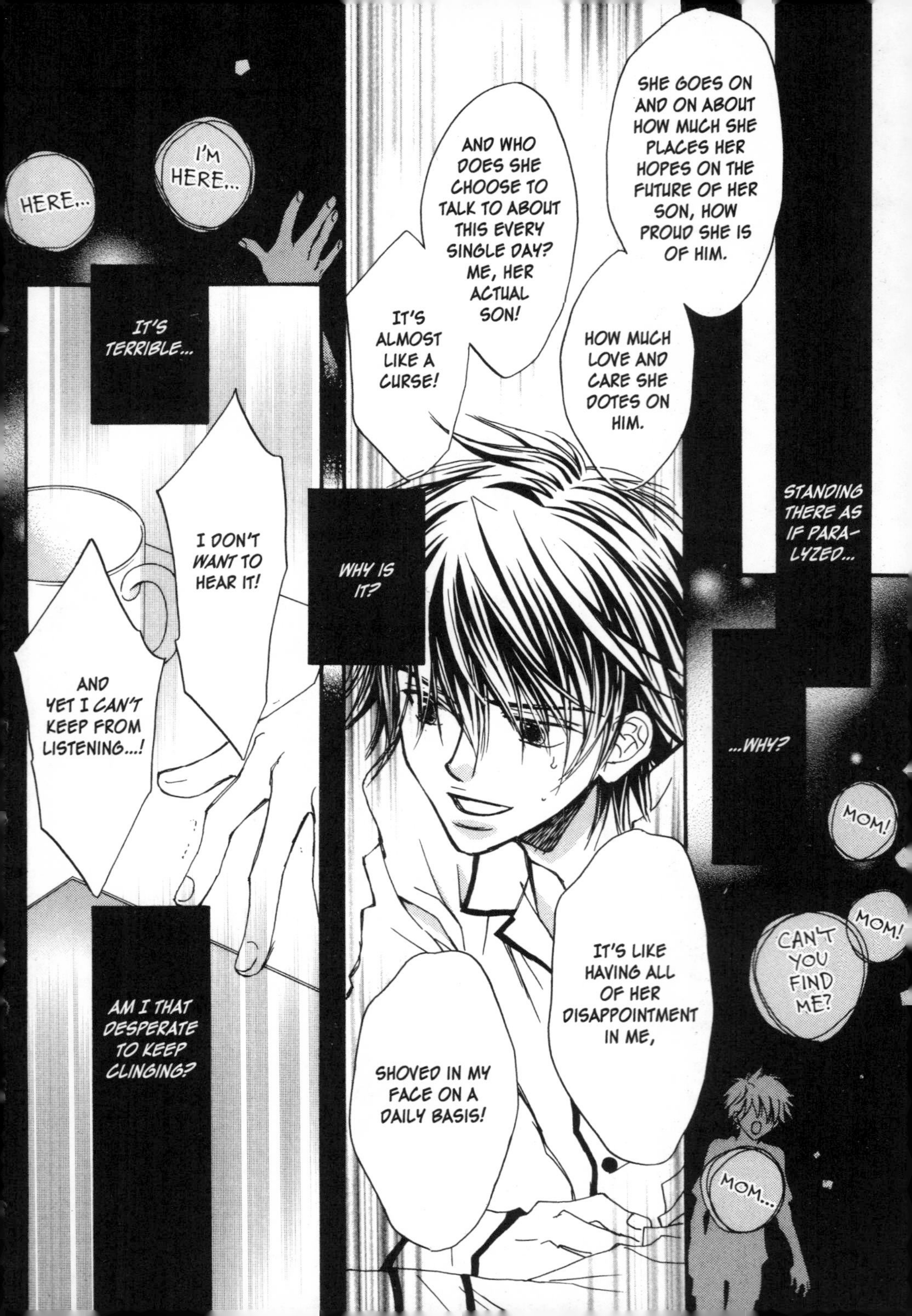
SHE GOES ON AND ON ABOUT HOW MUCH SHE PLACES HER HOPES ON THE FUTURE OF HER SON, HOW PROUD SHE IS OF HIM.
AND WHO DOES SHE CHOOSE TO TALK TO ABOUT THIS EVERY SINGLE DAY? ME, HER ACTUAL SON!
HOW MUCH LOVE AND CARE SHE DOTES ON HIM.
IT'S ALMOST LIKE A CURSE!
I'M HERE...
HERE...
IT'S TERRIBLE...
STANDING THERE AS IF PARA-LYZED...
...WHY?
MOM!
MOM!
CAN'T YOU FIND ME?
MOM...
WHY IS IT?
IT'S LIKE HAVING ALL OF HER DISAPPOINTMENT IN ME,
SHOVED IN MY FACE ON A DAILY BASIS!
I DON'T WANT TO HEAR IT!
AND YET I CAN'T KEEP FROM LISTENING...!
AM I THAT DESPERATE TO KEEP CLINGING?

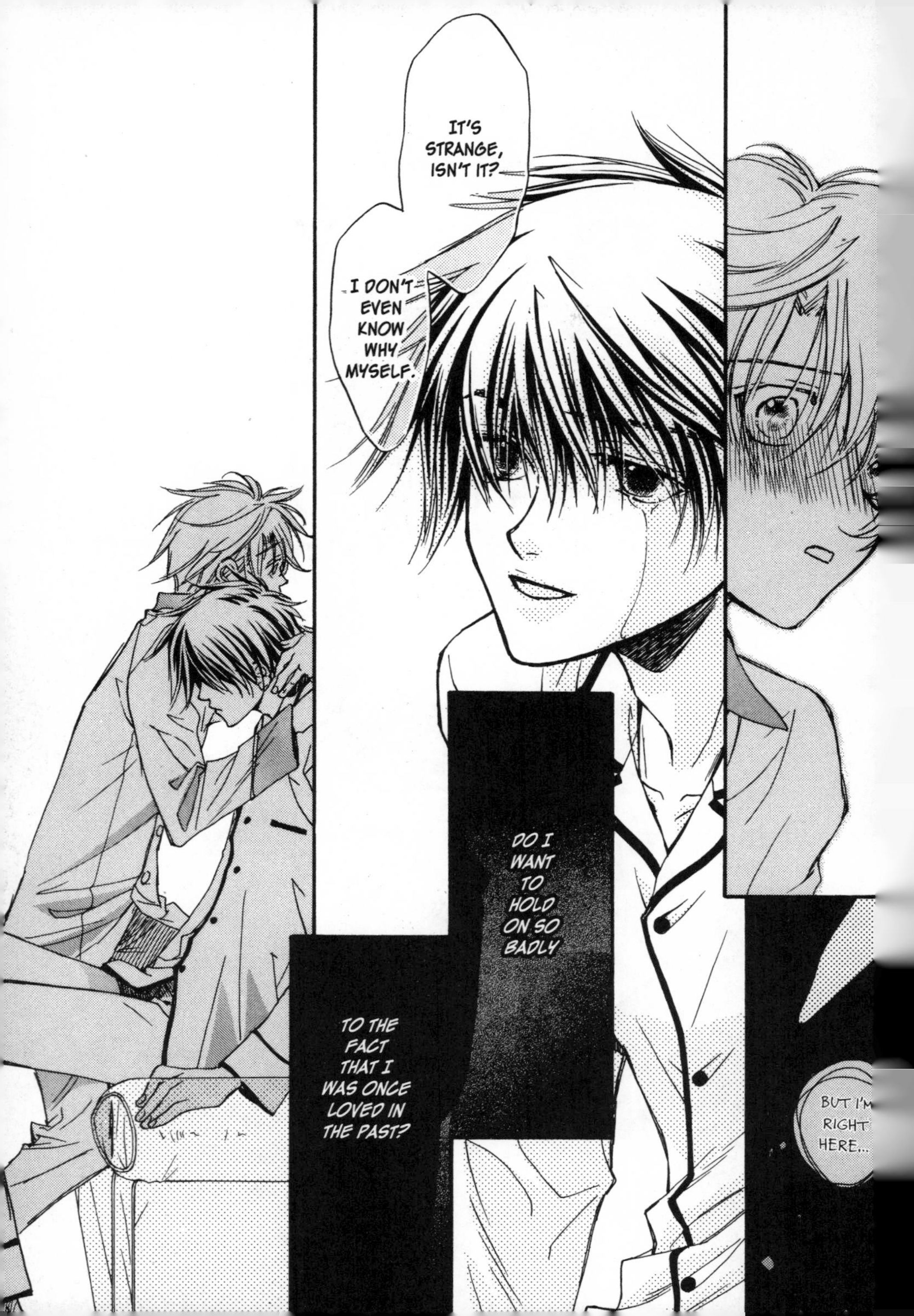
IT'S STRANGE, ISN'T IT?
I DON'T EVEN KNOW WHY MYSELF.
DO I WANT TO HOLD ON SO BADLY
TO THE FACT THAT I WAS ONCE LOVED IN THE PAST?
BUT I'M RIGHT HERE...

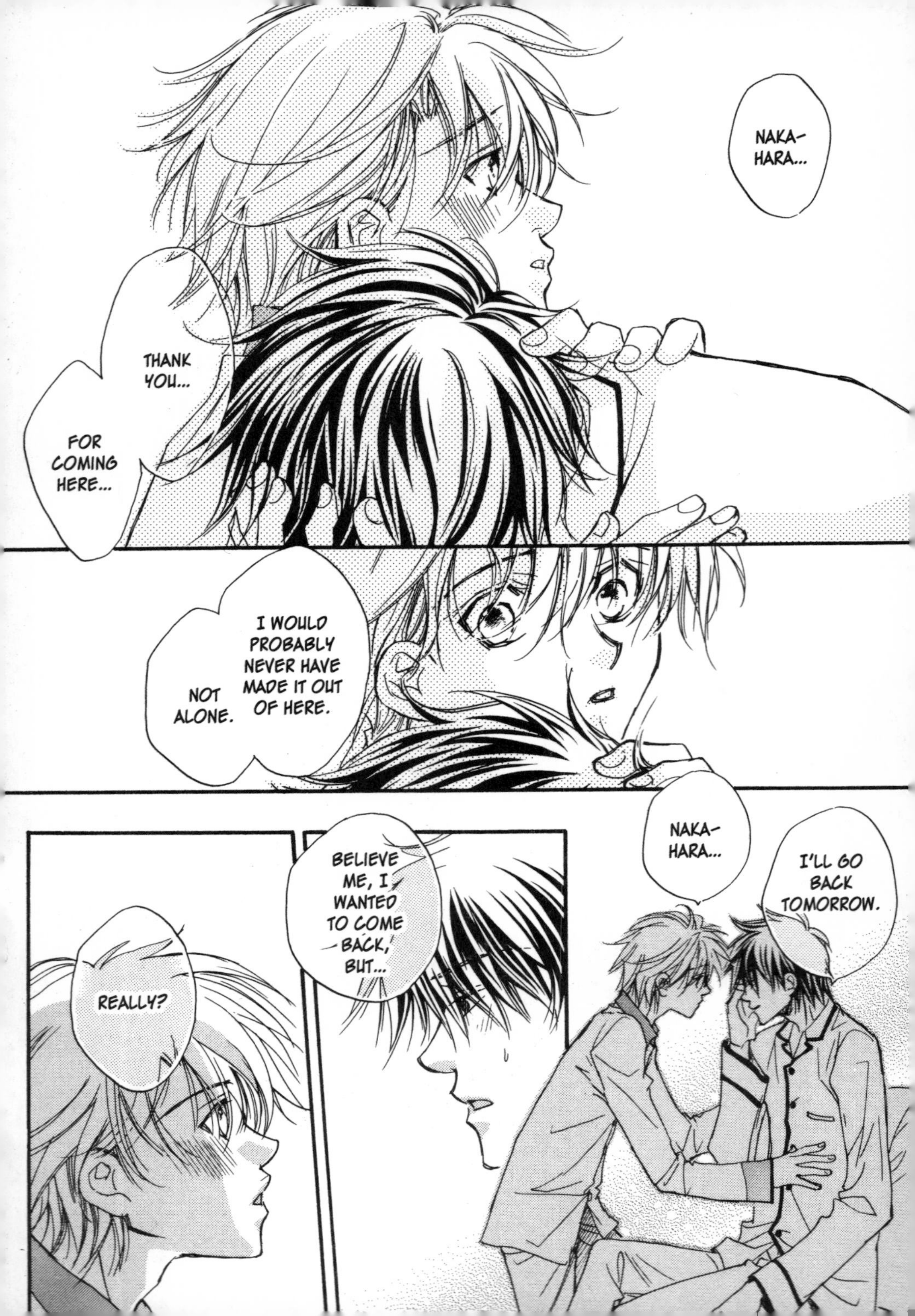
NAKA-HARA...
THANK YOU...
FOR COMING HERE...
I WOULD PROBABLY NEVER HAVE MADE IT OUT OF HERE.
NOT ALONE.
I'LL GO BACK TOMORROW.
NAKA-HARA...
BELIEVE ME, I WANTED TO COME BACK, BUT...
REALLY?

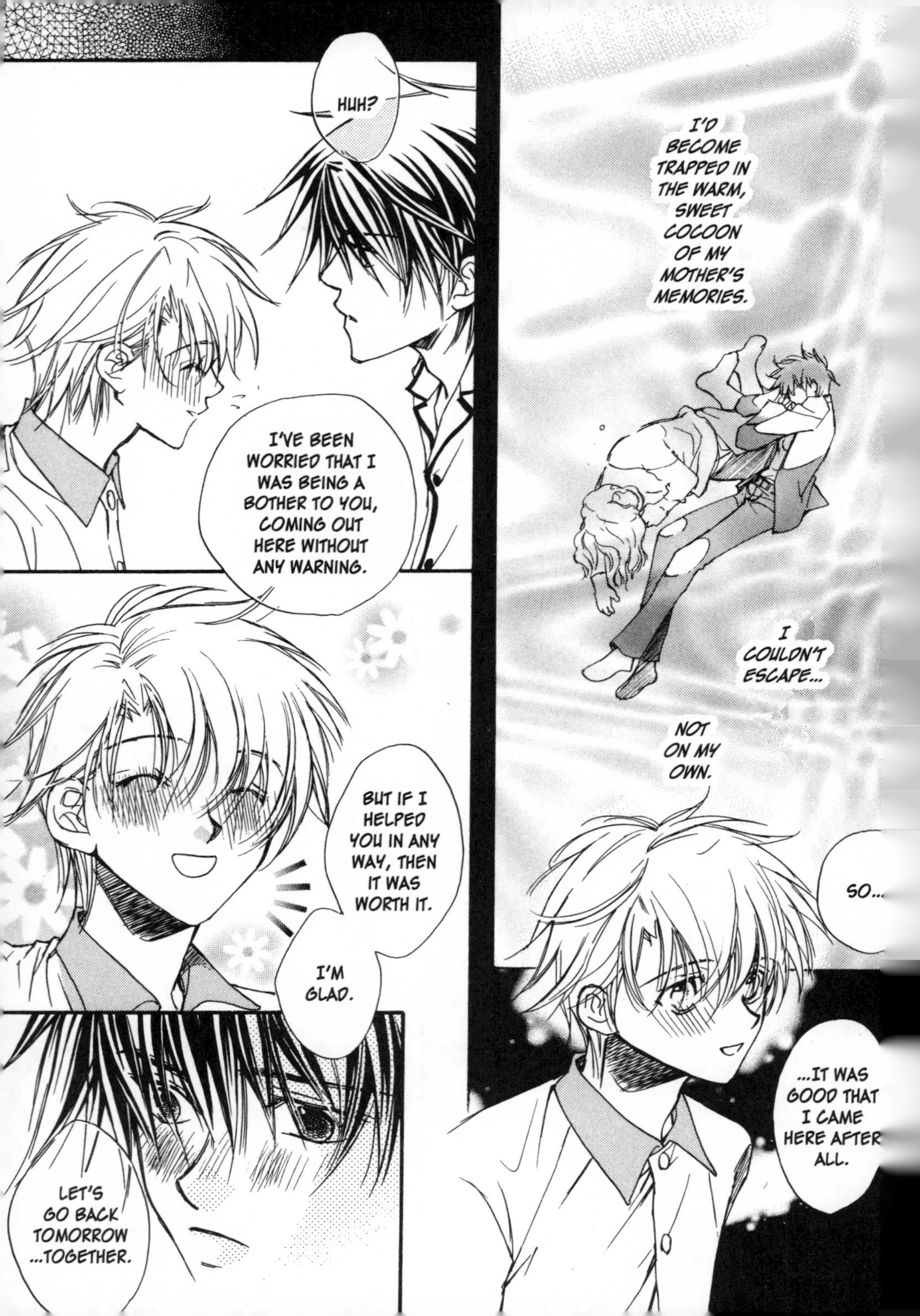
I'D BECOME TRAPPED IN THE WARM, SWEET COCOON OF MY MOTHER'S MEMORIES.
I COULDN'T ESCAPE...
NOT ON MY OWN.
SO...
...IT WAS GOOD THAT I CAME HERE AFTER ALL.
HUH?
I'VE BEEN WORRIED THAT I WAS BEING A BOTHER TO YOU, COMING OUT HERE WITHOUT ANY WARNING.
BUT IF I HELPED YOU IN ANY WAY, THEN IT WAS WORTH IT.
I'M GLAD.
LET'S GO BACK TOMORROW ...TOGETHER.

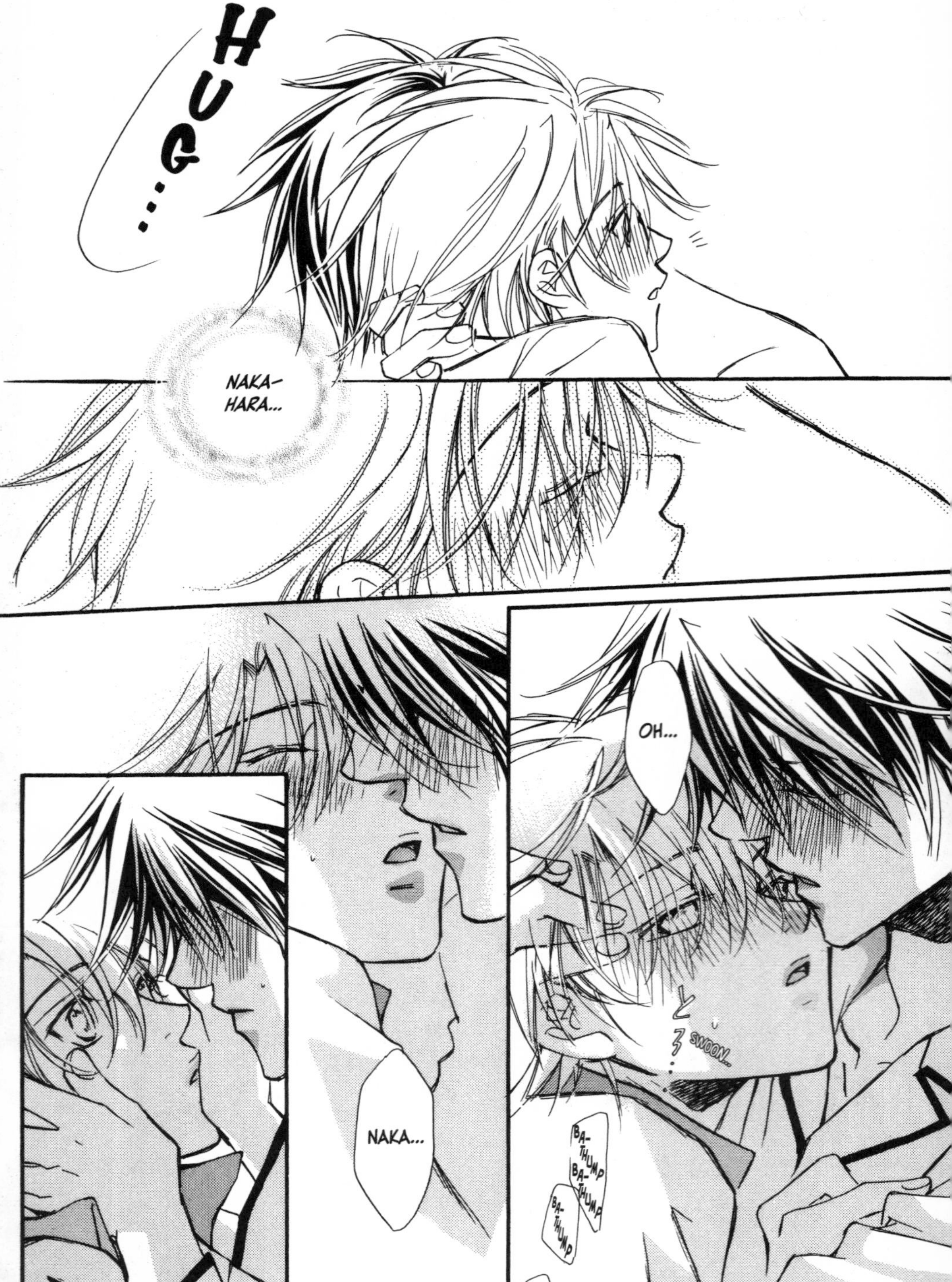
HUG...
NAKA-HARA...
OH...
SWOON...
BA-THUMP BA-THUMP
BA-THUMP
BA-THUMP
NAKA...

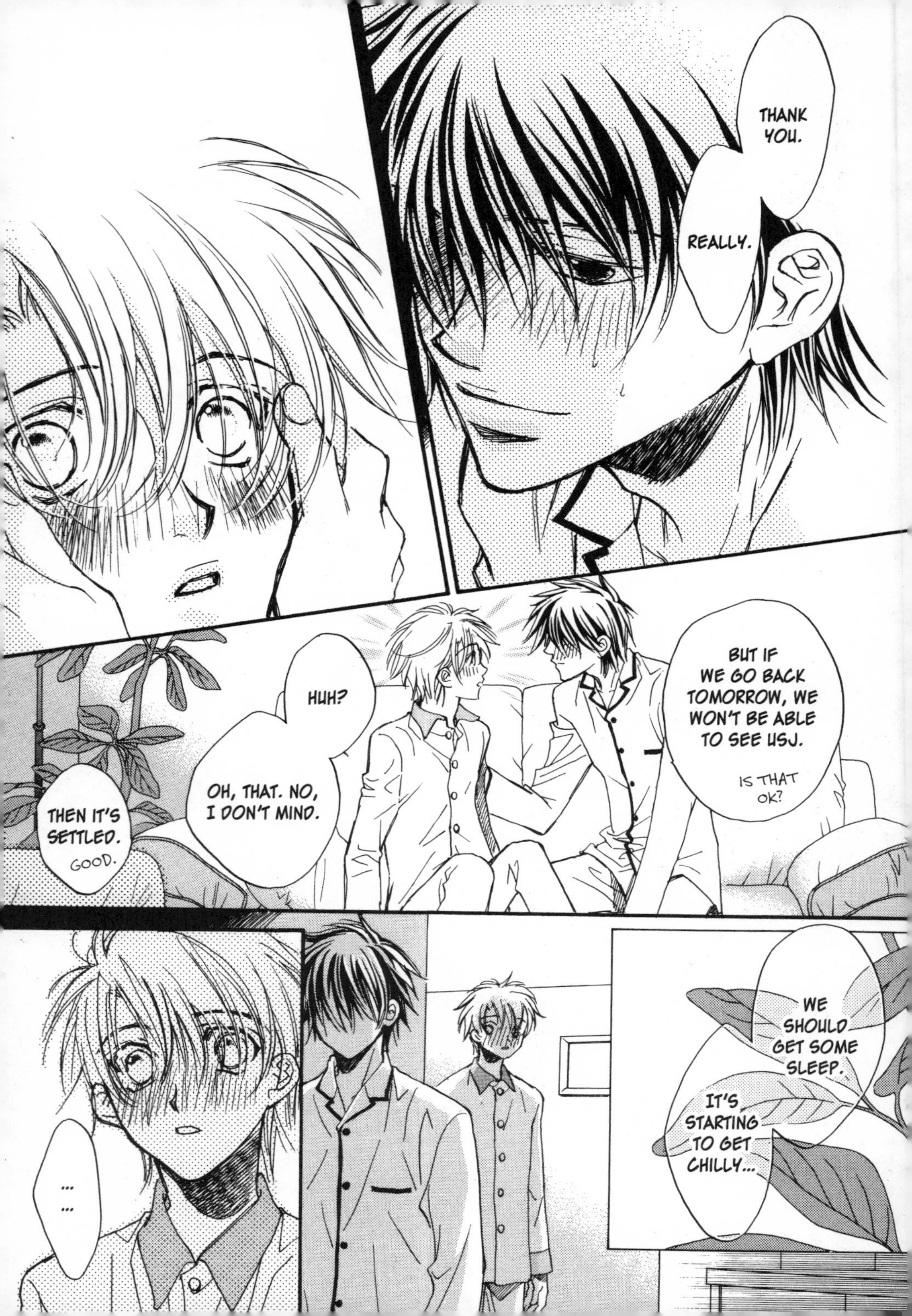
THANK YOU.
REALLY.
BUT IF WE GO BACK TOMORROW, WE WON'T BE ABLE TO SEE USJ.
IS THAT OK?
HUH?
OH, THAT. NO, I DON'T MIND.
THEN IT'S SETTLED.
GOOD.
WE SHOULD GET SOME SLEEP.
IT'S STARTING TO GET CHILLY...
... ...

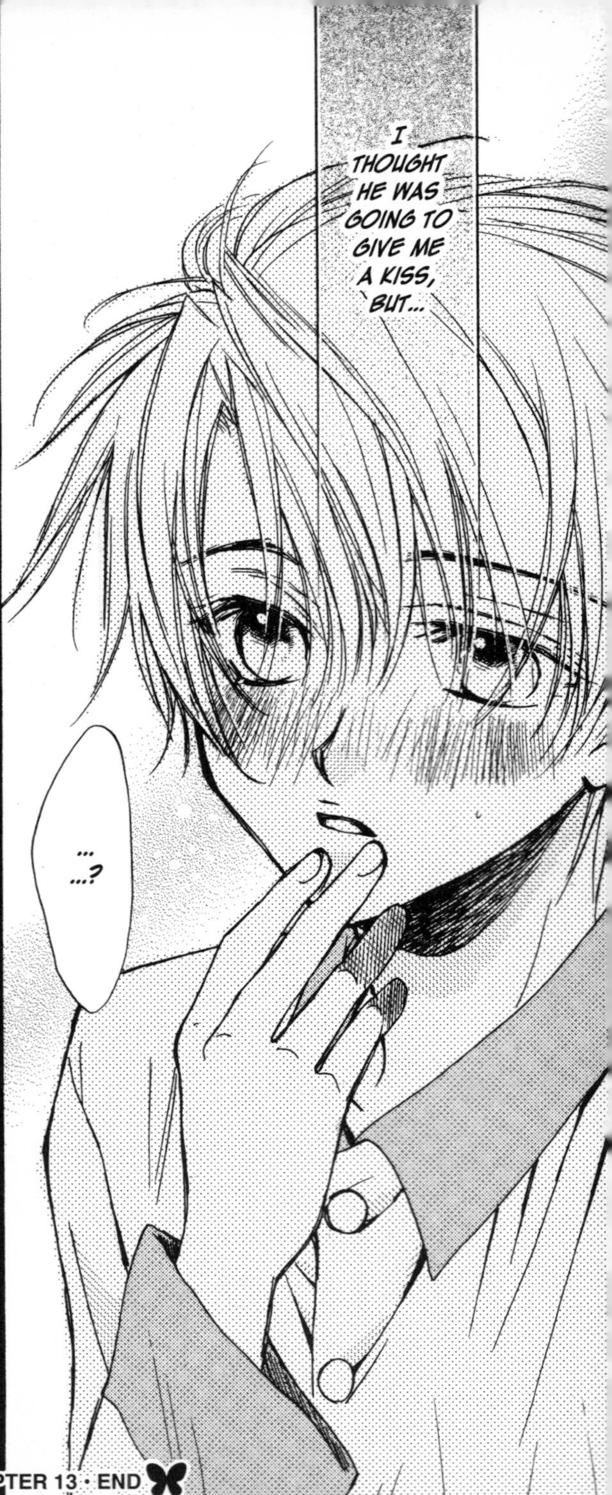
I THOUGHT HE WAS GOING TO GIVE ME A KISS, BUT...
... ...?

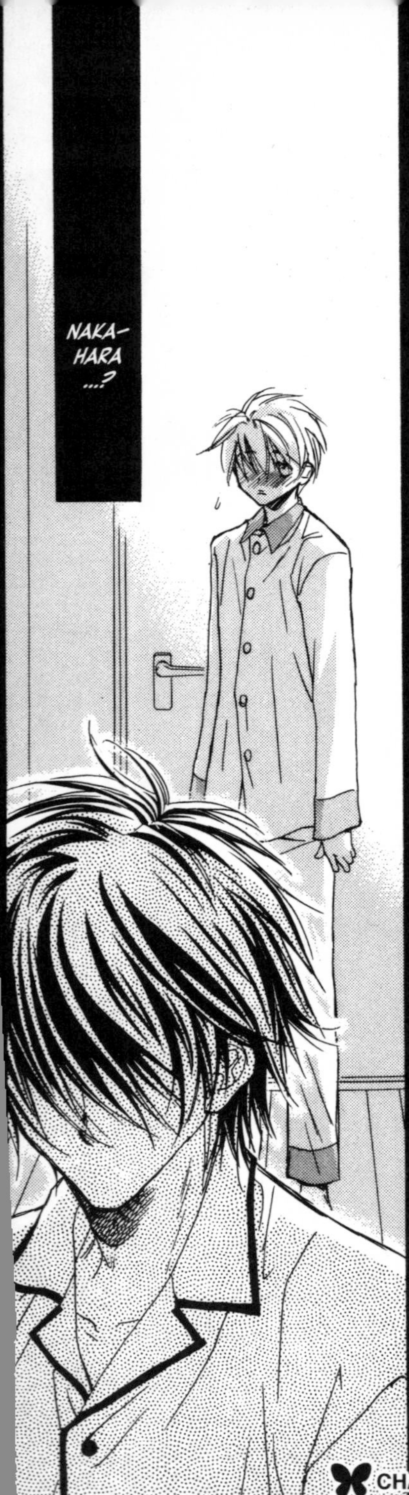
NAKA-HARA ...?

CHAPTER 13 • END

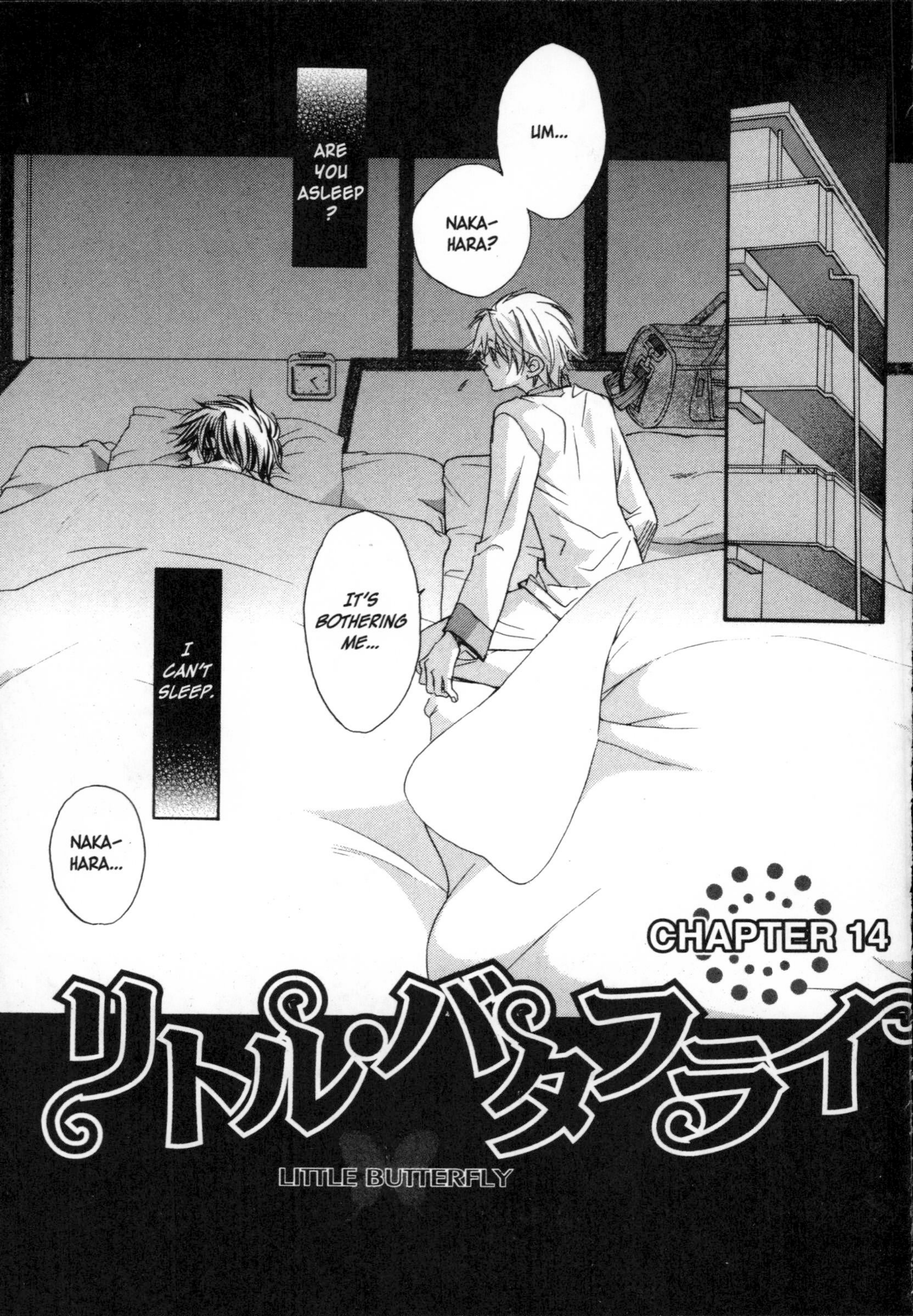
UM...
NAKA-HARA?
ARE YOU ASLEEP ?
IT'S BOTHERING ME...
I CAN'T SLEEP.
NAKA-HARA...
CHAPTER 14
リトル・バタフライ
LITTLE BUTTERFLY

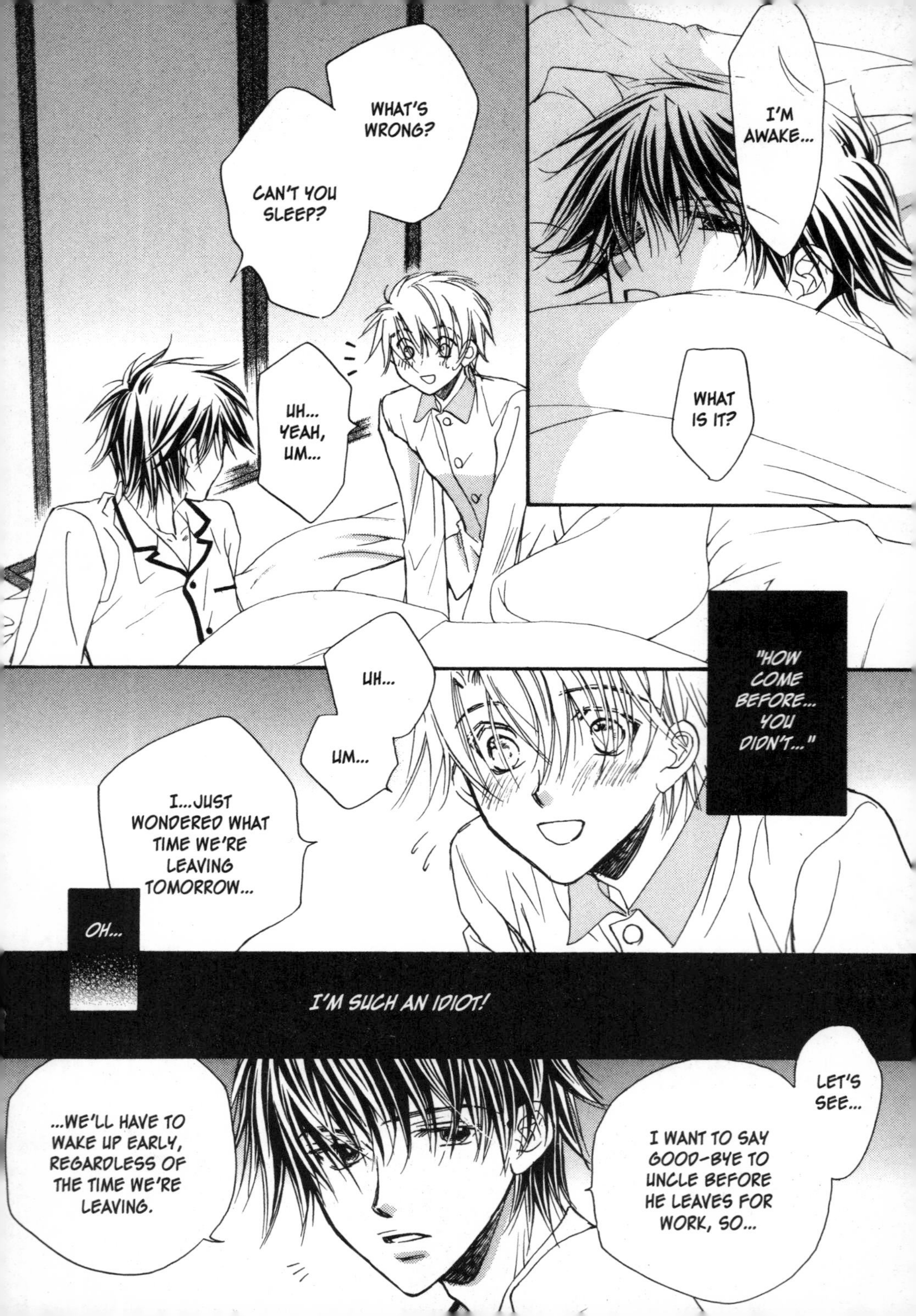
I'M AWAKE...
WHAT IS IT?
WHAT'S WRONG?
CAN'T YOU SLEEP?
UH... YEAH, UM...
"HOW COME BEFORE... YOU DIDN'T..."
UH...
UM...
I...JUST WONDERED WHAT TIME WE'RE LEAVING TOMORROW...
OH...
I'M SUCH AN IDIOT!
LET'S SEE...
I WANT TO SAY GOOD-BYE TO UNCLE BEFORE HE LEAVES FOR WORK, SO...
...WE'LL HAVE TO WAKE UP EARLY, REGARDLESS OF THE TIME WE'RE LEAVING.

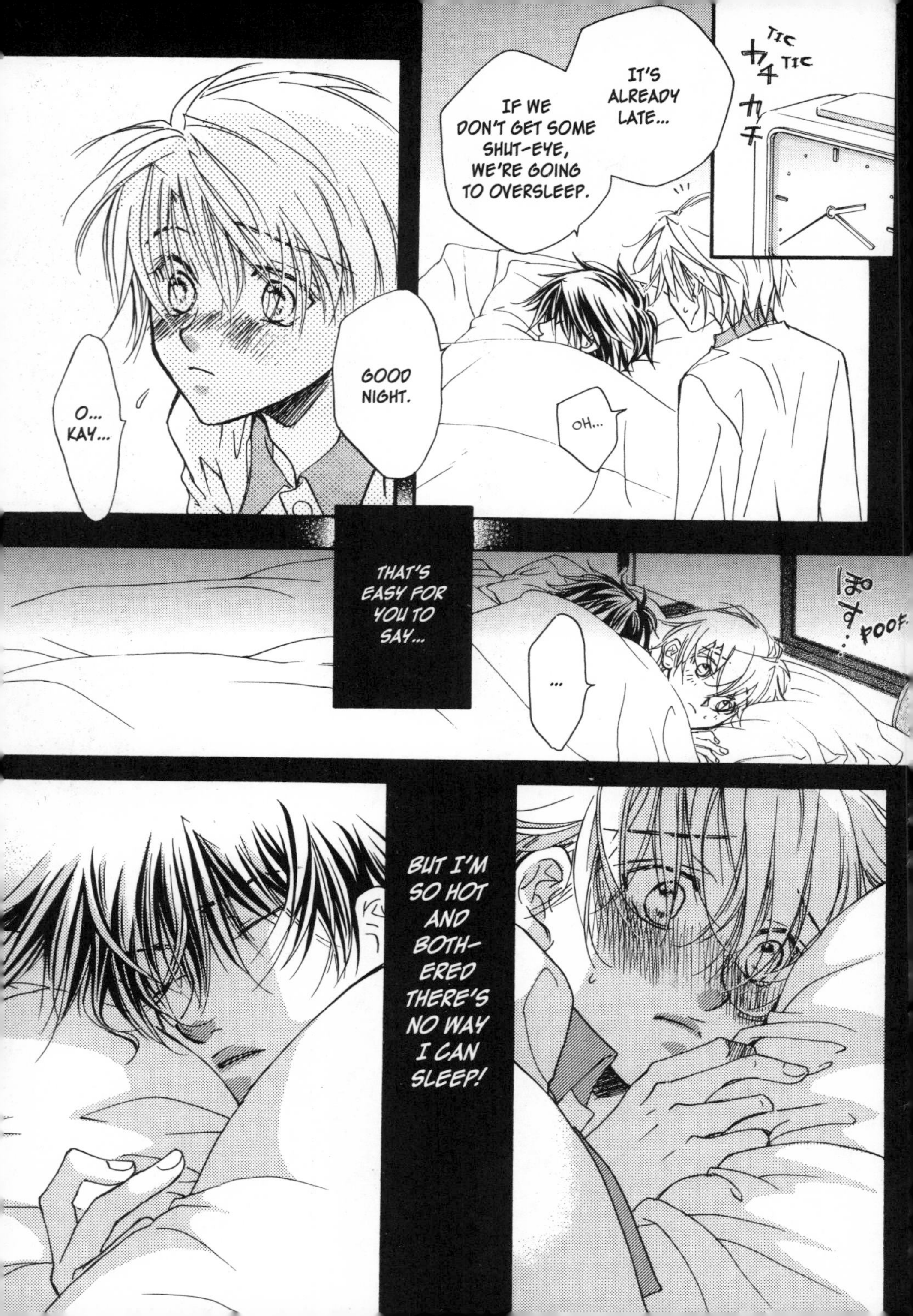
TIC TIC
IT'S ALREADY LATE...
IF WE DON'T GET SOME SHUT-EYE, WE'RE GOING TO OVERSLEEP.
OH...
GOOD NIGHT.
O... KAY...
POOF
...
THAT'S EASY FOR YOU TO SAY...
BUT I'M SO HOT AND BOTHERED THERE'S NO WAY I CAN SLEEP!

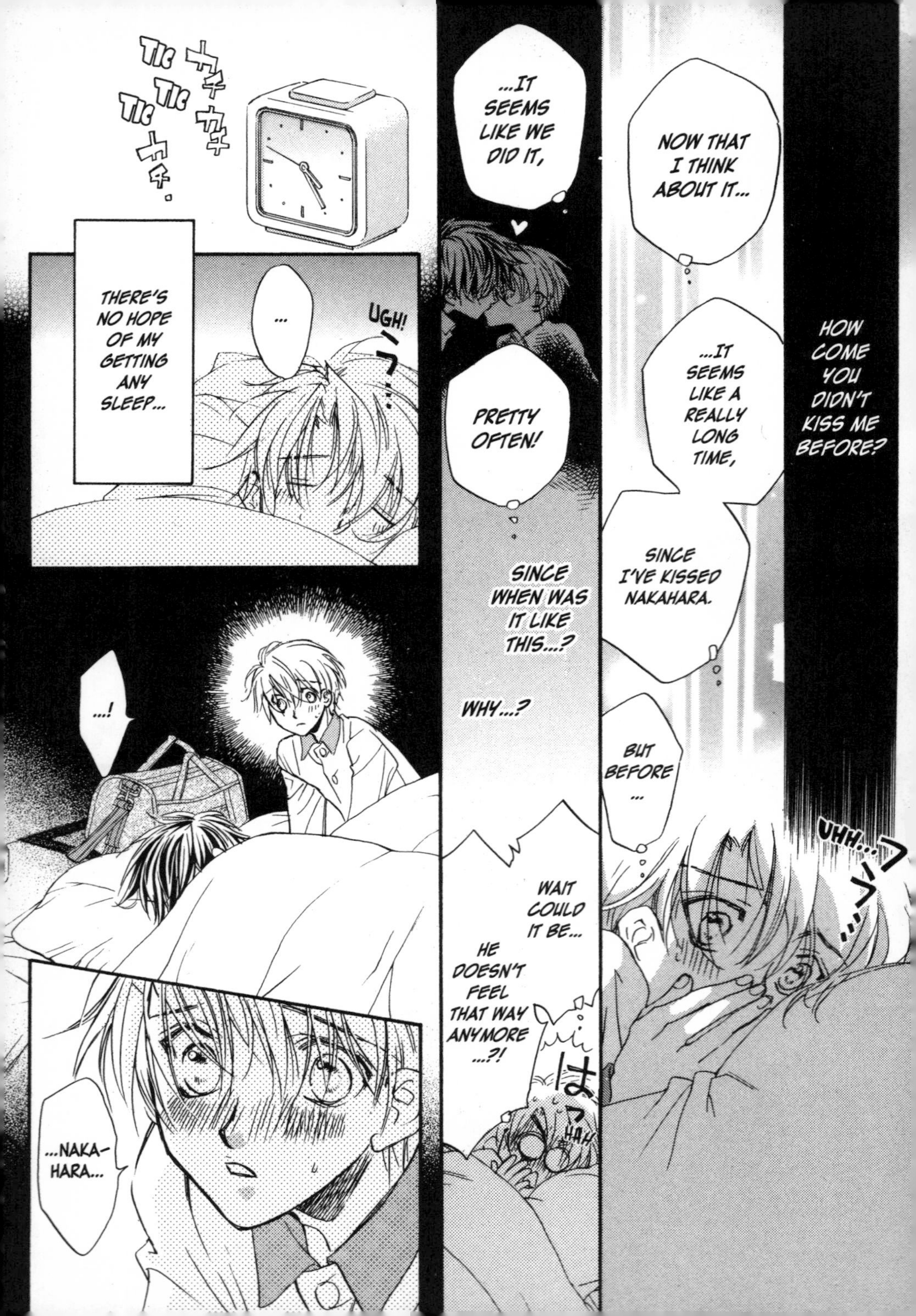
HOW COME YOU DIDN'T KISS ME BEFORE?
NOW THAT I THINK ABOUT IT...
...IT SEEMS LIKE A REALLY LONG TIME,
SINCE I'VE KISSED NAKAHARA.
BUT BEFORE ...
UHH...
...IT SEEMS LIKE WE DID IT,
PRETTY OFTEN!
SINCE WHEN WAS IT LIKE THIS...?
WHY...?
WAIT COULD IT BE...
HE DOESN'T FEEL THAT WAY ANYMORE ...?!
HAH
TIC TIC TIC
THERE'S NO HOPE OF MY GETTING ANY SLEEP...
...
UGH!
...!
...NAKA-HARA...

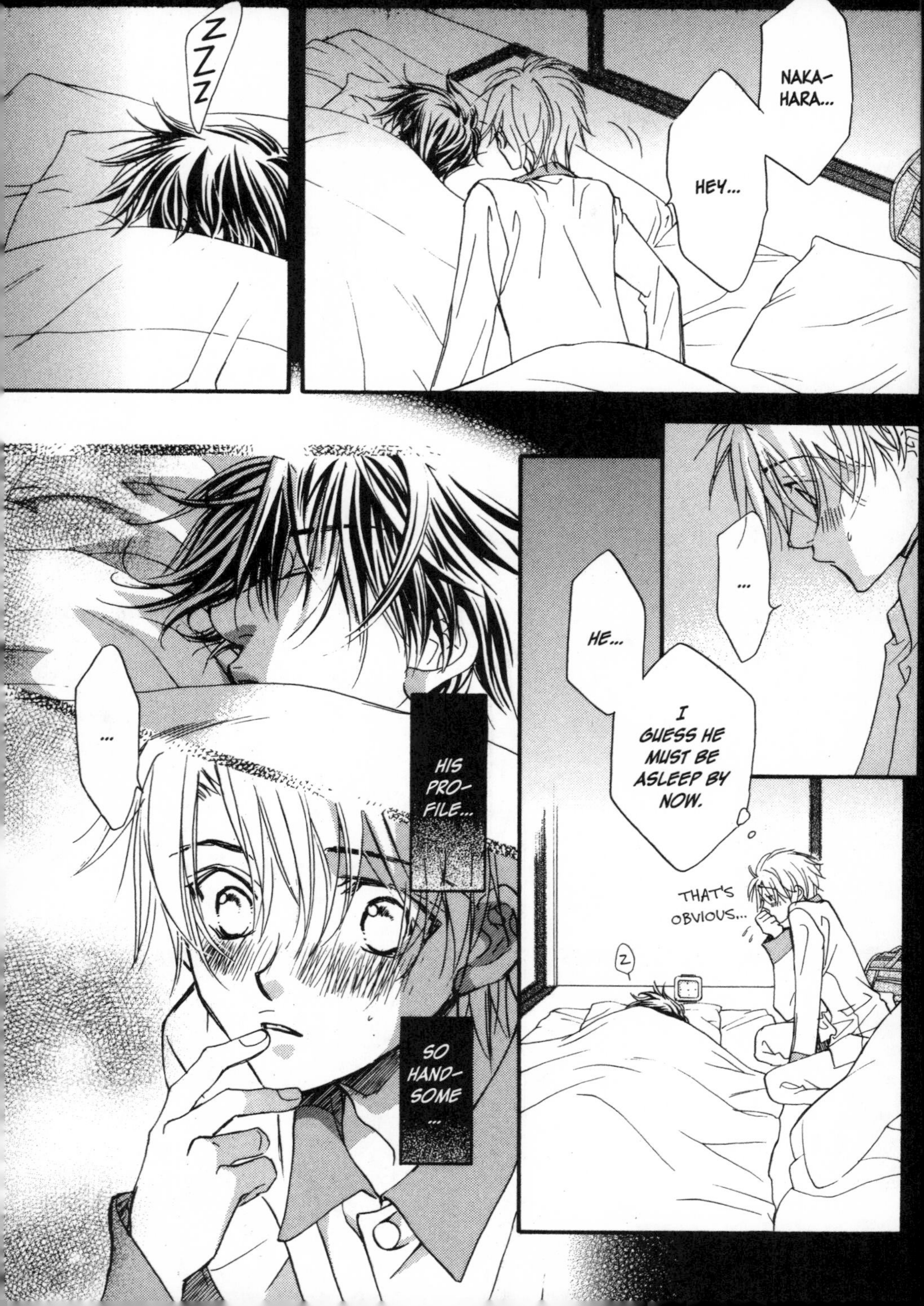
NAKA-HARA...
HEY...
ZZZ
...
HE...
I GUESS HE MUST BE ASLEEP BY NOW.
THAT'S OBVIOUS...
Z
...
HIS PRO-FILE...
SO HAND-SOME ...

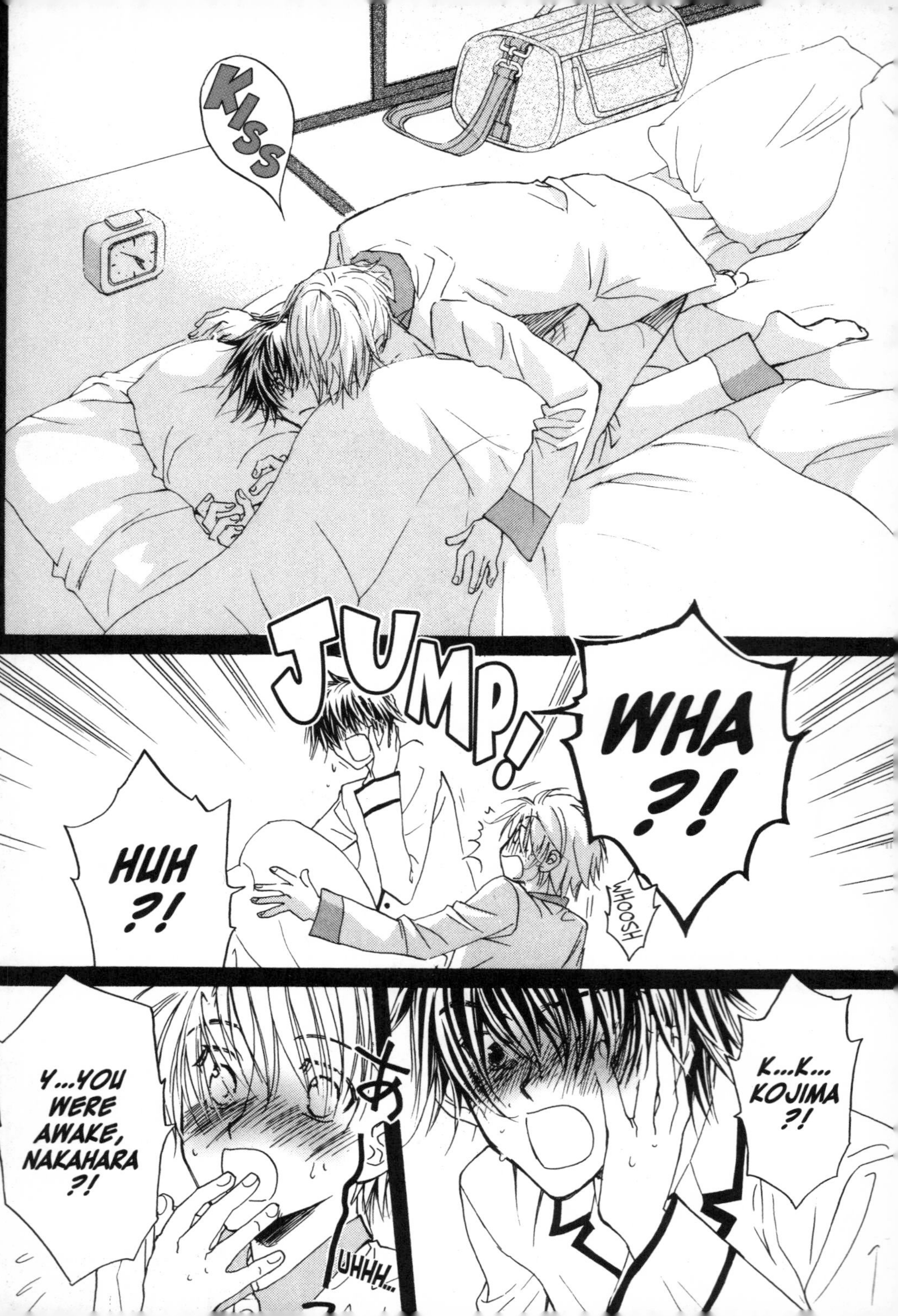
KISS
WHA ?!
JUMP!
WHOOSH
HUH ?!
K...K... KOJIMA ?!
あ
Y...YOU WERE AWAKE, NAKAHARA ?!
UHHH...

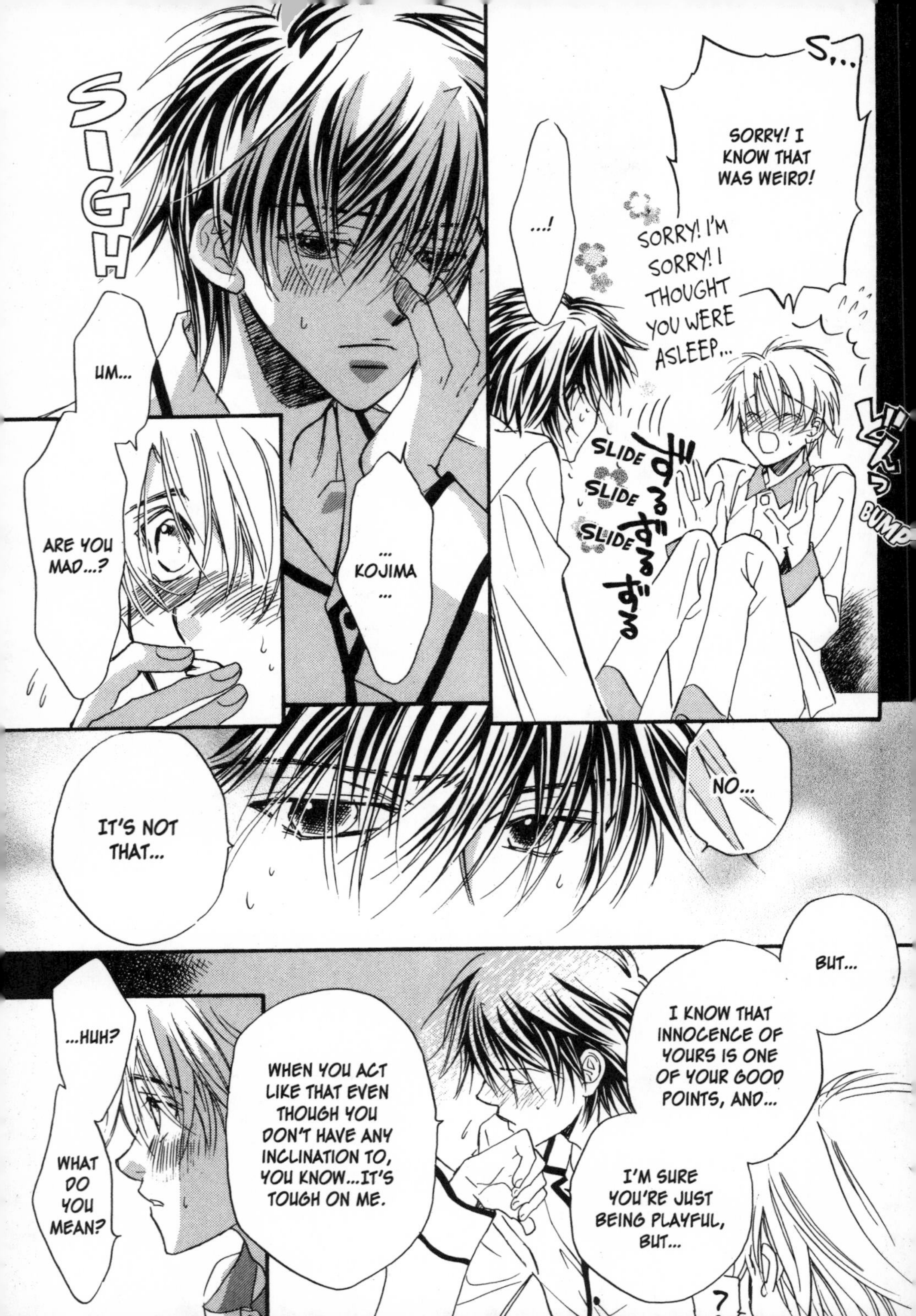
S,...
SORRY! I KNOW THAT WAS WEIRD!
...!
SORRY! I'M SORRY! I THOUGHT YOU WERE ASLEEP...
どんっ
BUMP
ずるずるずる
SLIDE SLIDE SLIDE
SIGH
UM...
...KOJIMA...
ARE YOU MAD...?
NO...
IT'S NOT THAT...
BUT...
I KNOW THAT INNOCENCE OF YOURS IS ONE OF YOUR GOOD POINTS, AND...
I'M SURE YOU'RE JUST BEING PLAYFUL, BUT...
WHEN YOU ACT LIKE THAT EVEN THOUGH YOU DON'T HAVE ANY INCLINATION TO, YOU KNOW...IT'S TOUGH ON ME.
...HUH?
WHAT DO YOU MEAN?

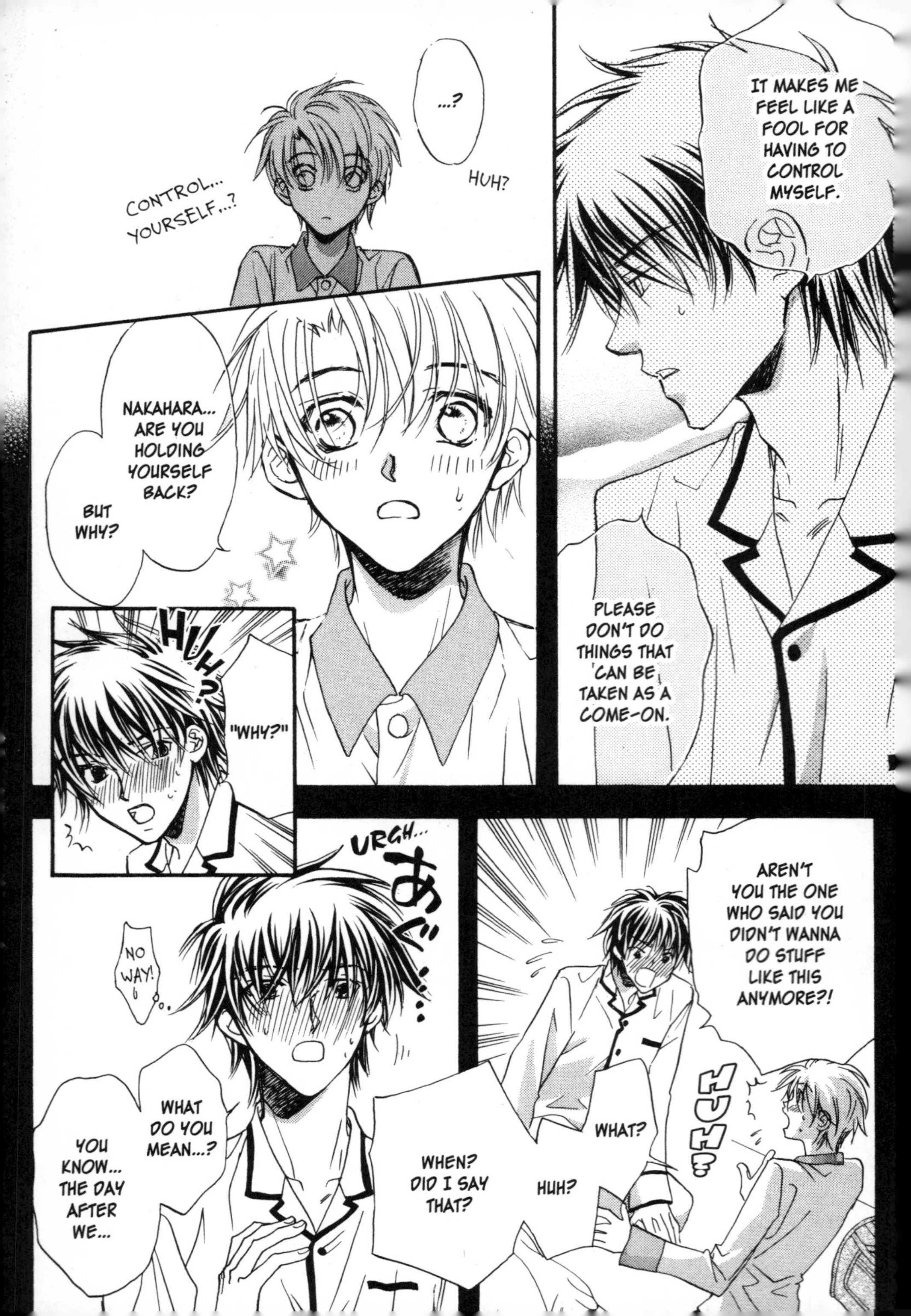
IT MAKES ME FEEL LIKE A FOOL FOR HAVING TO CONTROL MYSELF.
PLEASE DON'T DO THINGS THAT CAN BE TAKEN AS A COME-ON.
...?
HUH?
CONTROL... YOURSELF...?
NAKAHARA... ARE YOU HOLDING YOURSELF BACK?
BUT WHY?
HUH?
"WHY?"
AREN'T YOU THE ONE WHO SAID YOU DIDN'T WANNA DO STUFF LIKE THIS ANYMORE?!
HUH HUH?
WHAT?
HUH?
WHEN? DID I SAY THAT?
URGH...
あぐ…
NO WAY!
WHAT DO YOU MEAN...?
YOU KNOW... THE DAY AFTER WE...

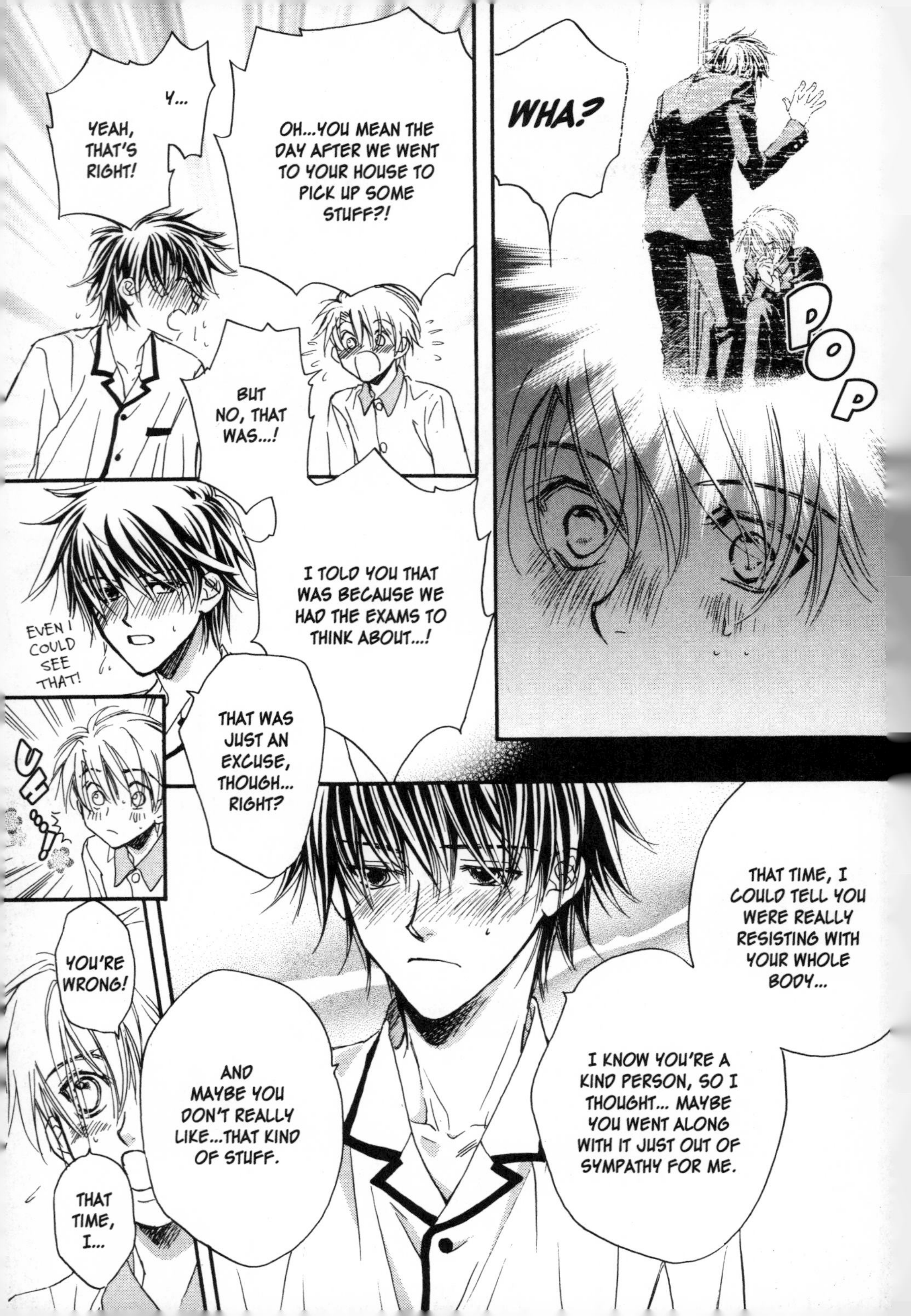
WHA?
POP
OH...YOU MEAN THE DAY AFTER WE WENT TO YOUR HOUSE TO PICK UP SOME STUFF?!
Y...
YEAH, THAT'S RIGHT!
BUT NO, THAT WAS...!
I TOLD YOU THAT WAS BECAUSE WE HAD THE EXAMS TO THINK ABOUT...!
EVEN I COULD SEE THAT!
THAT WAS JUST AN EXCUSE, THOUGH... RIGHT?
UH
THAT TIME, I COULD TELL YOU WERE REALLY RESISTING WITH YOUR WHOLE BODY...
I KNOW YOU'RE A KIND PERSON, SO I THOUGHT... MAYBE YOU WENT ALONG WITH IT JUST OUT OF SYMPATHY FOR ME.
AND MAYBE YOU DON'T REALLY LIKE...THAT KIND OF STUFF.
YOU'RE WRONG!
THAT TIME, I...

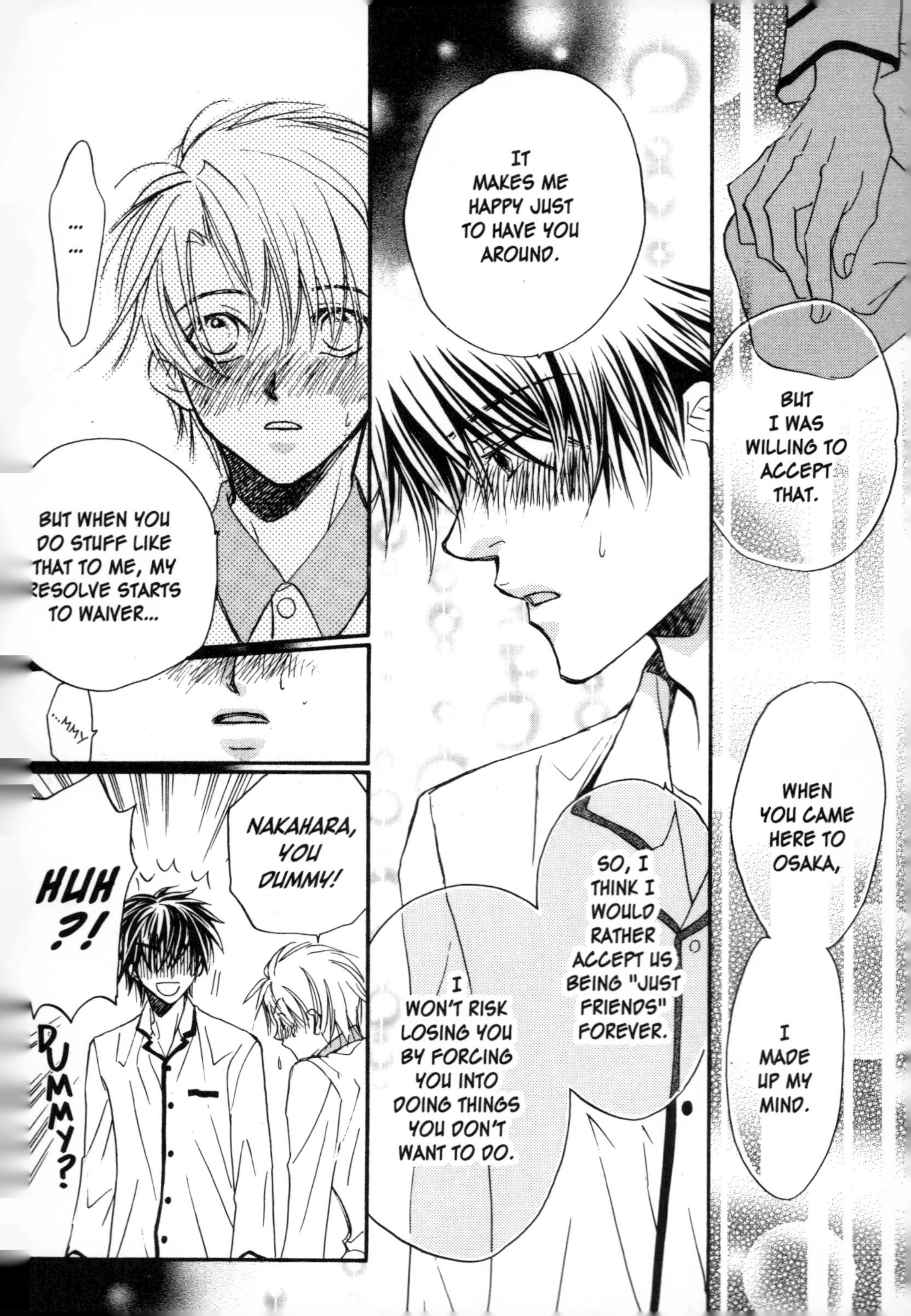
BUT I WAS WILLING TO ACCEPT THAT.
WHEN YOU CAME HERE TO OSAKA,
I MADE UP MY MIND.
IT MAKES ME HAPPY JUST TO HAVE YOU AROUND.
SO, I THINK I WOULD RATHER ACCEPT US BEING "JUST FRIENDS" FOREVER.
I WON'T RISK LOSING YOU BY FORCING YOU INTO DOING THINGS YOU DON'T WANT TO DO.
......
BUT WHEN YOU DO STUFF LIKE THAT TO ME, MY RESOLVE STARTS TO WAIVER...
...MMY
NAKAHARA, YOU DUMMY!
HUH?!
DUMMY?

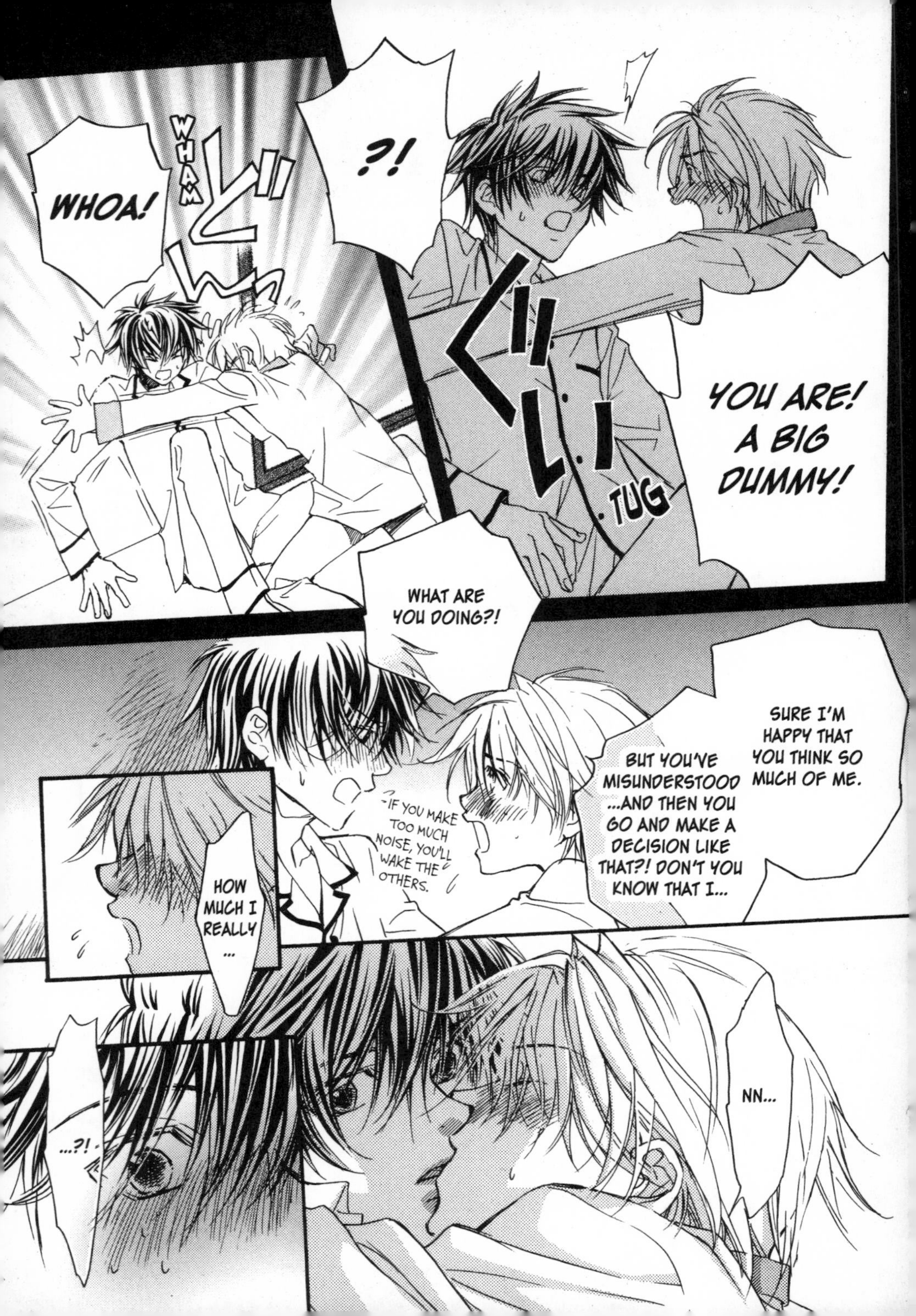
?!
YOU ARE! A BIG DUMMY!
TUG
WHOA!
WHAM
WHAT ARE YOU DOING?!
SURE I'M HAPPY THAT YOU THINK SO MUCH OF ME.
BUT YOU'VE MISUNDERSTOOD ...AND THEN YOU GO AND MAKE A DECISION LIKE THAT?! DON'T YOU KNOW THAT I...
IF YOU MAKE TOO MUCH NOISE, YOU'LL WAKE THE OTHERS.
HOW MUCH I REALLY ...
NN...
...?!

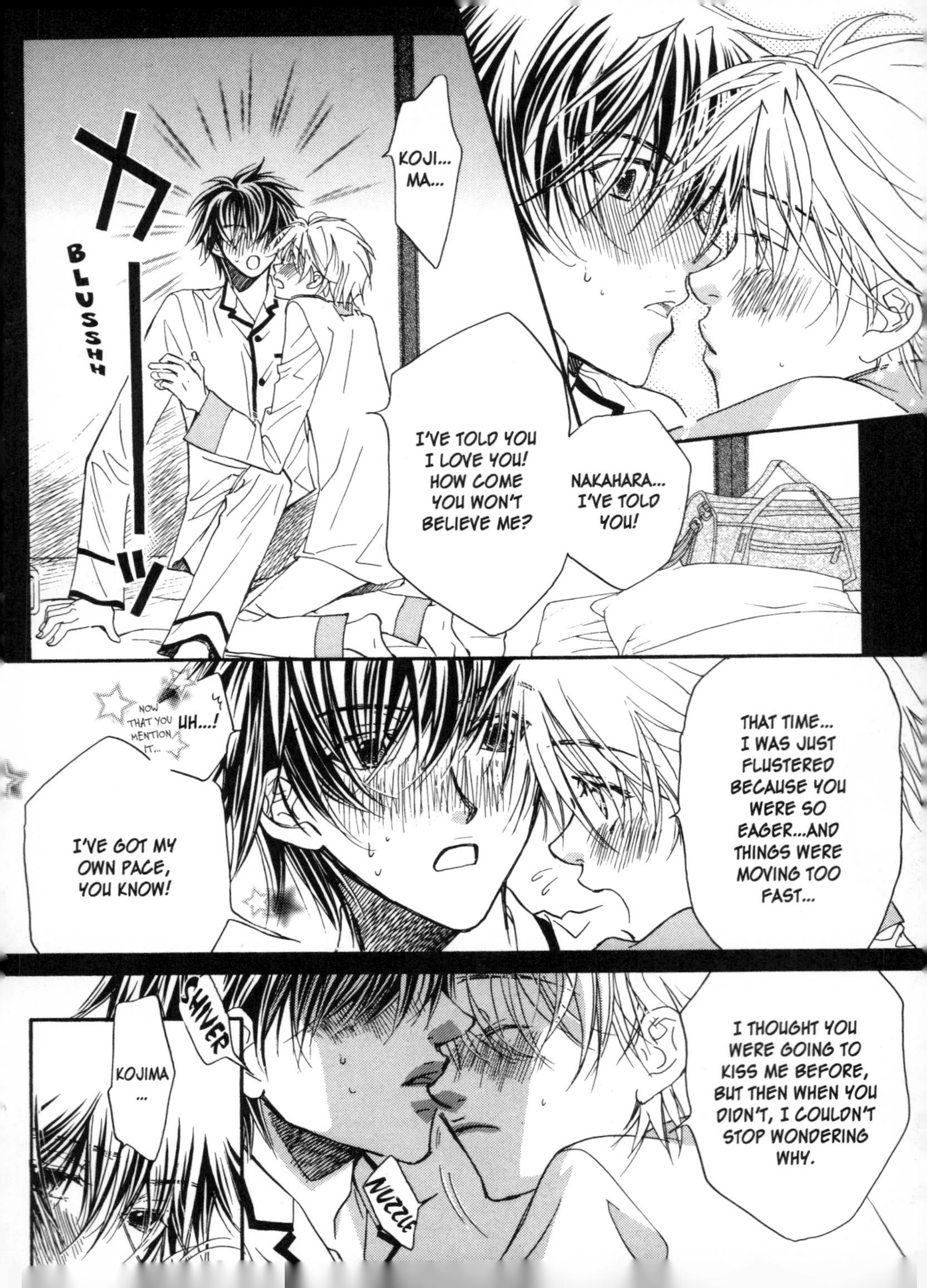
NAKAHARA... I'VE TOLD YOU!
I'VE TOLD YOU I LOVE YOU! HOW COME YOU WON'T BELIEVE ME?
KOJI... MA...
BLUSSHH
THAT TIME... I WAS JUST FLUSTERED BECAUSE YOU WERE SO EAGER...AND THINGS WERE MOVING TOO FAST...
UH...!
NOW THAT YOU MENTION IT...
I'VE GOT MY OWN PACE, YOU KNOW!
I THOUGHT YOU WERE GOING TO KISS ME BEFORE, BUT THEN WHEN YOU DIDN'T, I COULDN'T STOP WONDERING WHY.
SHIVER
NUZZLE
KOJIMA ...

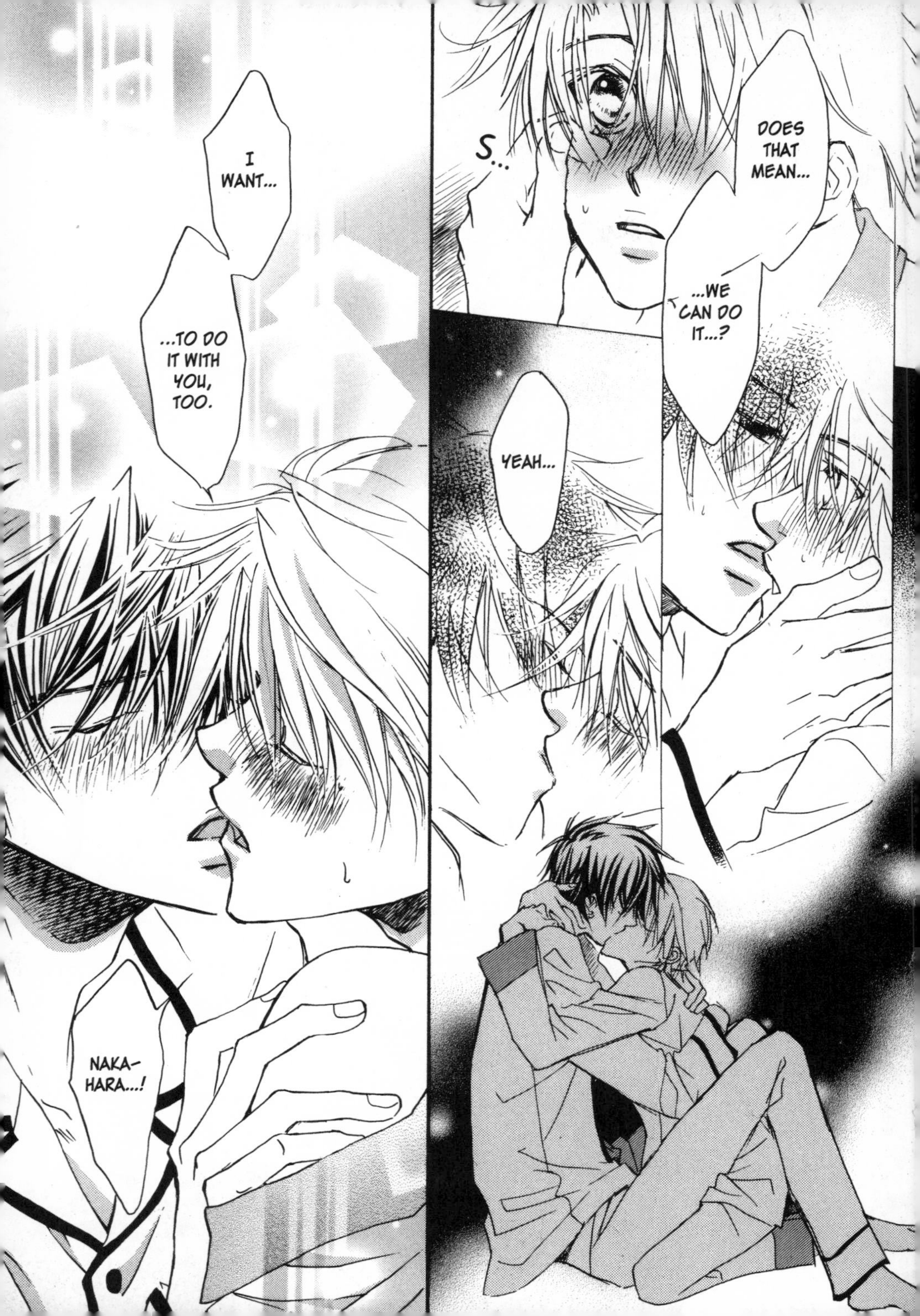
S...
DOES THAT MEAN...
...WE CAN DO IT...?
YEAH...
I WANT...
...TO DO IT WITH YOU, TOO.
NAKA-HARA...!

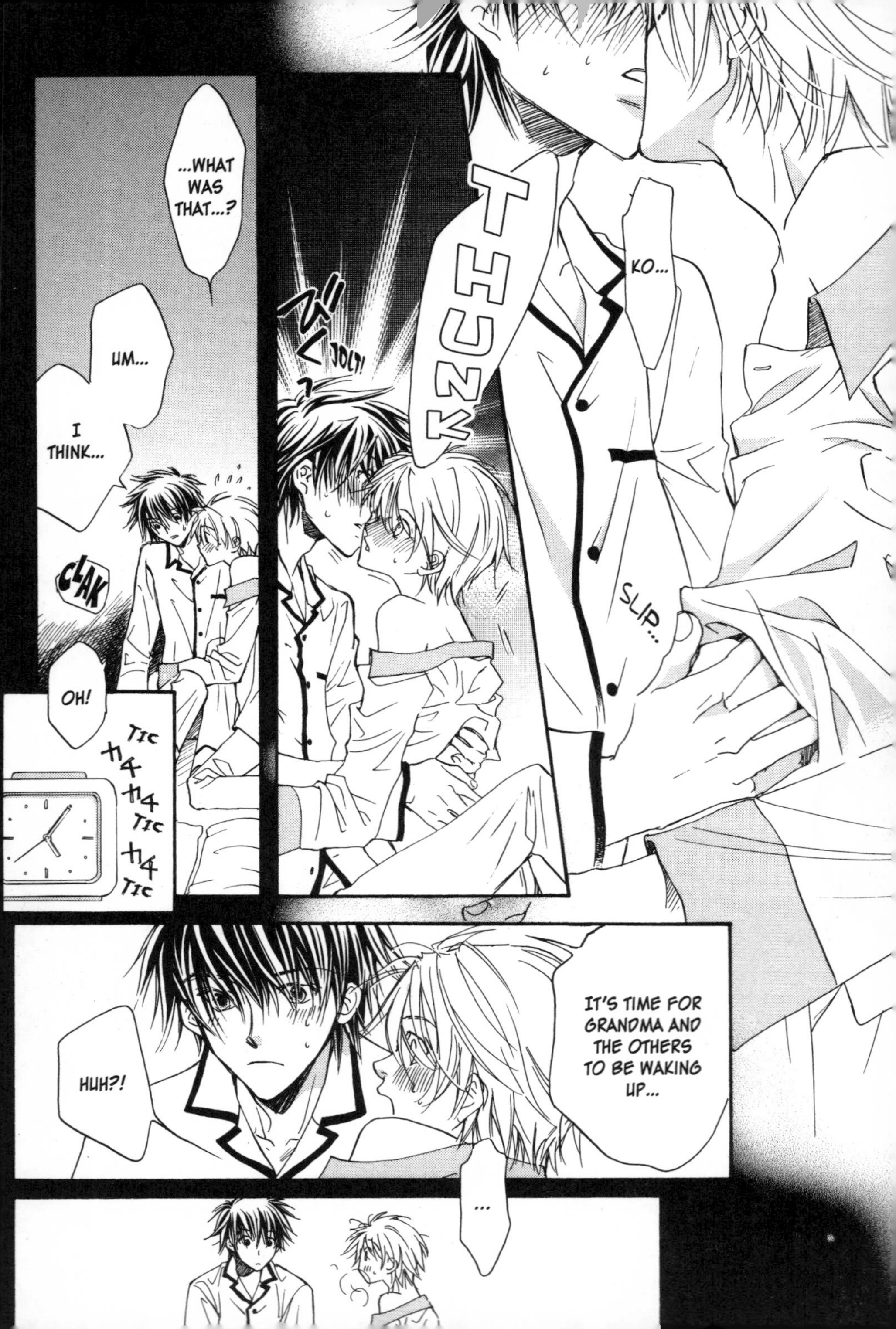
THUNK
KO...
SLIP...
JOLT!
...WHAT WAS THAT...?
UM...
I THINK...
CLAK
OH!
TIC
TIC
TIC
IT'S TIME FOR GRANDMA AND THE OTHERS TO BE WAKING UP...
HUH?!
...

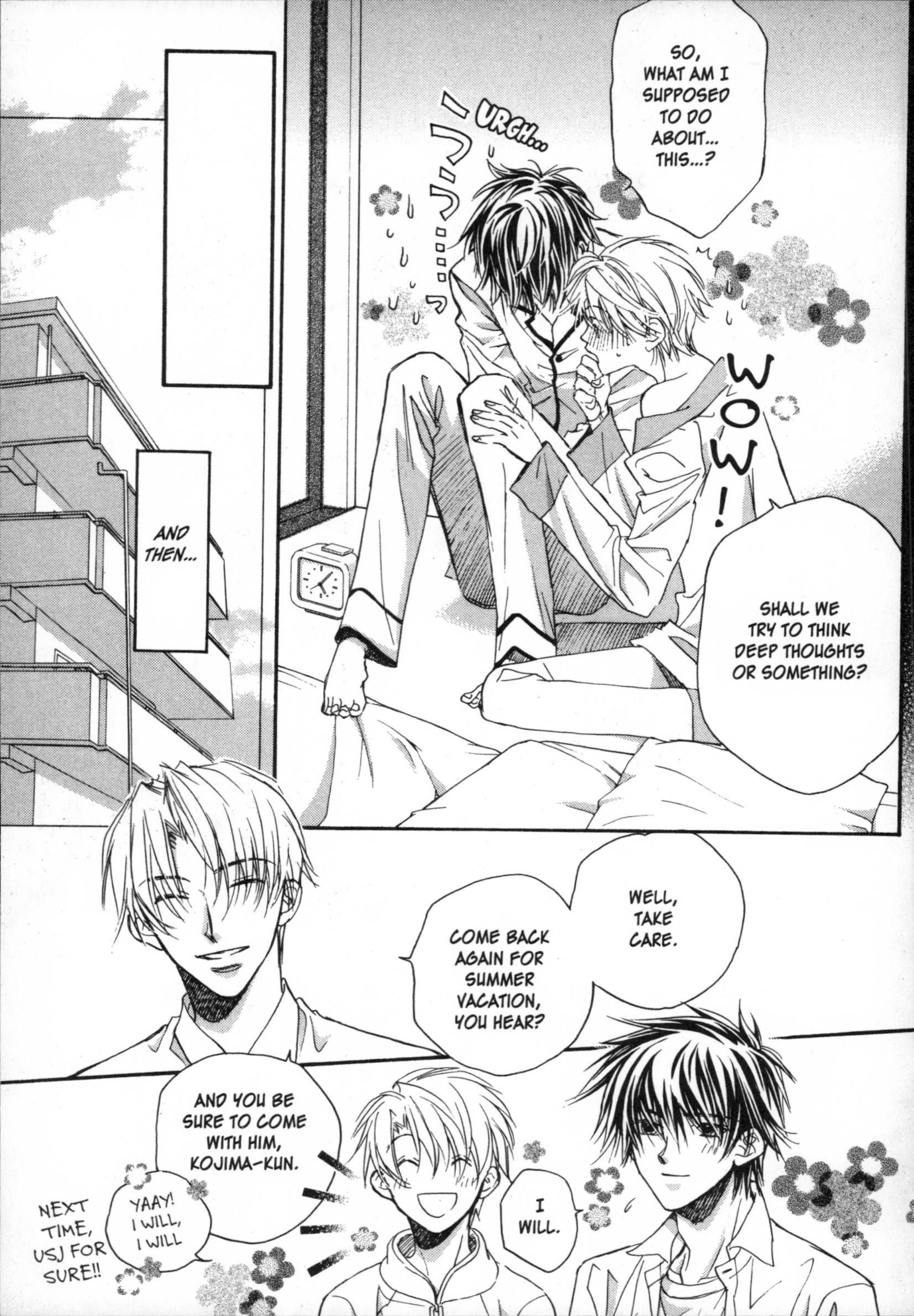
SO, WHAT AM I SUPPOSED TO DO ABOUT... THIS...?
URGH...
WOW!
SHALL WE TRY TO THINK DEEP THOUGHTS OR SOMETHING?
AND THEN...
WELL, TAKE CARE.
COME BACK AGAIN FOR SUMMER VACATION, YOU HEAR?
AND YOU BE SURE TO COME WITH HIM, KOJIMA-KUN.
I WILL.
YAAY! I WILL, I WILL
NEXT TIME, USJ FOR SURE!!

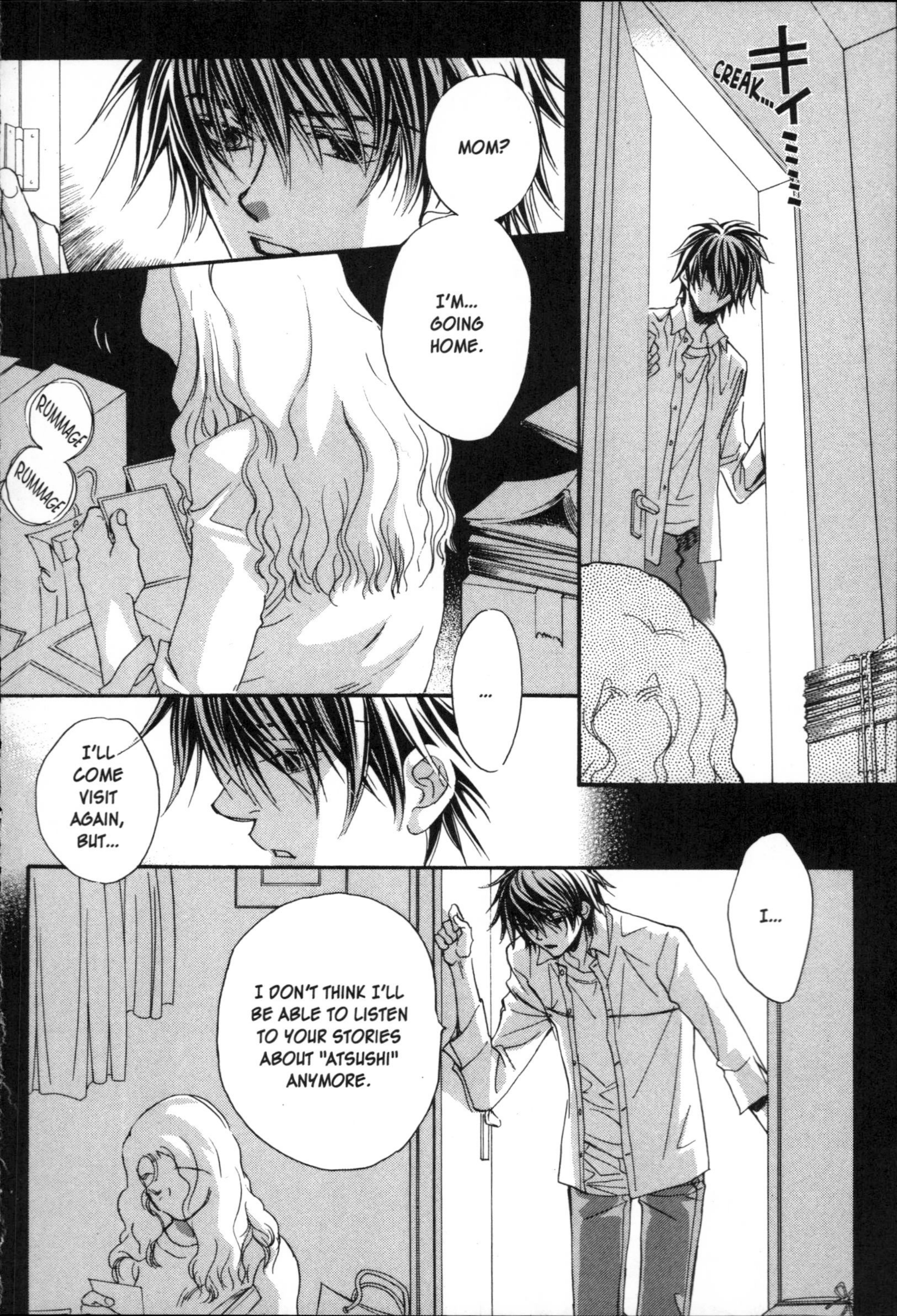
CREAK...
キイ
MOM?
I'M... GOING HOME.
RUMMAGE
RUMMAGE
...
I'LL COME VISIT AGAIN, BUT...
I...
I DON'T THINK I'LL BE ABLE TO LISTEN TO YOUR STORIES ABOUT "ATSUSHI" ANYMORE.

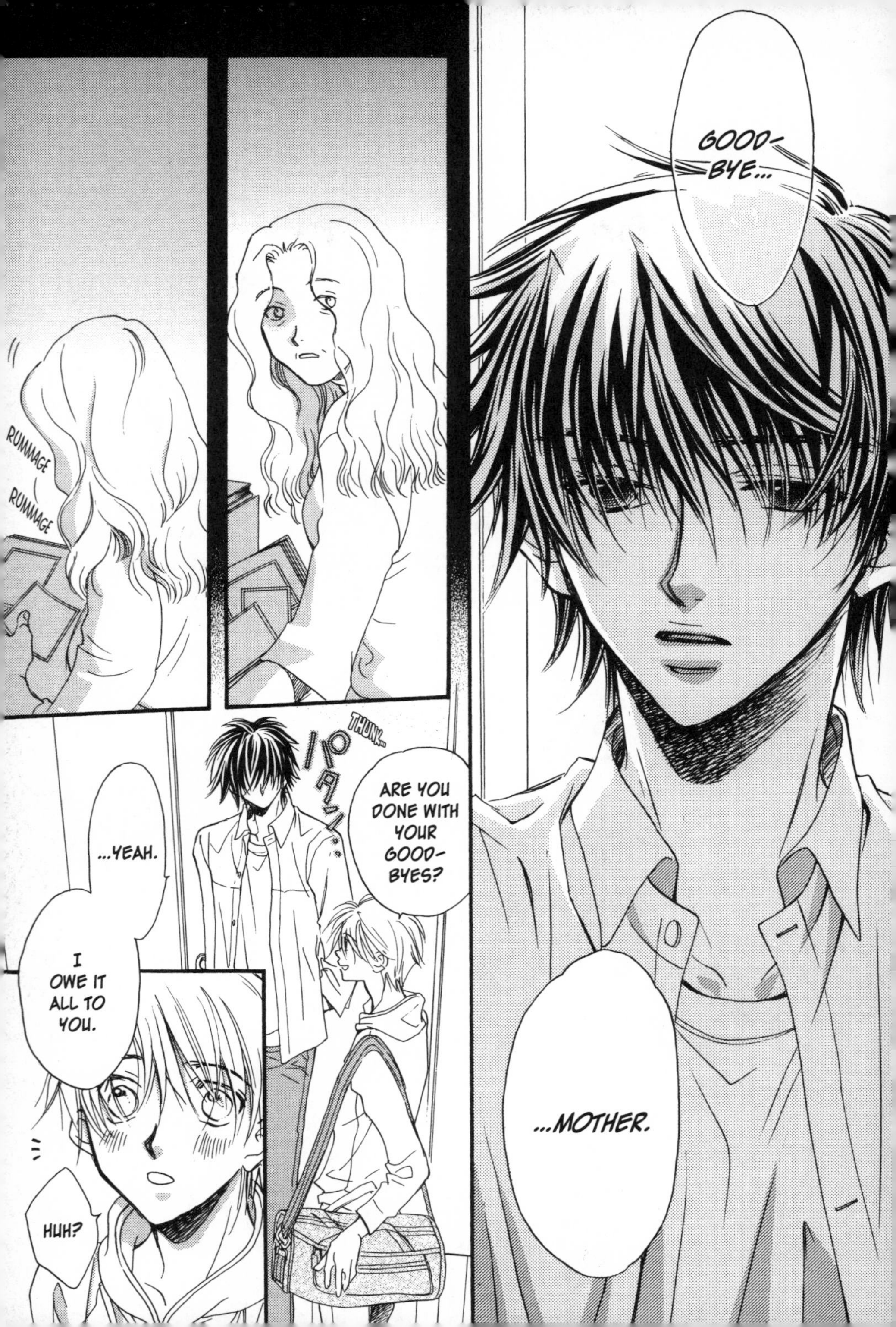
GOOD-BYE...
...MOTHER.
RUMMAGE
RUMMAGE
THUNK...
パタン
ARE YOU DONE WITH YOUR GOOD-BYES?
...YEAH.
I OWE IT ALL TO YOU.
HUH?

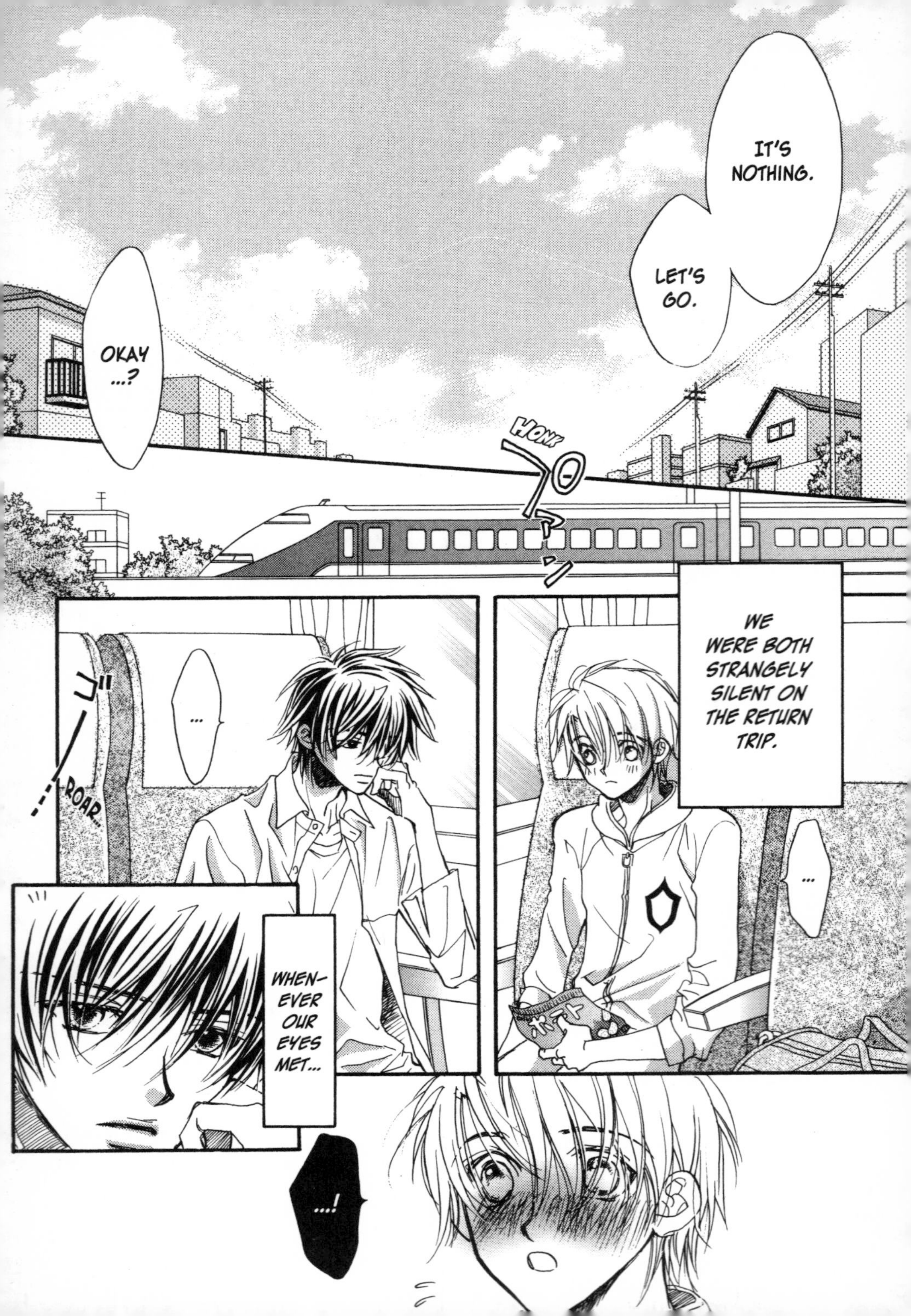
IT'S NOTHING.
LET'S GO.
OKAY ...?
HONK
WE WERE BOTH STRANGELY SILENT ON THE RETURN TRIP.
...
...
ROAR...
WHEN-EVER OUR EYES MET...
...!

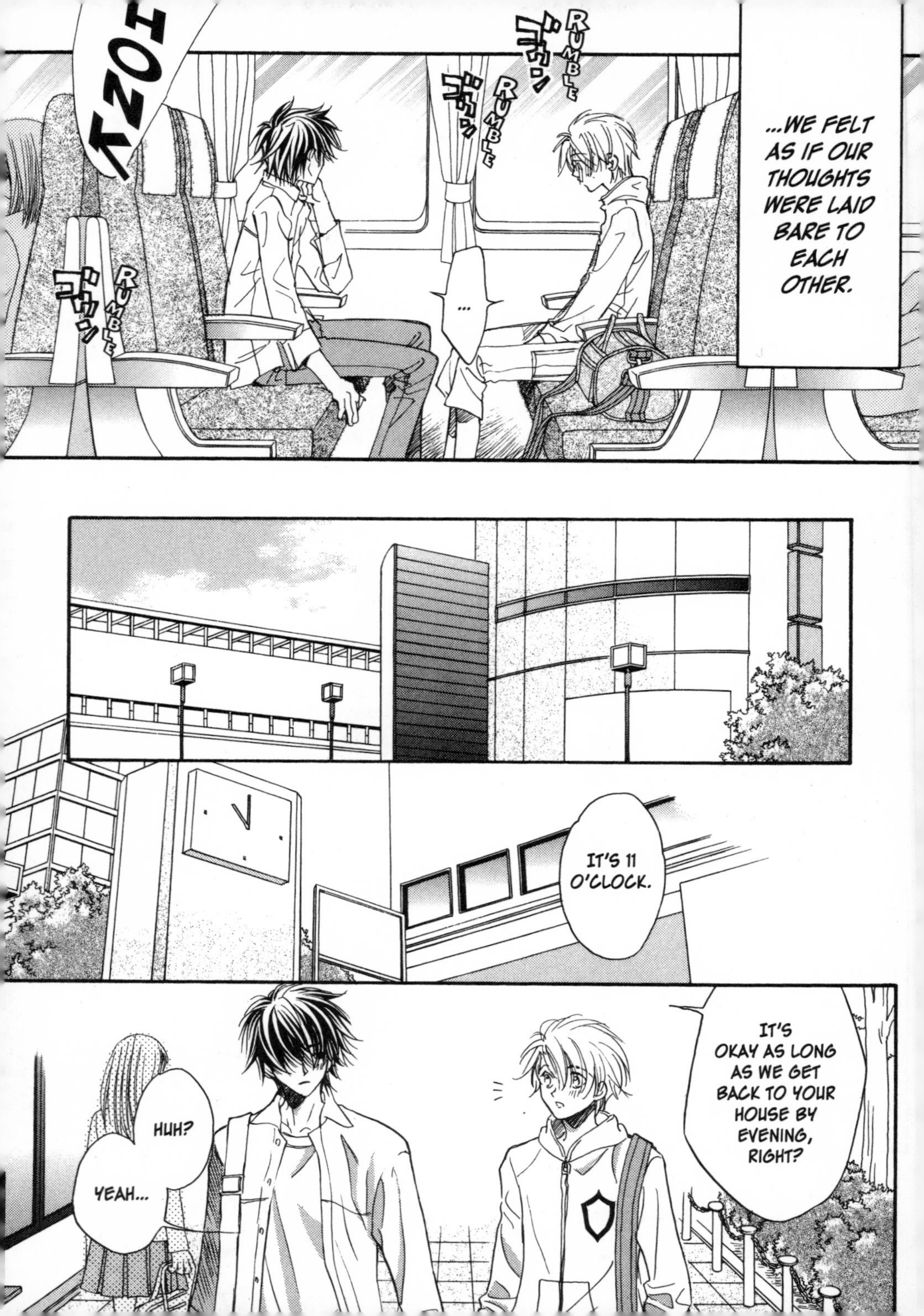
...WE FELT AS IF OUR THOUGHTS WERE LAID BARE TO EACH OTHER.
RUMBLE
RUMBLE
...
RUMBLE
HONK
IT'S 11 O'CLOCK.
IT'S OKAY AS LONG AS WE GET BACK TO YOUR HOUSE BY EVENING, RIGHT?
HUH?
YEAH...

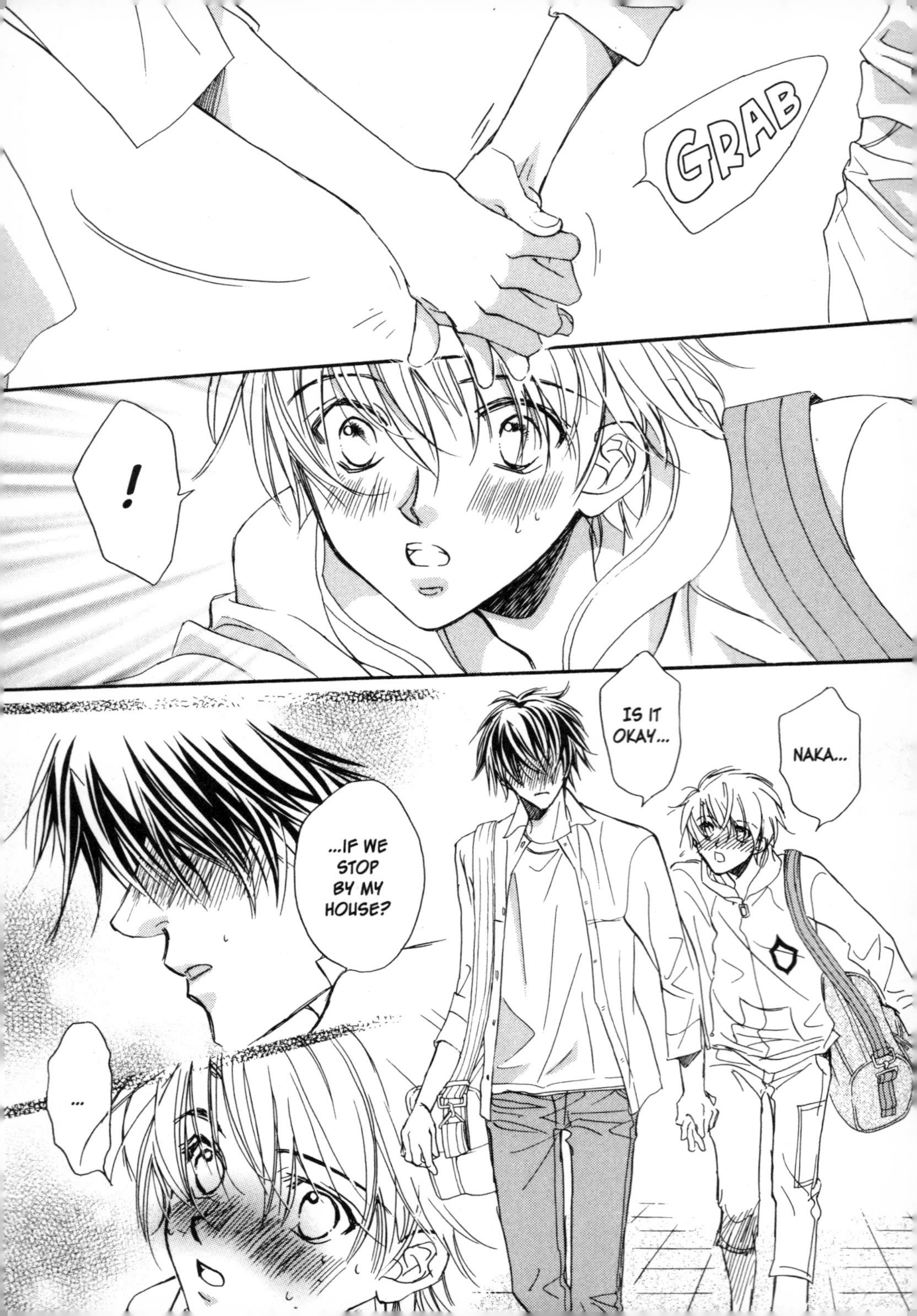
GRAB
!
NAKA...
IS IT OKAY...
...IF WE STOP BY MY HOUSE?
...

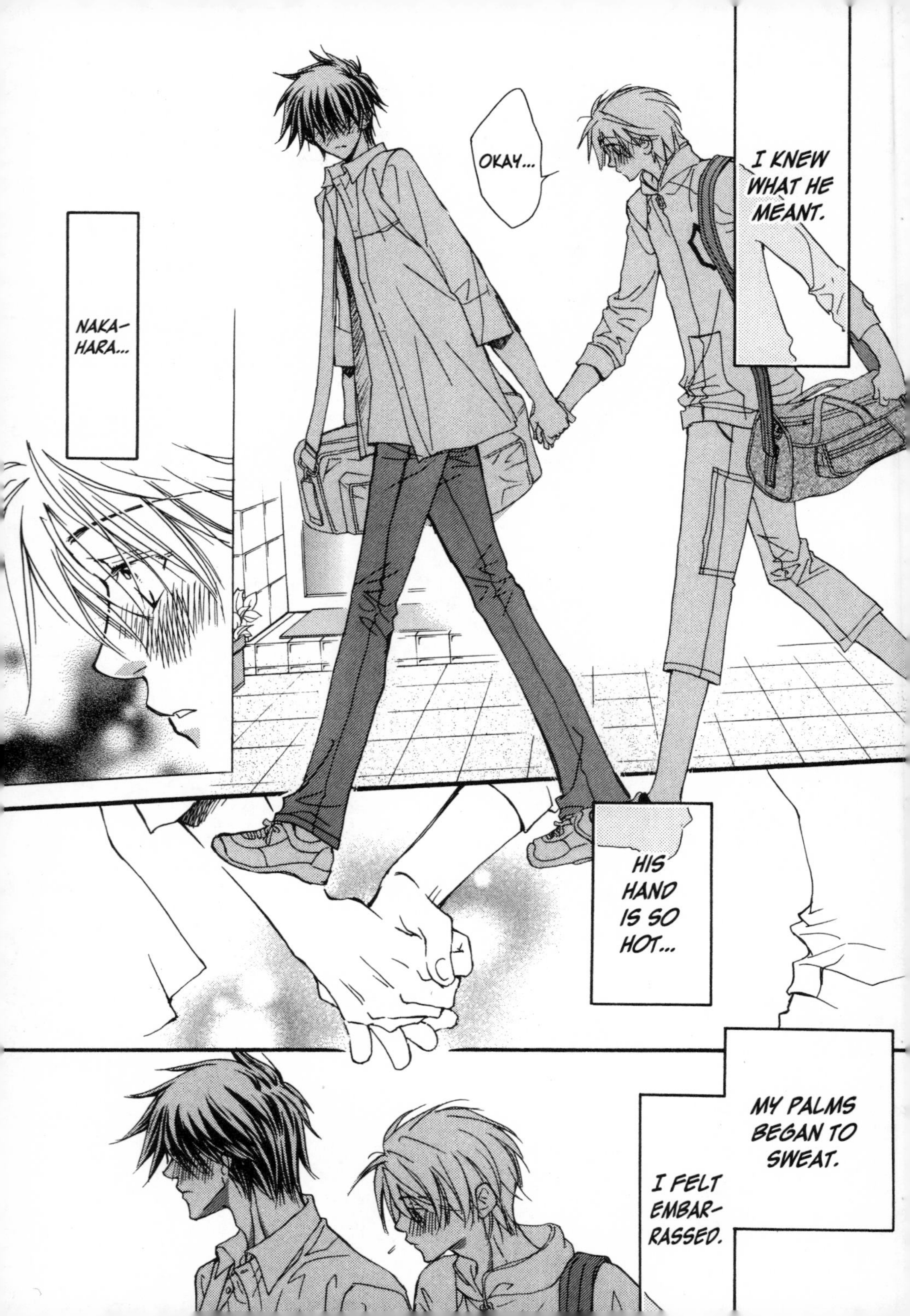
I KNEW WHAT HE MEANT.
OKAY...
NAKA-HARA...
HIS HAND IS SO HOT...
MY PALMS BEGAN TO SWEAT.
I FELT EMBARRASSED.

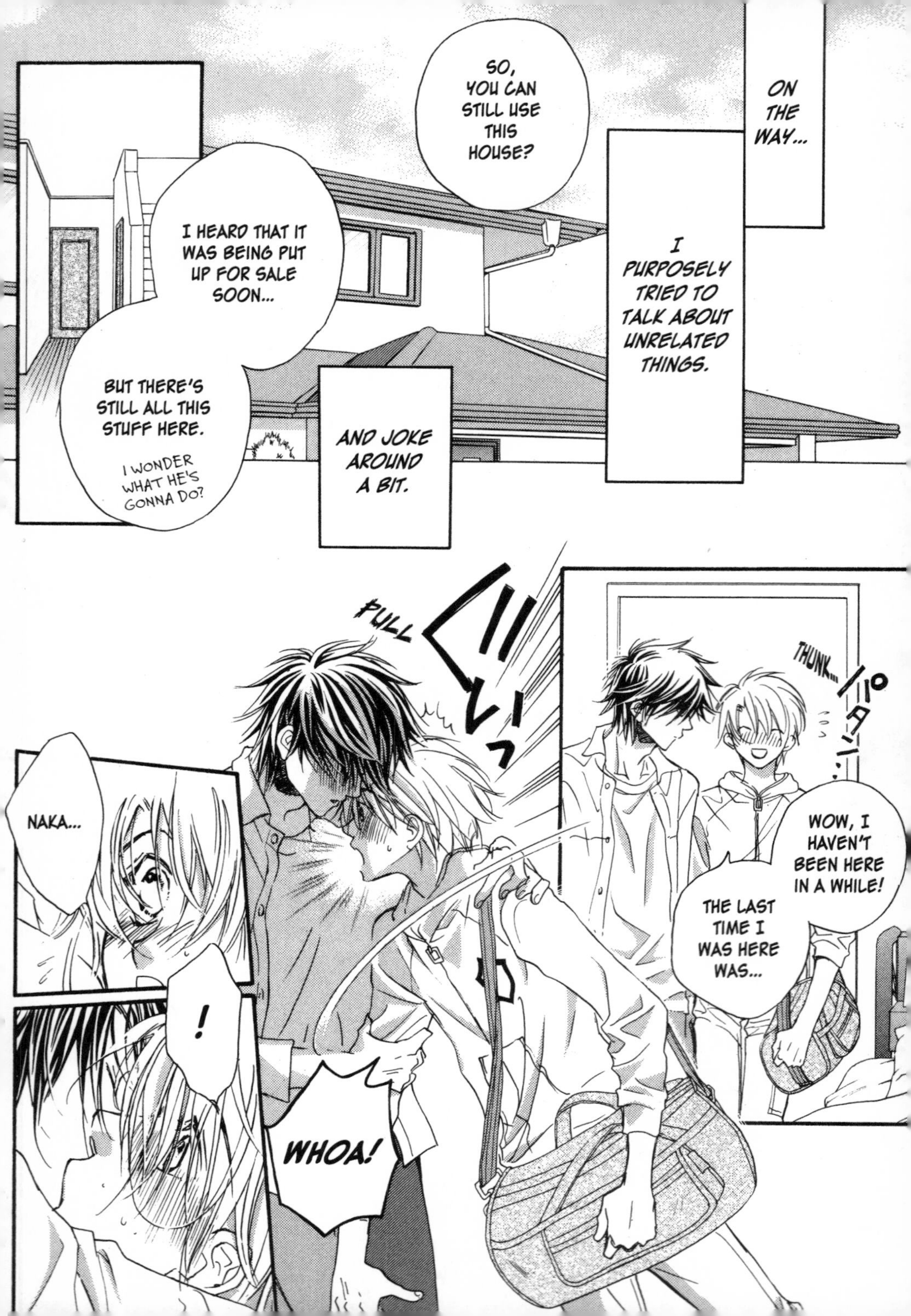

ON THE WAY...
I PURPOSELY TRIED TO TALK ABOUT UNRELATED THINGS.
SO, YOU CAN STILL USE THIS HOUSE?
AND JOKE AROUND A BIT.
I HEARD THAT IT WAS BEING PUT UP FOR SALE SOON...
BUT THERE'S STILL ALL THIS STUFF HERE.
I WONDER WHAT HE'S GONNA DO?
THUNK...
WOW, I HAVEN'T BEEN HERE IN A WHILE!
THE LAST TIME I WAS HERE WAS...
PULL
WHOA!
NAKA...
!

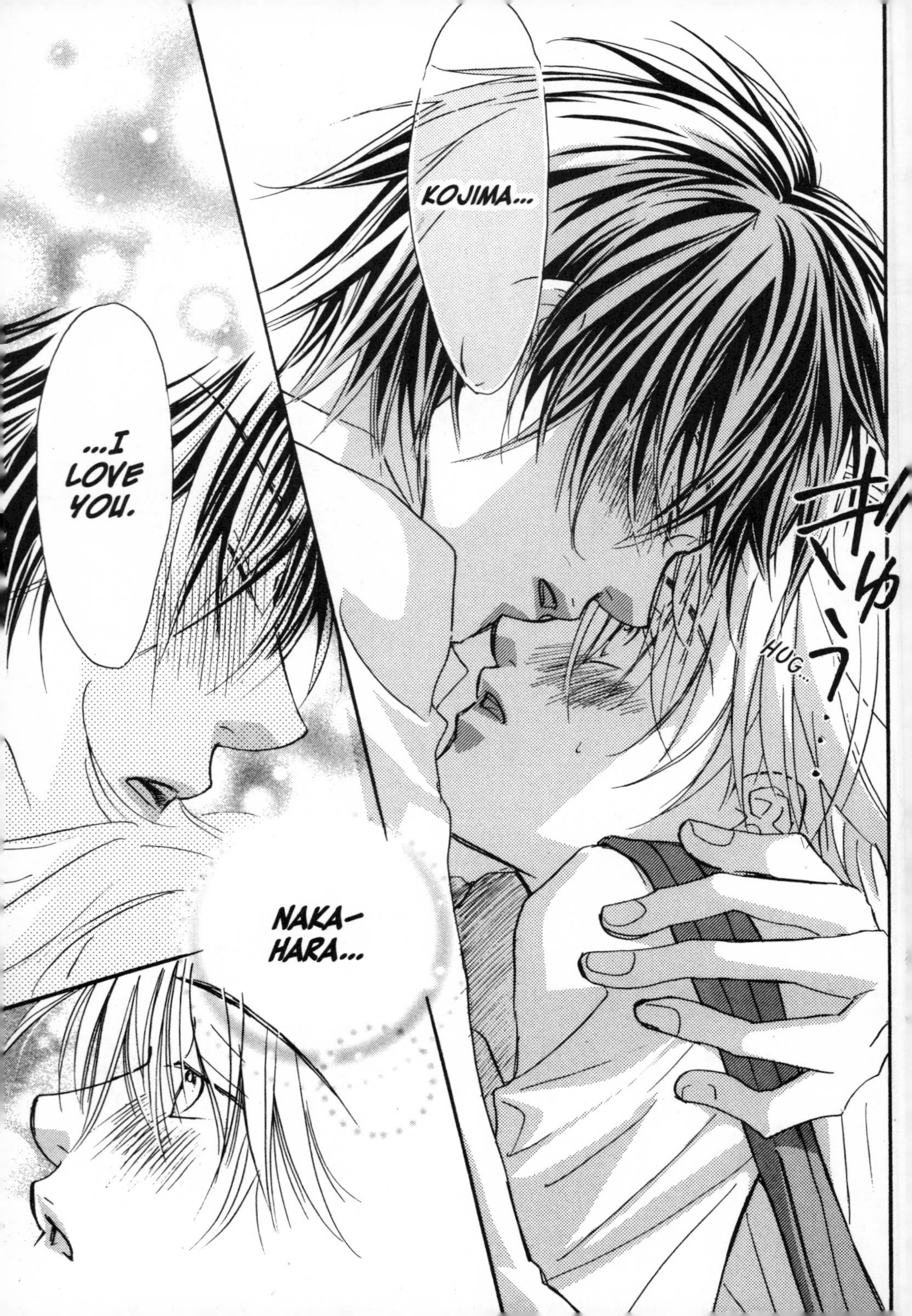
KOJIMA...
HUG...
...I LOVE YOU.
NAKA-HARA...

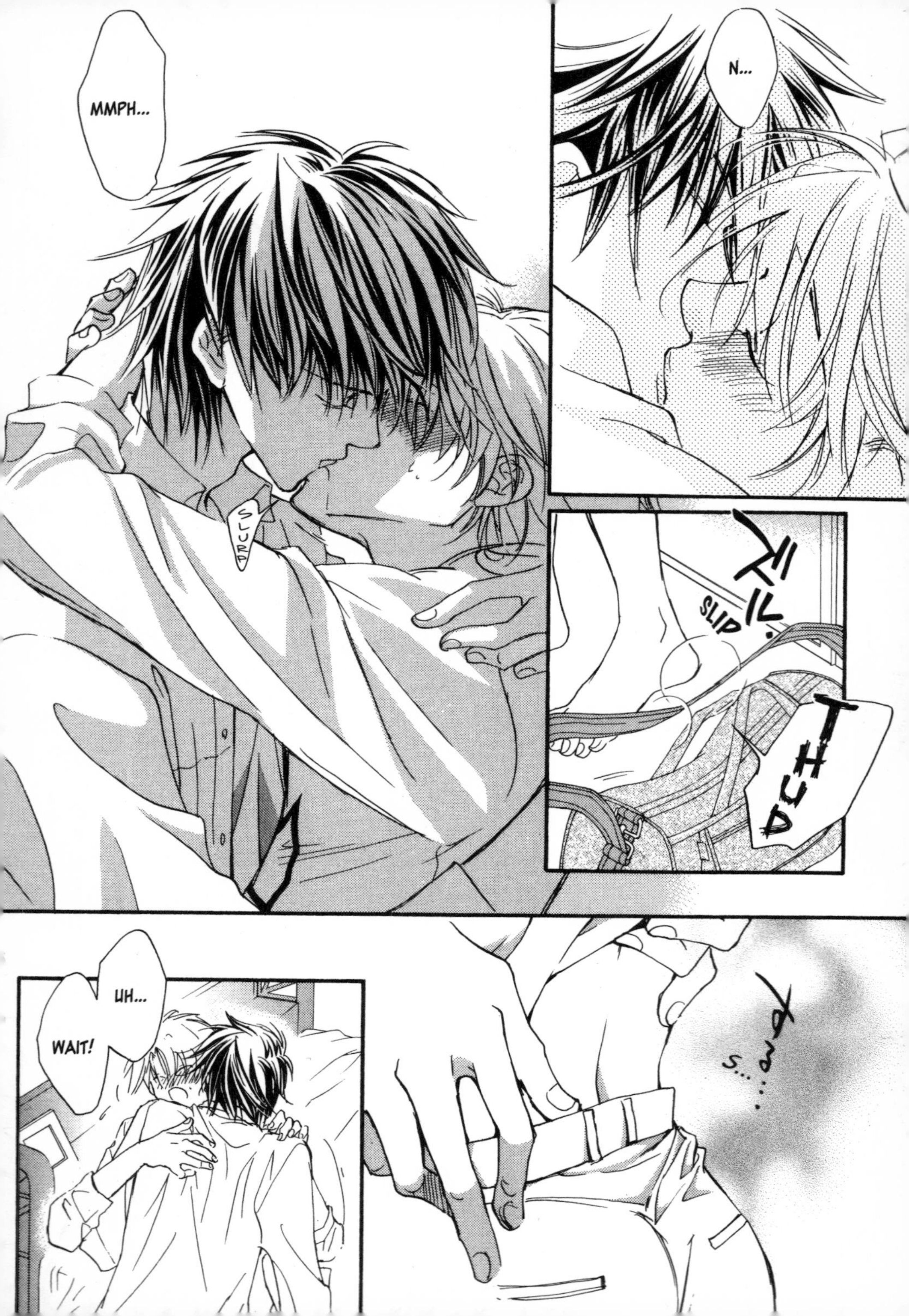
N...
SLIP
THUD
MMPH...
SLURP
UH...
WAIT!

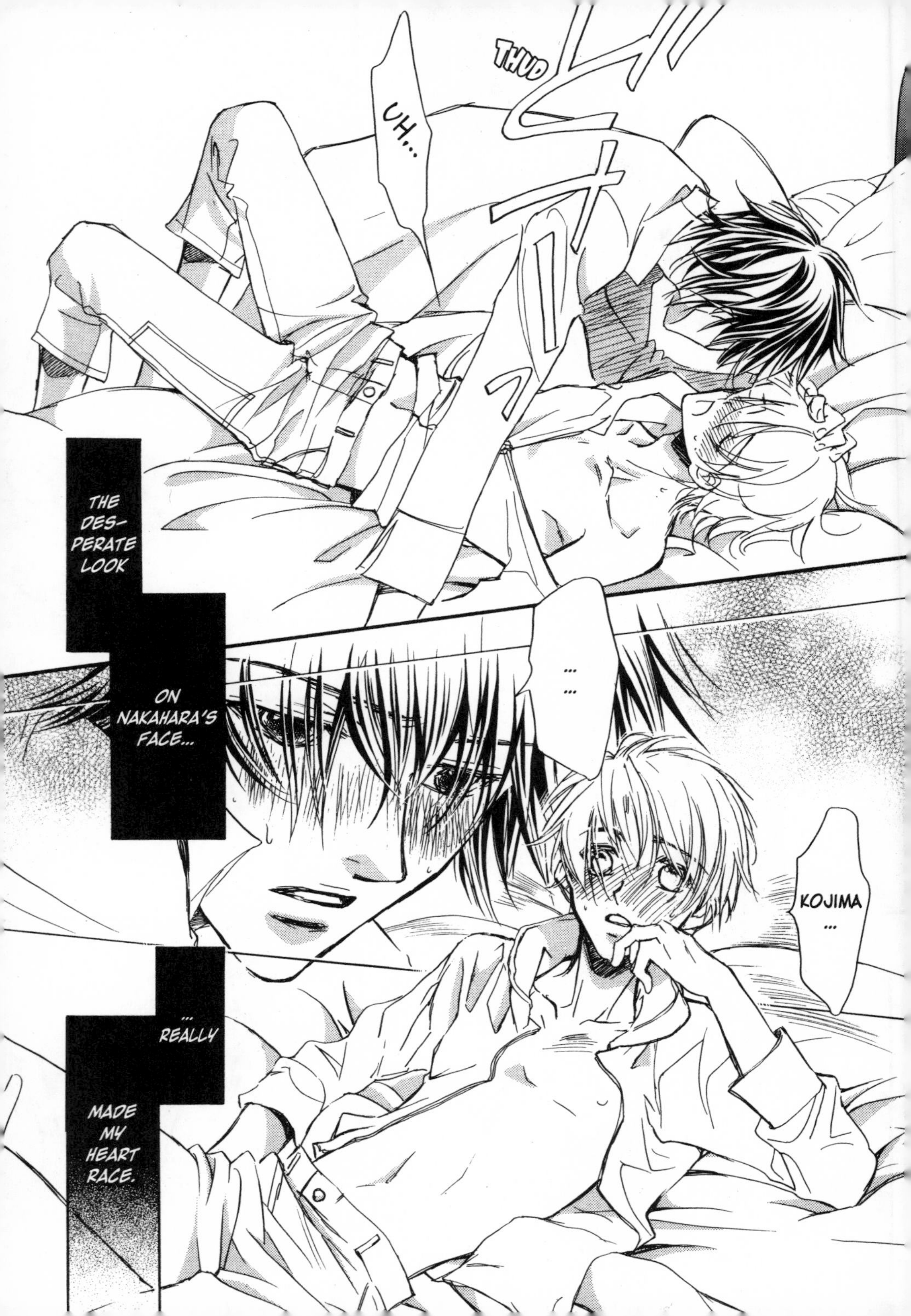
THUD
UH...
THE DES-PERATE LOOK
ON NAKAHARA'S FACE...
......
KOJIMA ...
... REALLY
MADE MY HEART RACE.

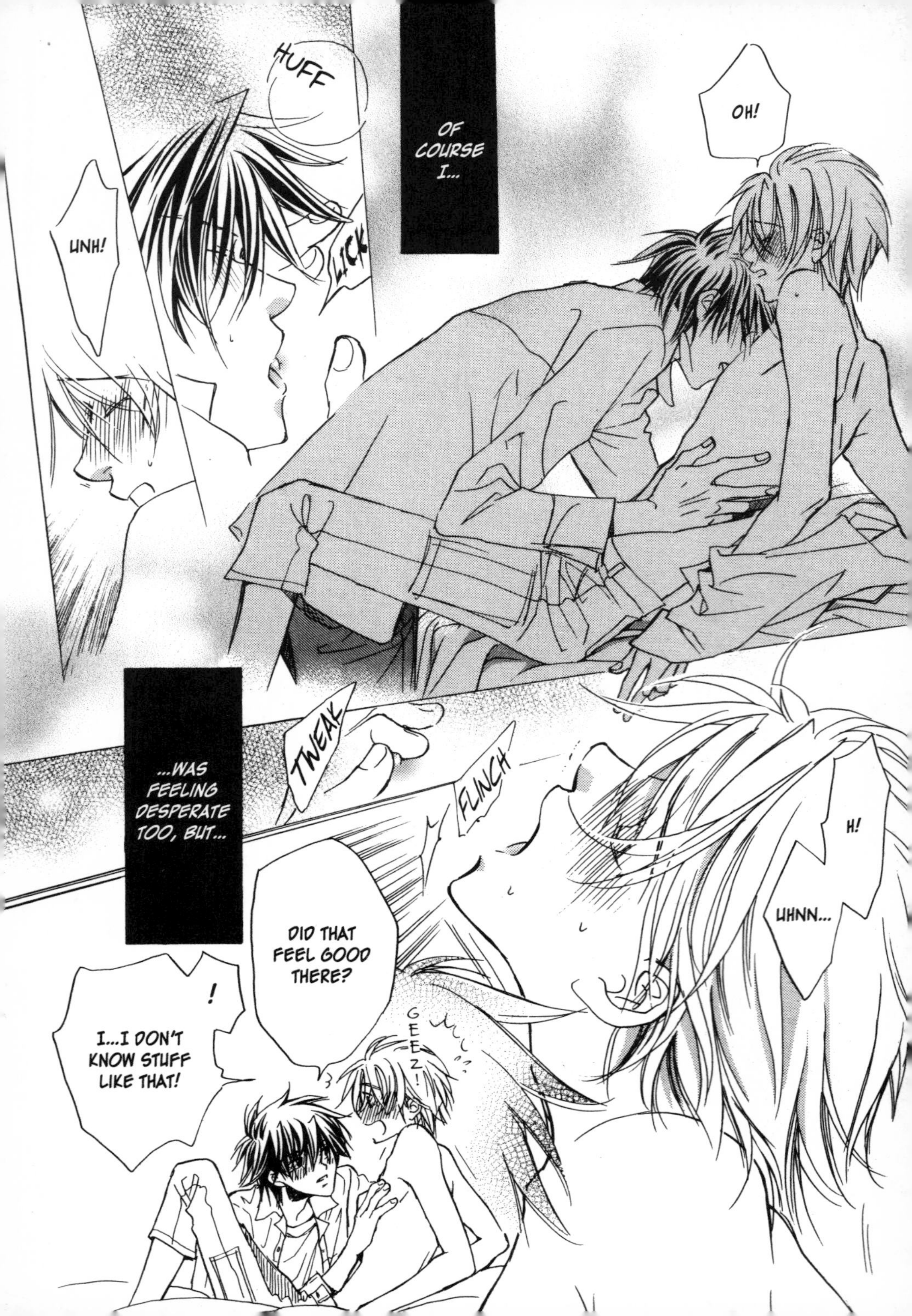
OH!
OF COURSE I...
HUFF
LICK
UNH!
H!
UHNN...
FLINCH
TWEAK
...WAS FEELING DESPERATE TOO, BUT...
DID THAT FEEL GOOD THERE?
!
I...I DON'T KNOW STUFF LIKE THAT!
GEEZ!

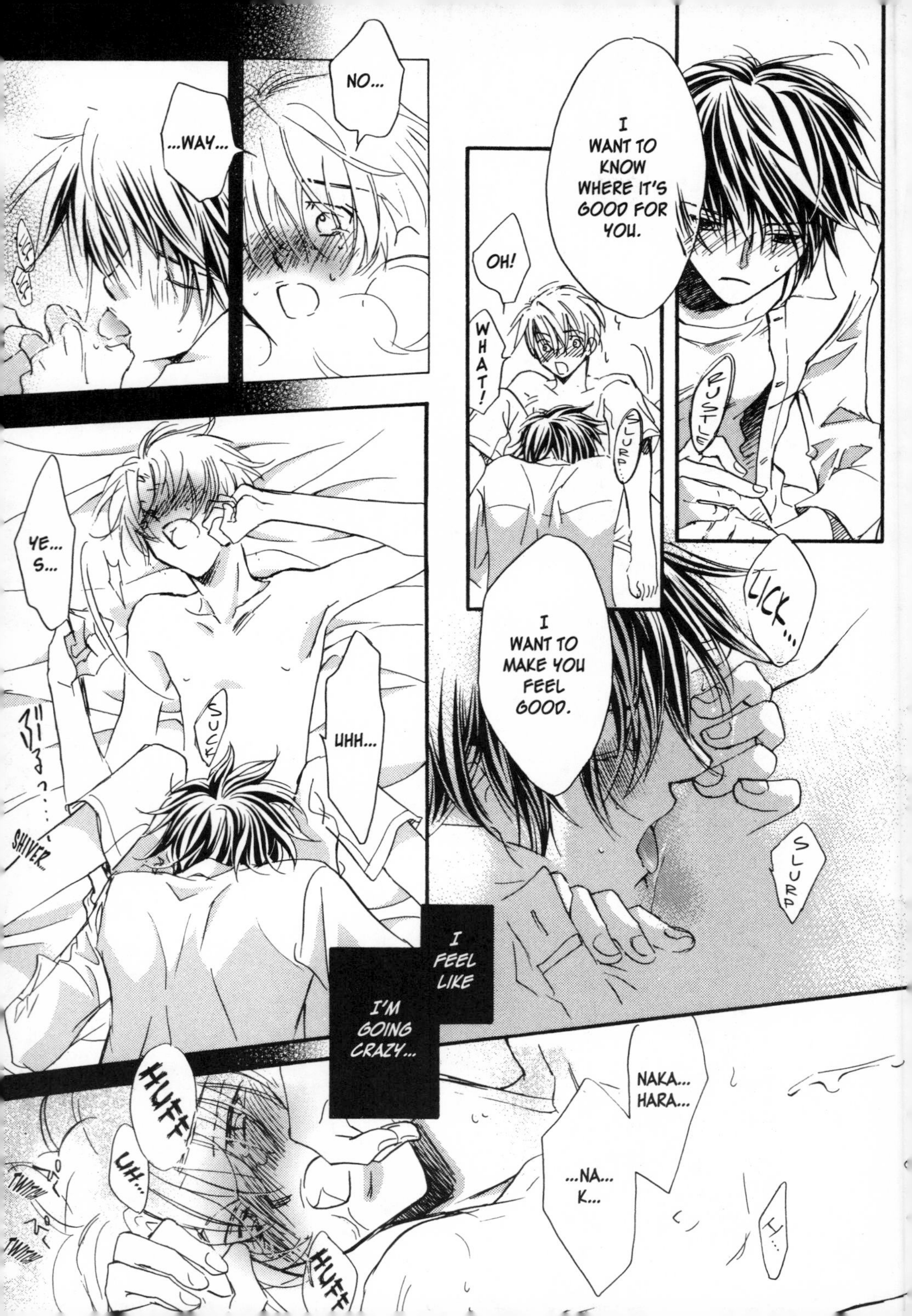
RUSTLE
I WANT TO KNOW WHERE IT'S GOOD FOR YOU.
OH!
WHAT!
SLURP...
NO...
...WAY...
LICK LICK
I WANT TO MAKE YOU FEEL GOOD.
LICK...
SLURP
YE... S...
UHH...
SUCK
SHIVER...
I FEEL LIKE
I'M GOING CRAZY...
NAKA... HARA...
...NA... K...
I...
HUFF
UH...
HUFF
TWITCH
TWITCH

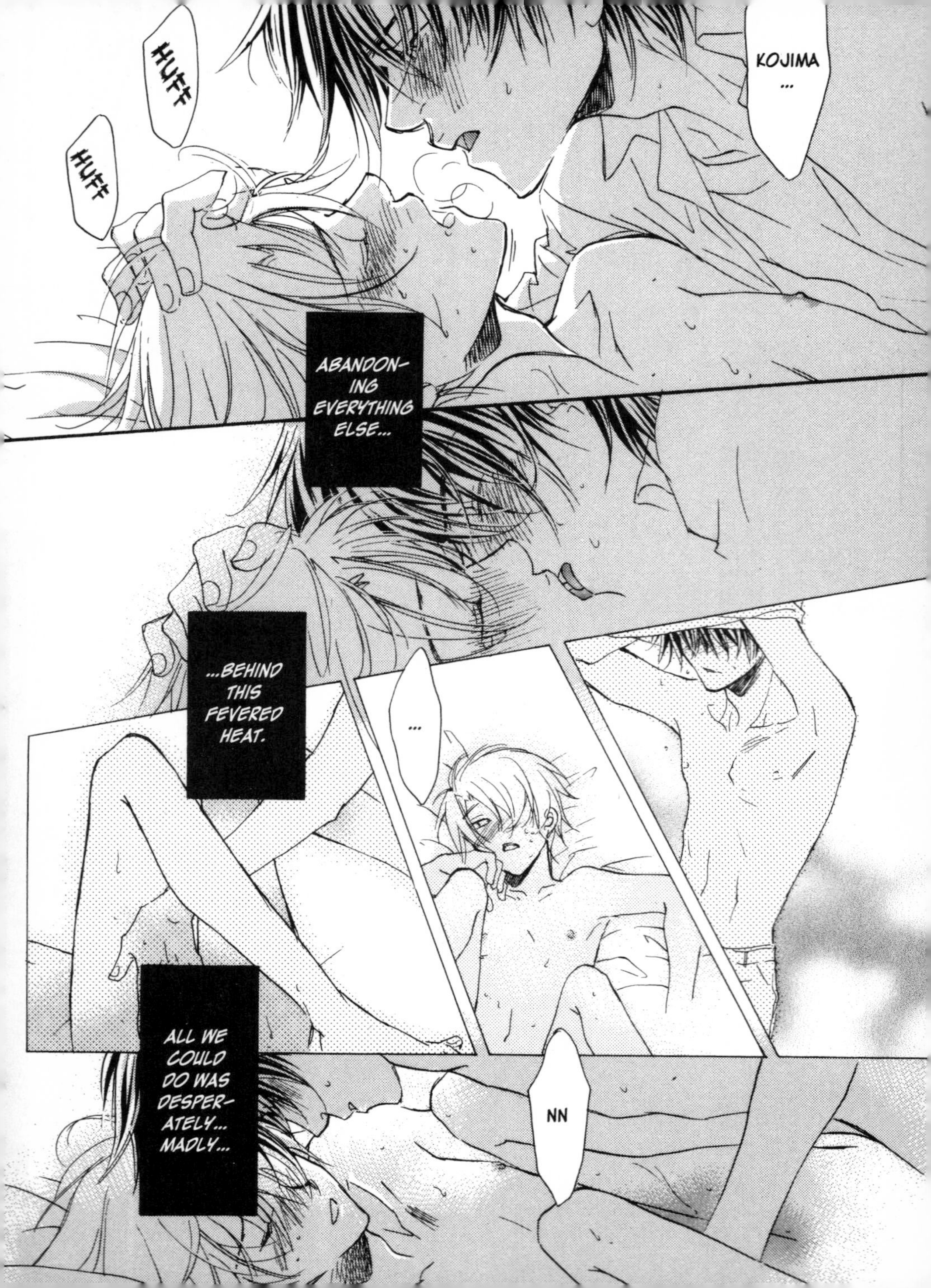
KOJIMA ...
HUFF
HUFF
ABANDON-ING EVERYTHING ELSE...
...BEHIND THIS FEVERED HEAT.
...
NN
ALL WE COULD DO WAS DESPER-ATELY... MADLY...

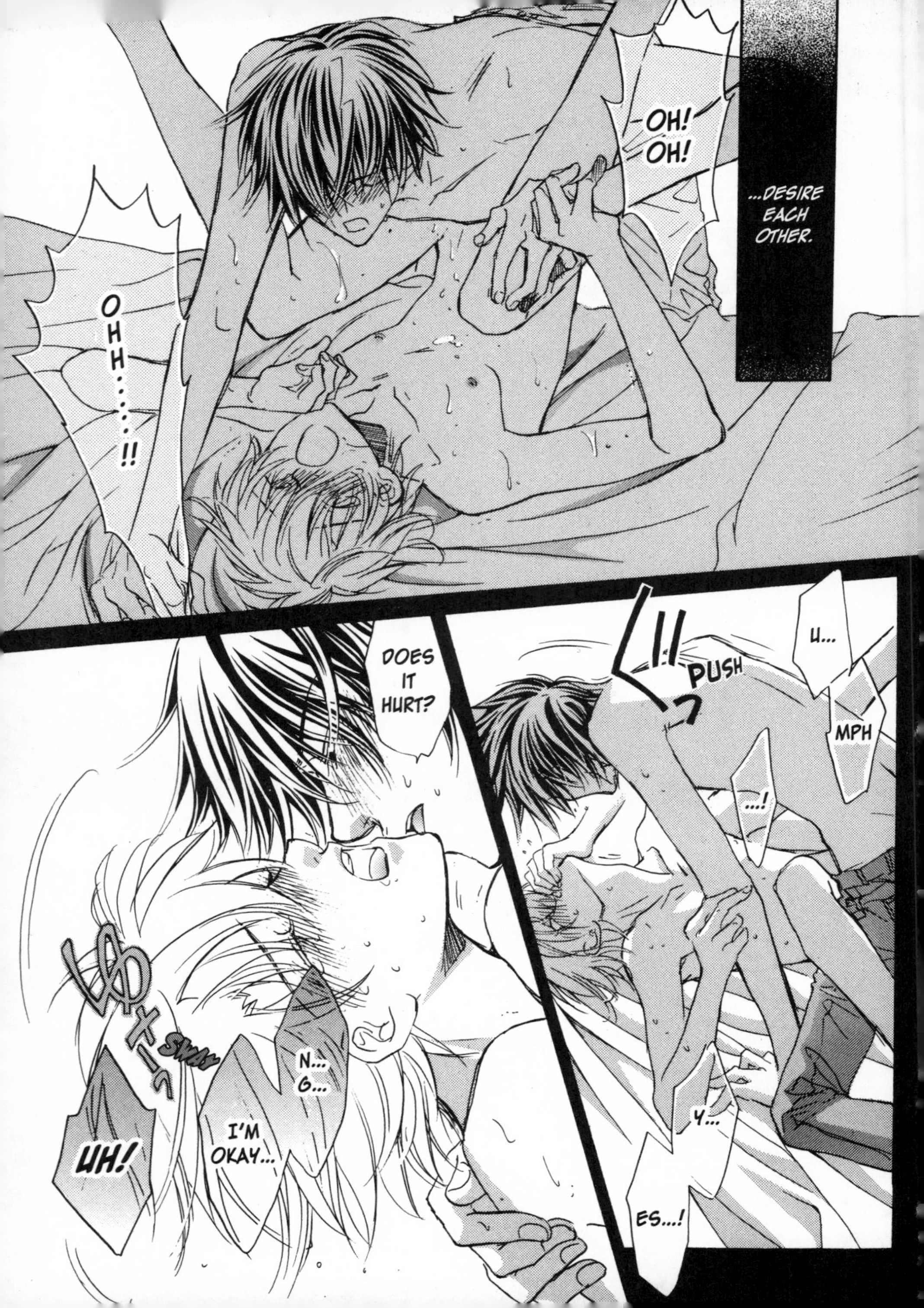
...DESIRE EACH OTHER.
OH! OH!
OHH......!!
U...
PUSH
MPH
...!
Y...
ES...!
DOES IT HURT?
N... G...
SWAY
I'M OKAY...
UH!

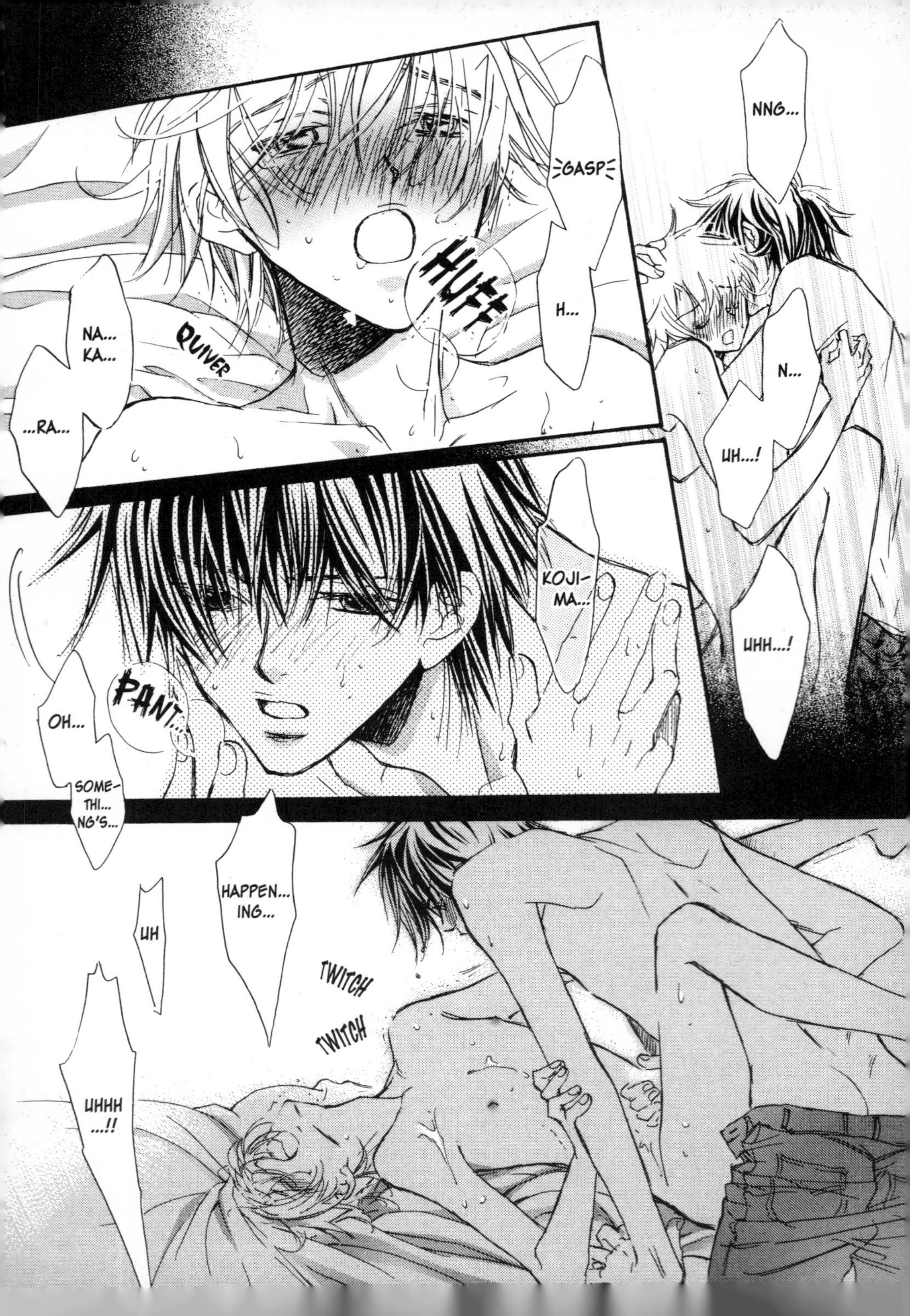
NNG...
N...
UH...!
UHH...!
GASP
H...
HUFF
NA... KA...
QUIVER
...RA...
KOJI-MA...
PANT...
OH...
SOME-THI... NG'S...
HAPPEN... ING...
UH
TWITCH
TWITCH
UHHH ...!!

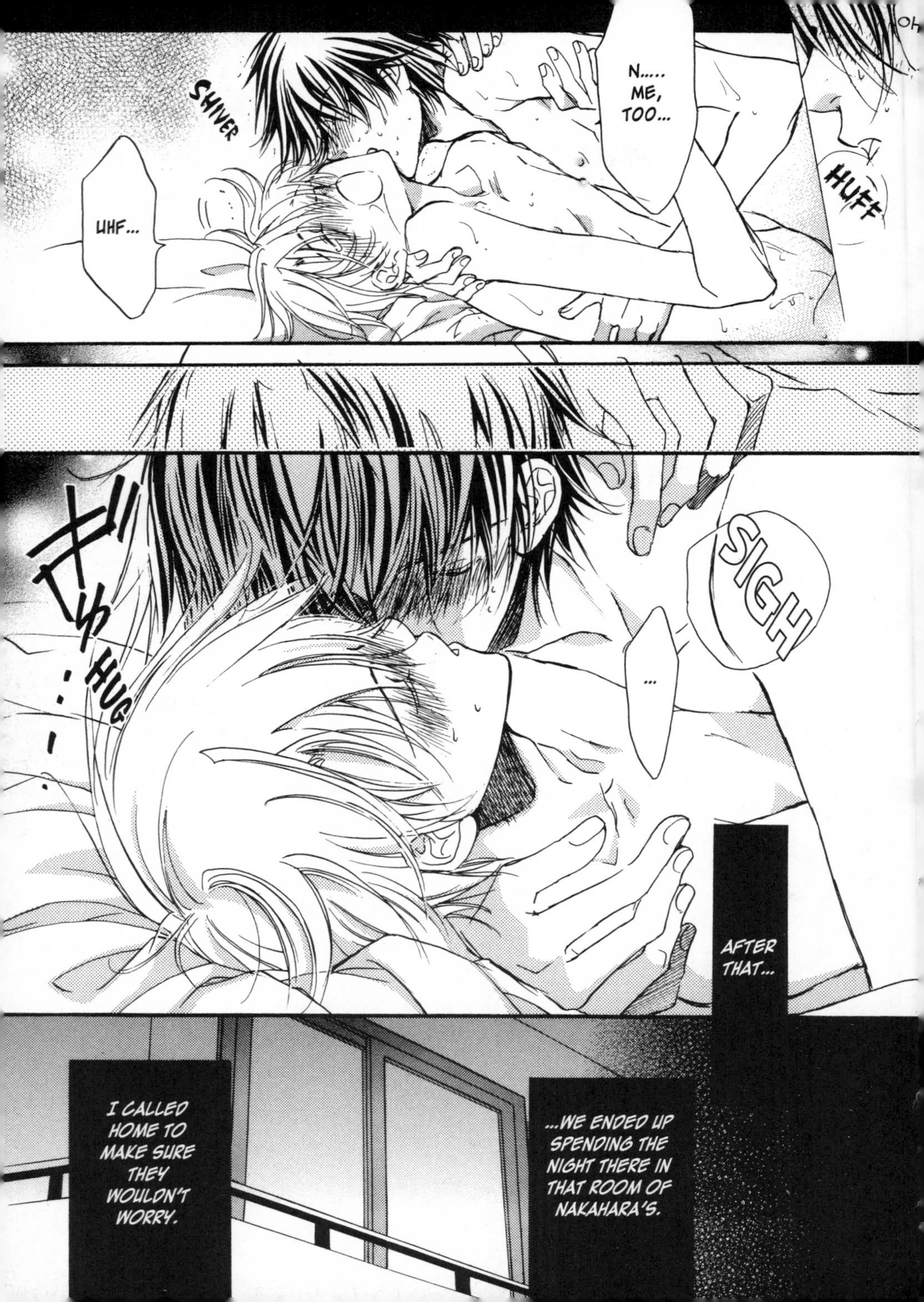
OH
HUFF
N..... ME, TOO...
SHIVER
UHF...
SIGH
...
HUG
AFTER THAT...
...WE ENDED UP SPENDING THE NIGHT THERE IN THAT ROOM OF NAKAHARA'S.
I CALLED HOME TO MAKE SURE THEY WOULDN'T WORRY.

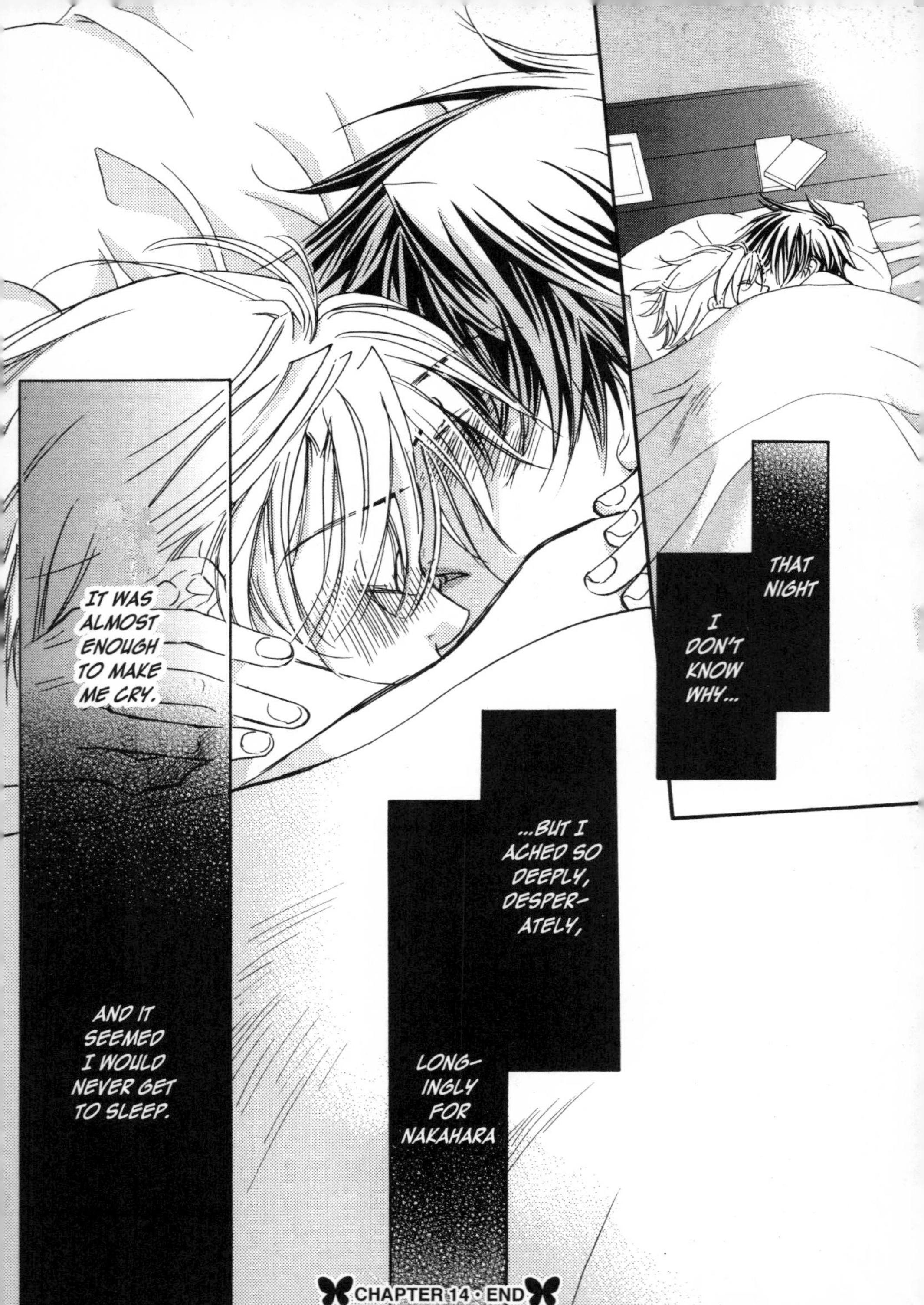
THAT NIGHT
I DON'T KNOW WHY...
...BUT I ACHED SO DEEPLY, DESPER-ATELY,
LONG-INGLY FOR NAKAHARA
IT WAS ALMOST ENOUGH TO MAKE ME CRY.
AND IT SEEMED I WOULD NEVER GET TO SLEEP.

CHAPTER 14 • END

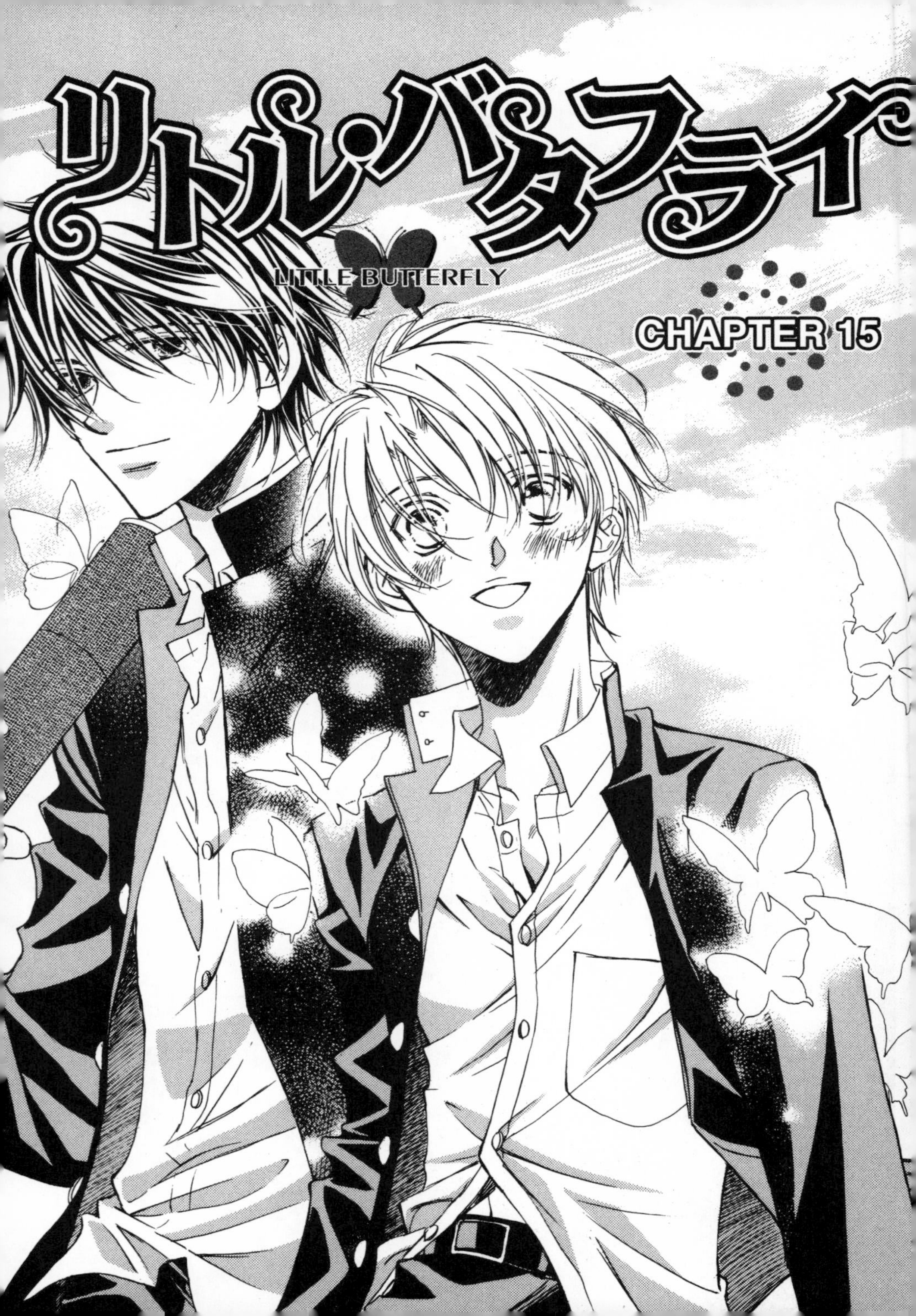
リトル・バタフライ
LITTLE BUTTERFLY
CHAPTER 15

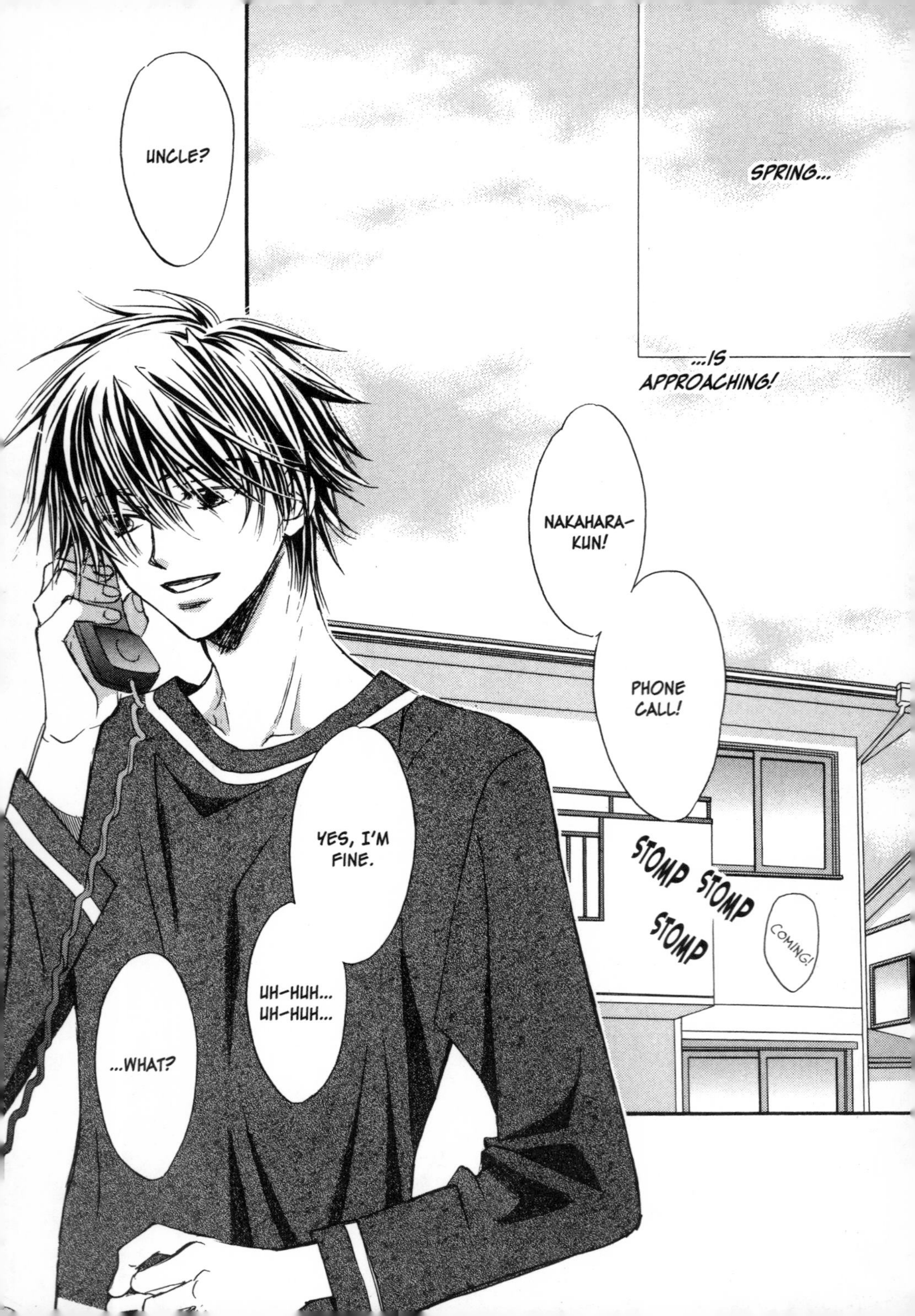
SPRING...
...IS APPROACHING!
NAKAHARA-KUN!
PHONE CALL!
STOMP STOMP STOMP
COMING!
YES, I'M FINE.
UH-HUH... UH-HUH...
...WHAT?
UNCLE?

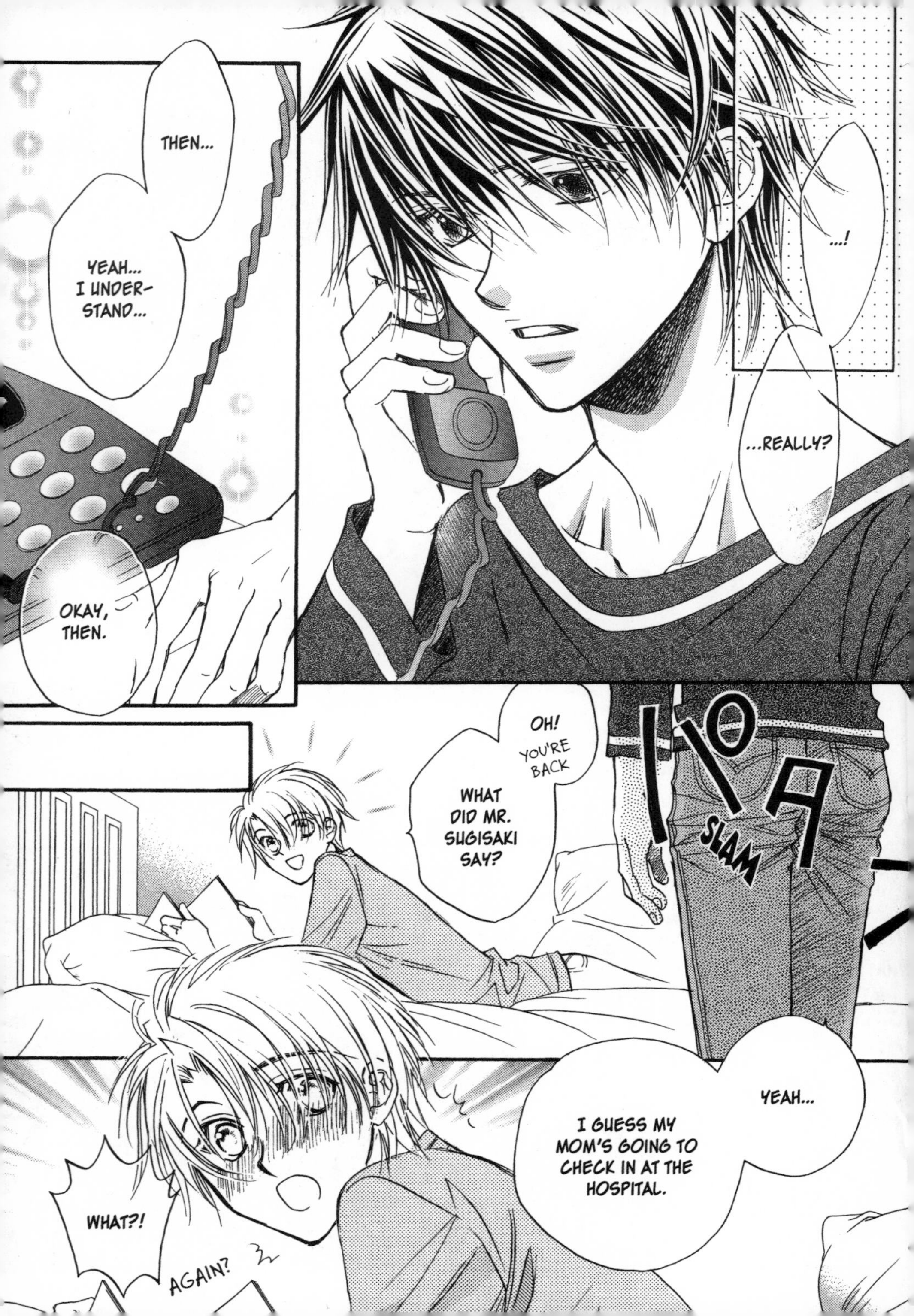
...!
...REALLY?
THEN...
YEAH... I UNDER-STAND...
OKAY, THEN.
SLAM
OH! YOU'RE BACK
WHAT DID MR. SUGISAKI SAY?
YEAH...
I GUESS MY MOM'S GOING TO CHECK IN AT THE HOSPITAL.
WHAT?!
AGAIN?

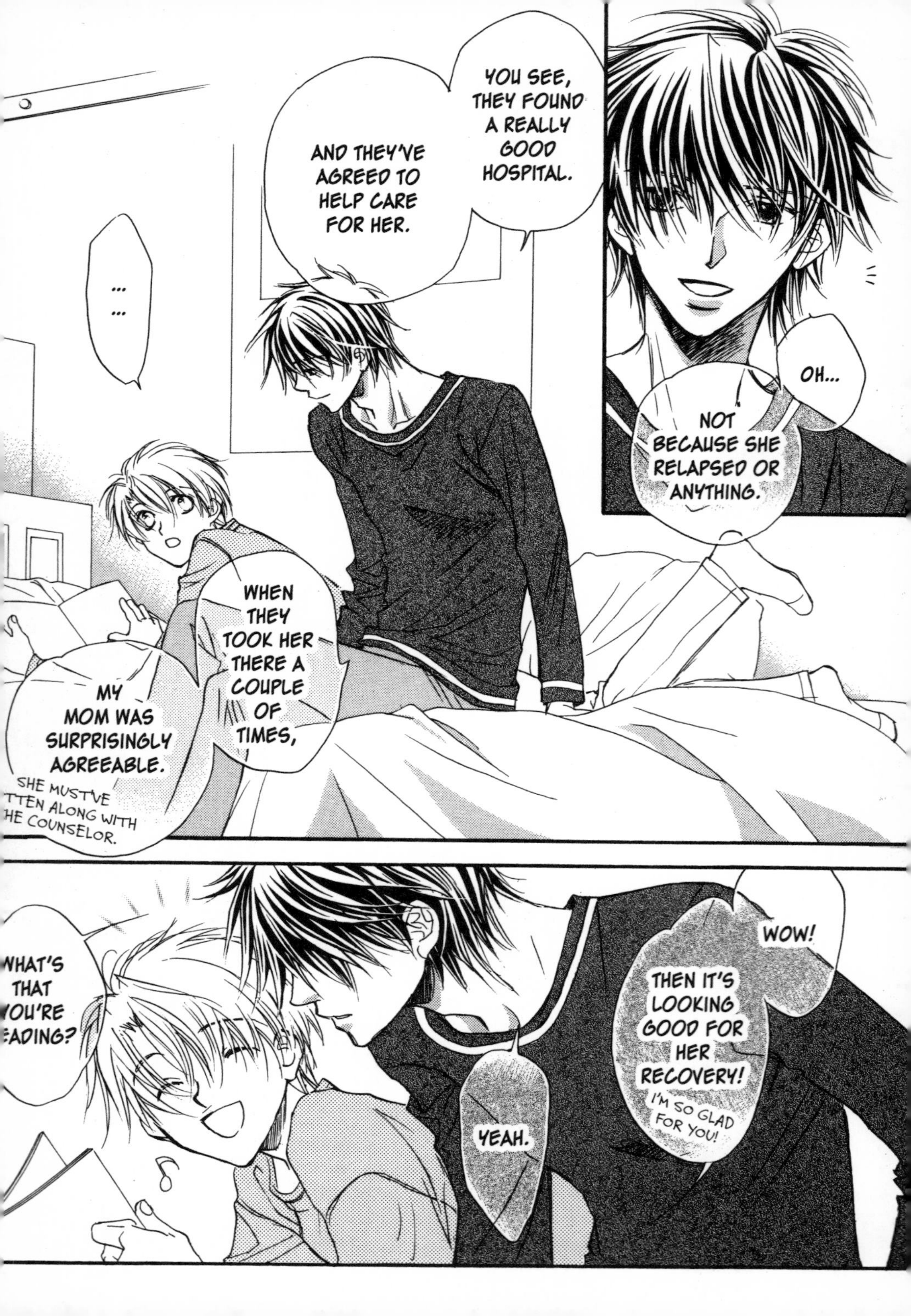
OH...
NOT BECAUSE SHE RELAPSED OR ANYTHING.
YOU SEE, THEY FOUND A REALLY GOOD HOSPITAL.
AND THEY'VE AGREED TO HELP CARE FOR HER.
... ...
WHEN THEY TOOK HER THERE A COUPLE OF TIMES,
MY MOM WAS SURPRISINGLY AGREEABLE.
SHE MUST'VE TTEN ALONG WITH HE COUNSELOR.
WOW!
THEN IT'S LOOKING GOOD FOR HER RECOVERY!
I'M SO GLAD FOR YOU!
YEAH.
WHAT'S THAT OU'RE EADING?

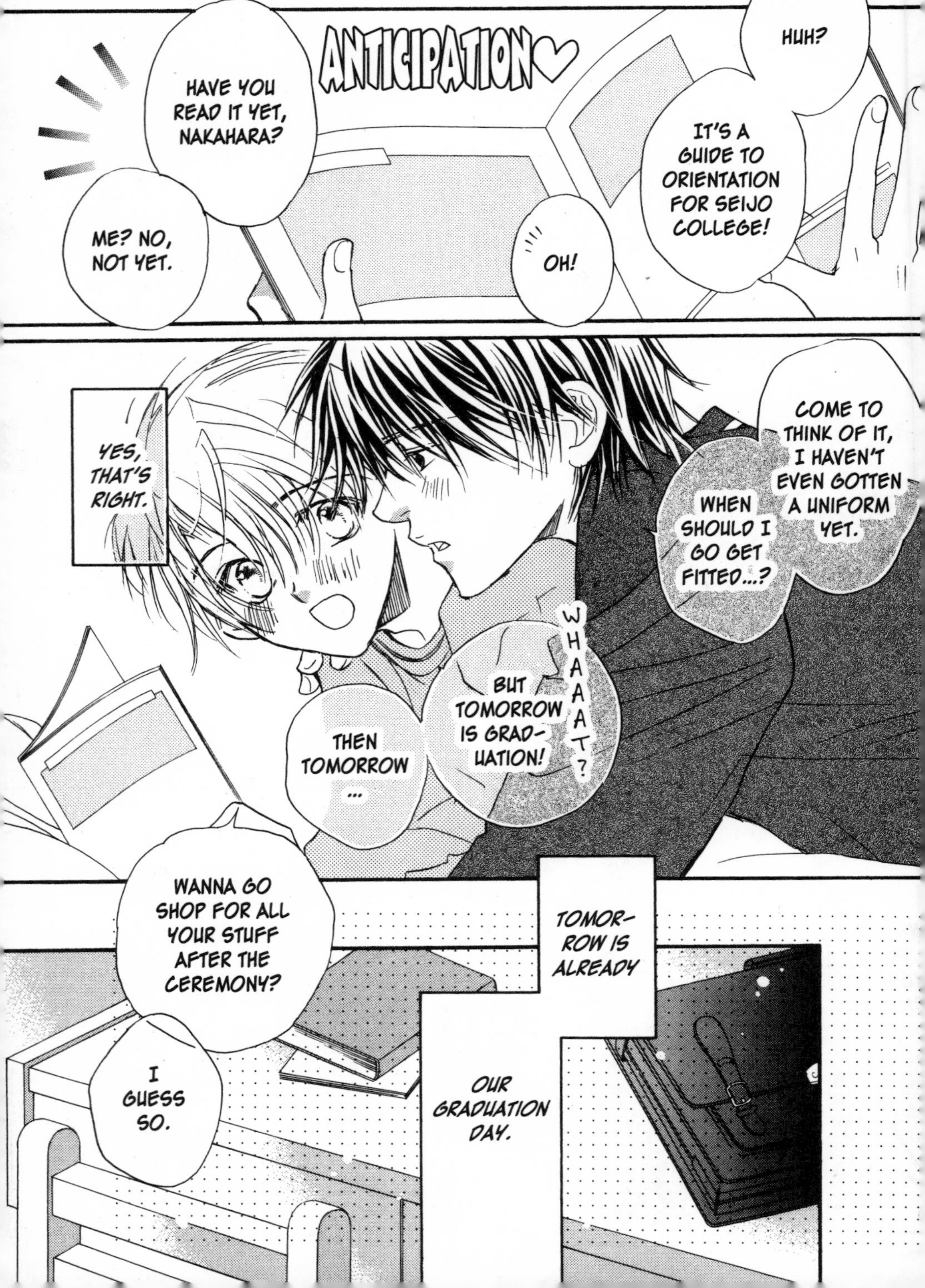
ANTICIPATION♥
HUH?
IT'S A GUIDE TO ORIENTATION FOR SEIJO COLLEGE!
OH!
HAVE YOU READ IT YET, NAKAHARA?
ME? NO, NOT YET.
COME TO THINK OF IT, I HAVEN'T EVEN GOTTEN A UNIFORM YET.
WHEN SHOULD I GO GET FITTED...?
YES, THAT'S RIGHT.
WHAAAAT?
BUT TOMORROW IS GRAD-UATION!
THEN TOMORROW ...
TOMOR-ROW IS ALREADY
OUR GRADUATION DAY.
WANNA GO SHOP FOR ALL YOUR STUFF AFTER THE CEREMONY?
I GUESS SO.

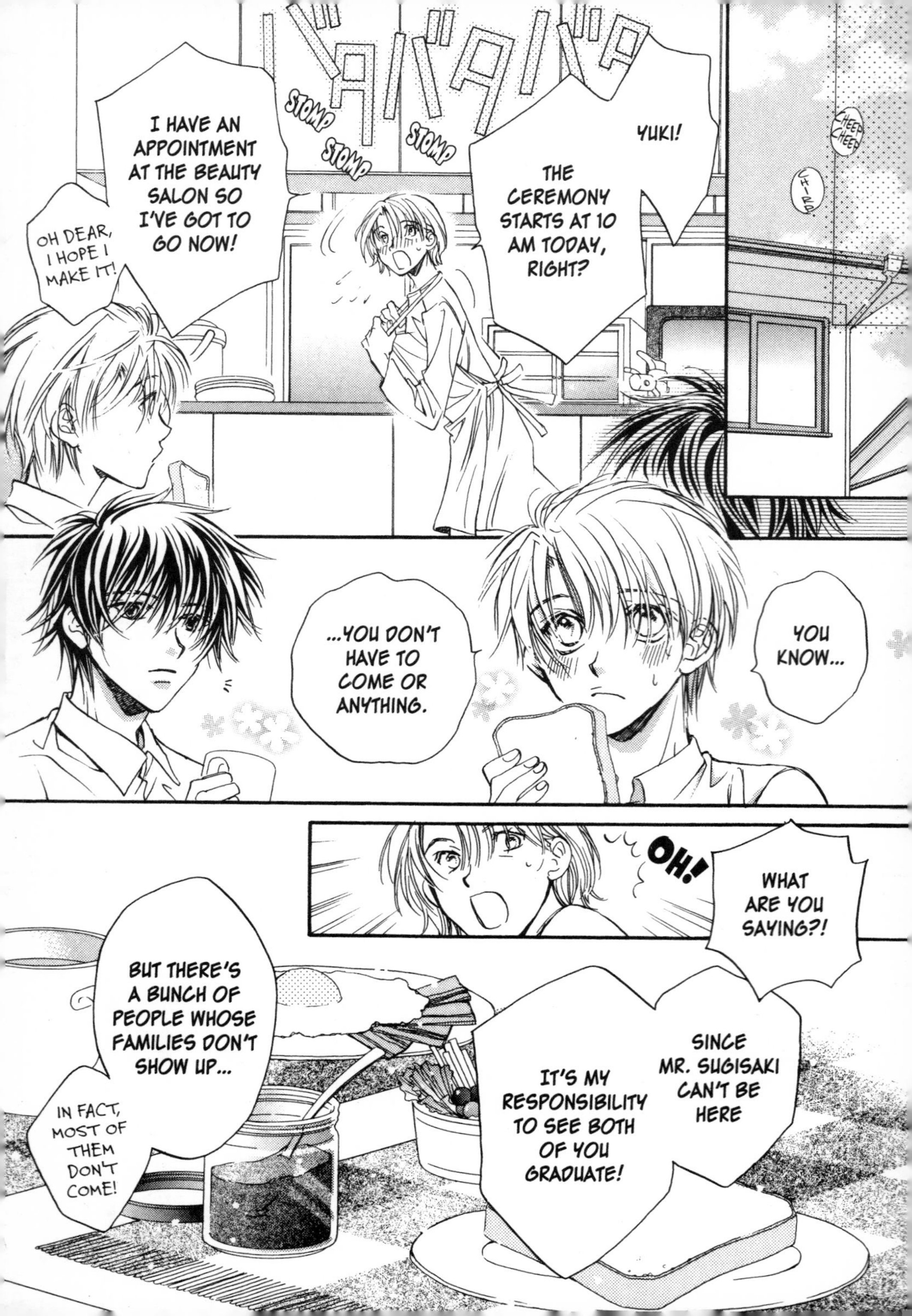
YUKI!
THE CEREMONY STARTS AT 10 AM TODAY, RIGHT?
CHEEP CHEEP
CHIRP
STOMP
STOMP
STOMP
I HAVE AN APPOINTMENT AT THE BEAUTY SALON SO I'VE GOT TO GO NOW!
OH DEAR, I HOPE I MAKE IT!
YOU KNOW...
...YOU DON'T HAVE TO COME OR ANYTHING.
OH!
WHAT ARE YOU SAYING?!
SINCE MR. SUGISAKI CAN'T BE HERE
IT'S MY RESPONSIBILITY TO SEE BOTH OF YOU GRADUATE!
BUT THERE'S A BUNCH OF PEOPLE WHOSE FAMILIES DON'T SHOW UP...
IN FACT, MOST OF THEM DON'T COME!

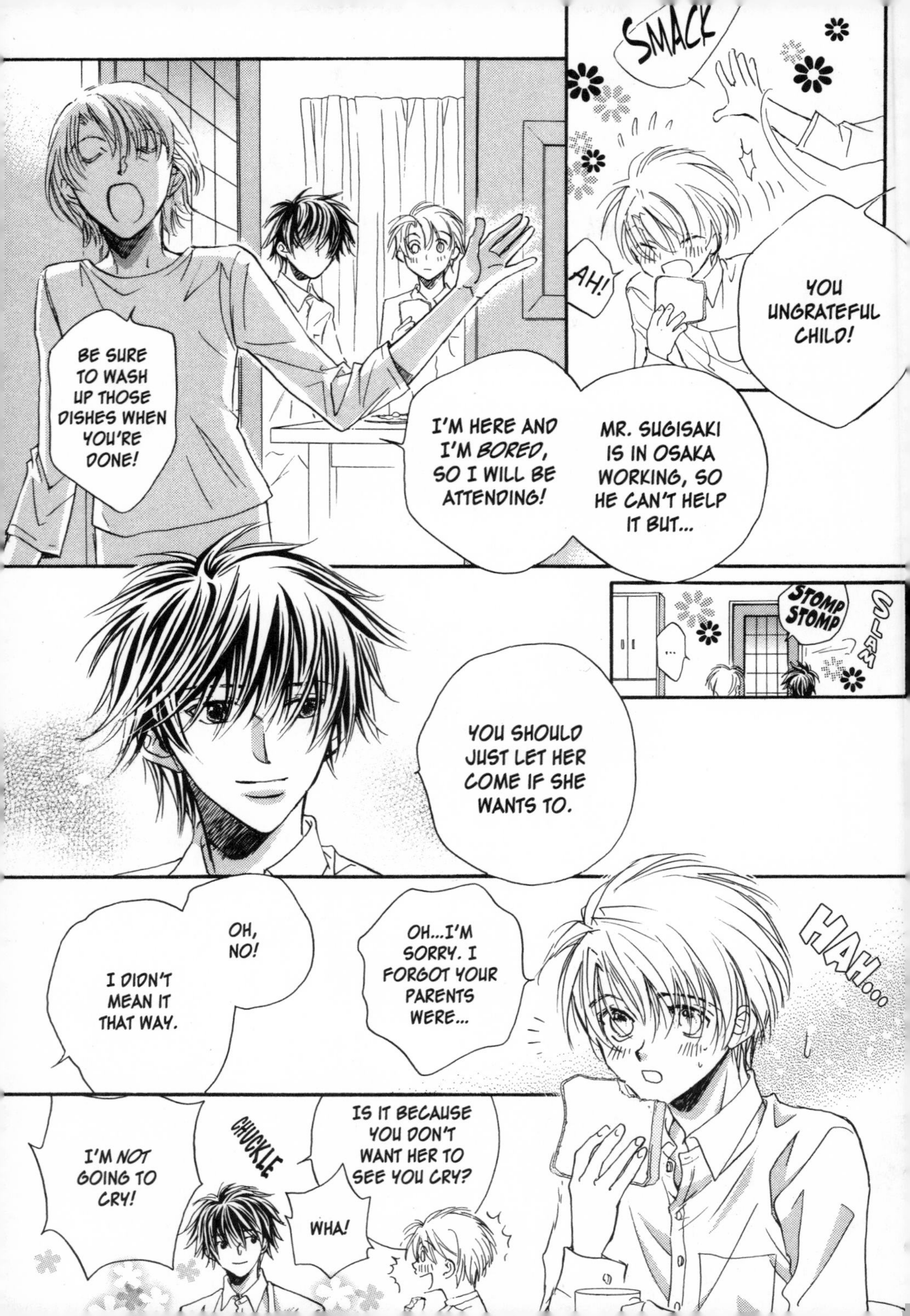
SMACK
AH!
YOU UNGRATEFUL CHILD!
MR. SUGISAKI IS IN OSAKA WORKING, SO HE CAN'T HELP IT BUT...
I'M HERE AND I'M *BORED*, SO I WILL BE ATTENDING!
BE SURE TO WASH UP THOSE DISHES WHEN YOU'RE DONE!
STOMP STOMP
SLAM
...
YOU SHOULD JUST LET HER COME IF SHE WANTS TO.
HAH...
OH...I'M SORRY. I FORGOT YOUR PARENTS WERE...
OH, NO!
I DIDN'T MEAN IT THAT WAY.
IS IT BECAUSE YOU DON'T WANT HER TO SEE YOU CRY?
CHUCKLE
WHA!
I'M *NOT* GOING TO CRY!

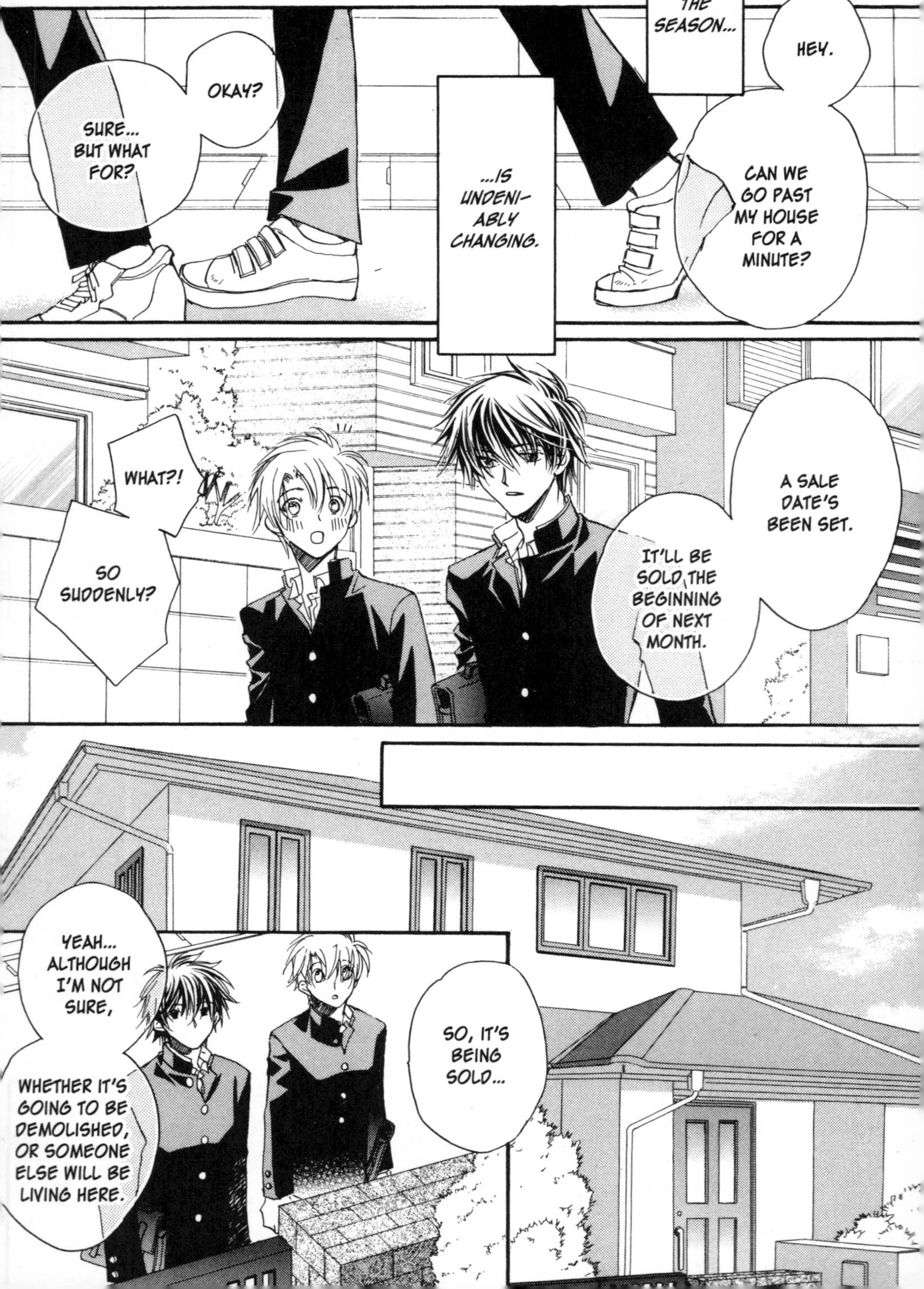
THE SEASON...
HEY.
CAN WE GO PAST MY HOUSE FOR A MINUTE?
...IS UNDENI-ABLY CHANGING.
OKAY?
SURE... BUT WHAT FOR?
A SALE DATE'S BEEN SET.
IT'LL BE SOLD THE BEGINNING OF NEXT MONTH.
WHAT?!
SO SUDDENLY?
SO, IT'S BEING SOLD...
YEAH... ALTHOUGH I'M NOT SURE,
WHETHER IT'S GOING TO BE DEMOLISHED, OR SOMEONE ELSE WILL BE LIVING HERE.

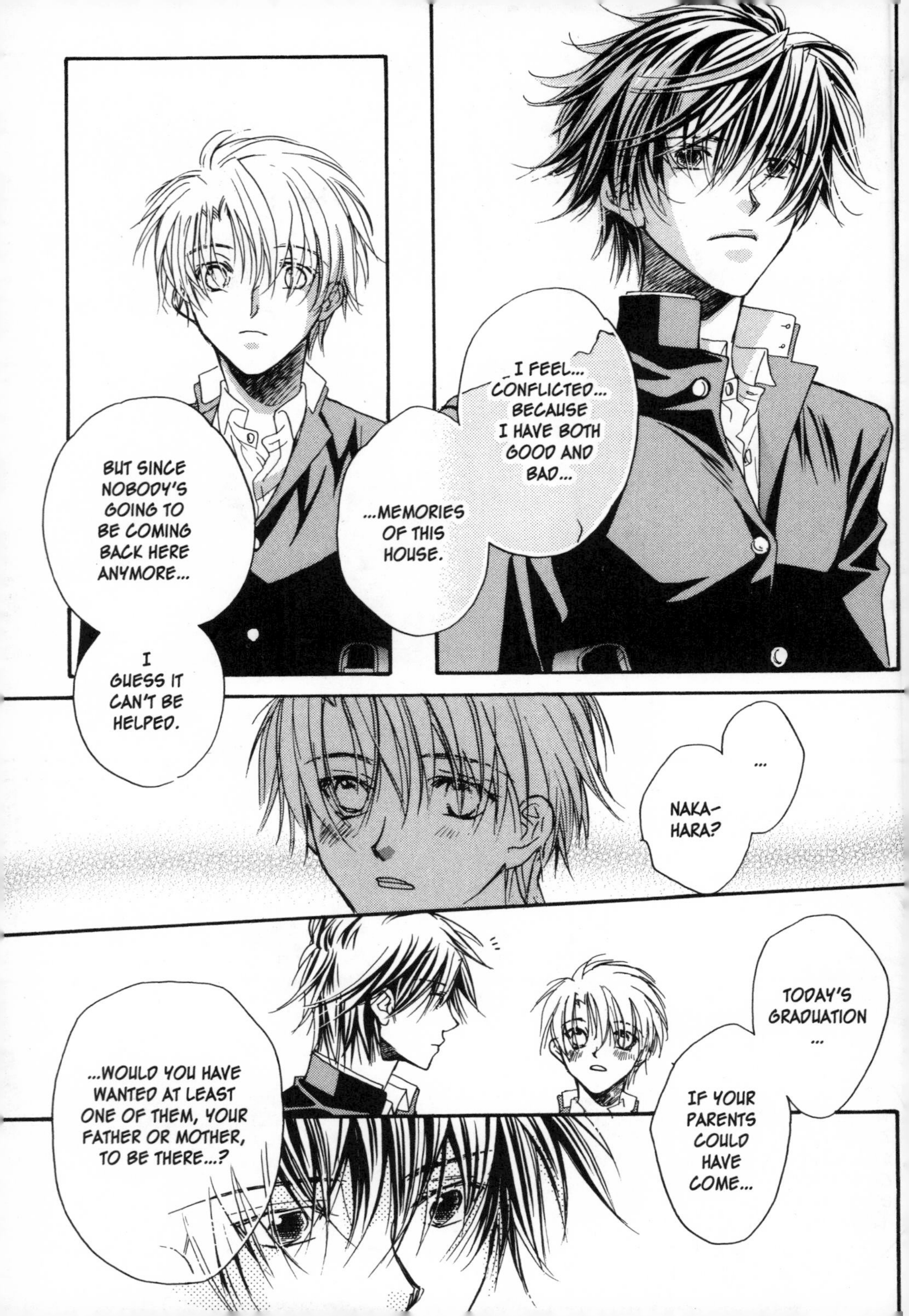
I FEEL... CONFLICTED... BECAUSE I HAVE BOTH GOOD AND BAD...
...MEMORIES OF THIS HOUSE.
BUT SINCE NOBODY'S GOING TO BE COMING BACK HERE ANYMORE...
I GUESS IT CAN'T BE HELPED.
...
NAKA-HARA?
TODAY'S GRADUATION ...
IF YOUR PARENTS COULD HAVE COME...
...WOULD YOU HAVE WANTED AT LEAST ONE OF THEM, YOUR FATHER OR MOTHER, TO BE THERE...?

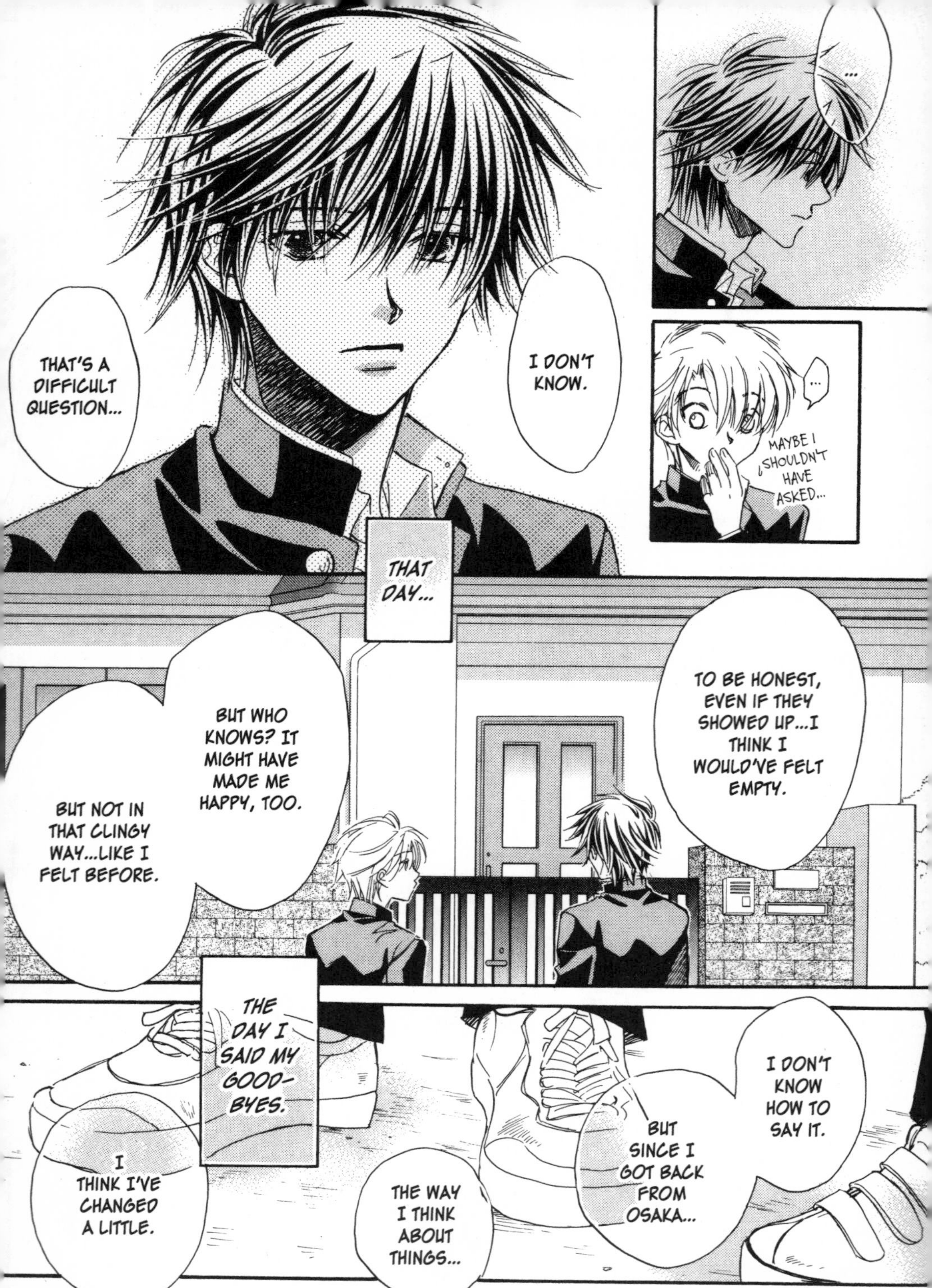
...
...
MAYBE I SHOULDN'T HAVE ASKED...
I DON'T KNOW.
THAT'S A DIFFICULT QUESTION...
THAT DAY...
TO BE HONEST, EVEN IF THEY SHOWED UP...I THINK I WOULD'VE FELT EMPTY.
BUT WHO KNOWS? IT MIGHT HAVE MADE ME HAPPY, TOO.
BUT NOT IN THAT CLINGY WAY...LIKE I FELT BEFORE.
THE DAY I SAID MY GOOD-BYES.
I DON'T KNOW HOW TO SAY IT.
BUT SINCE I GOT BACK FROM OSAKA...
THE WAY I THINK ABOUT THINGS...
I THINK I'VE CHANGED A LITTLE.

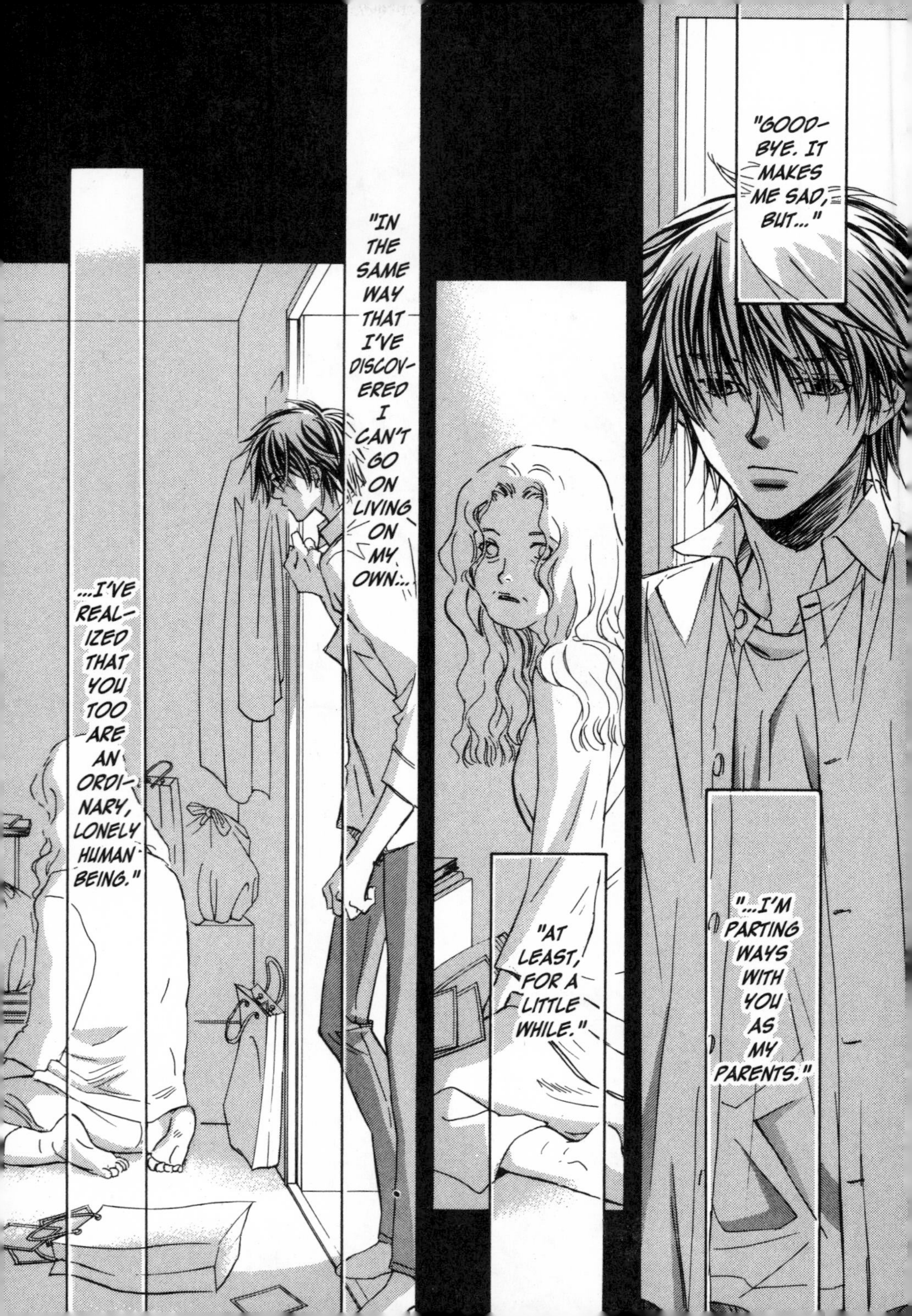
"GOOD-BYE. IT MAKES ME SAD, BUT..."
"...I'M PARTING WAYS WITH YOU AS MY PARENTS."
"AT LEAST, FOR A LITTLE WHILE."
"IN THE SAME WAY THAT I'VE DISCOVERED I CAN'T GO ON LIVING ON MY OWN...
...I'VE REALIZED THAT YOU TOO ARE AN ORDINARY, LONELY HUMAN BEING."

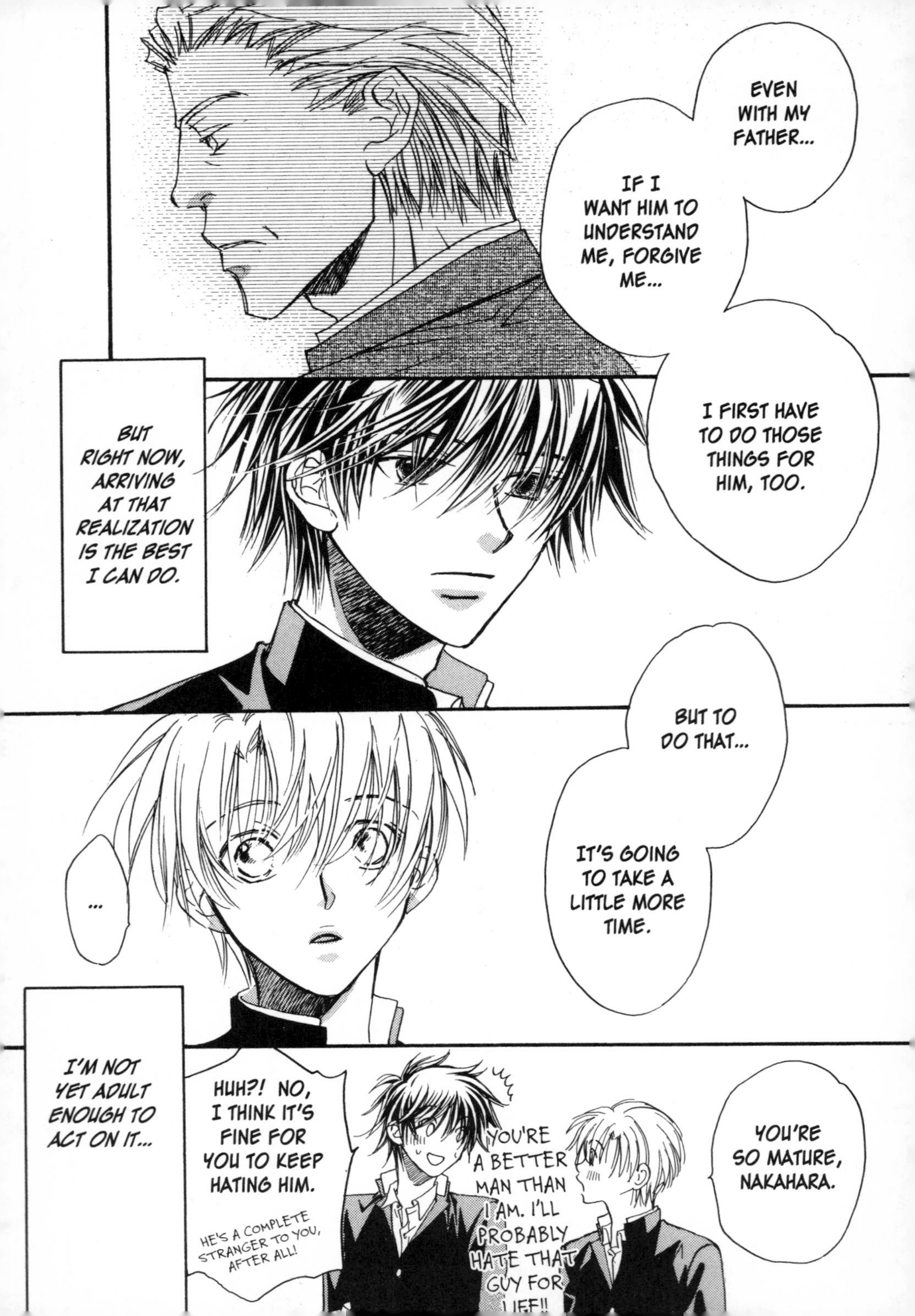
EVEN WITH MY FATHER...
IF I WANT HIM TO UNDERSTAND ME, FORGIVE ME...
I FIRST HAVE TO DO THOSE THINGS FOR HIM, TOO.
BUT RIGHT NOW, ARRIVING AT THAT REALIZATION IS THE BEST I CAN DO.
BUT TO DO THAT...
IT'S GOING TO TAKE A LITTLE MORE TIME.
...
YOU'RE SO MATURE, NAKAHARA.
YOU'RE A BETTER MAN THAN I AM. I'LL PROBABLY HATE THAT GUY FOR LIFE!!
HUH?! NO, I THINK IT'S FINE FOR YOU TO KEEP HATING HIM.
HE'S A COMPLETE STRANGER TO YOU, AFTER ALL!
I'M NOT YET ADULT ENOUGH TO ACT ON IT...

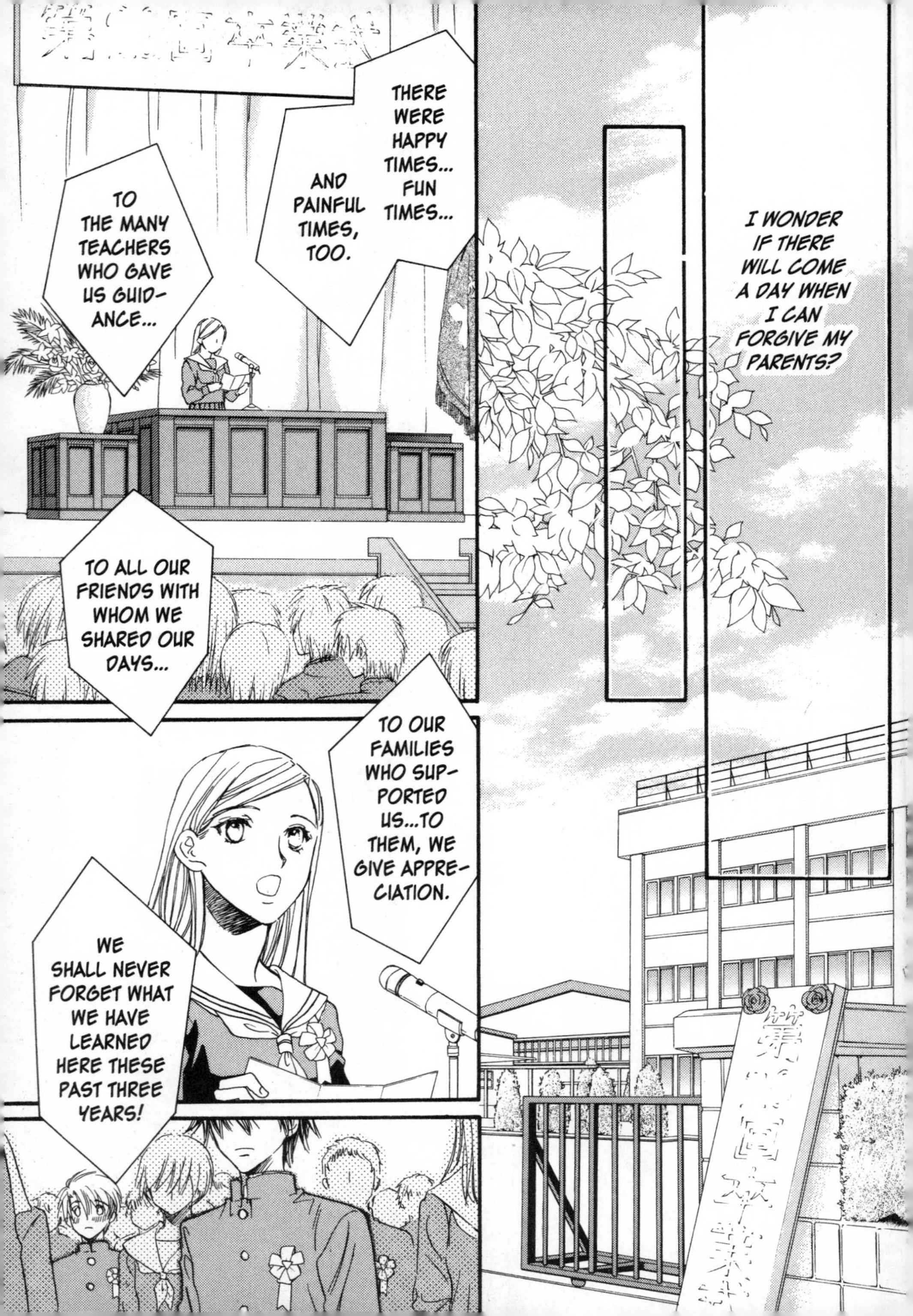
I WONDER IF THERE WILL COME A DAY WHEN I CAN FORGIVE MY PARENTS?
THERE WERE HAPPY TIMES... FUN TIMES...
AND PAINFUL TIMES, TOO.
TO THE MANY TEACHERS WHO GAVE US GUID-ANCE...
TO ALL OUR FRIENDS WITH WHOM WE SHARED OUR DAYS...
TO OUR FAMILIES WHO SUP-PORTED US...TO THEM, WE GIVE APPRE-CIATION.
WE SHALL NEVER FORGET WHAT WE HAVE LEARNED HERE THESE PAST THREE YEARS!

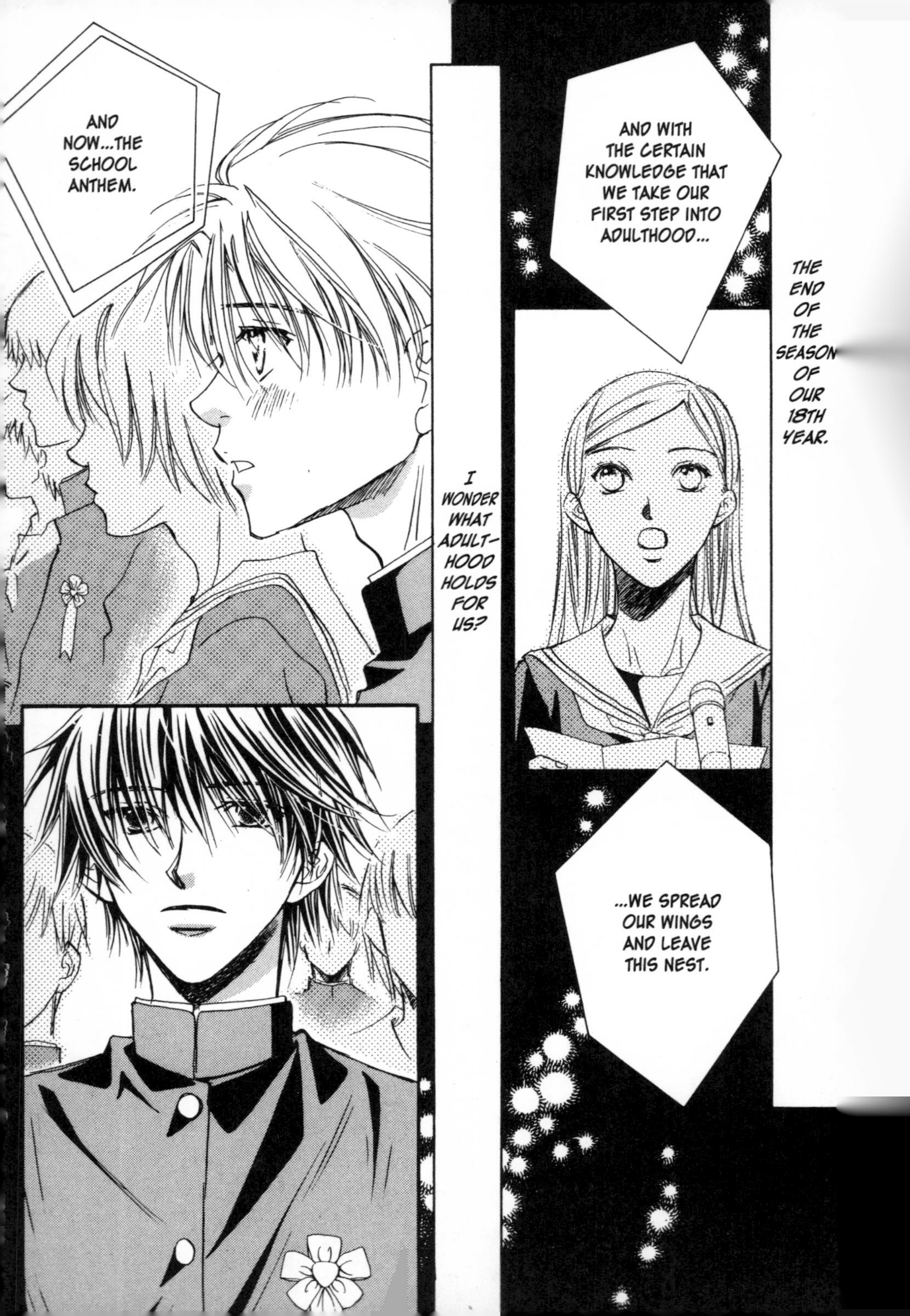
AND WITH THE CERTAIN KNOWLEDGE THAT WE TAKE OUR FIRST STEP INTO ADULTHOOD...
THE END OF THE SEASON OF OUR 18TH YEAR.
...WE SPREAD OUR WINGS AND LEAVE THIS NEST.
I WONDER WHAT ADULT-HOOD HOLDS FOR US?
AND NOW...THE SCHOOL ANTHEM.

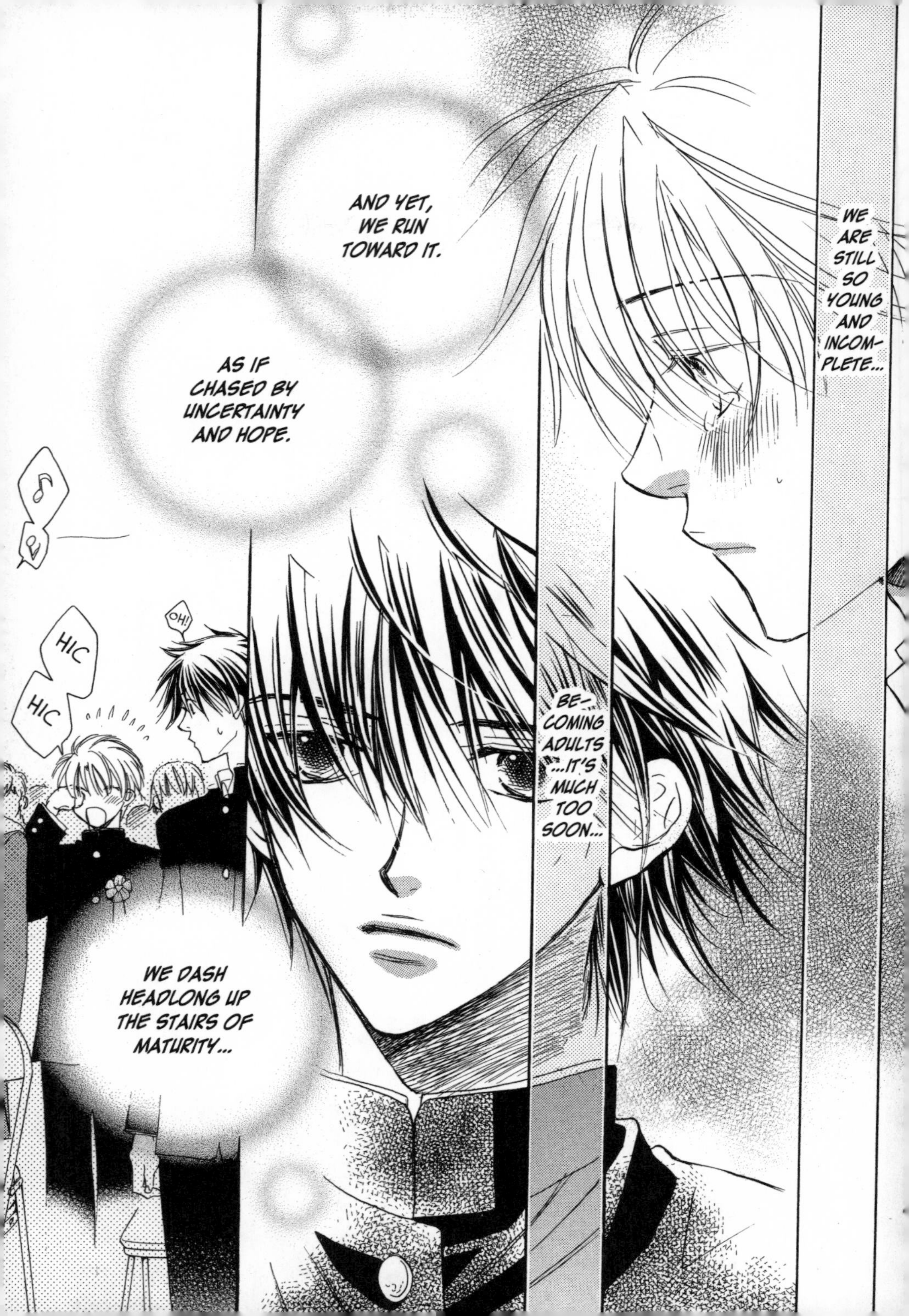
WE ARE STILL SO YOUNG AND INCOMPLETE...
BE-COMING ADULTS ...IT'S MUCH TOO SOON...
AND YET, WE RUN TOWARD IT.
AS IF CHASED BY UNCERTAINTY AND HOPE.
WE DASH HEADLONG UP THE STAIRS OF MATURITY...
OH!
HIC HIC

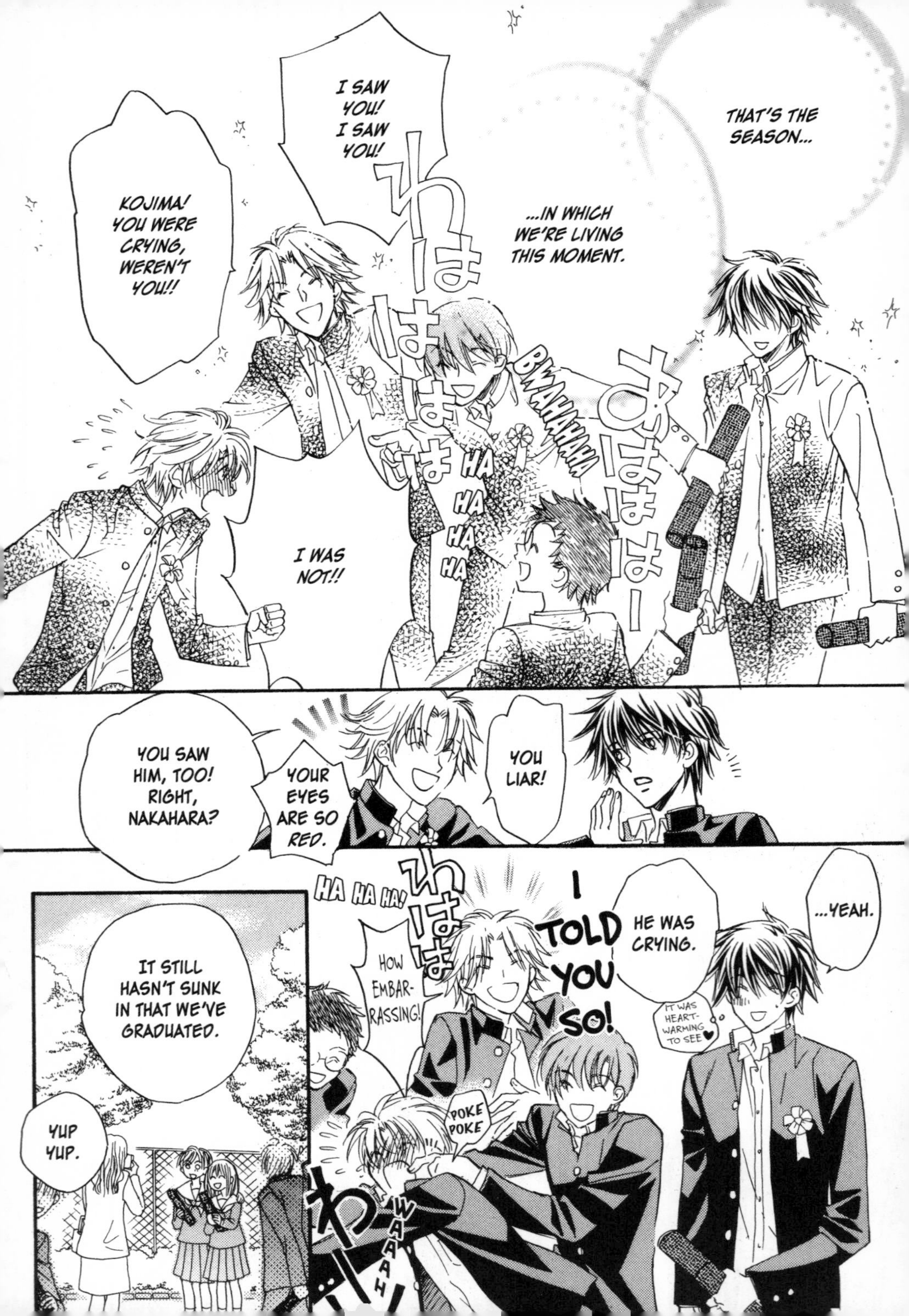
THAT'S THE SEASON...
...IN WHICH WE'RE LIVING THIS MOMENT.
あははははー
BWAHAHAHA
I SAW YOU! I SAW YOU!
わははは
KOJIMA! YOU WERE CRYING, WEREN'T YOU!!
HA HA HA HA
I WAS NOT!!
YOU LIAR!
YOUR EYES ARE SO RED.
YOU SAW HIM, TOO! RIGHT, NAKAHARA?
...YEAH.
HE WAS CRYING.
IT WAS HEART-WARMING TO SEE♥
I TOLD YOU SO!
わはは
HA HA HA!
HOW EMBAR-RASSING!
POKE POKE
わー
WAAAAH
IT STILL HASN'T SUNK IN THAT WE'VE GRADUATED.
YUP YUP.

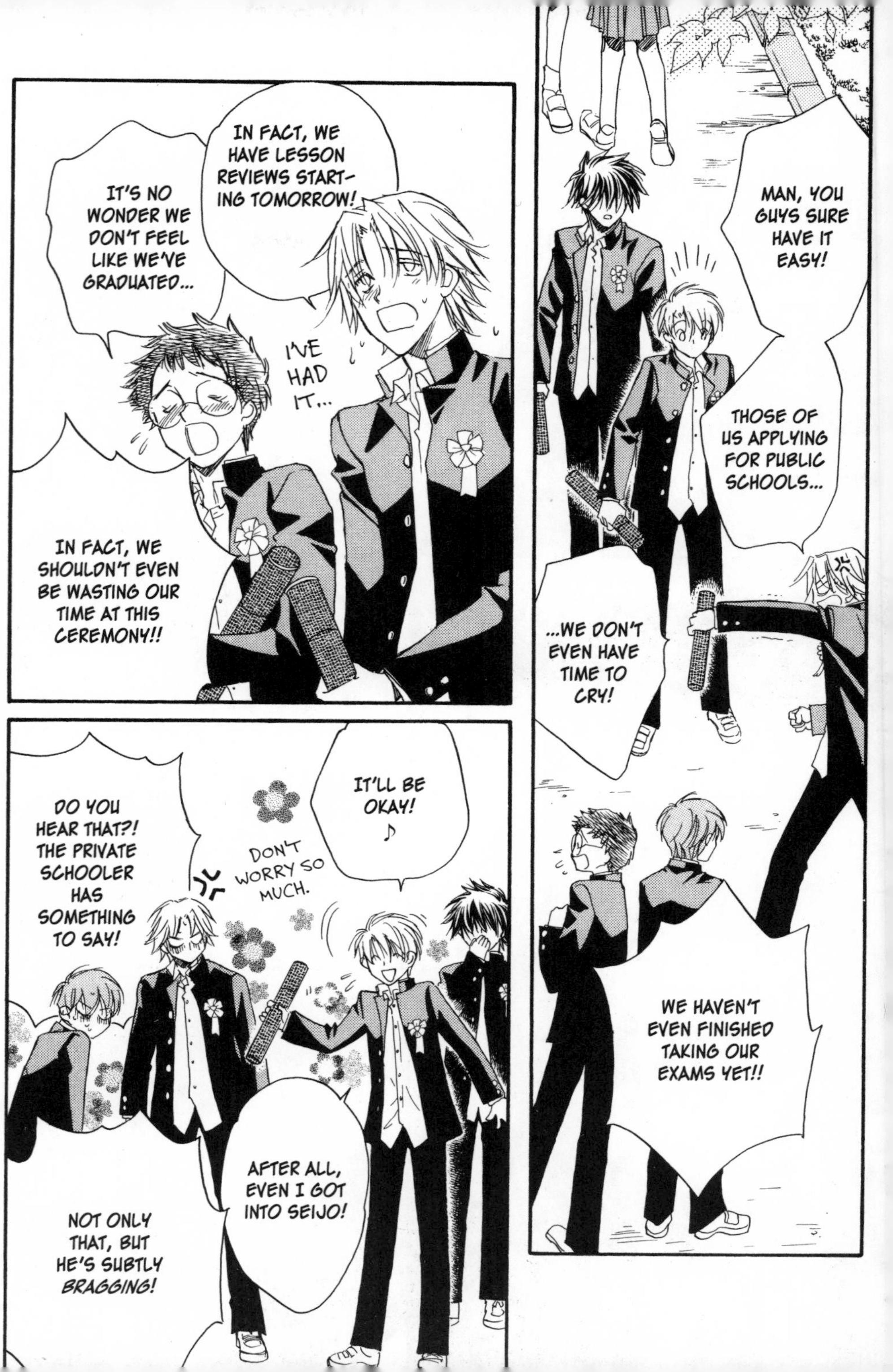
MAN, YOU GUYS SURE HAVE IT EASY!
THOSE OF US APPLYING FOR PUBLIC SCHOOLS...
...WE DON'T EVEN HAVE TIME TO CRY!
WE HAVEN'T EVEN FINISHED TAKING OUR EXAMS YET!!
IN FACT, WE HAVE LESSON REVIEWS STARTING-ING TOMORROW!
I'VE HAD IT...
IT'S NO WONDER WE DON'T FEEL LIKE WE'VE GRADUATED...
IN FACT, WE SHOULDN'T EVEN BE WASTING OUR TIME AT THIS CEREMONY!!
IT'LL BE OKAY! ♪
DON'T WORRY SO MUCH.
DO YOU HEAR THAT?! THE PRIVATE SCHOOLER HAS SOMETHING TO SAY!
AFTER ALL, EVEN I GOT INTO SEIJO!
NOT ONLY THAT, BUT HE'S SUBTLY *BRAGGING!*

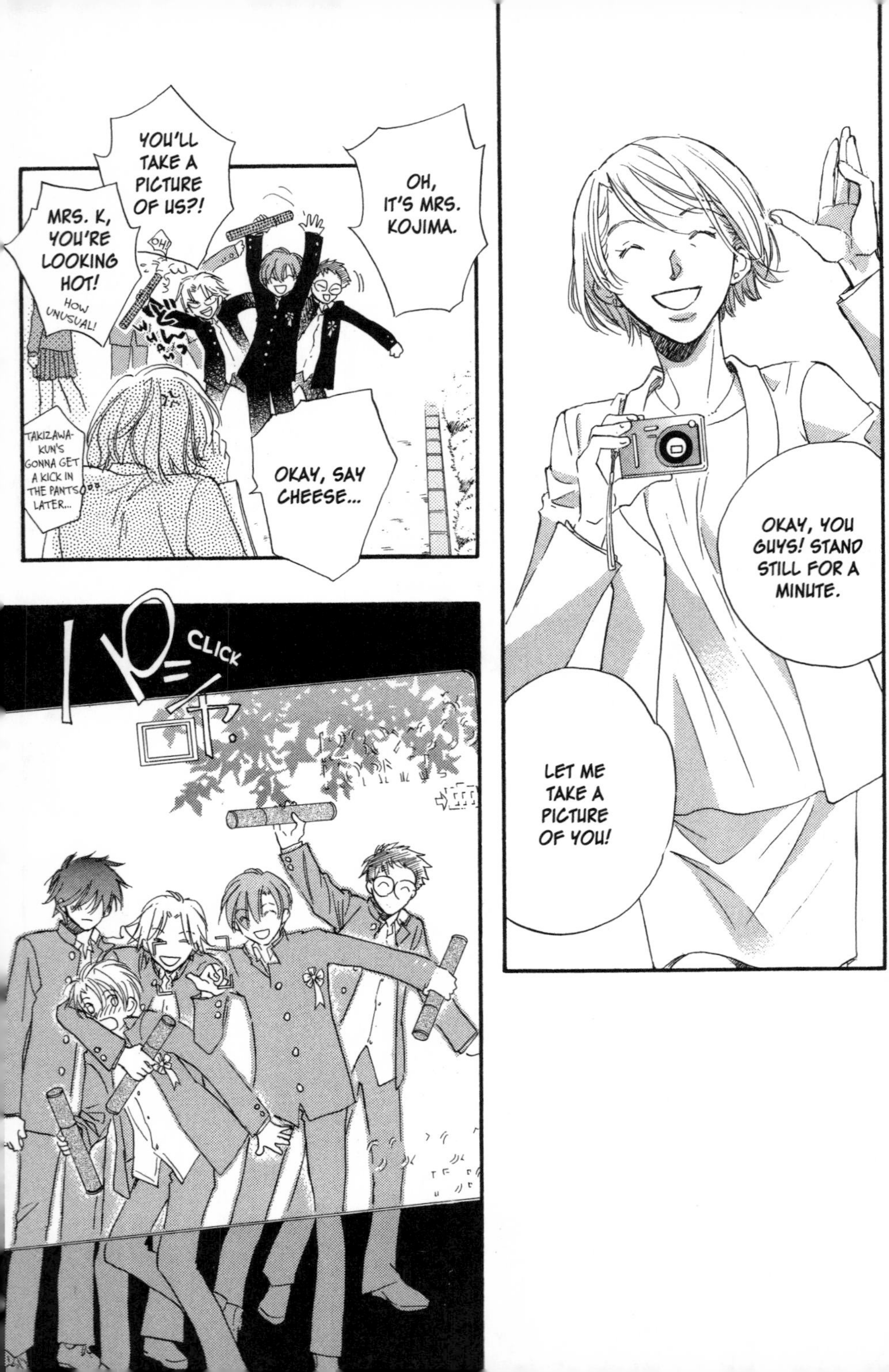
OKAY, YOU GUYS! STAND STILL FOR A MINUTE.
LET ME TAKE A PICTURE OF YOU!
OH, IT'S MRS. KOJIMA.
YOU'LL TAKE A PICTURE OF US?!
MRS. K, YOU'RE LOOKING HOT!
HOW UNUSUAL!
OH!
OKAY, SAY CHEESE...
TAKIZAWA-KUN'S GONNA GET A KICK IN THE PANTS LATER...
CLICK

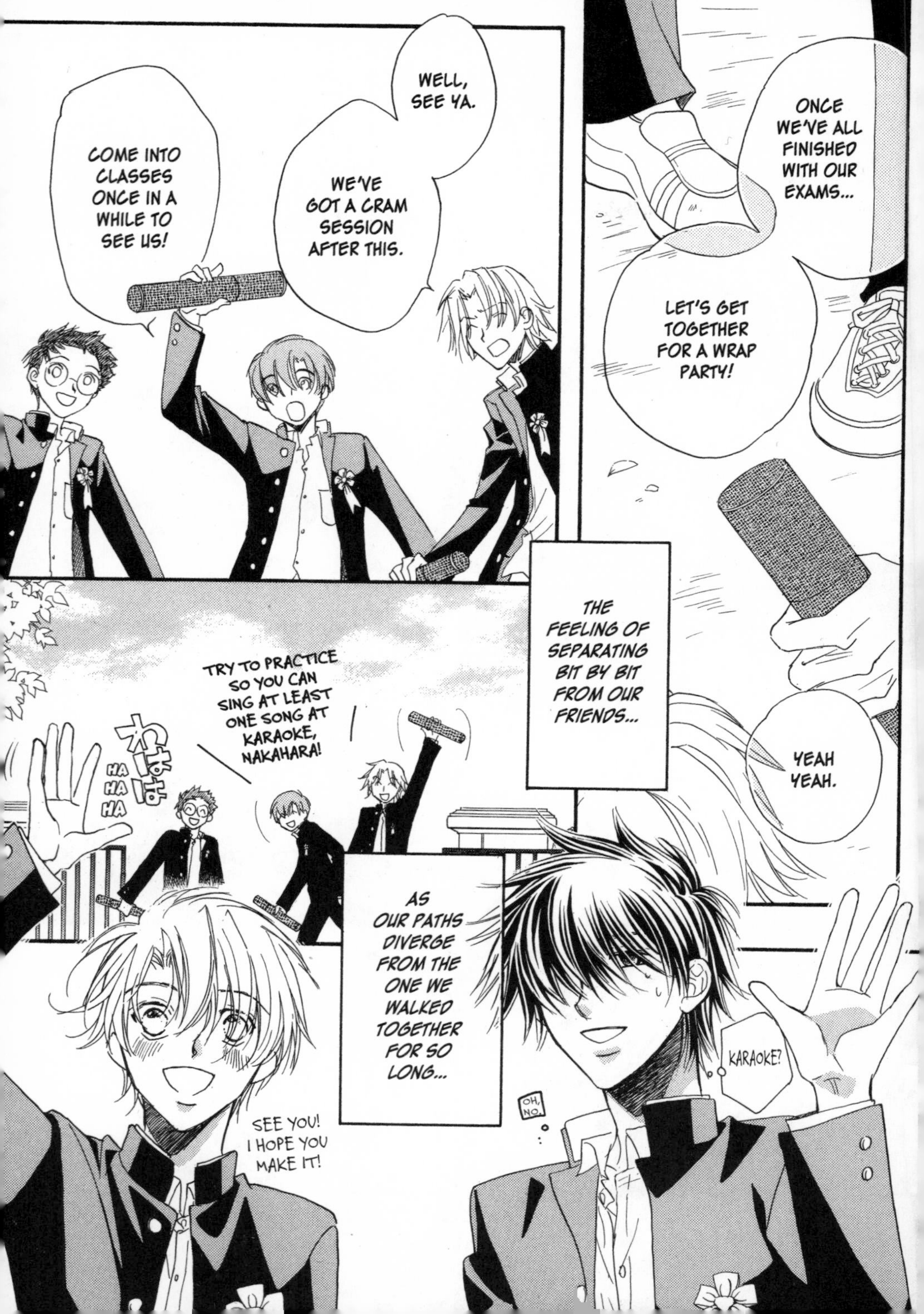
ONCE WE'VE ALL FINISHED WITH OUR EXAMS...
LET'S GET TOGETHER FOR A WRAP PARTY!
YEAH YEAH.
WELL, SEE YA.
WE'VE GOT A CRAM SESSION AFTER THIS.
COME INTO CLASSES ONCE IN A WHILE TO SEE US!
THE FEELING OF SEPARATING BIT BY BIT FROM OUR FRIENDS...
TRY TO PRACTICE SO YOU CAN SING AT LEAST ONE SONG AT KARAOKE, NAKAHARA!
わはは
HA HA HA
AS OUR PATHS DIVERGE FROM THE ONE WE WALKED TOGETHER FOR SO LONG...
KARAOKE?
OH, NO.
SEE YOU! I HOPE YOU MAKE IT!

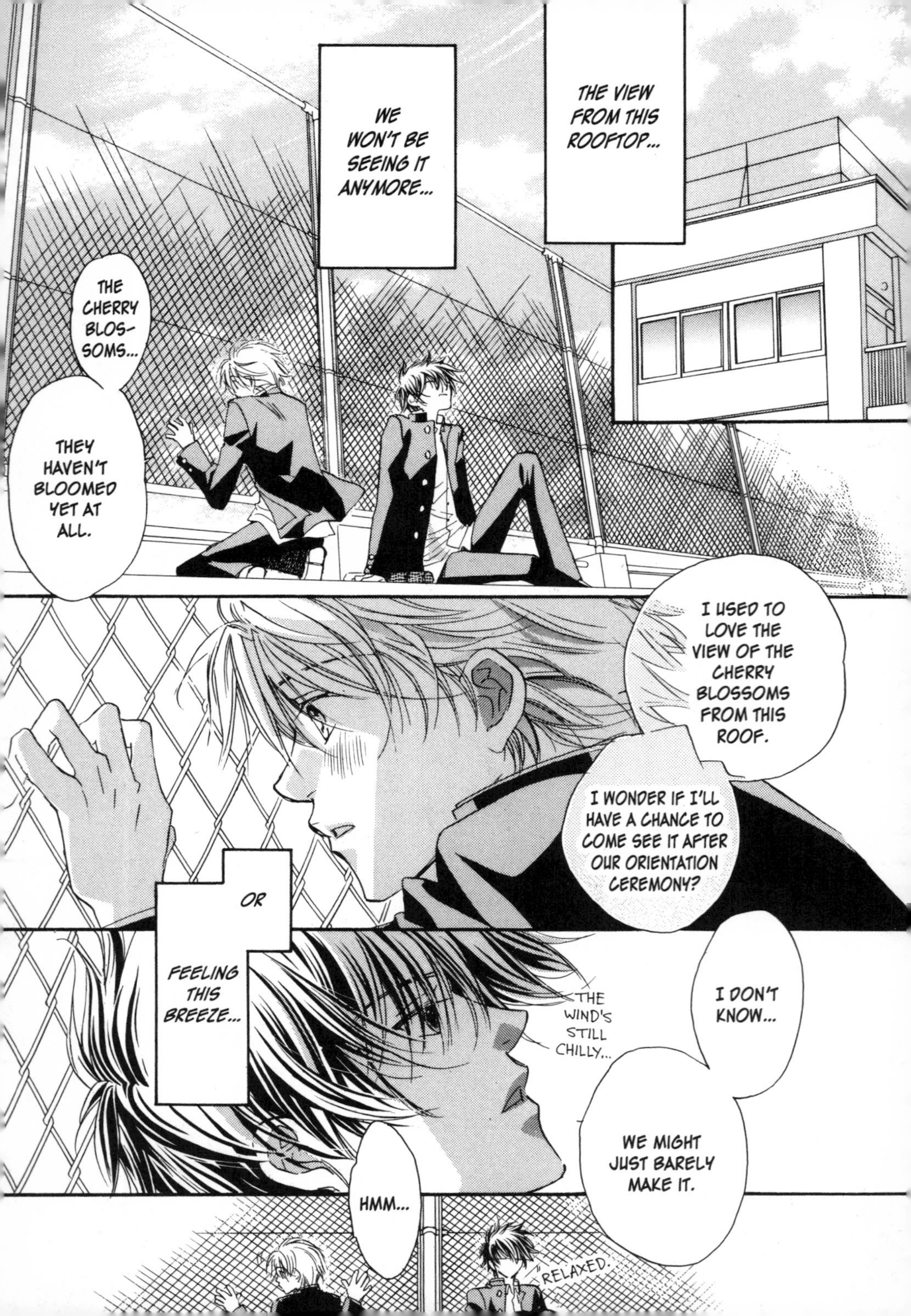
THE VIEW FROM THIS ROOFTOP...
WE WON'T BE SEEING IT ANYMORE...
THE CHERRY BLOSSOMS...
THEY HAVEN'T BLOOMED YET AT ALL.
I USED TO LOVE THE VIEW OF THE CHERRY BLOSSOMS FROM THIS ROOF.
I WONDER IF I'LL HAVE A CHANCE TO COME SEE IT AFTER OUR ORIENTATION CEREMONY?
OR
I DON'T KNOW...
WE MIGHT JUST BARELY MAKE IT.
THE WIND'S STILL CHILLY...
FEELING THIS BREEZE...
RELAXED.
HMM...

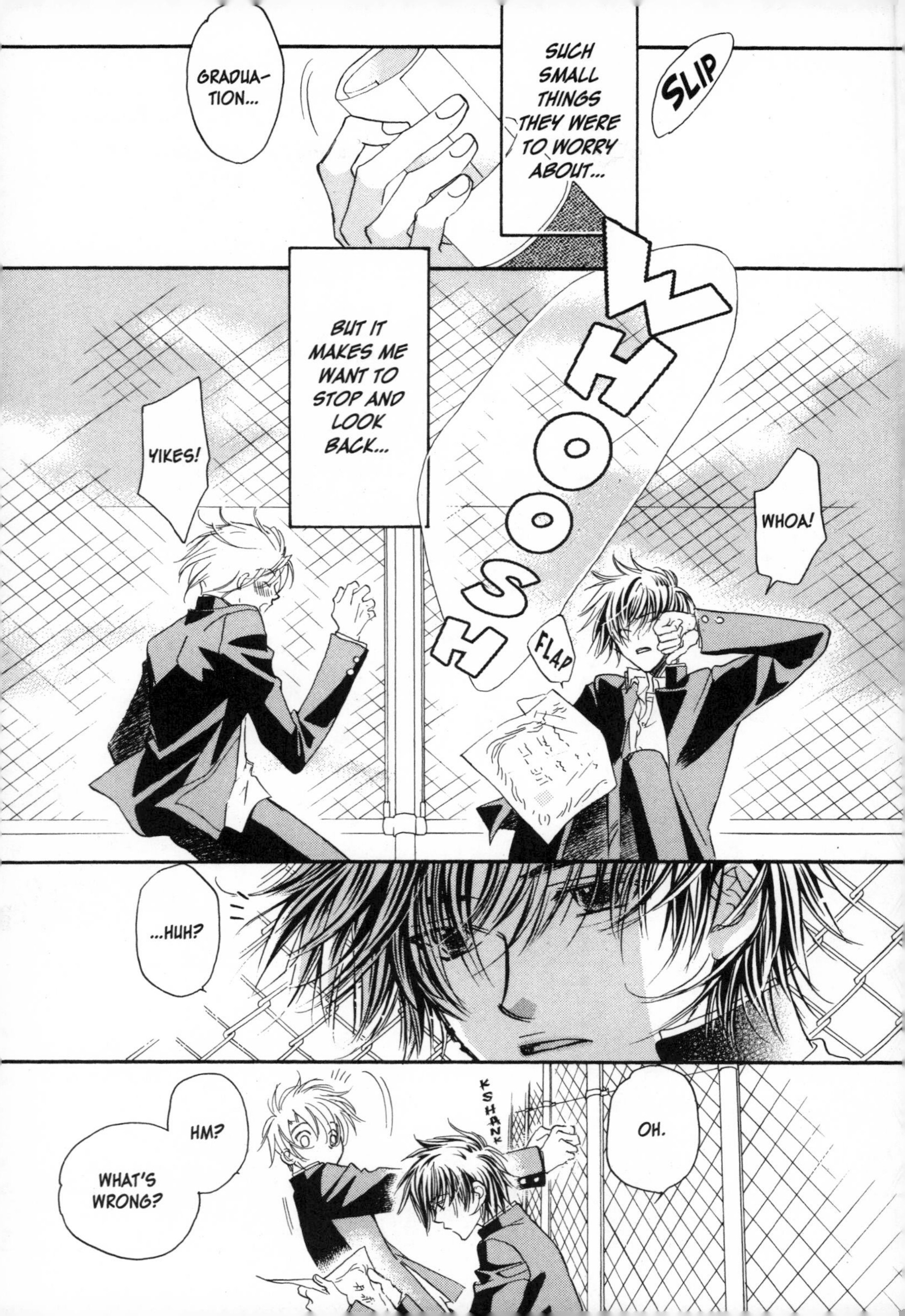
SLIP
SUCH SMALL THINGS THEY WERE TO WORRY ABOUT...
GRADUA-TION...
WHOOSH
BUT IT MAKES ME WANT TO STOP AND LOOK BACK...
WHOA!
FLAP
YIKES!
...HUH?
OH.
KSHANK
HM?
WHAT'S WRONG?

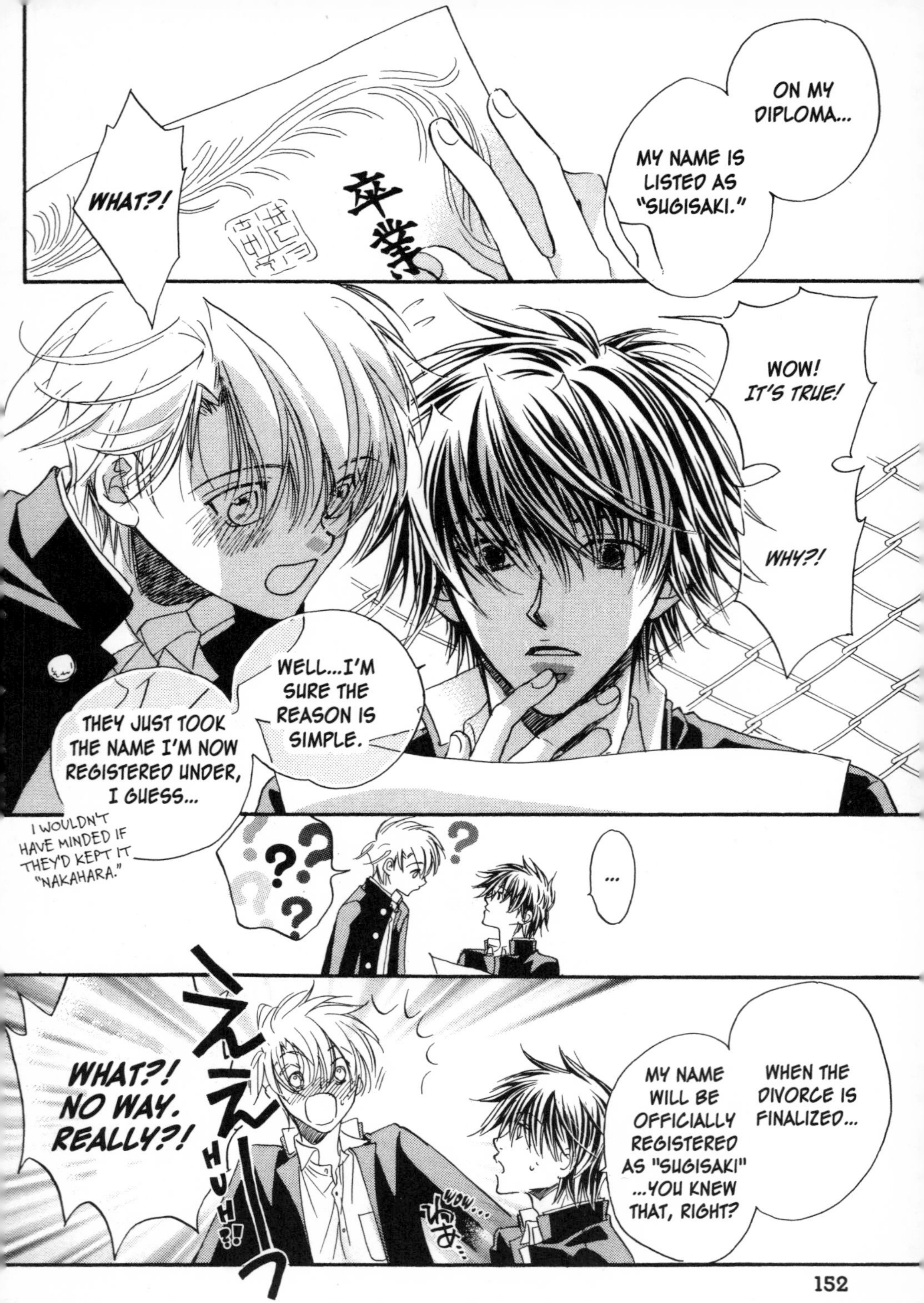
ON MY DIPLOMA...
MY NAME IS LISTED AS "SUGISAKI."
卒業
WHAT?!
WOW! IT'S TRUE!
WHY?!
WELL...I'M SURE THE REASON IS SIMPLE.
THEY JUST TOOK THE NAME I'M NOW REGISTERED UNDER, I GUESS...
I WOULDN'T HAVE MINDED IF THEY'D KEPT IT "NAKAHARA."
...
? ? ? ?
WHEN THE DIVORCE IS FINALIZED...
MY NAME WILL BE OFFICIALLY REGISTERED AS "SUGISAKI" ...YOU KNEW THAT, RIGHT?
WOW...
わあ...
HUH?!
WHAT?! NO WAY. REALLY?!

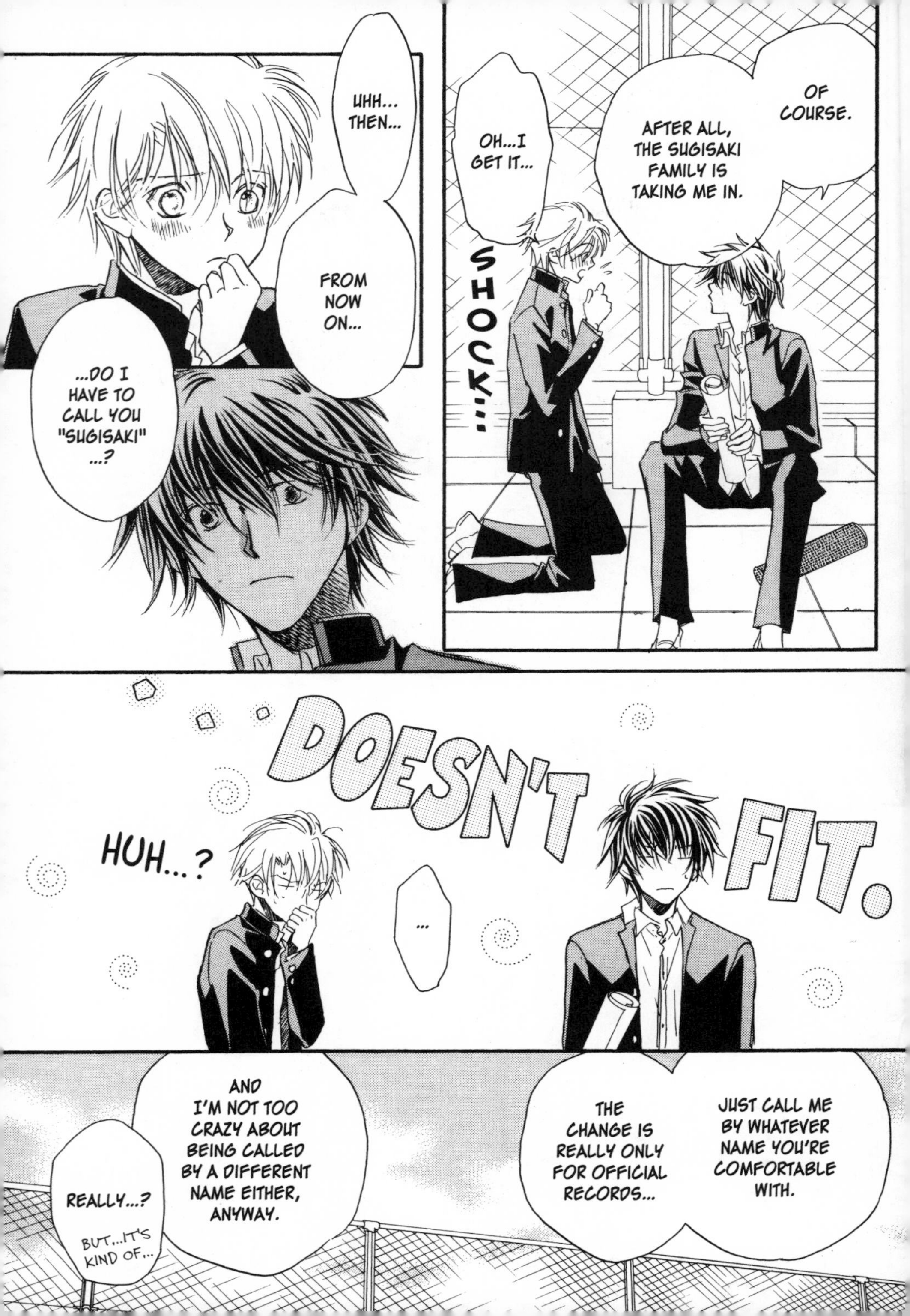
OF COURSE.
AFTER ALL, THE SUGISAKI FAMILY IS TAKING ME IN.
OH...I GET IT...
SHOCK!!
UHH... THEN...
FROM NOW ON...
...DO I HAVE TO CALL YOU "SUGISAKI" ...?
DOESN'T FIT.
...
HUH...?
JUST CALL ME BY WHATEVER NAME YOU'RE COMFORTABLE WITH.
THE CHANGE IS REALLY ONLY FOR OFFICIAL RECORDS...
AND I'M NOT TOO CRAZY ABOUT BEING CALLED BY A DIFFERENT NAME EITHER, ANYWAY.
REALLY...?
BUT...IT'S KIND OF...

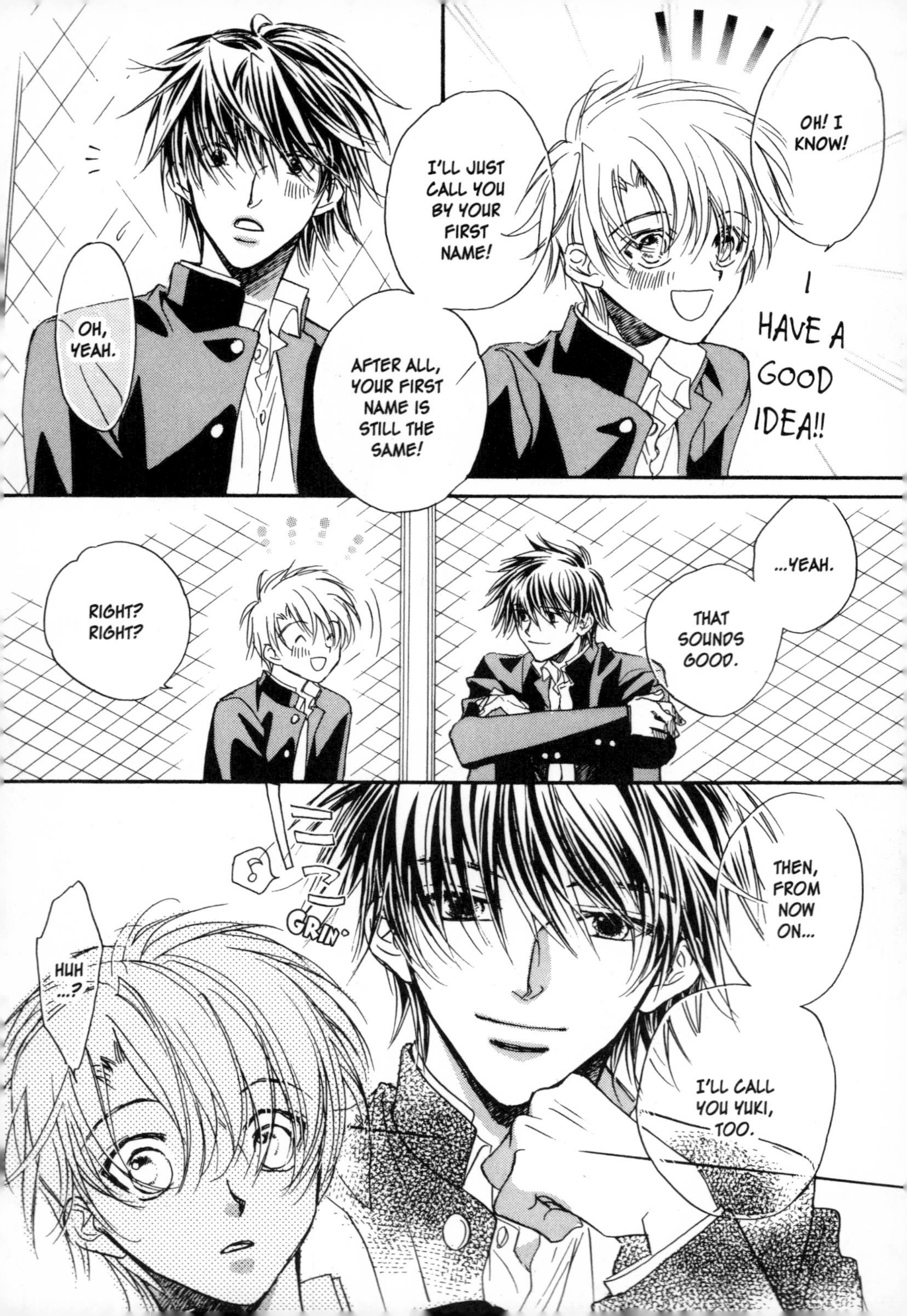
OH! I KNOW!
I HAVE A GOOD IDEA!!
I'LL JUST CALL YOU BY YOUR FIRST NAME!
AFTER ALL, YOUR FIRST NAME IS STILL THE SAME!
OH, YEAH.
...YEAH.
THAT SOUNDS GOOD.
RIGHT? RIGHT?
THEN, FROM NOW ON...
I'LL CALL YOU YUKI, TOO.
GRIN
HUH ...?

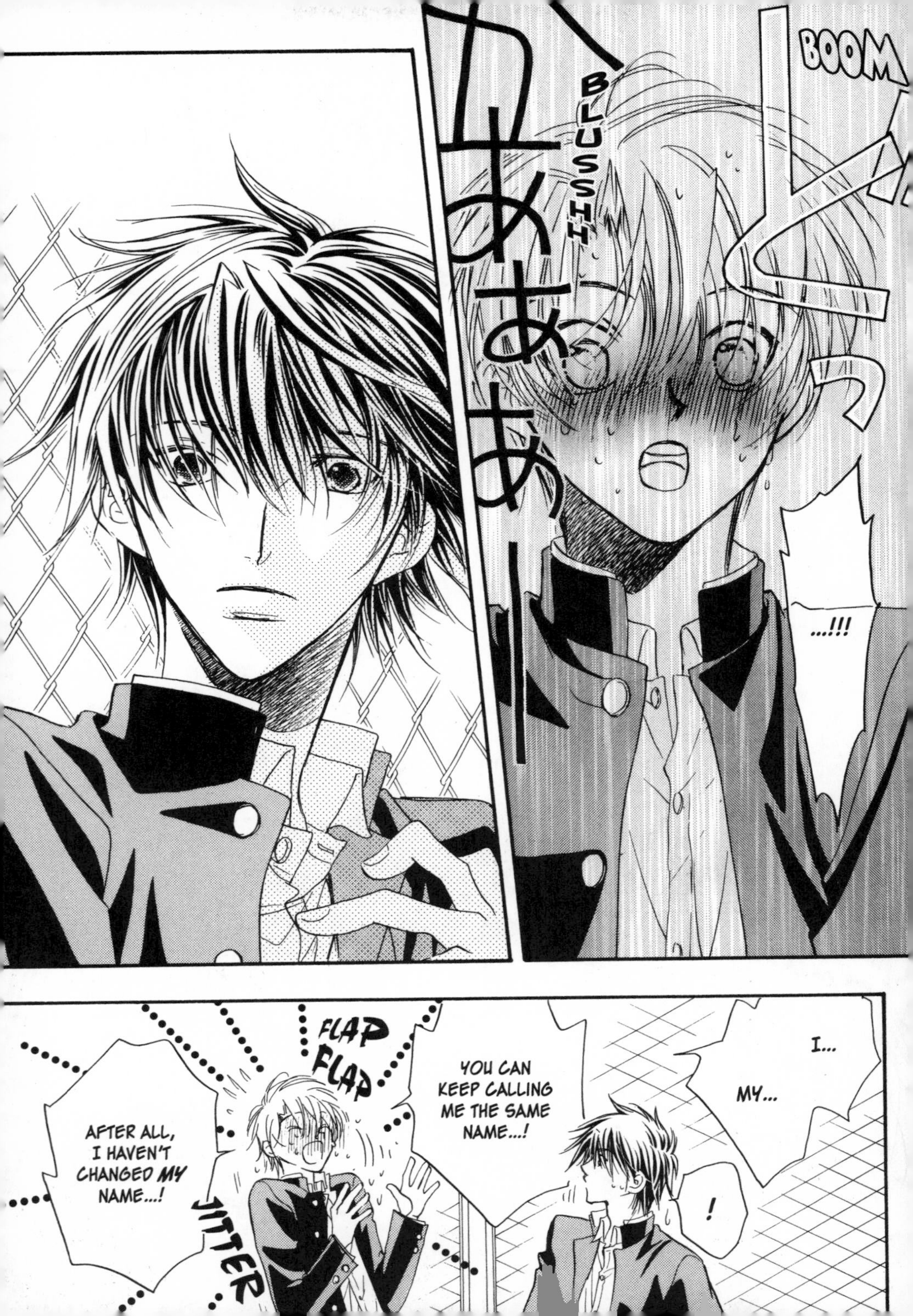
BOOM
BLUSSHH
...!!!
I...
MY...
!
YOU CAN KEEP CALLING ME THE SAME NAME...!
FLAP FLAP
AFTER ALL, I HAVEN'T CHANGED *MY* NAME...!
JITTER

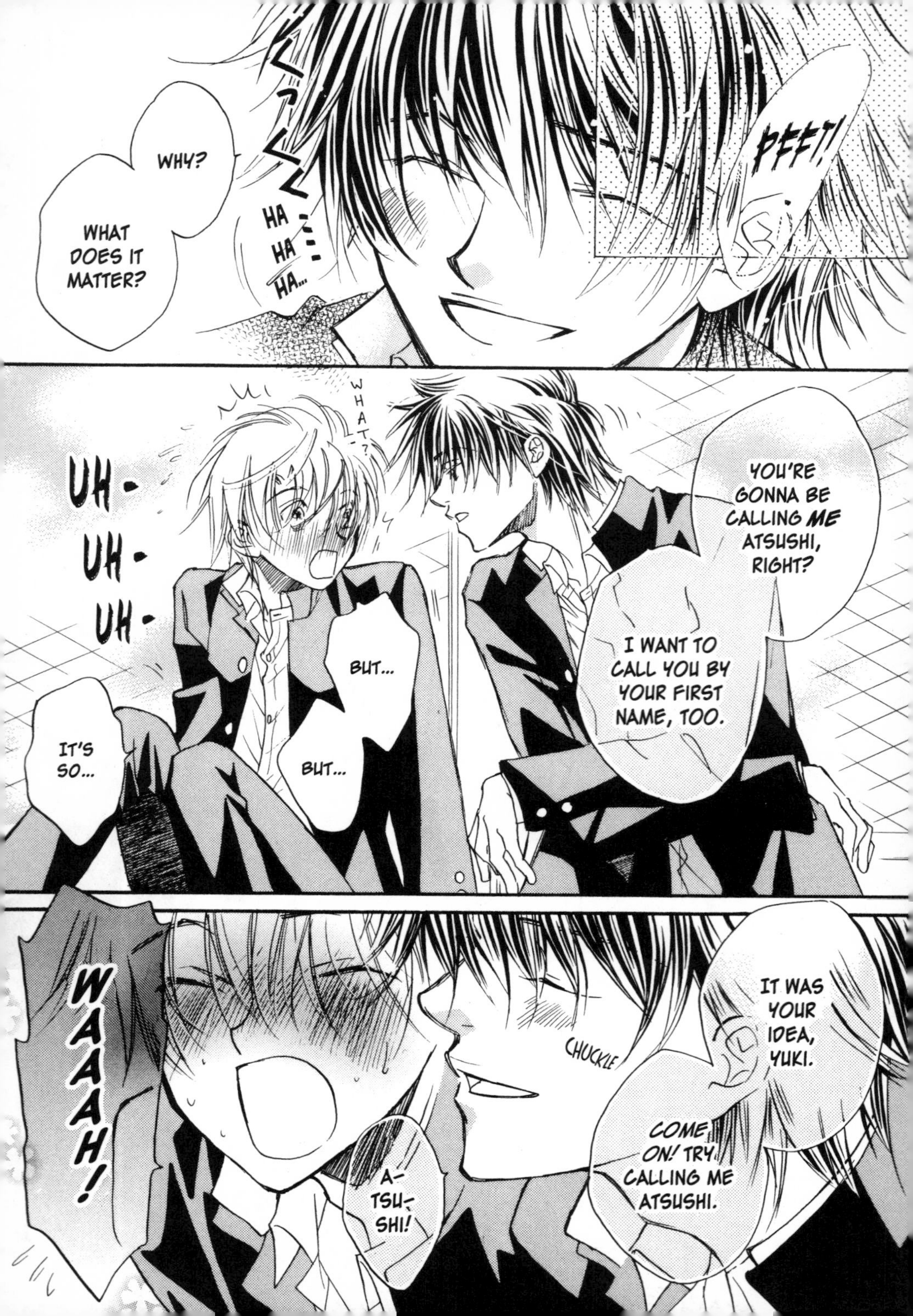
PFFT!
HA HA HA...
WHY?
WHAT DOES IT MATTER?
YOU'RE GONNA BE CALLING *ME* ATSUSHI, RIGHT?
I WANT TO CALL YOU BY YOUR FIRST NAME, TOO.
WHAT?
BUT...
BUT...
IT'S SO...
UH- UH- UH-
IT WAS YOUR IDEA, YUKI.
COME ON! TRY CALLING ME ATSUSHI.
CHUCKLE
A-TSU-SHI!
WAAAAH!

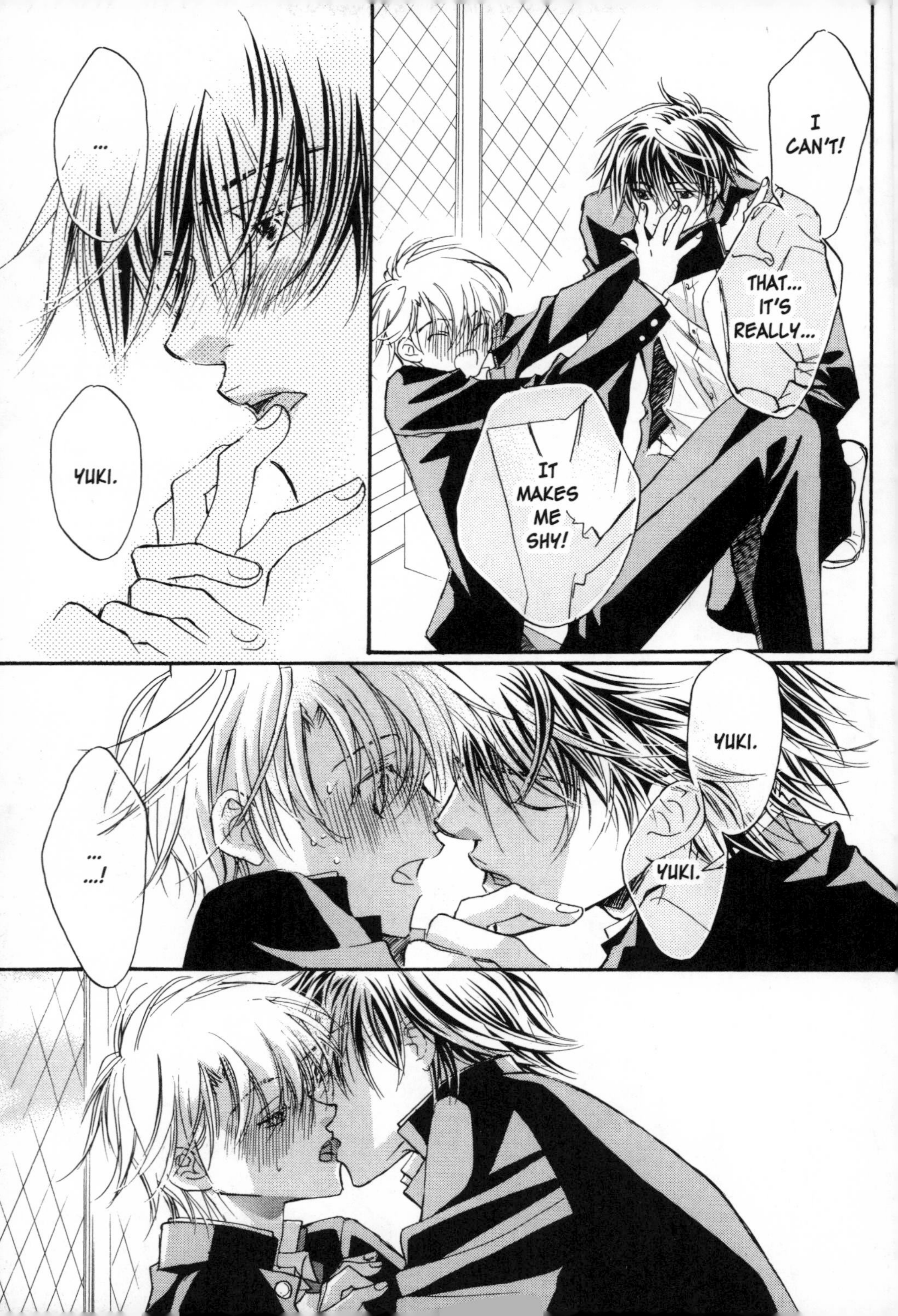
I CAN'T!
THAT... IT'S REALLY...
IT MAKES ME SHY!
...
YUKI.
YUKI.
YUKI.
... ...!

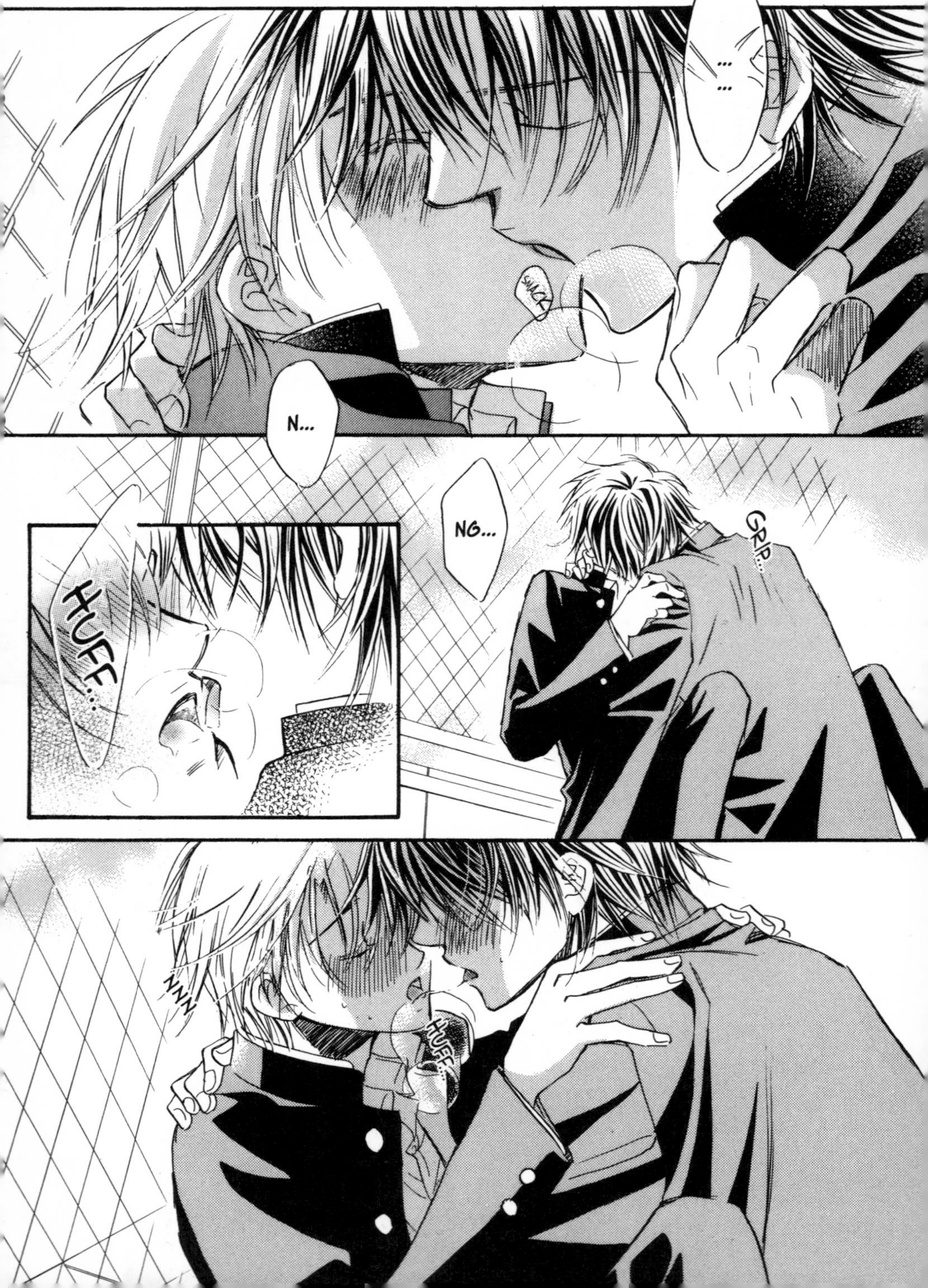
...
...
SMACK
N...
GRIP...
NG...
HUFF...
NNN
HUFF...

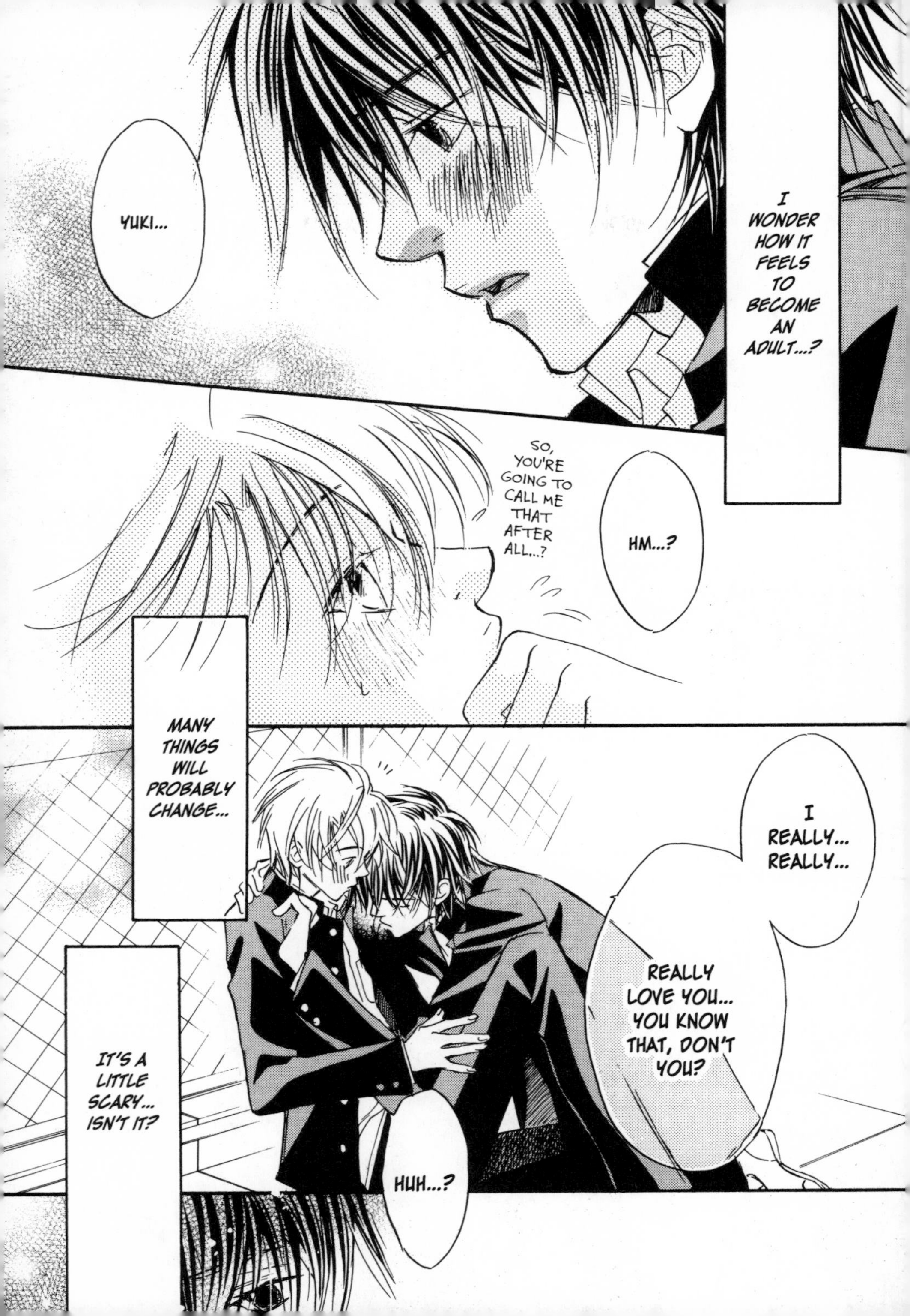
I WONDER HOW IT FEELS TO BECOME AN ADULT...?
YUKI...
HM...?
SO, YOU'RE GOING TO CALL ME THAT AFTER ALL...?
MANY THINGS WILL PROBABLY CHANGE...
I REALLY... REALLY...
REALLY LOVE YOU... YOU KNOW THAT, DON'T YOU?
IT'S A LITTLE SCARY... ISN'T IT?
HUH...?

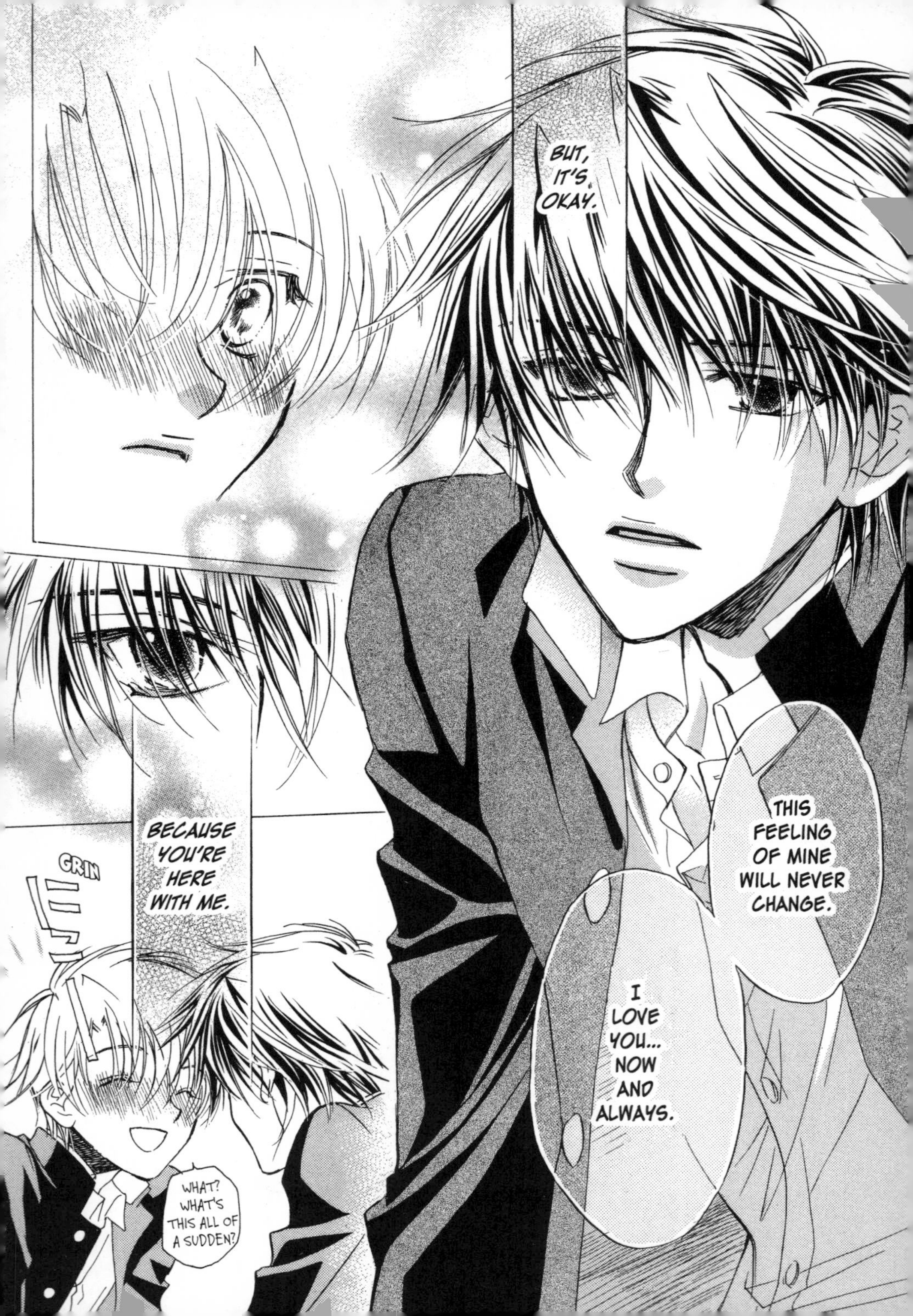
BUT, IT'S OKAY.
THIS FEELING OF MINE WILL NEVER CHANGE.
I LOVE YOU... NOW AND ALWAYS.
BECAUSE YOU'RE HERE WITH ME.
GRIN
WHAT? WHAT'S THIS ALL OF A SUDDEN?

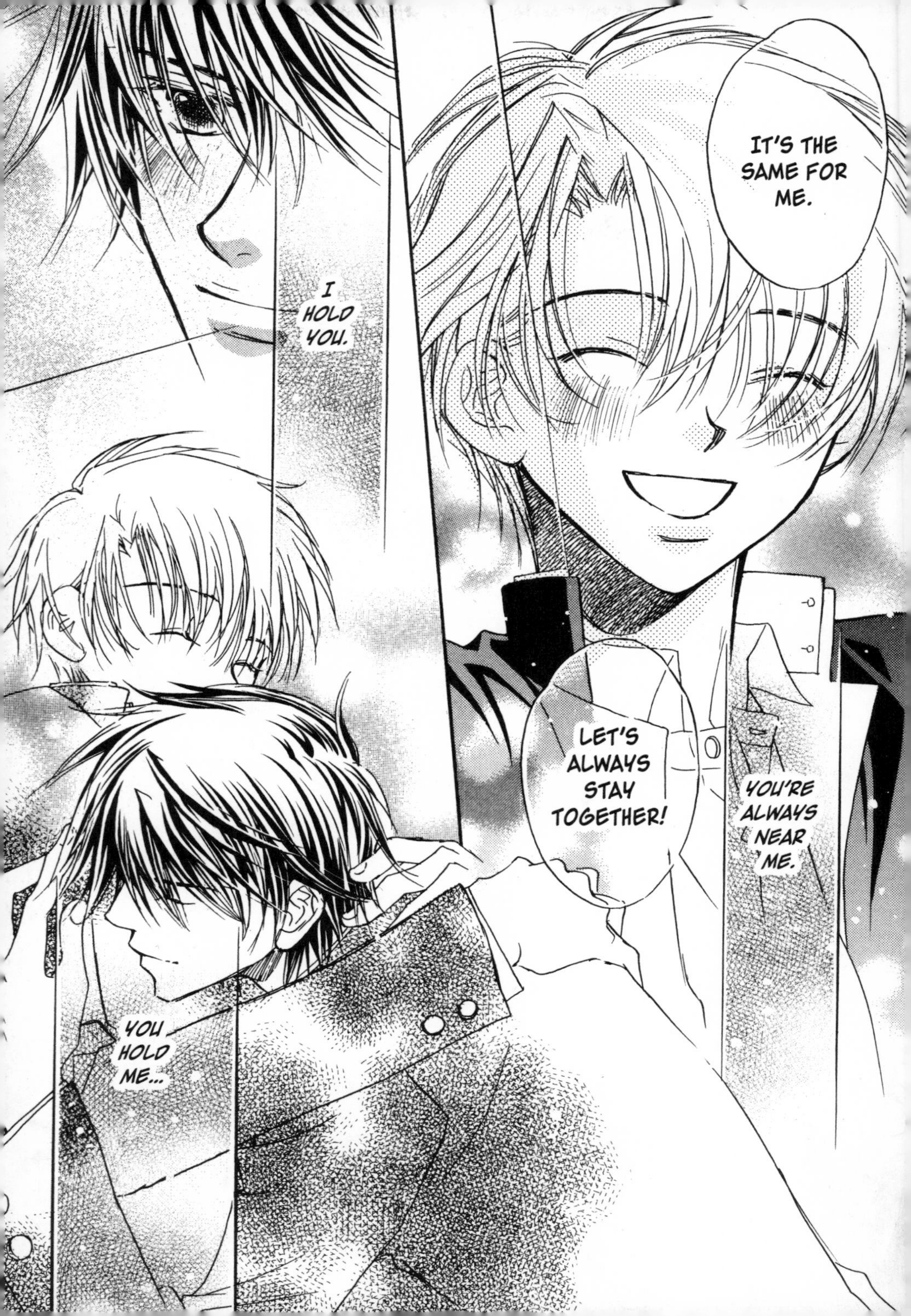
IT'S THE SAME FOR ME.
YOU'RE ALWAYS NEAR ME.
LET'S ALWAYS STAY TOGETHER!
I HOLD YOU.
YOU HOLD ME...

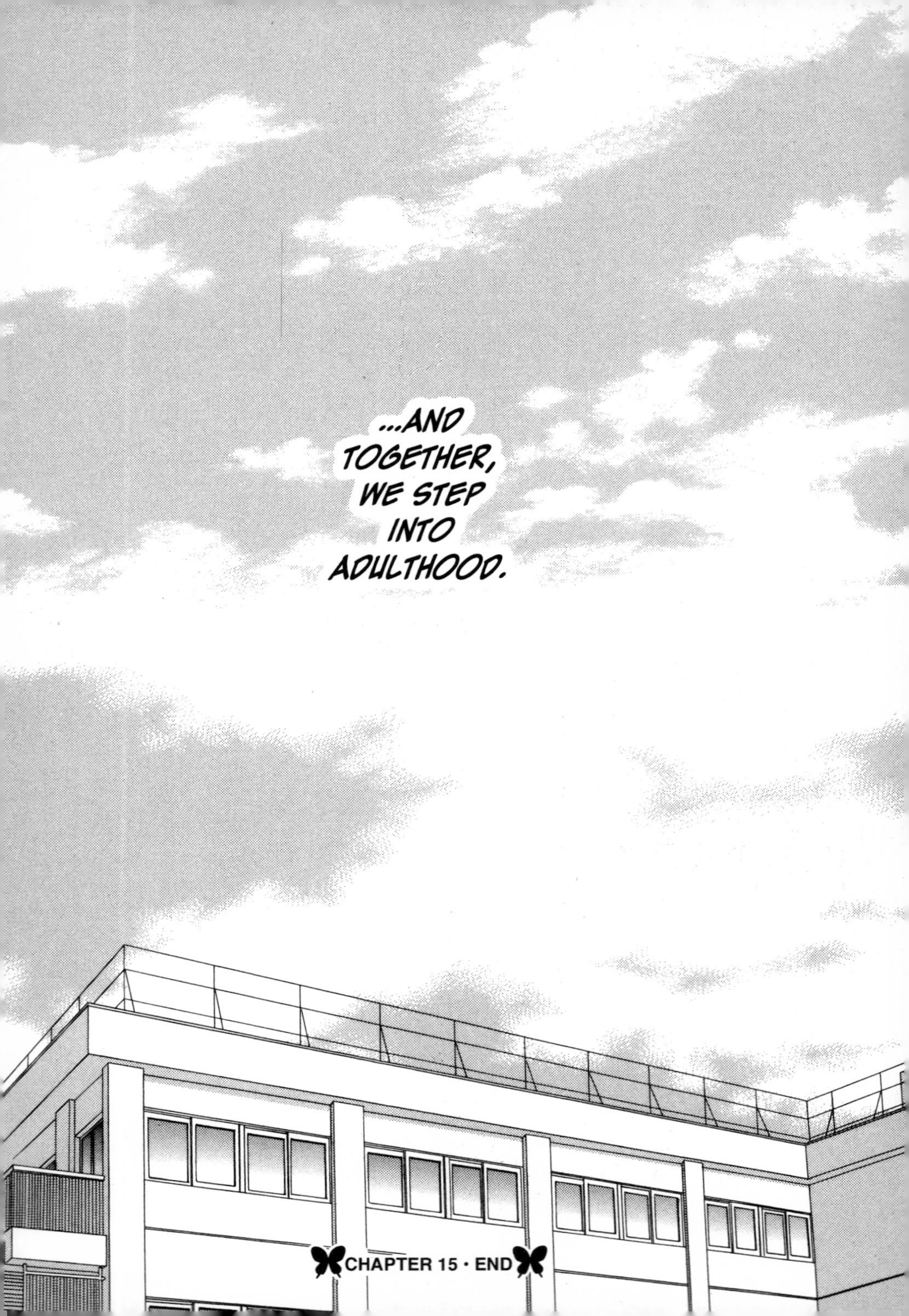
...AND TOGETHER, WE STEP INTO ADULTHOOD.
CHAPTER 15 • END

SEE
YOU!
I HOPE
YOU
MAKE
IT!

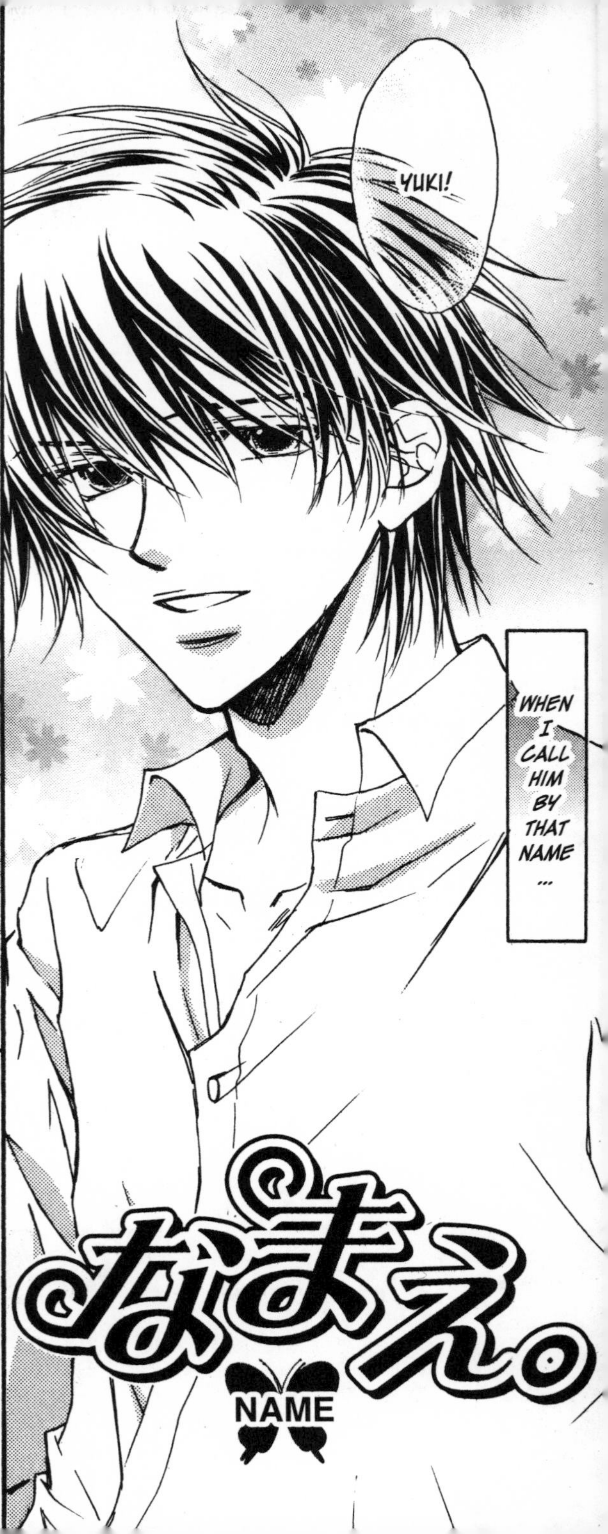
YUKI!
WHEN I CALL HIM BY THAT NAME...
なまえ。
NAME

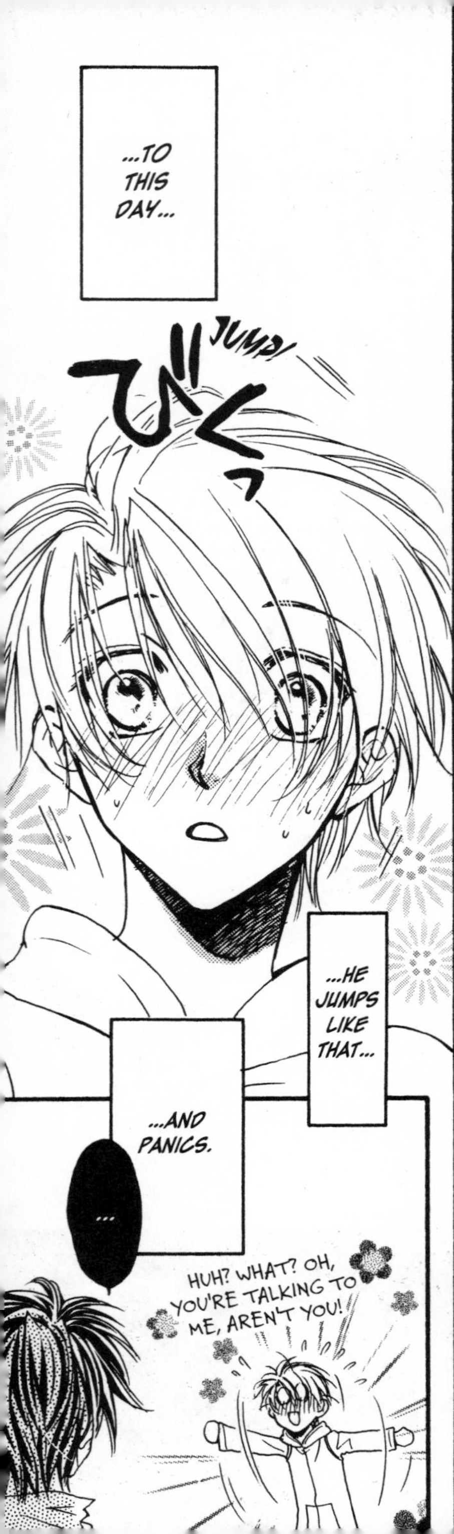
...TO THIS DAY...
びくっ
JUMP!
...HE JUMPS LIKE THAT...
...AND PANICS.
...
HUH? WHAT? OH, YOU'RE TALKING TO ME, AREN'T YOU!

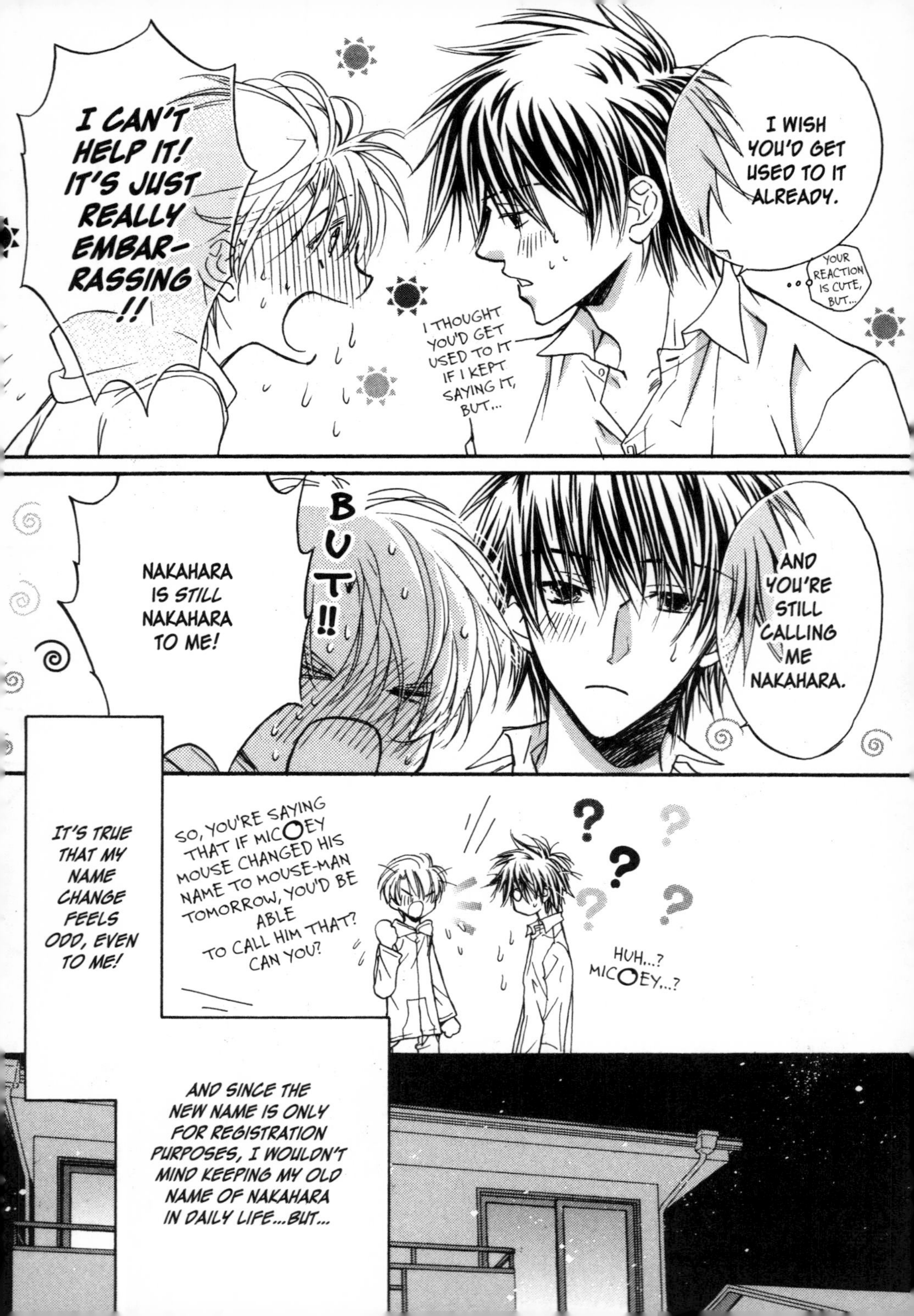
I WISH YOU'D GET USED TO IT ALREADY.
...YOUR REACTION IS CUTE, BUT...
I THOUGHT YOU'D GET USED TO IT IF I KEPT SAYING IT, BUT...
I CAN'T HELP IT! IT'S JUST REALLY EMBARRASSING!!
AND YOU'RE STILL CALLING ME NAKAHARA.
BUT!!
NAKAHARA IS STILL NAKAHARA TO ME!
HUH...? MIC○EY...?
SO, YOU'RE SAYING THAT IF MIC○EY MOUSE CHANGED HIS NAME TO MOUSE-MAN TOMORROW, YOU'D BE ABLE TO CALL HIM THAT? CAN YOU?
IT'S TRUE THAT MY NAME CHANGE FEELS ODD, EVEN TO ME!
AND SINCE THE NEW NAME IS ONLY FOR REGISTRATION PURPOSES, I WOULDN'T MIND KEEPING MY OLD NAME OF NAKAHARA IN DAILY LIFE...BUT...

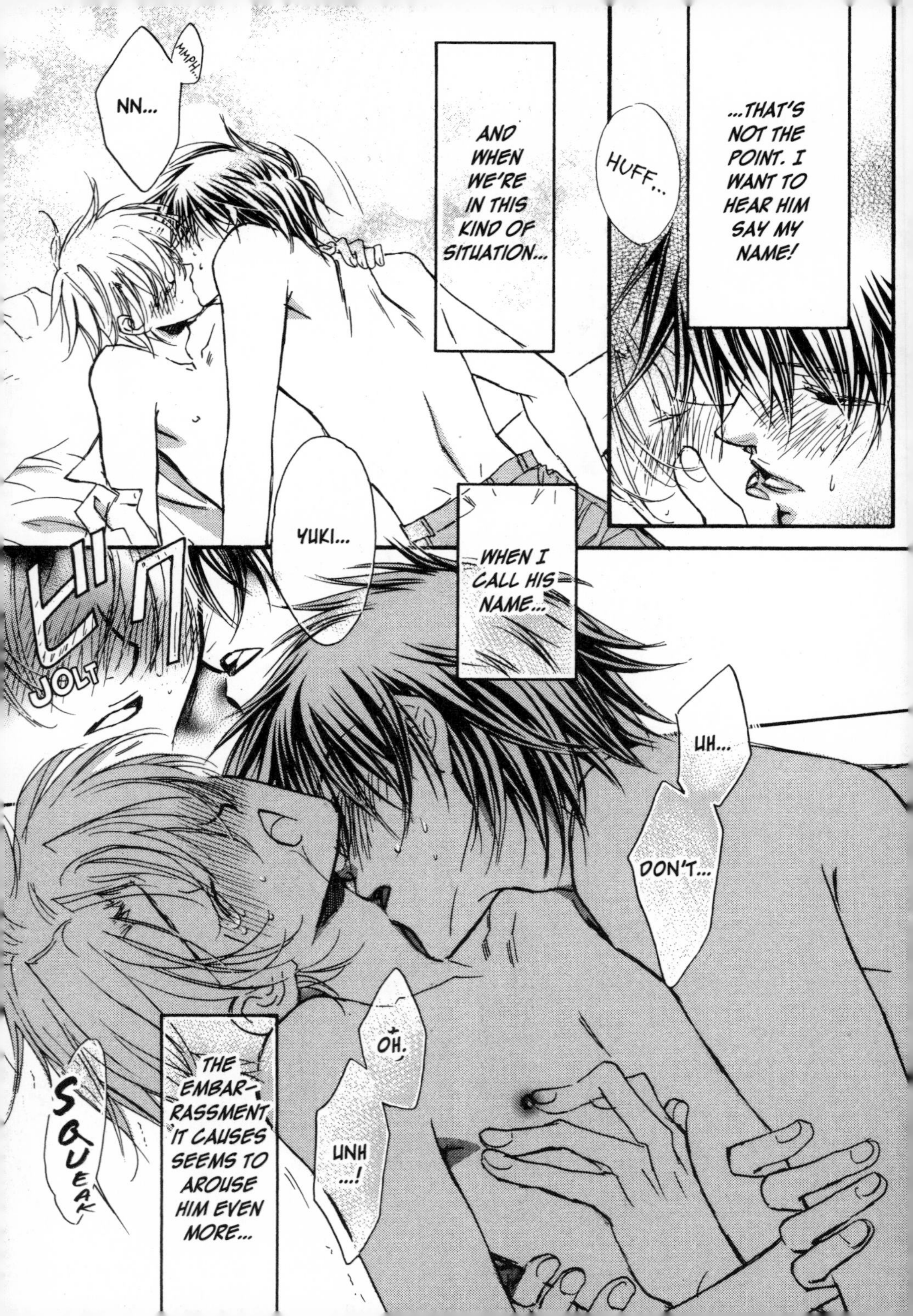
...THAT'S NOT THE POINT. I WANT TO HEAR HIM SAY MY NAME!
HUFF...
AND WHEN WE'RE IN THIS KIND OF SITUATION...
MMPH...
NN...
YUKI...
WHEN I CALL HIS NAME...
ビク
JOLT
UH...
DON'T...
OH.
UNH ...!
THE EMBAR-RASSMENT IT CAUSES SEEMS TO AROUSE HIM EVEN MORE...
SQUEAK

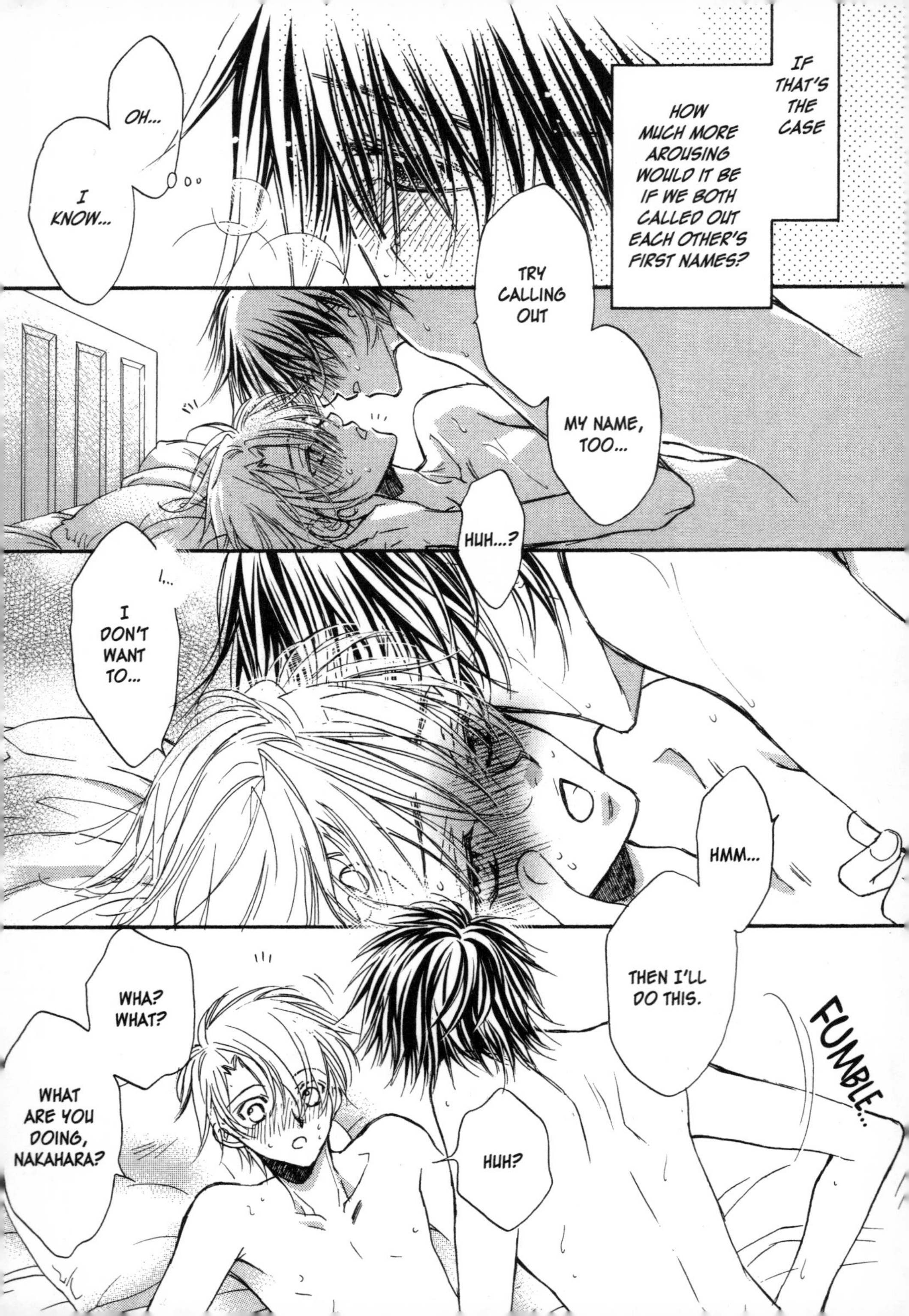
IF THAT'S THE CASE
HOW MUCH MORE AROUSING WOULD IT BE IF WE BOTH CALLED OUT EACH OTHER'S FIRST NAMES?
OH... I KNOW...
TRY CALLING OUT
MY NAME, TOO...
HUH...?
I... I DON'T WANT TO...
HMM...
THEN I'LL DO THIS.
FUMBLE...
WHA? WHAT?
HUH?
WHAT ARE YOU DOING, NAKAHARA?

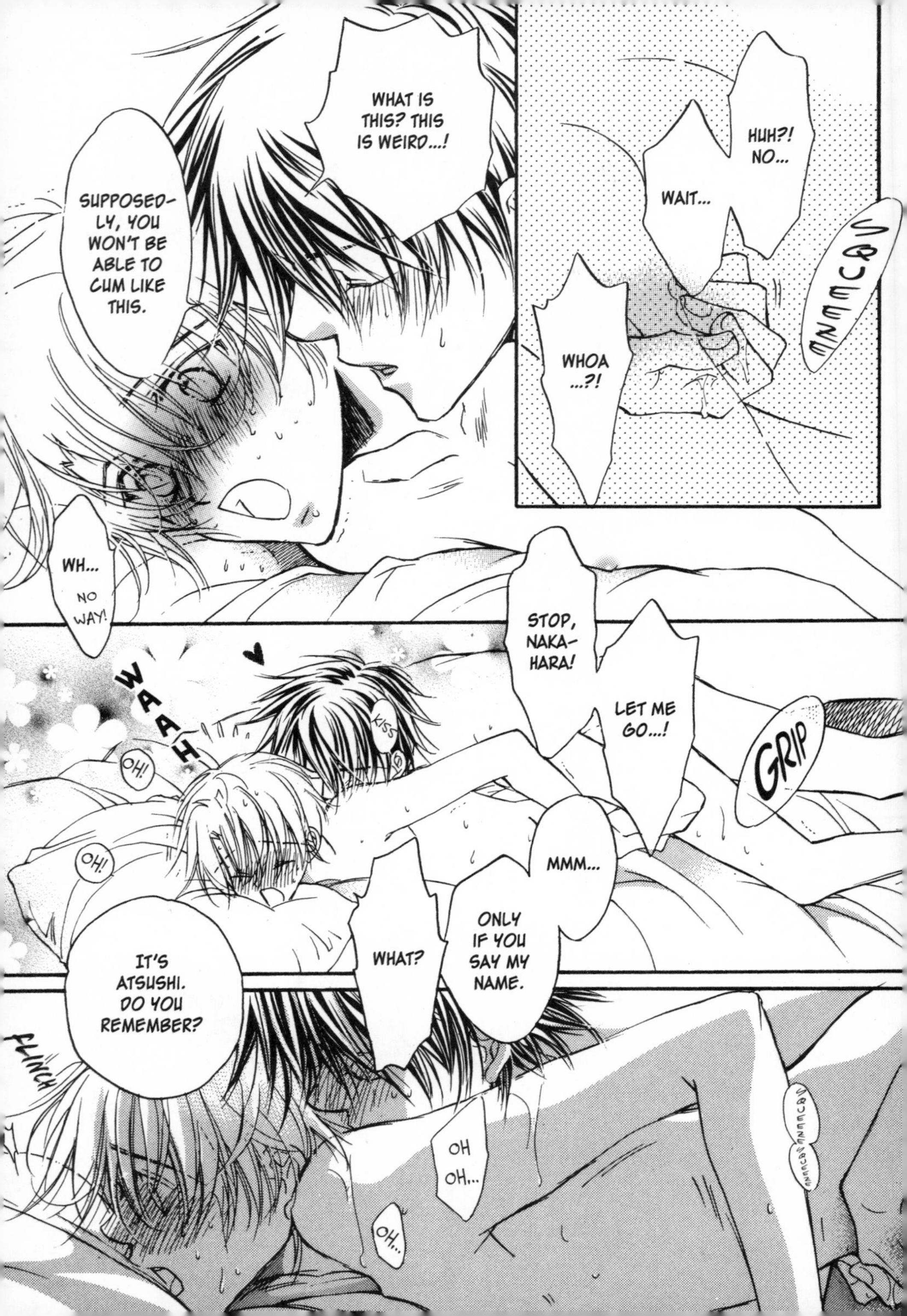
HUH?! NO...
WAIT...
SQUEEZE
WHOA ...?!
WHAT IS THIS? THIS IS WEIRD...!
SUPPOSED-LY, YOU WON'T BE ABLE TO CUM LIKE THIS.
WH... NO WAY!
STOP, NAKA-HARA!
LET ME GO...!
GRIP
WAAAH
KISS
OH!
OH!
MMM...
ONLY IF YOU SAY MY NAME.
WHAT?
IT'S ATSUSHI. DO YOU REMEMBER?
SQUEEZE SQUEEZE
OH OH...
OH...
FLINCH

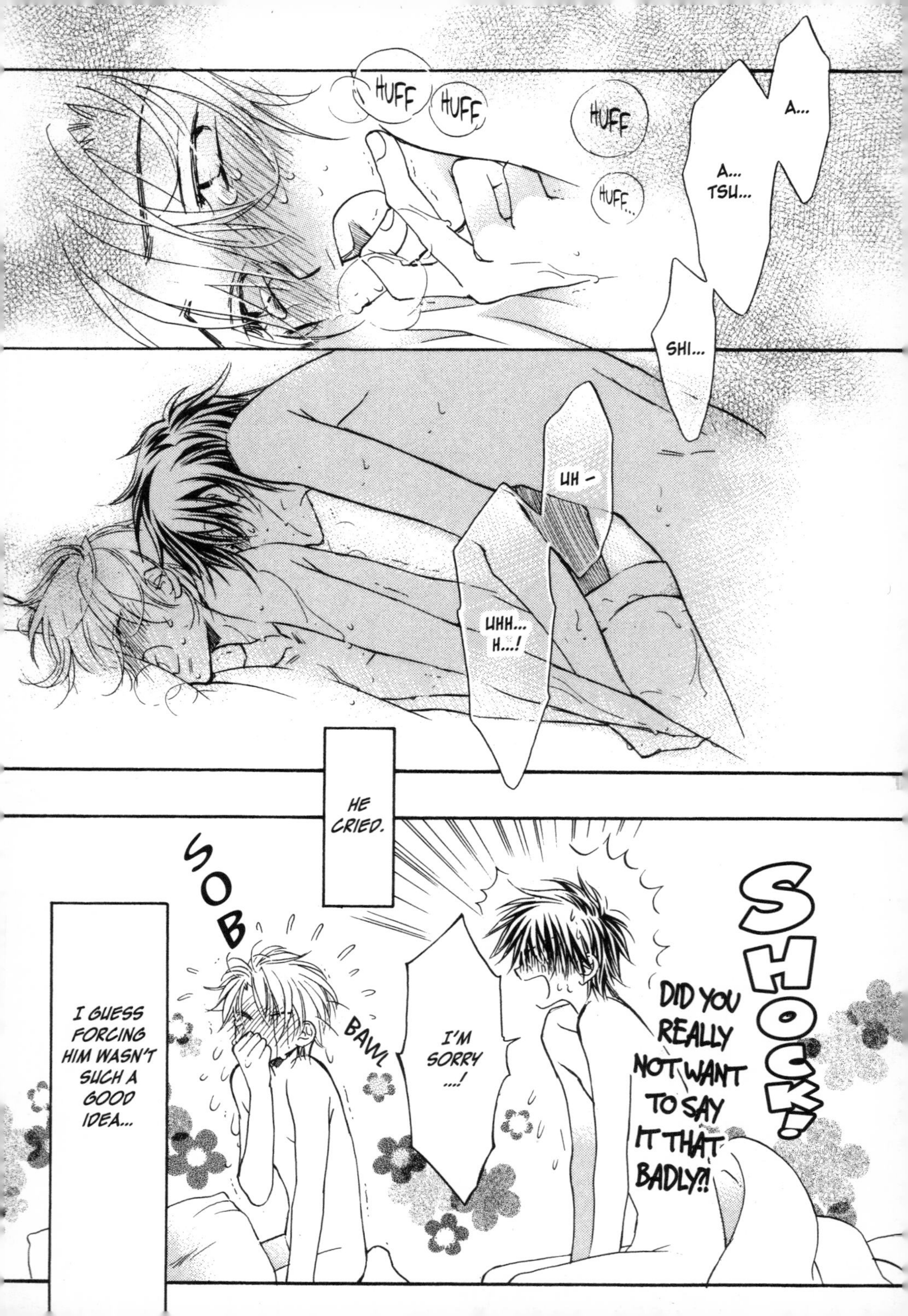
A...
A... TSU...
HUFF
HUFF...
HUFF
HUFF
SHI...
UH –
UHH... H...!
HE CRIED.
SHOCK!
DID YOU REALLY NOT WANT TO SAY IT THAT BADLY?!
I'M SORRY ...!
BAWL
SOB
I GUESS FORCING HIM WASN'T SUCH A GOOD IDEA...

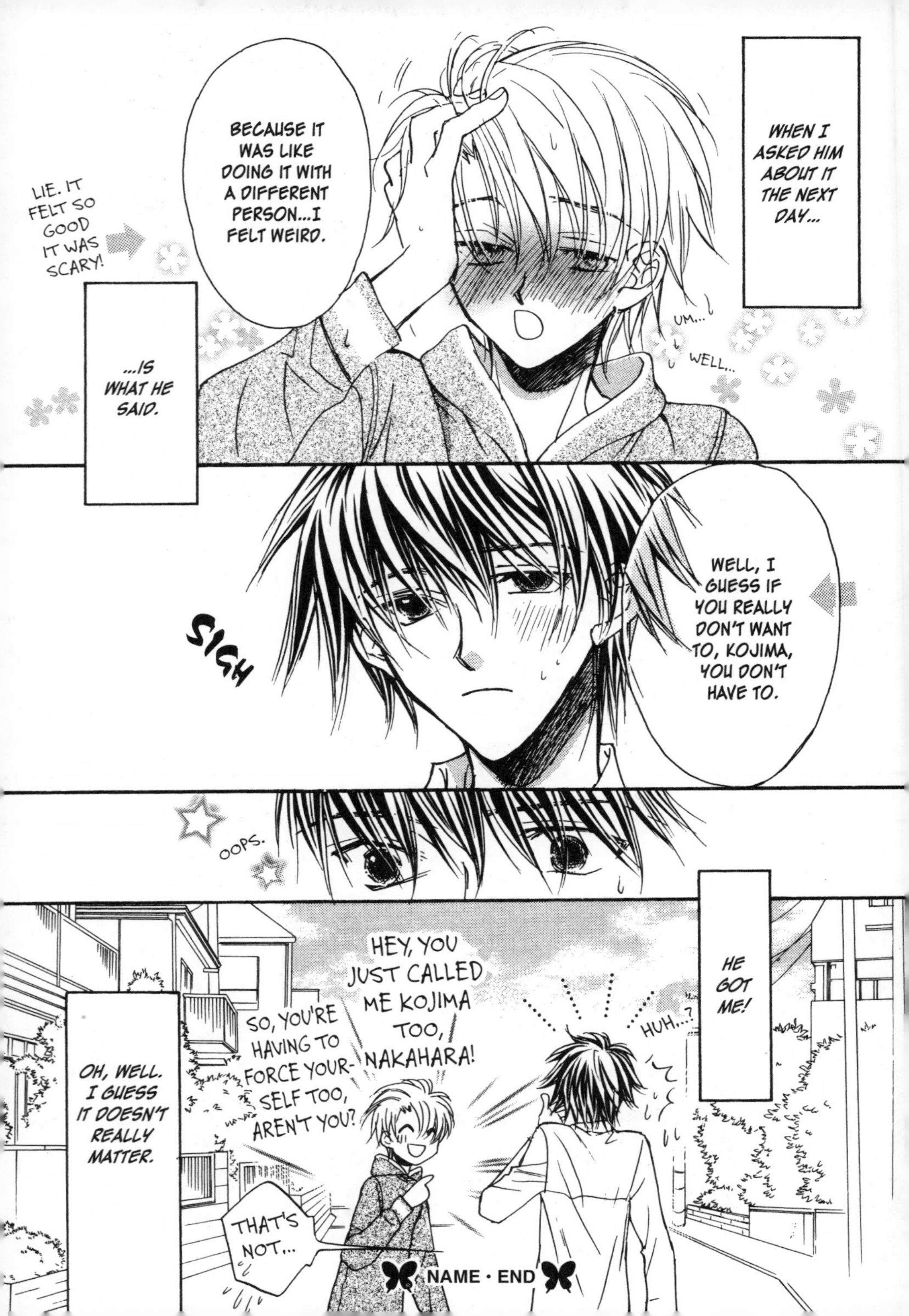
WHEN I ASKED HIM ABOUT IT THE NEXT DAY...
UM... WELL...
BECAUSE IT WAS LIKE DOING IT WITH A DIFFERENT PERSON...I FELT WEIRD.
LIE. IT FELT SO GOOD IT WAS SCARY!
...IS WHAT HE SAID.
WELL, I GUESS IF YOU REALLY DON'T WANT TO, KOJIMA, YOU DON'T HAVE TO.
SIGH
OOPS.
HE GOT ME!
HUH...?
HEY, YOU JUST CALLED ME KOJIMA TOO, NAKAHARA!
SO, YOU'RE HAVING TO FORCE YOUR-SELF TOO, AREN'T YOU?
OH, WELL. I GUESS IT DOESN'T REALLY MATTER.
THAT'S NOT...
NAME · END

HELLO. THIS IS HINAKO TAKANAGA. "LITTLE B..." HAS NOW REACHED ITS THIRD VOLUME - THANK YOU VERY MUCH FOR YOUR SUPPORT! AT THE TIME THE CHAPTERS CONTAINED IN THIS VOLUME WERE BEING SERIALIZED IN THE MAGAZINE, THERE WERE MANY... INCIDENTS. THE MAGAZINE CHANGED PUBLISHERS, THE SERIES WAS DELAYED FOR ABOUT SIX MONTHS, AND I WAS EVEN IN A CAR ACCIDENT... THANKFULLY, I ONLY SUFFERED MINOR INJURIES BUT SINCE I HAD TO POSTPONE THE SERIES BECAUSE OF IT, THE SCHEDULE AFTERWARDS BECAME ALL MUDDLED AND IT WAS TRULY A HECTIC PERIOD. THOSE DAYS WERE FILLED WITH CONSTANT BATTLES TO OVERCOME...AND, WELL, BECAUSE OF THAT, I HAVE MANY MEMORIES OF THE MAKING OF THIS SECOND HALF OF THE "LITTLE B..." SERIES. DESPITE EVERYTHING, I WAS ABLE TO CARRY THROUGH TO THE ENDING I HAD PLANNED. (*ABOUT THE ENDING: THERE ARE MORE THAN LIKELY SOME OF YOU WHO ARE DISSATISFIED WITH THIS CONCLUSION, BUT I HAVE PURPOSELY DECIDED TO END IT IN THIS WAY. AFTER ALL, THE CHARACTERS ARE STILL YOUNG... AND THEY'VE ONLY JUST STARTED ON THE ROAD TO ADULTHOOD. OH, I KNOW I'M BEING UNFAIR FOR WRITING THIS - I'M SORRY! BUT I JUST WANTED TO EXPLAIN AT LEAST THIS MUCH...) TO ALL THOSE WHO HAVE FOLLOWED THIS STORY FROM THE BEGINNING, THANK YOU VERY MUCH. (AND TO ALL THE PEOPLE I TROUBLED, MY APOLOGIES...)

WHEN THE DECISION FOR A "PART TWO" FOR THIS SERIES WAS MADE, I UNDERSTAND THAT ON A QUESTIONNAIRE, MANY OF YOU SAID THAT YOU WANTED TO SEE THE TWO BOYS' LIVES IN COLLEGE. (THANK YOU♡) THIS SEEMS ONLY NATURAL, FOLLOWING THE WAY VOLUME ONE ENDS, AND AT THE TIME I WAS ALSO PLOTTING THE STORY THAT WAY, TOO...BUT... HUH? ...THEY ENDED UP BEING IN HIGH SCHOOL TO THE END...DIDN'T THEY... THE STORYLINE PROGRESSED ACCORDING TO PLAN, THOUGH... STRANGE, ISN'T IT? APPARENTLY, SOME PEOPLE CONTINUED CLAMORING, "WE'RE LOOKING FORWARD TO SEEING THE TWO'S LIFE TOGETHER IN THE DORMITORY!" UNTIL ALMOST THE VERY END OF THE SERIES AND

WHEN I HEARD THIS, IT BROKE MY HEART...IN A BAD WAY. I'M SO SORRY FOR CONTINUING TO DISAPPOINT YOU, MY FANS. DID YOU WANT TO SEE THEM LOVEY-DOVEY IN THE DORMS? OH - SOME PEOPLE SAID THEY WERE FIRED UP TO SEE THEM IN UNIFORMS...I GUESS I COULD'VE GIVEN THEM COLLEGE UNIFORMS... (IF THE OPPORTUNITY TO CONTINUE THIS SERIES COMES UP, I'LL BE SURE TO FOLLOW YOUR REQUEST.)

ABOUT THE ORIGINAL SHORT STORIES ADDED TO THIS VOLUME...THIS TIME, IN ALL THE SHORT STORY ADDITIONS FOR VOLUME THREE, I DECIDED TO MAKE THEM FROM NA-KAHARA-KUN'S VANTAGE POINT. (THE LAST SCENE IN THE MAIN STORY SEEMS TO LEAN HEAVILY TOWARD NAKAHA-RA-KUN, TOO, BUT THAT WAS SUPPOSED TO BE MORE OF A NEUTRAL NARRATION.) AFTER READING THEM, MY EDITOR SAID TO ME, "THE TWO ARE ALREADY QUITE ADULT, AREN'T THEY (TWINKLE)!" (LAUGH) PERHAPS THERE ARE SOME PEOPLE WHO CAN'T TAKE THOSE TWO IN THAT TYPE OF SITUATION...? I'M SORRY... BUT TO ME, NAKAHA-RA-KUN JUST SEEMS LIKE HE'D BE QUITE...LUSTY...(OH DEAR!) AND HERE'S ONE THING I'M CURIOUS ABOUT: I WONDER WHERE NAKAHARA-KUN GETS HIS KNOWLEDGE ABOUT ALL THAT (GAY) SEX STUFF...? TO MY MIND, AFTER HE REALIZED HE MIGHT BE ABLE TO GET TOGETHER WITH KOJIMA-KUN AFTER ALL, HE PROBABLY DID SOME RE-SEARCH ON THE NET...LIKE, ON HIS NOTEBOOK PC OR SOMETHING... I CAN JUST IMAGINE A SHOCKED NAKAHARA-KUN AS HE ACCIDENTALLY CLICKS ON SOME HARDCORE GAY PORN SITE...NICE...HEH HEH. (HEY, THAT MIGHT HAVE BEEN A GOOD SHORT STORY SUBJECT, TOO!)

ALSO, A NAKAHARA-KUN WHO HAS SEEN A YAOI SEX SITE...

AND SO, "LITTLE B..." HAS REACHED ITS CONCLUSION FOR THE TIME BEING. APOLOGIES TO MY EDITOR FOR CAUS-ING TROUBLE ALL THE TIME...AND THANKS TO MY ASSIS-TANTS FOR ALL THEIR HELP. AND FINALLY, TO ALL OF YOU READERS WHO STUCK WITH ME TO THE END, I THANK YOU FROM THE BOTTOM OF MY HEART. I WOULD GREATLY AP-PRECIATE IT IF YOU WOULD SEND ME ANY COMMENTS YOU MAY HAVE...! ALSO, I'LL STILL HAVE OPPORTUNITIES TO KEEP DRAWING THESE TWO AT CONVENTIONS AND SO ON, SO IF WE HAPPEN TO MEET AGAIN SOMEWHERE, PLEASE COME AND SAY HI TO THEM!

XXX HINAKO TAKANAGA XXX

ADDITIONAL EXTRA STORY IDEAS:

NAKAHARA-KUNS WE DON'T WANT TO SEE

A NAKAHARA-KUN WHO FINDS A YAOI SEX SITE WHILE SURFING THE NET.

A NAKAHARA-KUN WHO FINDS A "FAVORITE" SITE BY ACCIDENT.

A NAKAHARA-KUN WHOSE "FAVORITES" FOLDER BECOMES FILLED WITH YAOI SITES.

AN EMBARRASSED NAKAHARA-KUN WHO CAUSES KOJIMA-KUN TO BE DISGUSTED WITH HIM WHEN THOSE SITES ARE DISCOVERED ON HIS COMPUTER.

POOR GUY...
(HEY, THIS IS FUN.)

◆ PLEASE VISIT MY SITE ◆

"ANAGURANZ"
http://cgi2.it-serve.ne.jp/~anaguranz/

[LITTLE BUTTERFLY 3] HINAKO TAKANAGA PRESENTS

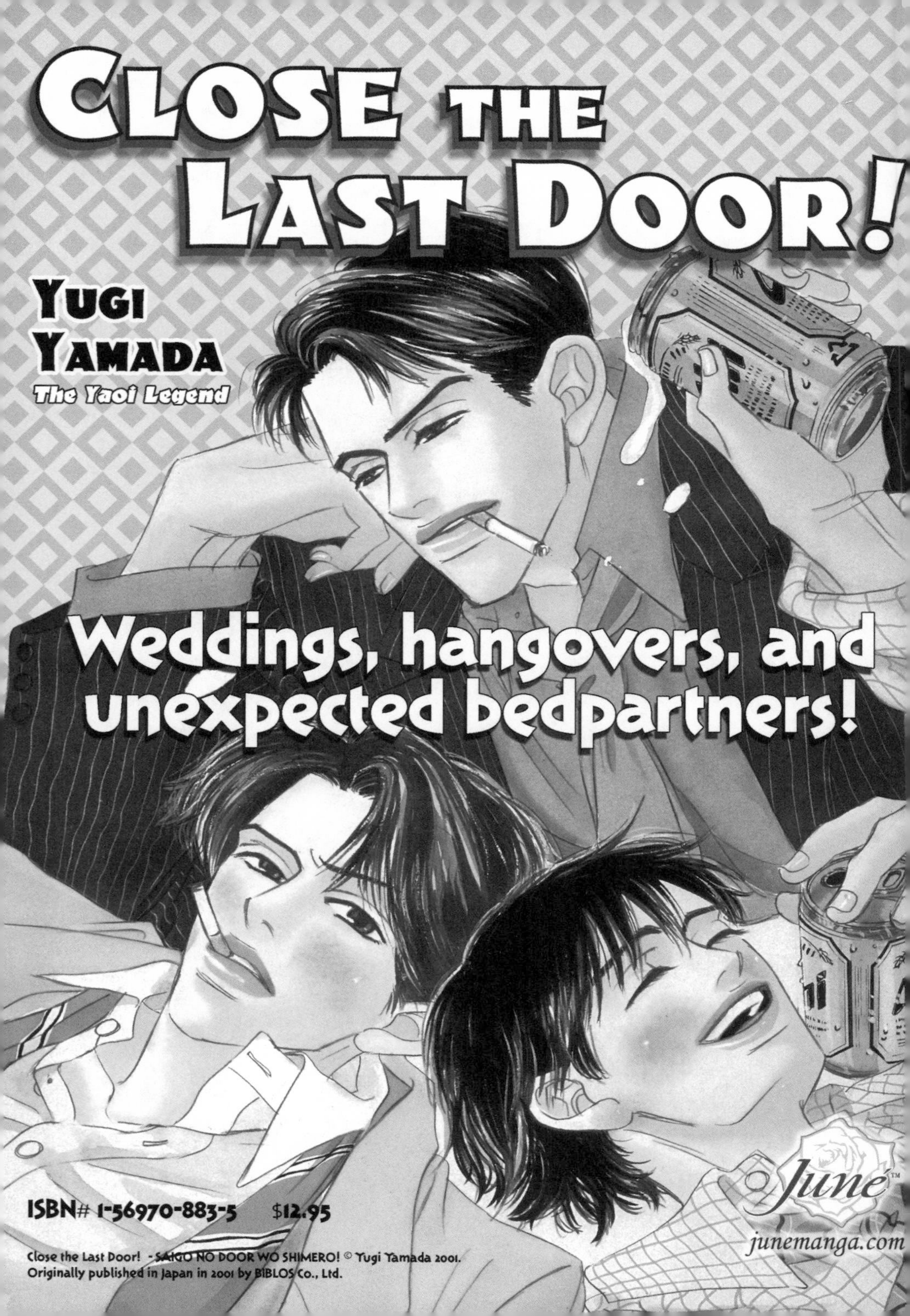
CLOSE THE LAST DOOR!
YUGI YAMADA
The Yaoi Legend
Weddings, hangovers, and unexpected bedpartners!
ISBN# 1-56970-883-5 $12.95
June
junemanga.com
Close the Last Door! - SAIGO NO DOOR WO SHIMERO! © Yugi Yamada 2001.
Originally published in Japan in 2001 by BIBLOS Co., Ltd.

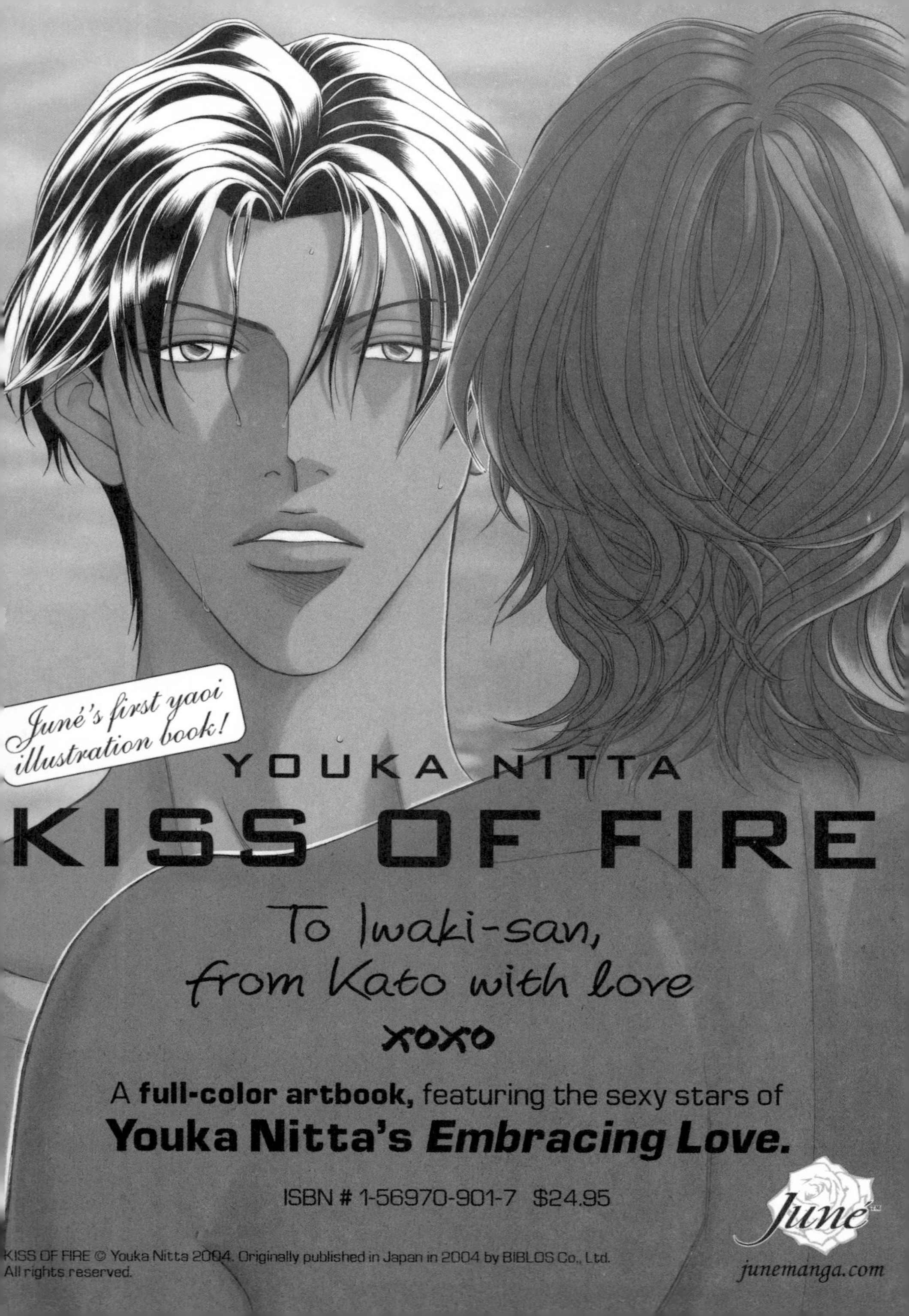
June's first yaoi illustration book!
YOUKA NITTA
KISS OF FIRE
To Iwaki-san,
from Kato with love
XOXO
A full-color artbook, featuring the sexy stars of
Youka Nitta's Embracing Love.
ISBN # 1-56970-901-7 $24.95
June
junemanga.com
KISS OF FIRE © Youka Nitta 2004. Originally published in Japan in 2004 by BIBLOS Co., Ltd.
All rights reserved.

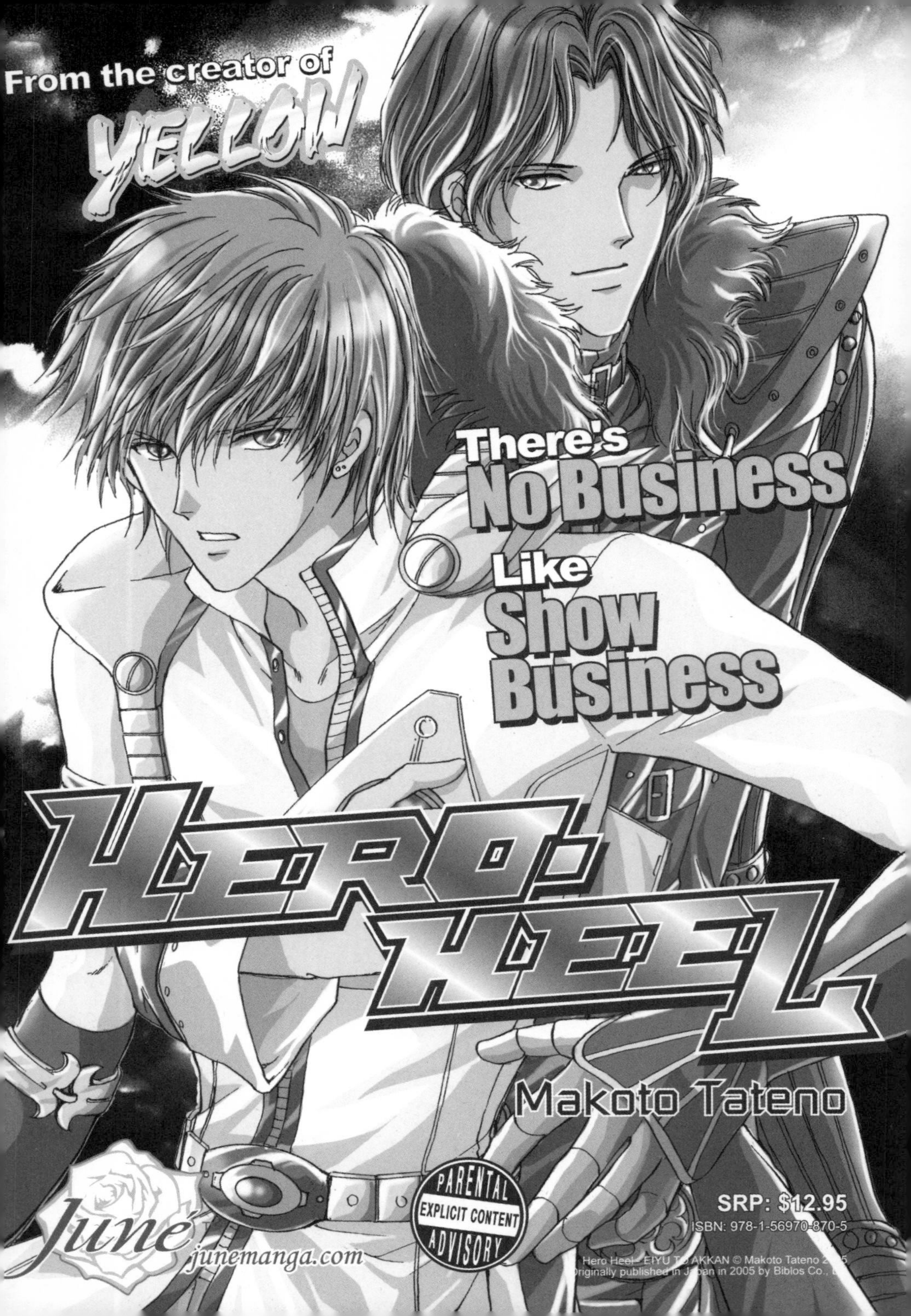
From the creator of
YELLOW
There's
No Business
Like
Show
Business
HERO HEEL
Makoto Tateno
June
junemanga.com
PARENTAL
EXPLICIT CONTENT
ADVISORY
SRP: $12.95
ISBN: 978-1-56970-870-5
Hero Heel - EIYU TO AKKAN © Makoto Tateno 2005
Originally published in Japan in 2005 by Biblos Co., Ltd.

Princess·Princess

By MIKIYO TSUDA

Peer pressure...
has never been this intense!

When students need a boost, the Princesses arrive in gothic lolita outfits to show their school spirit! Join Kouno and friends in this crazy, cross-dressing comedy.

VOLUME 1 - ISBN# 978-1-56970-856-9 $12.95
VOLUME 2 - ISBN# 978-1-56970-855-2 $12.95
VOLUME 3 - ISBN# 978-1-56970-852-1 $12.95
VOLUME 4 - ISBN# 978-1-56970-851-4 $12.95
VOLUME 5 - ISBN# 978-1-56970-850-7 $12.95

DMP
DIGITAL MANGA
PUBLISHING
www.dmpbooks.com

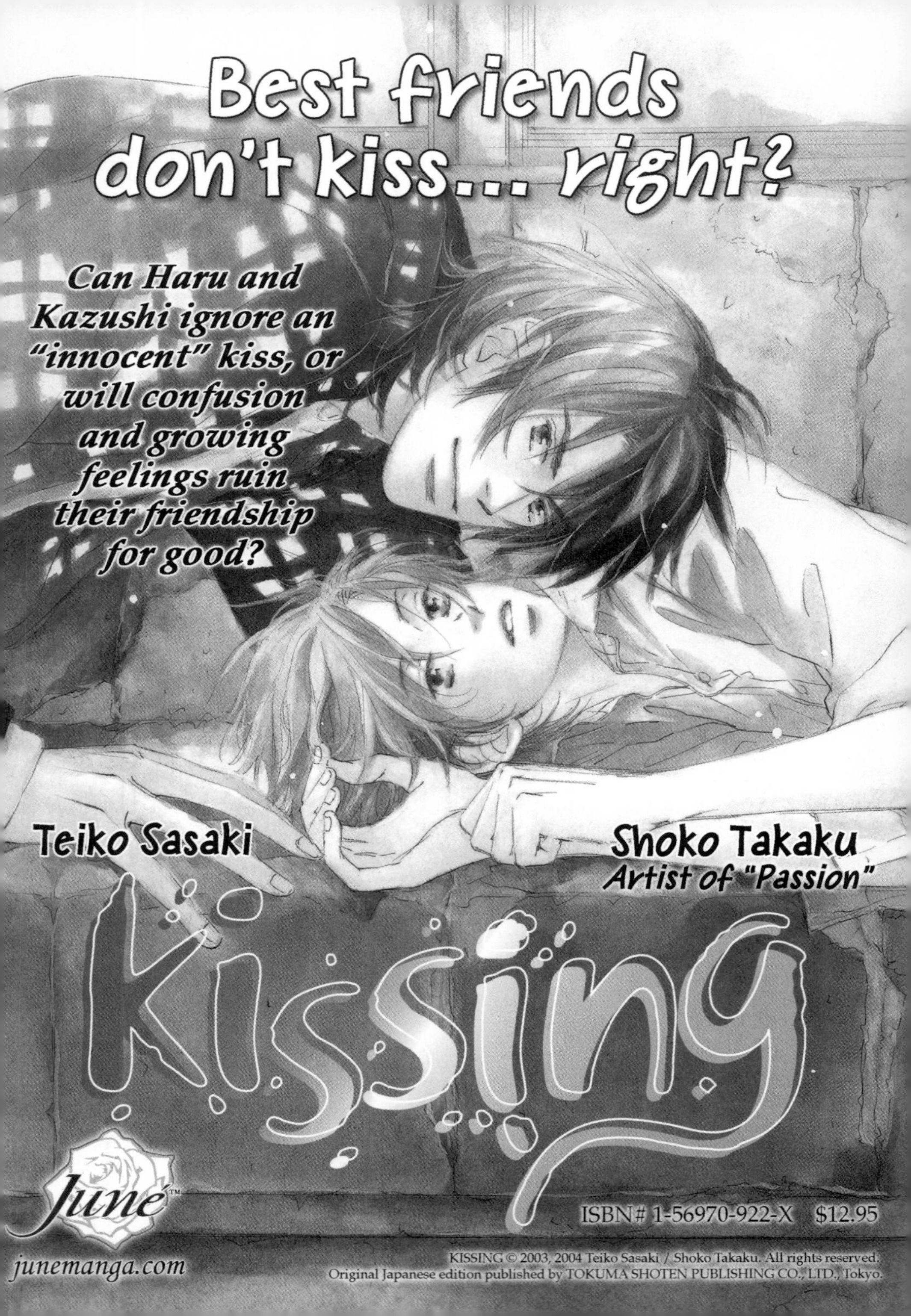
Best friends don't kiss... right?
Can Haru and Kazushi ignore an "innocent" kiss, or will confusion and growing feelings ruin their friendship for good?
Teiko Sasaki
Shoko Takaku
Artist of "Passion"
Kissing
June™
junemanga.com
ISBN# 1-56970-922-X $12.95
KISSING © 2003, 2004 Teiko Sasaki / Shoko Takaku. All rights reserved.
Original Japanese edition published by TOKUMA SHOTEN PUBLISHING CO., LTD., Tokyo.

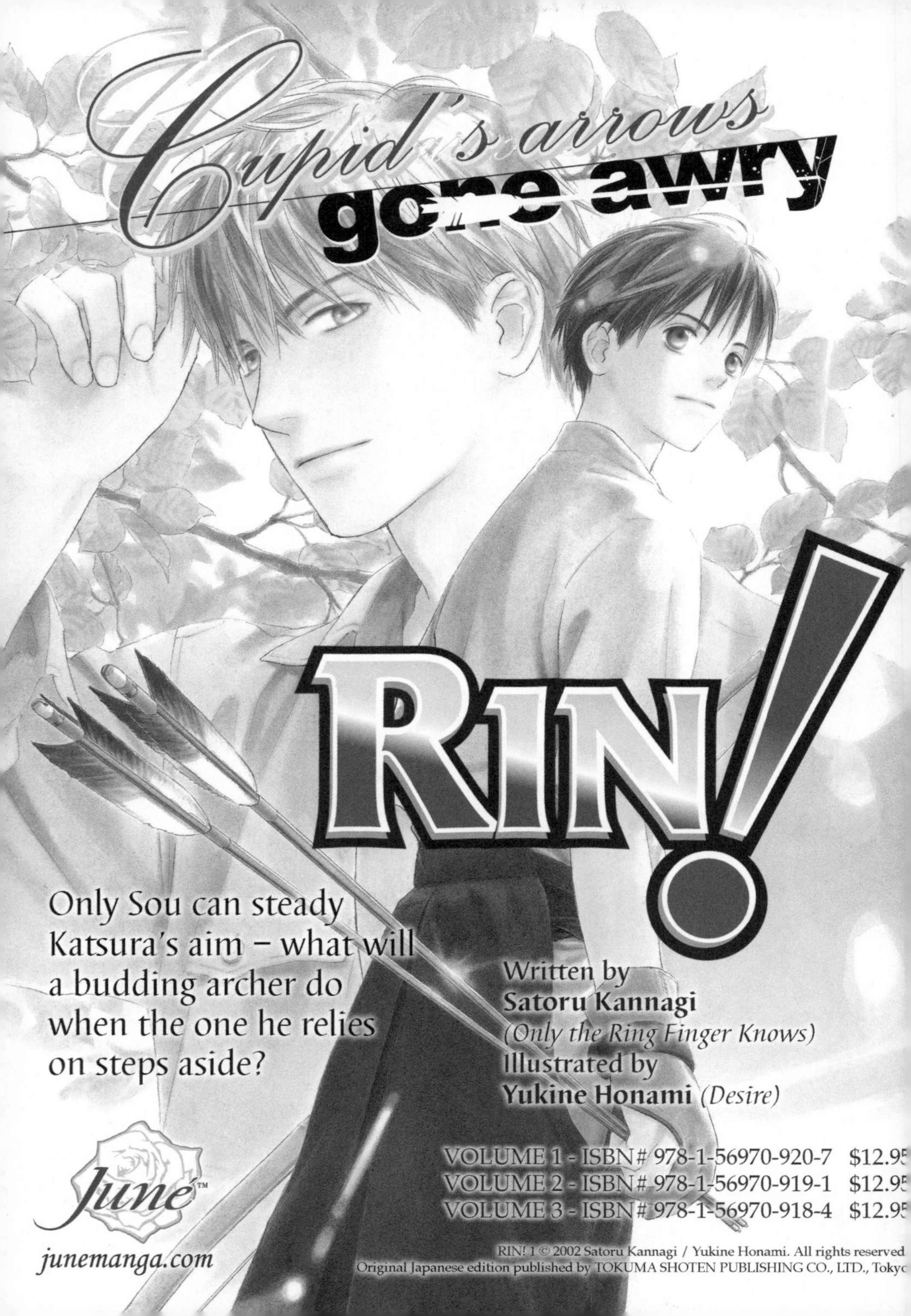
Cupid's arrows
gone awry
RIN!
Only Sou can steady Katsura's aim – what will a budding archer do when the one he relies on steps aside?
Written by
Satoru Kannagi
(Only the Ring Finger Knows)
Illustrated by
Yukine Honami (Desire)
VOLUME 1 - ISBN# 978-1-56970-920-7 $12.95
VOLUME 2 - ISBN# 978-1-56970-919-1 $12.95
VOLUME 3 - ISBN# 978-1-56970-918-4 $12.95
June™
junemanga.com
RIN! 1 © 2002 Satoru Kannagi / Yukine Honami. All rights reserved
Original Japanese edition published by TOKUMA SHOTEN PUBLISHING CO., LTD., Tokyo

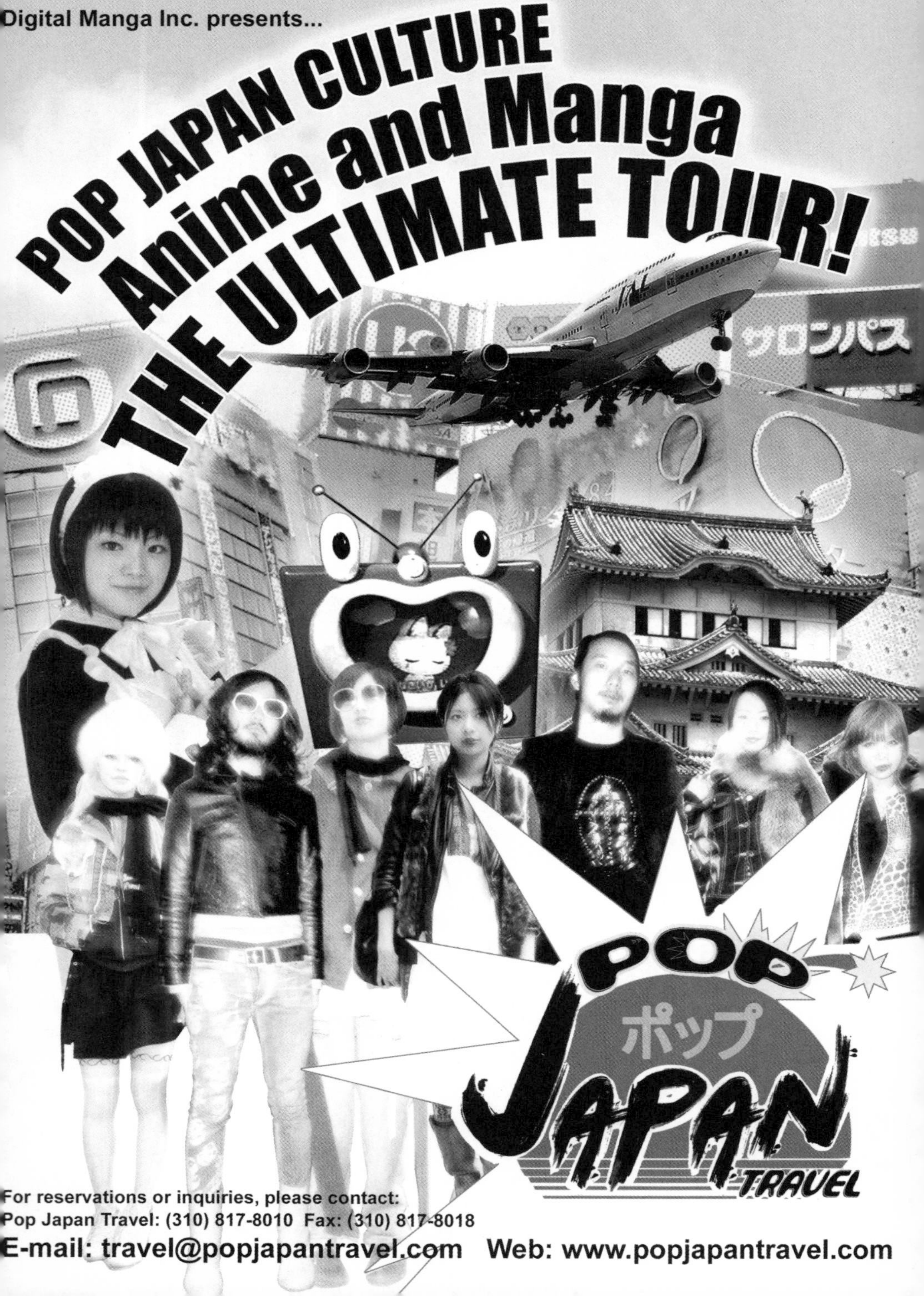
Digital Manga Inc. presents...
POP JAPAN CULTURE
Anime and Manga
THE ULTIMATE TOUR!
サロンパス
POP
ポップ
JAPAN
TRAVEL
For reservations or inquiries, please contact:
Pop Japan Travel: (310) 817-8010 Fax: (310) 817-8018
E-mail: travel@popjapantravel.com Web: www.popjapantravel.com

STOP

This is the back of the book! Start from the other side.

NATIVE MANGA readers read manga from *right to left*.

If you run into our *Native Manga* logo on any of our books... you'll know that this manga is published in it's true original native Japanese right to left reading format, as it was intended. Turn to the other side of the book and start reading from right to left, top to bottom.

Follow the diagram to see how its done. *Surf's Up!*

NATIVE MANGA

READ RIGHT TO LEFT